The Quest of the Attal

A Michael Chrome Novel

Copyright © 2017 Michael Chrome

ISBN: 978-1-945642-05-0
Editor: J. Arthur's Edits (www.jaedits.com).
All edits were approved by the author.
All rights reserved.

Dedication

With supportive family and friends even the unbelievable is possible. I dedicate this novel to one of my biggest supporters who lost his battle with leukemia before I finished the Attal series.

Thank you, Ivan Glen Hargis, for your support and example.

Contents

Dedication 5
Chapter I 9
Chapter II 14
Chapter III 22
Chapter IV 32
Chapter V 43
Chapter VI 52
Chapter VII 62
Chapter VIII 72
Chapter IX 85
Chapter X 93
Chapter XI 100
Chapter XII 110
Chapter XIII 119
Chapter XIV 130
Chapter XV 136
Chapter XVI 145
Chapter XVII 154
Chapter XVIII 164
Chapter XIX 172
Chapter XX 182
Chapter XXI 193
Chapter XXII 202
Chapter XXIII 212
Chapter XXIV 222
Chapter XXV 231

Chapter XXVI ... 241
Chapter XXVII ... 251
Chapter XXVIII ... 261
Chapter XXIX ... 271
Chapter XXX ... 280
Chapter XXXI ... 291
Chapter XXXII ... 305
Chapter XXXIII ... 314
Chapter XXXIV ... 324
Chapter XXXV ... 334
Chapter XXXVI ... 341
Chapter XXXVII ... 351
Chapter XXXVIII ... 360
Authors' Note ... 366
Authors' Biography ... 367

Chapter I

Gary White, a fifty-year-old, bald store owner with bags under his eyes revealing his lack of sleep, put his car in park and waited for the train to pass. He looked over to Maria, his thin, blonde wife who appeared at least ten years younger than him.

"I've been thinking about my buddy Bill a lot lately. It's been almost two years since he went to South America. He should have been home by now."

"That's random," Maria said. "I've known you since middle school. You don't do random. What you do is think about something for days then pretend to have a casual thought. What's wrong?

"I just miss him," Gary said.

"Me, too. But we stay in touch," she said, playing with her enhanced, full-moon, cat-claw necklace used for instant communication with their alien friend. "I know our life's been complicated ever since he walked into our store. When he revealed the secret, alien society living on Earth and recruited us to help discover its corrupted leadership, we knew things would get a little crazy."

"I don't mind the crazy," Gary said, "but we've identified the malicious members of the Attal, and most of them have been captured. He should have caught the last two by now."

"Maybe," Maria said. "They did have a huge head start. At least we still get to see his son. Between Elaine's Attal technology lessons and Eddie's Wright State Racing Team consults, our kids see Pax almost every week."

"I know, and I love having the big, brilliant goof around. I just wonder—"

The horn from the car behind him interrupted Gary's thought. He waved out the window and put his car in drive.

"Let's go get some dessert."

"You know Eddie's coming home for break next week," Maria reminded him. "Let's ask Elaine to come over for dinner, and we'll have a quiet family dinner, just the four of us."

"Quiet family dinner with Elaine in the room. Have you met your daughter?" Gary asked as he laughed at the impossibility.

"Yea, I've met her. She takes after her father."

"Really?" Gary said, rubbing his bald head. "Just like me? What color is her hair this week?"

"According to her latest selfie, it's a greenish-blue," she answered. "Just because she's a colorful person who talks too loud and fast doesn't mean we can't have a fun family dinner."

"Fun—absolutely," Gary said. "But quiet—doubtful."

After sitting in their favorite booth at Lucy's Bakery, the restaurant Maria's mom owned and operated, they ordered a slice of apple pie with two forks and two cups of coffee.

"This is the second time this week I woke up without you beside me. What's really bothering you?" Maria asked.

"I'm fine," he assured her. "It's just lately I've been waking up after only a couple hours of sleep and can't slow down my mind. I don't want to wake you, so I go downstairs and watch TV until I fall back asleep."

"What do you watch?"

"I look for something I've already seen. Something I don't have to stay awake for, but entertaining enough to stop my mind from wandering. Last night, I watched *The Breakfast Club*."

"Good movie, but why can't you sleep? What are you worrying about?" she asked.

"I have no idea. I'm not really worried. I'd describe it more as unsettled. For a couple years, we had Pax's Galtri coming-of-age tournament and Bill's leadership problems to solve."

Gary looked around to make sure he wouldn't be overheard and dropped his voice.

"I think I'm just having adventure withdrawal."

"I certainly miss the world travel and fancy dinner parties, but let's not forget we also aren't spending our days getting shot at in English pubs or having our kids speed down the expressway trying to get aliens to their high-tech transporter pod anymore either," Maria said.

"I know. I think half of my problem is I feel guilty for wanting more adventure," Gary admitted. "I liked being included in the alien culture and feeling like the hero solving the world's problems, but I'm not sure it didn't come at the kids' expense. I'm afraid I've changed our kids' lives forever."

"Maybe, but I think they will be much better when all is said and done," Maria said. "I know Elaine has been struggling with relationships and Eddie with his studies, but they are doing pretty good. From what I hear, maybe even better than most of their friends, who haven't had to deal with an alien society and death-defying missions. And maybe someday, Pax and Elaine will, you know—"

"No. I don't know," Gary interrupted. He pointed to his temple. "Up here, I know they're both doing okay, but my gut still keeps me up at night. Relationships are hard enough when two people have a lot in common. I can't imagine trying to be romantic with an alien. I liked how Vinnie treated Elaine. And Eddie's really been sidetracked lately. He's become obsessed with building and driving cars, instead of nursing and his studies. I just wonder if my actions change their fate."

"Nah, you were just being you. How could we choose to not help Bill? He needed us, and all of our lives are better by helping him," Maria said. "Besides, it doesn't help to dwell on the past. You can only change the future."

"I know worrying is irrational, hence my frustrations," Gary said.

"Did someone say irrational?" Lucy asked as she slid into the booth beside her daughter. "You wouldn't be talking about me, would you?"

"Hey, Mom. Not this time," Gary said with a smile. "I just haven't been sleeping very well. I wake up in the middle of the night and start thinking about the kids."

"They're doing fine," Lucy said. "Elaine stopped in the other day for a lemon square, and she seemed great. Speaking of lemon squares, I made some fresh this morning. Let me get you one."

"See? Listen to Mom," Maria said. "All you need is dessert and a cup of coffee and you will be fine."

"Any more desserts and you're going to need to buy me new clothes. Gary said.

12

"I have a crazy idea," Maria said, ignoring his comment. "Maybe you should embrace the past instead of worrying about it. Why don't you write about our adventure? It will help you analyze and maybe appreciate what we did for the Attal and for Earth."

"Except we promised to keep the Attal's secret existence a secret. Remember? I'm sure they wouldn't appreciate a novel revealing their presence and the fact that their so-called peaceful race caused havoc on Earth."

"You don't have to publish or advertise it," Maria explained.

"Maybe," Gary said, contemplating the idea. "But I'm not a writer and I would feel wrong sharing their story."

"Sharing whose story?" Lucy asked, sitting back down and giving Gary a double serving of her lemon squares. "Are you finally going to write a book about Riverside Market? I've said for years that what goes on in your store would make a great story."

"You have no idea," Gary said. "But I'll leave the writing to someone else. I'm more of a talker than an author."

While Lucy and Maria talked about something Gary neither cared about nor paid attention to, he grinned at the potential adventures waiting for him and his family and then thought, "Besides, how could I write a book when the ending isn't finished?"

Chapter II

  Juanita, being skilled at manipulating her Earthly body to operate at near peak efficiency and preferring the outdoors if given a choice, was one of only three people sitting at the pool in the midday sun. The 34°C temperature and lack of a Brazilian ocean breeze kept most guests inside the air-conditioned resort, allowing Juanita to receive more of the staff's attention.

  "*Obrigada*," she said, thanking the waiter for bringing her a fresh, chilled mineral water.

  She smiled as the nervous waiter blushed at getting caught making eye contact with her $200, black bikini. She waited for his gaze to come back up to her sunglass-covered eyes. She winked at the smile he gave as he hastily returned to the bar. Almost two years ago, Juanita had gladly left behind the strict dress and behavior codes of the Pacific station and continued to master using the freedom and power the female body had on the surface, especially when dealing with men.

Being on the run from her fellow Attal, an advanced, normally peaceful race secretly inhabiting the earth, forced her to adapt quickly. When she left the station for the last time to live in exile, she manipulated the transporter and changed her appearance from a white, English male named Barry to the 35-year-old Latina woman named Juanita sitting pool side and enjoying luxuries reserved for the rich and powerful.

Concentrating on her information device, she contemplated her next move. Positive the Attal leadership would send someone to apprehend her and Carlos—her partner, friend, and fellow fugitive—she was equally confident they had left no clues to their current location, appearance, or goals. She covered her tracks well, hiding her relationship with both the drug lord and the evangelist, whom they were almost done using. Her current problem was whether to allocate her available resources to the International South America Shipping Partnership (ISASP) or to fund the political efforts of Argentina's leader's main competition in the upcoming election. She sat deep in concentration when the waiter interrupted her thoughts.

"Ma'am, I'm about to end my shift. Can I be of any further assistance before I leave?" he asked.

She wanted to laugh as he made sure to look directly at her Bulgari sunglasses.

"Yes, Manny. You can apply lotion on my back before you leave. I believe this midday sun is drying my skin," she answered, sitting up, removing her sunglasses, and looking up at him with her large, brown, penetrating eyes.

"M-Ma'am, the last time you—well, last time—Ma'am, I almost lost my job," he said, breaking eye contact to study the stitching of his white denim loafers.

Juanita flipped over to expose her back and the bikini strings she expected Manny to untie before applying her lotion and asked, "And what happened after I talked to your boss, Manny?"

Before he could answer, she removed the lotion from her tote bag and lifted it above her head, emphasizing that he had no input in this decision. Although she did not get the same pleasure from the service as the obviously nervous but excited Manny, who undid the ties and applied the lotion to her naked back, she did love the ease with which she could control Terra men. Although no one could see her face, she had a slight smile when Manny finally answered.

"I got a raise and now all the other waiters are mad at me."

"Don't forget my legs, Manny"

****

Eddie sat alone on an upside-down milk crate in the recently emptied bay of the Bullet Hole Garage, reading a report he hoped would explain his loss to the University of Akron racing team. Even though his transcripts listed him as a sophomore nursing student, he had a long and well documented love for horsepower and fine-tuned machines. As the founder of the Wright State Racing team, he took every loss personally, but this one hurt a little more due to the trash talking he had done to Jenny Summers, his childhood friend, engineering student, and contributing member of Akron U's race team. Now, he had to face a second consecutive year of having dinner with the Summers as the head of the loosing team.

The orange trouble light, normally used for those hard-to-see repairs to the latest Wright State racer or one of Eddie's project cars, supplemented the uncovered, eight-foot, fluorescent, overhead bulbs in the cluttered garage. The mess revealed his team's need to adjust their car right up to the last minute. His thick, brown hair was unusually messy, and he had a grease stain in what he would exaggeratingly call a beard. He intently studied each lap's split time when the appearance of an unannounced visitor surprised him. He jumped about an inch off his makeshift chair, tossing his report in the air and knocking over his diet cola.

"Sorry. I didn't mean to startle you," Pax said.

"You didn't startle me," Eddie corrected him as he turned and grabbed a blue, grease-stained shop rag. "You scared the shit out of me!"

"I just wanted to congratulate you on the improvement you showed against Akron this year," Pax offered as an explanation for his interruption. "Last year, they crushed you. This year, you were making up time every lap. I think you might have won if the race had been a lap longer. How much behind were you this year?"

"1.4 seconds," Eddie answered, not sharing Pax's positive assessment.

"If I may be so bold," Pax said before leaning on a stack of three tires and continuing without waiting for a response. "Your design and driving are fine. You just need to concentrate on getting off the line a little quicker. You beat them on every lap except the first. Work on your 0-30 time."

"Thanks. How about you do some of the voodoo stuff you do to make my car faster off the line?" Eddie asked with raised eyebrows and a closed-mouth smile.

"First, I don't know any voodoo, just advanced technology," Pax corrected him. "Secondly, you know I would never give you an unfair advantage in a fair competition."

"I didn't ask you for some secret fuel to shoot my car to the finish line in two seconds, but if one of your rich, technology friends happens to know about combustion engines and happens to make a stop by my garage and happens to make a suggestion or two about improvements, where's the harm? The rules allow for outside consults. Let the other schools get their own rich, powerful sponsor. It's a competition thing."

"I know something about competition," Pax rebutted. "Having been in a couple very important—"

"And if memory serves me right, I broke about fifty traffic laws helping you with your last competition, and now I get a lecture about fair play?" Eddie interrupted. "If you don't want to help, just say no. I get plenty of lectures from Dad."

After a few seconds, Pax conceded, "You are right. I'm sorry, but my situation is different. It's a—"

"—very long and complicated story. I know. Funny how, when explaining *your* actions, it's long and complicated, yet mine are always so simple. But Dad did tell me what you are doing is of vital importance."

He chuckled to himself before repeating the last comment, "Vital importance. Who uses the phrase *vital importance?*"

After taking a moment to laugh at his Dad's expense, he added, "It's not you. I just hate losing. I know you are smarter and richer than me, but all things being equal, I'm not in the mood for an ethics lesson."

"Agreed. I came to congratulate you and get caught up, not to teach. How about some dinner?" Pax suggested.

Being dirty, tired, and stressed from his loss did not add to Eddie's appetite, but hoping some company might improve his mood, he suggested they simply walk over to the Arby's and grab a quick bite.

Halfway through his French dip sandwich, Eddie asked without looking up or swallowing all his food, "So, you comin' to Mom and Dad's on Saturday for dinner with the Summers?"

"I don't think so," Pax answered in a quiet, melancholy tone. "I get the feeling Elaine's a little…a little uncomfortable around me lately."

"Nah, she's fine. Marshall feels uncomfortable with you being around. Can ya blame him?" Eddie said with much less interest in the topic than he had in the black Honda Civic pulling out of the parking lot with an after-market rear spoiler and barely legal Magna Flow muffler he would have described as "a little ricey."

"Why does Marshall not want me around?" Pax asked, confused.

"Oh, I don't know. Let's see," Eddie said before turning to face Pax. "You are rich, generous, and well connected. You're also insanely smart and, if I can say so without sounding gay, a good-looking guy who started his own charity. Marshall could never compete with you. Can you really be that clueless?"

"Yes," Pax answered, suddenly very interested in the lettuce in his side salad.

"You've got to be the dumbest smart person I've ever met. Come to the party, Pax," Eddie said with a shake of his head. "Besides, I get the feeling Marshall won't be around for long."

"Why?" Pax asked, looking up with a renewed interest in the conversation. "What makes you think Marshall will be leaving?"

"Really?" Eddie said as a commentary on Pax's lack of understanding about relationships. "You like to study. Why don't you read some romance novels, watch a couple chick flicks, or something."

"It's not that simple," Pax tried to explain. "Interpersonal relationships and communication is a learned art. I study constantly, but I really don't have any practical experience in relationship talks with anyone other than Bill and your family. I have some experience talking to women at work, but zero experience talking to any women about deep or personal matters other than Elaine and Lizzy."

"And they both love you," Eddie said as a fact he thought just as obvious as stating his curly fries were an unhealthy yet enjoyable side dish. "So there you go."

"What?"

"Oh, my God. Really? Lizzy turned down two better offers to continue working with you at Moonlight. Elaine broke up with Vinnie because he had no drive and then dated a couple losers before seeing Jesse; she broke up with Jesse because of his partying. And now there's Marshall. He and Elaine share a love for music, but he doesn't care about things like—oh, I don't know—money or a real job. Face it, Pax, you ruin it for the rest of us."

"What?" he asked, clearly confused and not sounding anything like an intelligent member of an advanced, alien race. "But I would never—"

"I know," Eddie said, anticipating his response. "You would never do anything to harm us or anyone else, cuz you're THAT guy. Kinda my point here. Quit obsessing and just do what feels right in your heart…or better yet, that big, old head of yours. Elaine will someday realize no one will ever meet your standards and find someone who accepts her friendship with you. Or maybe someday, you and Elaine will wake up and you'll end up my brother."

Blushing and rolling the cherry tomato back and forth in his salad, Pax said, "Regardless of my apparently transparent feelings for your sister, that can never happen. I know you hear this too often with me, but it's a—"

"I know. One of these days, you will tell me why everything is so damn complicated with you. But you're wrong about this. *This* isn't complicated. You just gotta quit being a pussy and ask the girl out. There's a big difference between something being complicated and just plain scary."

"Sometimes it's both," he said quietly without looking up. "And Eddie, you are my brother." Seeing Eddie squirm a little with his last comment, Pax quickly changed the subject.

"Thanks for the lesson. You want any dessert?"

Chapter III

Eddie stood in the kitchen, arguing with Jenny about race theory. "Engineering takes seconds off of the time—which is obvious by our loss—but a good driver can make up the time. A bad one will piss his advantage away and cost you much more in the long run."

"It's not too obvious you're the driver, is it?" Jenny asked.

"And you the engineer," Eddie rebutted. "Why don't you just transfer to Wright so we can win the whole thing? I'll even let you drink out of the trophy cup."

"The year isn't over, yet," she reminded him. "With a little luck, Akron could still win this thing. I'll send you a pic of me drinking out of the cup."

"Not with your driver you won't," Eddie said.

"You kids play nice," Maria interrupted, entering the kitchen with two pizza boxes and some chicken wings.

Eddie served Jenny her first helping of pizza and wings with a fake and exaggerated bow. Everyone sat in the Whites' sunroom, eating pizza and talking about Marshall's new music video. They were laughing about the videos Elaine and Lizzy used to make in their early teens, when Pax appeared at the back door.

Elaine, excited to see her friend, hopped off the couch and greeted Pax at the door with a hug so big it almost spilled the veggie tray he had brought to share.

"Pax," Maria said, pausing long enough to take the veggie tray and give him a kiss on the cheek. "I'm so glad you could make it. It's great to see you. How long has it been?"

"Twenty-six days," he answered immediately. "It's great to see you, too."

"How was your trip to England? How's Aggie doing?" Marie asked, using Elaine's nickname for Agrata, her Attal friend who partnered with Pax on the Co-Habitat Relations Department and lived just outside of London as a 22-year-old, skinny, Indian girl.

"She's having the same struggles I am, but it's always good to see her, and she sends her best," he answered before looking back to Elaine. "She told me to tell you, and I quote, 'It's about time for another trip over the pond, bitch.'"

"Oh. Okay. Wait 'til I call her tonight," Elaine said with a smile only Pax and her parents understood. Using slang was rare for a member of the Attal. Impressively, she had even used it correctly.

Elaine sat down next to Marshall, whose demeanor had changed from a few minutes ago.

"What is he doing here?" he asked sternly but only loud enough for her to hear.

"Why wouldn't he be here? He started Moonlight Trail with Lizzy, and he's Eddie's race sponsor," she answered rudely and not nearly quietly enough. "What are you, sixteen?"

"May I have a word with you in private, please?" Marshall whispered.

They both got up and headed upstairs to talk in her old bedroom, which Gary and Maria kept as a spare and Elaine used to store some of her extra clothes. On the way, Elaine got a feeling Pax wanted to speak to her. Accepting his communication with her technology-enhanced, antique necklace that resembled a full moon with a cat-claw overlay, she heard him speak telepathically.

"Would you like me to leave? We can get caught up another time."

"Oh, hell no. You aren't going anywhere. I'll be back down in a second," she answered before turning on Marshall.

"What the hell is wrong with you?" she demanded. "You know our family is close to Pax and his Dad. I've told you about him many times."

"Yea, I know," Marshall countered. "You tell me about him every day. Your obsession with him is very…um...unhealthy."

"Don't you think about your sister in LA a lot? Talk about your friend Max a hundred times a day? Obsess about your band schedule? I don't mind," she countered in a volume not quite a yell for her, but may have been described as such.

"It's not the same. They aren't 24-year-old, single guys in love with someone's girlfriend," he answered, not caring about the fight he knew he would be starting.

"Bullshit! It's not like that," she said, allowing her frustration to show.

"Oh, come on. One sight of him had you jumping out of your seat."

"That's cuz…Well, it's been a while since—you know what? Kiss my ass! Maybe if you were a little more like him, we wouldn't be having this ridiculous conversation. He offered to leave because it made you uncomfortable. Doesn't sound like some sort of secret love to me."

"I don't want to be like him. If you like him so much, why don't you just date him?" Marshall asked, irritated with the direction of the conversation.

"It's not like that with us, and never could be."

"So you say, but I see what I see."

"You know what, Marshall," she said, dropping the anger out of her voice. "I could see this coming. We're at two different places in life. I don't think this is going to work."

Marshall, trying to protect his ego, responded, "You're damn right this isn't going to work. You don't even live in reality. He never offered to leave!"

"He would have," she responded. "I'm sorry it didn't work out."

"You're going to be sorry. Bitch! You better get used to being alone," he said and left her room without waiting for a response.

Before Marshall made it down the steps and out the front door, Elaine heard Gary in her mind.

"Everything okay up there, or do you need a little Daddy help? And do I need to bring Eddie?"

"No, everything is fine now," Elaine responded. *"I won't be having any more trouble from Marshall. I'll be down in a couple minutes."*

Elaine sat in her room for a bit to collect her thoughts and had to chuckle to herself for being called a bitch twice in ten minutes. She concentrated on communicating with Aggie.

"'Time for another trip over the pond, bitch.' Really? How are you doing, girl?"

"I'm doing okay," Aggie answered in a melancholy tone. *"Still unsure about who to pick for the council, and I'm getting pressure from Ivan to complete my task."*

"Need a little help?" Elaine asked. *"I find myself recently single, and I could use a break. You want some company?"*

"Absolutely," she answered with a much improved tone. *"I need a change of pace, and I miss my girl. Look in the mirror so I can see you. When do you want to come?"*

Walking over to the mirror so Aggie could see through her eyes, Elaine turned to show off her light brown hair with pink and blue, cotton candy-like streaks. *"I have a couple things to do here first. Make reservations for me in a week or two. I'll re-arrange my work schedule."*

"Okay. I'll fly you out a week from Thursday. I can't wait to see you again. I love your bubble gum hair," Aggie responded, going to the mirror herself so Elaine could see her waving and smiling.

"It's cotton candy—bitch," Elaine said loftily to her friend, then blew her a kiss in the mirror a second before leaving her mind.

Elaine went downstairs to join the party and picked up her striped tabby cat, Buddy, who waited for her at the bottom step. He rested in her arms, purring in response to her long, manicured nails gently scratching under his chin.

"You make me feel better, too," she said, knowing exactly how he felt thanks to Pax's help reading his mind a couple years ago.

She sat down and heard her mother's gentle voice in her mind.

"Are you okay, honey?"

Without answering in kind, she made eye contact and nodded her head, letting Maria know she would be fine.

The remainder of the party was enjoyable and uneventful. Elaine's disposition improved every hour. Truth be told, her new relationship status gave her a sense of freedom she hadn't felt in a while. She decided the time had come to take her position in what she referred to as "the new order of things" much more seriously. And honestly, it would probably be easier for her if she wasn't in a relationship.

Knowing there were aliens in the universe powerful enough to travel to Earth was one thing. Living and interacting with them on a daily basis was quite another. Ivan, Bill, and AJ before them thought of themselves as 100% Attal living with the Terra. Her parents were comfortable being 100% Terra living with the Attal. Both groups were at peace with their role in the new order. She, Pax, and Aggie, however, were in turmoil about all the secrets and felt a great deal of pressure to create a smooth, orderly transition for peaceful co-habitation on Earth. Gary would say the stress and discomfort were because she, Pax, and Aggie were all in their mid-twenties without enough life experience, while he and the others were mature adults. She disagreed. Her parents failed to understand the responsibility to help her friends when it came to decisions concerning the Terra and the difficulty surrounding those decisions.

She decided to resume her Attal training classes every other week with Pax and focus her energy on helping Aggie and Pax with their assignments of choosing a Terra to join the recently founded Terra Relations Council. It had been almost a year since Ivan, the station leader, had chosen his two Attal members to join Pax and Aggie. The younger Attal were each responsible for choosing a Terra to join Gary as the last two members of the Council. After two years, neither was any closer to choosing a Terra than the day AJ, their friend and homeland delegate, gave them their assignments.

After the Summers said goodbye, during which Eddie promised next year's dinner would take place at Jenny's house, Elaine instructed Pax to follow her upstairs. Maria glanced at Gary and gave him the "I told you so" look. Gary responded in her mind.

"Slow your row. You're way ahead of yourself."

"We'll see," she countered with a smile, showing she obviously knew more than her husband and proving her point by adding, *"And for the record it's 'slow your roll', bun, not 'slow your row.'"*

Once upstairs, Elaine informed Pax about her new relationship status and her plans to visit Aggie in England. She asked, "How is your Terra selection going? Aggie is really struggling and is catching flack about it from Ivan."

"Me, too," Pax replied. "We have agreed I will choose someone successful and possibly wealthy, while she concentrates on an averagely successful, possibly blue-collar, worker. We Attal tend to all have similar morals and personalities. You Terra, however, are much more diverse. We were hoping to choose one person below your Dad's social status and one above. Not that your Dad is—Well…"

"I understand," Elaine offered, letting him off the hook.

"Beyond that agreement, we are both stuck. There are way too many consequences to consider. I don't know how Bill ever chose your Dad—although I'm really glad he did," he quickly added.

"Just a thought, but if you are looking for diversity, you might also consider picking one male and one female. Why don't you ask Bill for help? He's the only person who has been through this. Plus, it would make him feel needed."

"I'll give it some thought," Pax answered, nodding in agreement. "I wanted to avoid dividing his concentration. He has been alone and concentrating on the Seretus for so long I don't want to bother him with my responsibilities. His work is too important. "

"Alone?" Elaine scoffed. "Have you not met my mom and dad? I'd bet my right pinky Dad checks on Bill and offers unsolicited advice every day."

"I'll contact him tomorrow," Pax conceded. "It can only help. Besides, I miss him."

"So tonight, you take me out on the town. Tomorrow, we get down to business," Elaine said, staring into her old closet and looking for something to wear.

"Oh, um, well…I…um…I didn't know we were going out tonight," Pax stuttered, never comfortable being in Terra social situations.

"That's because I hadn't told you, yet," she answered with a smile as she took off her top and tried on an old button-up blouse resembling a hybrid of a southwestern style and the tie-dyed, 60s, hippie look. "This doesn't make you uncomfortable, does it?"

"You know we transport naked. Vanity and embarrassment are rare for Attal. You're fine," he answered intellectually, but not convincingly to either him or her.

"You're lucky," she said, taking off her shorts and trying on a skirt.

"Maybe," he admitted. "But there is nothing wrong with stronger emotions. Emotions can be motivating and protective."

He turned to give her some seemingly unnecessary privacy, but found himself peeking in the mirror at her matching black bra and thong and noticing the cat tattoo she had on her right shoulder blade.

"I guess, but I wish I could control my emotions a little more. I feel out of control sometimes and often regret my actions. This doesn't work," she added to herself as she took off the colorful top and tossed it on the floor.

"We can concentrate on those skills during your lessons if you want, but I like your emotional outbursts. They entertain me," he said before quickly adding, "And help with my Terra education."

"I'm glad I can keep you entertained," she said. "The mind blocks and personal healing lessons are probably more important."

She retrieved a black-and-white-striped blouse with a kitten pirate embroidered on the pocket.

"And I like being able to supplement my sleep," she said as she laid the blouse on the bed and went to a chest of drawers, where she found a black camisole. "Wow. I didn't think I still had any of these here. Whoever said being lazy and sloppy doesn't have benefits didn't know what they were talking about."

Even though she felt Pax would get no more physical enjoyment from her nudity than Aggie or Lizzy might, she turned and faced away from him as she took off her bra and put on the cami and blouse.

She was wrong. She noticed his inability to not only look away but to move. His breathing became shorter, and his cheeks turned pink.

"Really? A nude Terra body does nothing for you, and you big, tough, Attal guys never get embarrassed, huh?" she said, shocking him back to reality.

After Elaine transformed from her 'get-together with the family' look to her 'going out to the club' look, she and Pax went downstairs and found Maria at the sink, finishing the dishes.

"We're going out for a little while, and Pax is gonna drive. I'll come get my car tomorrow."

Maria looked at her fishnet stockings, short, black skirt, and her black-and-white-striped, kitten-pirate blouse.

"Well, you sure look different than when you went up there."

Although Elaine seemed unfazed, Gary still instructed his wife telepathically, "*Be nice.*"

Chapter IV

  Wednesday morning, Maria stopped by Riverside Market, their family's neighborhood store, for a cup of coffee and to give Gary some time away from the register before heading to the beauty shop to start work. He stayed in the cooler, pricing the recent beer order, while she sat near the counter, enjoying her morning coffee and latest romance novel on her Kindle. Interrupted by the electronic beep of a customer entering the store, she dropped her reader.
  "Oh, my God. Bill!" she yelled, somewhere between a squeal and a scream. Within ten seconds, she made her way around the counter and hugged the middle-aged, tan, bald man she hadn't seen in almost two years.
  "Oh, my God. It's so good to see you. What are you doing here? Is everything okay? Gary is going to be so surprised. Are you okay?" she exclaimed in rapid fire.

"Everything is fine. I really missed you guys," he said. His voice shifted to a loud, raspy whisper simulating airless lungs when he added, "And your hugs."

"Oh, sorry," she said, releasing her grip. "It's just such a surprise. Why didn't you tell us you were coming home?"

"I hoped for a response like this," Bill answered.

After another few minutes of catching up, she opened the large, wooden, insulated cooler door.

"Bun, there is someone out here who needs to talk to you."

"Okay. I'll be right out. Who is it?" Gary asked, out of breath from his cold workout.

"Some 40-year-old bald guy claiming to be an old friend of yours," she answered, not wishing to ruin Bill's surprise.

"Yea, more likely some guy wanting to sell me something or borrow money. Tell him to hold on a second. I'll be right out," he instructed.

"Okey-dokey," she responded, closing the cooler door with a smile.

He continued pricing the last case of beer, broke down the cardboard box, and added it to the pile on his way to the register.

As soon as he heard the door open, Bill used some vis stored in his antique necklace to contact Gary.

Recognizing Bill's request, Gary decided to make his unknown visitor wait and chose instead to stay in the back room and accept Bill's communication.

"Hey, buddy. What's up?"

Bill answered, *"I've had my first hug and kiss from a girl in almost two years. I wanted you to see her. She's beautiful."*

"What? You contacted me just to show me a girl? Um...I appreciate the thought, but what does that have to do with catching the Seretus Ligare?"

"Nothing," he conceded. *"But wait 'til you see this girl."*

Gary concentrated on looking through Bill's eyes and saw his friend lean in and kiss Maria's cheek.

Not missing a beat, he said to his friend, *"You better be careful. She looks cute, but trust me, if you get any closer it will cost you a lifetime of hard labor to keep a woman like her happy."*

He left his friend's mind and hurried through the swinging door. Embracing his alien friend, he said, "Oh, man, it's good to see you. It has been too long."

"You have no idea. Even with Maria's daily updates, it's been extremely lonely," Bill admitted. "I really missed you guys."

"Us, too," Gary said. "Don't get me wrong; we are thrilled to see you. But what brings the unannounced visit?"

"I'm hungry," Bill said with a smile. "I thought we could have dinner tonight."

"Sure," Maria said. "Should I invite anyone else?"

"Absolutely. Let's invite the whole Pride," Bill answered, using Gary's latest nickname for their group of earthlings and aliens who all wore the modified, antique, Mooncat necklaces.

Maria quickly contacted the whole team. Within seconds, Pax, Elaine, Ivan, Aggie, Bill, and Gary were all accepting her communication request.

"We haven't had a full team chat in a long time," Ivan pointed out the obvious.

"Is everyone okay?" Pax interrupted.

"Everything is fine," Maria answered. *"Excellent, actually. I just wanted to invite everyone over for dinner tonight."*

"Oh. Okay," Ivan said, clearly puzzled. *"Why tonight? And why the whole team?"* He asked what everyone wondered.

"Because we have an unexpected guest in town. Besides, we haven't all been together in over a year," she said as she turned and looked at Gary and Bill who were standing arm-in-arm and waving to Maria.

Everyone euphorically agreed to meet at the Whites' house at 7:00 p.m.

****

Not surprising to anyone in the room, Elaine arrived last at 7:08p.m. She had big hugs for Bill and Aggie and a smaller, but heartfelt hug for Ivan, the station leader, whom Elaine still pictured as the 75-year-old she had met a couple years ago instead of the 35-year-old man in front of her who could easily pass as Pax's older brother. Elaine handed a wrapped present to Bill.

"I got you something I thought you might enjoy. You can open it after dinner."

"I don't need presents," Bill said while excitedly accepting the gift. "Just seeing you all makes this the best day I've had in years."

"Yea, but presents make any occasion better," she argued with a wink.

After dinner, Bill told everyone the real reason for his visit. "As you know, I've been in communication with AJ, our delegate. We have agreed my search for our Seretus friends has gone about as far as it can as a solo act. They have used their time away from the station well and have done an admirable job hiding and protecting themselves. AJ feels—and I agree—the odds of my bringing them to justice alone are minuscule."

"How minuscule?" Pax interrupted.

"Estimates are at about two percent. Personally, I feel it is less. They have become very powerful."

"How can we help?" Pax asked while everyone nodded, offering any necessary assistance.

"Ivan, Aggie, and Pax—the Delegate hopes you will offer your allegiance to me and my assignment."

"Of course, we will," Ivan said. "What can we do?"

"Hold on," Elaine interrupted. "You're not going to exclude us again. You tried that a couple years ago in jolly, old England. I almost ruined the mission trying to learn your secrets, Aggie got poisoned and almost died, Eddie got shot, and some chick named Rosa died. For better or worse, we're a team."

Bill listened to Elaine's rant, but instead addressed Gary. "It's your call. This will be more dangerous than the night at The Grey Wolf Pub."

Although unnecessary, Gary looked at Maria, who gave him the slightest of nods and a hint of a smile before he said, "You know me better than that. What kind of secret club would we be if we didn't save the world every couple years? Count us in. Now, who needs a cup of coffee with dessert?"

"I knew you would help, and I'm glad to have you on board. Before we go forward, we need to discuss a couple of situations," Bill said, turning serious. "AJ and I are considering some changes so extreme they could risk your planet's leadership and possibly its evolutionary process. It's important we do this our way and by our rules."

"Geez, Bill. It's not like you're going to create a society of evil monkeys to take back the world. Let's just team up and go get the bastards instead of mucking up the waters with rules and bureaucracy."

"It's not that simple," Bill countered. "To use a Terra phrase, we are talking about upping the ante here. We've already broken our rules to include you in our secrets and introduce you to our technology. What we are planning next is a much bolder move. We do not intend to simply tell you our secrets; we want to *give* you our secrets. Big difference."

"Okay," Gary said slowly. "Maybe you should tell us your plan and some of these rules of yours before we agree to proceed."

"Hence the visit," Bill said with a smile. "As you all know, Wendy and Barry changed their appearance and fled our station almost two years ago. I have not been able to find out much about Barry other than *he* is now *she*. When he left the station, he chose a female form."

As a reminder to the Whites, he turned his IDC and showed them a picture of a thin, 35-year-old Latina woman with long, straight, jet-black hair.

"I expect her to have changed her appearance, but the body height and basic size should still be similar. I don't know much about her other than she's content hiding in the shadows and is apparently making the major decisions.

"Wendy, who also changed gender, is much more visible."

Bill showed them a dark-skinned, thin, 5'9" Latino with short, straight hair and slightly sunken eyes.

"He has chosen the name Carlos and changed his appearance greatly."

His device now showed two pictures, side by side. The man on the left showed the body shape of an Attal immediately after transport, a thin man with darkly tanned, blemish free skin and medium-length, straight, black hair. The man on the right had a couple of visible tattoos, a short, military haircut, and a scar on his neck, mostly covered by a shirt that struggled to contain his muscles. He looked so menacing; Maria felt he might kill her if she made eye contact for too long.

"Wow. What a change," she said out loud to herself with the silent agreement of everyone in the room.

Bill continued, "His moves are much more documented. I'm sure my list is incomplete, but he is absolutely responsible for the bombing of a drug lord's village, assassinating a Chilean leader, and maintaining the security detail for the most well-known, South American evangelist. It appears he is the face and ground troops of the *Seretus Ligare*, while our Latina, lady friend chooses to remain hidden and protected. I'm not implying Carlos isn't protected. He has created and surrounded himself with a heavily armed group of militant, Terra fighters. Their numbers have been estimated at between fifty and sixty."

"Jesus," Gary interrupted. "Maybe we do need an army of evil monkeys."

"We were thinking a small group of well-trained cats. Although I must admit, that doesn't sound very menacing," Bill said with a chuckle

"How can—" Gary looked up and did a quick body count. "—four Attal and three Terra ever match two Attal and what I assume will be a hundred, elite, Terra soldiers?"

"Normally, they couldn't," Bill answered. "Hence our plan to change the game. We need to stop these two before they complete their mission, and we would prefer not exposing ourselves to the world in the process. We're convinced our plan is the best way to remove them from power and return control back to the Terra."

"What's this plan of yours, and what is the Seretus' mission?" Gary asked.

"I'm confident they're no longer content hiding and running their non-sanctioned, Galtri-style games. As best we can tell, their mission is to possibly expose, but ultimately overthrow the Attal and take over vis production. They could then use the vis to topple the Terra leadership. Essentially, although it sounds very Terra cliché, they want to take over the world."

"Oh, is that all?" Gary asked. "And what is your plan to stop them?"

"You're always kidding about saving the world. Well, here's your chance," Bill said with a smile to his best friend. "We are creating a secret Attal station with access from the surface and using it for sophisticated vis training in advanced functions. We are *not* going to use conventional Terra weapons, but rather the advanced technology and energy we have and they so desperately desire."

After a short pause, Bill gave a devious, closed-mouth smile and added, "Just because we're a peaceful, non-violent race, doesn't mean we don't have certain, useful skills."

"I understand and agree with your logic," Pax intervened. "And I mean this with all due respect, but why include the Whites? Why not just train eight Attal, give them the more powerful, homeland vis, and send them after Carlos and the Lady?"

"Kinda thinking the same thing," Gary added.

"We considered that with three different models," Bill admitted. "Each one had a lower chance of success than including the Whites. Out of necessity, the Seretus has surrounded themselves with Terra: people, weapons, and technology. They are attempting to use Terra laws, politics, and fears to become strong enough to combat the Attal. A loyal, secret, well-trained team, able to successfully operate in the Terra world, is essential to our plan.

"Additionally, Ivan and AJ feel it would be better not to include too many Attal. We can't be completely certain there are no more Seretus supporters at the station, and the leadership is embarrassed by their success. We don't want their efforts to become a primer for future revolutions, and it would be catastrophic to include one of their sympathizers in our plan and give them a special, vis-enhanced skill.

"Using the Terra also gives us the advantage of surprise. And although we hope they will be peaceful teammates, they will not be governed by our rules against harming Terra. What we need is a small, dedicated group of people who think like and are intimately knowledgeable about the Terra yet have the full power of the Attal. What we need are the people in this room.

"We will hopefully be adding one more to our group."

He turned to face Maria.

"We think it's time to bring Eddie into our club. We could use his help, and the necessary training schedule will be difficult to keep secret from him. Also, we feel he would be safer as a part of our effort rather than an unprepared, weak link. The *Seretus* could use him as a bargaining chip if they learn of our relationship with your family."

Maria nodded, acknowledging that she understood his logic and request, although not fully convinced his assumptions were correct.

"If you still choose to help us, we will supply you with much more *vis* and will give you technology and training beyond your current comprehension. But you must agree to follow our rules."

Bill faced Gary, leaned in, and said, "Not your interpretation of what is best for the group."

Addressing the whole group again, he continued, "You each must accept our authority over the use of our technology and our punishment if you choose not to follow that authority. If you do decide to join us again, you will be agreeing to put your lives on hold and help us until the end of this mission."

After an awkward silence a little too long for Elaine's comfort, Gary finally said, "So, who wants coffee with their brownies?"

They ate brownies, promised by Maria to be baked with vegan ingredients, and discussed non-life-changing events:

Elaine's hair, Bill's physical appearance, Riverside Market, and Pax's lack of dance skills.

Pax took advantage of this time to have a short, private conversation with both Bill and Aggie. Bill advised his son about his task of revealing his secret to a Terra.

"The best you can do is pick a Terra you respect for the Council and hope for the best. Trust your instincts. You're the smartest person I know."

"It is really good to see you again," Pax said.

"My best day in years," Bill added, ending the conversation with a hug.

As the evening wound down, Elaine sensed Aggie in her mind.

"Whatcha need?" she asked.

"Do you know why Pax wants me to stop by his apartment before transporting back?"

"No idea, but I hope it's to help him with his dance moves. Check out Bill's present," she added, standing by herself and laughing out loud.

"Hey, Bill," Aggie said loudly so everyone could hear. "What did Elaine bring for you, and why didn't I get a present?"

"Good question. Let's see."

As he unwrapped his gift, Elaine chimed in.

"Just a small thank-you for bringing Pax and Aggie into my life and a reminder of how much more work they need to truly become Terra."

They passed around Elaine's gift and laughed for fifteen minutes at the framed picture of Elaine and Pax at the club, proving that dancing is not an intellectual activity.

Gary watched his friends share a laugh at Pax's expense. He could never choose to not help this group, but as always, he needed time to think and discuss his options with Maria. Before parting ways for the night, they all agreed Ivan and Bill would

41

continue their efforts to create the secret, Attal surface station while Pax and Aggie chose their Terra for the Council and the Whites made changes so their businesses would operate smoothly in their absence. They scheduled another meeting in a month to discuss what role, if any, the Whites would play in saving the world one more time.

"But most importantly," Gary informed the group. "If we choose to join you, we will need to come up with a cool name for our new clubhouse."

Chapter V

    Manny sat at the end of the bar, waiting to make his next rounds and monitoring the guests, when he saw the muscular, dark-skinned man enter. Even though they had a cordial relationship, Carlos frightened the young waiter, who avoided eye contact with him if at all possible.
    "Where's Juanita?"
    "She's in her cabana. Can I bring you a beverage this afternoon, sir?" Manny asked, smiling but focusing on Carlos' large, menacing figure more than his dark, terrifying eyes.
    "A bottle of water," he answered, walking without the need for directions to the cabana Juanita rented by the week. He entered her private, outdoor oasis and stood over her.
    Juanita lifted her sunglasses and rested them on her head. "How are you, brother?"

"I'm hot. Why do you insist on sitting in this heat? There's an air-conditioned building fifty feet away. And quit calling me 'brother.' It's Carlos."

"After two hundred years of station life, I love the weather and the sky. Besides, look at how I'm treated. With my money and this Terra body, I feel like a Pat."

"I *was* a Pat. It's nothing like this," he corrected her. "Also, Terra brothers and sisters don't call each other that. Call me Carlos."

Manny interrupted their Terra lesson, uncapped the bottle of water, and poured it in a glass. Laying it on the table closest to Carlos, he asked Juanita, "Ma'am, can I get you anything at this time?"

"No, but after my brother leaves, maybe you can help me with my lotion," she said, lowering her glasses over her eyes.

"As you wish, ma'am," Manny responded as he turned and headed back to his stool at the worker's end of the bar.

"I don't need a Terra lesson, *Carlos*," she said. "I've spent more time on the surface than you and have orchestrated everything perfectly thus far. If we survive our little game, I'll serve you again when the Attal are in charge. For now, just do what you're told."

She paused long enough for him to respond, but realizing one would not be coming, she asked, "Did you confirm our assumptions? And what is our vis balance?"

"I'm confident we will not have to assassinate our opponent to win the Argentinean election," Carlos answered. "Our lead is almost insurmountable. With the addition of our evangelistic friend's recent support, I'm predicting a win."

"And vis?" she asked, unimpressed with Carlos' success.

"I used .04u guaranteeing our friend's support and .06u on other military needs."

"Acceptable," Juanita affirmed. "So our balance is 18u?"

"18.54, assuming you didn't use any more convincing Manny's boss he could continue to serve your every need."

"No, and I fear it's time for me to give up my residence at this fine establishment. It's by far my favorite, but I don't want to get complacent and caught by the leadership. We agreed it would be best to change locations every six Terra weeks. I've been here almost seven. Next week, I move."

"Then you want to continue with ISASP?" he asked.

"Yes. Do you think we can get control of them using minimal vis?" she asked.

"Rumor has it they are having big security issues on their ships and at the docks in North America. I also heard they are seeking more Terra money," Carlos explained without actually answering her question.

"Excellent. I'll meet with them next week to offer a plausible, but risky option to minimize their monetary worries and insist my protection company help with their security problems. We should be able to control them with no vis."

"I think I can spare some men. Not only will we be able to watch and control ISASP, but if we have men on his ships and at the world's largest docks, we will have a more impressive disbursement of troops."

"Nice, ancillary benefit, but we need to lock up Brazil first. After Chile and Argentina, we will have the whole ABC union locked. With South America under our control, we are halfway to our goal," Juanita stated, turning her attention to her IDC.

"I'm more concerned about our vis level. We are going to need much more when we turn our attention to North America. Have we had any success with our source at the station?"

"Ivan has done a good job protecting his energy," Carlos explained. "But we have found out some interesting information. It seems the technology labs have been Ivan's main priority over the last couple years. He has been developing some new devices and possible weapons."

Thinking out loud, Juanita said, "We are definitely going to need substantially more vis against our old friends to gain control of North America. I have an idea on how to acquire it, but we are going to need those ships for my plan. Make sure ISASP realizes how much they need our protection."

Realizing she digressed, she brought the conversation back to their current situation, suddenly anxious things weren't going as well as she thought they were a couple minutes ago.

"Do we know what these new weapons are? How to beat them? And can we get a hold of any?"

"Not yet, but we do know they have been concentrating on tools used on the surface. Also, it appears you assumed correctly. Someone who reported as returning to the homeland stayed on the surface and has been hunting us since our departure."

"Do we know who? And were they successful?" she asked.

"It's Bill," he answered. "We do not know how much information he has gathered, but we know he has been on an unsupported assignment to apprehend us."

"Logical move," Juanita conceded. "Let's revamp our schedule and move locations every three weeks. I'll change locations tomorrow, and we should put someone on a search-and-destroy assignment for Bill. Does our contact know if he still looks the same? Is he even male?"

"We do not know, but we have confirmed he is still in communication with Ivan," Carlos admitted. "Our guy will continue to work on procuring vis and gathering information. I have another meeting scheduled with him in thirty moons."

"You work on convincing ISASP their security is understaffed," Juanita instructed. "I will schedule a meeting with their president. We will talk again in seven moons at my new location."

"Okay, sis," he said as he got up and headed out to start his assignment.

On the way out, he passed Manny heading toward Juanita's cabana with some suntan lotion and a bottle of mineral water.

****

Aggie arrived at Pax's apartment and found him uncharacteristically nervous and waiting for her at the door.

"Please, come in, and thanks so much for helping me."

"You're welcome for coming," she said. "But I haven't done anything to help you, yet. Whatcha need?"

"Well, I've had a hard time concentrating and—it's quite personal and embarrassing. I didn't know who to ask, and…um…I'd really rather you not say anyth—"

"Geez, Pax," Aggie interrupted. "You sound like a nervous Terra kid trying to talk his way out of trouble. Quit stuttering and just ask your question."

Realizing she was right, he took a deep breath and said, "I want you to get naked and try to seduce me."

"You want me to do what?" Aggie asked in a surprised squeal two octaves higher than her usual tone.

"You asked me to be direct," Pax said. "I've been struggling to concentrate recently due to unstoppable and illogical thoughts about Terra sex and intimacy."

"We are both trying to become more Terra, but that doesn't mean we should sleep together," Aggie said, surprised by his suggestion.

"It makes the most sense," Pax disagreed. "We are of similar age and are the two Attal most familiar with the Terra. We have been on the surface about the same amount of time and are both comfortable with nudity. More importantly, neither of us has any experience with Terra sex, and we are both curious."

"I would be lying if I told you I didn't think about trying Terra sex," Aggie admitted. "And I have been successful in arousing Terra men with my body, but they were strangers and usually under the influence of alcohol."

"But were *you* aroused?" Pax asked.

"Um…I'm not sure," she answered in embarrassment. "I think so. Maybe. Even though I ended the test, I secretly planned for more studies."

She looked down at the floor.

"But having sex with you seems wrong."

"Why?" Pax asked. "You just said what I'm feeling. Think of your efforts to arouse me as another test."

"First, to feel more Terra and get proper experience, you would need to sleep with a Terra. But much more importantly, unless I'm an idiot, the Terra girl causing your arousal is my best friend, and it just wouldn't be right."

"I understand, but I'm struggling with this question: Is my curiosity about the Terra culture getting the better of me, like you admit is your situation, or is it based on my feelings for a particular Terra? You're attractive, and men find in you a cause for arousal. I am looking for a controlled situation with a trusted friend to determine if my feelings are normal, young adult, Terra feelings or a specific feeling about a specific person."

"Or maybe both. But can't you just watch pornography or something?" she asked.

"I've already watched enough. This is the most logical next step," Pax answered honestly.

"Sleeping with someone might be the next step, but don't you think sleeping with Elaine's best friend would be wrong?" she asked, questioning his logic.

"Maybe. The difference is I'm not trying to sleep with Elaine's friend; I'm trying to test myself with my Attal friend. You are the only person qualified to understand my feelings and not be offended by the request," Pax explained.

They sat in silence for a couple of minutes, finally interrupted by a soft-spoken and apologetic Pax.

"I'm sorry to make you uncomfortable. I don't ever think about sleeping with you—although you are very attractive," he quickly added. "I wanted to know if I, like most Terra men I read about, would be excited by any attractive, sexy woman trying to seduce me or am I just unable to control my emotions around Elaine. Your Attal familiarity with my body and ability to control your emotions just seemed safe. But of course, you are right. I'm very sorry."

"Honestly," Aggie said after a few more seconds of silent reflection. "I have been extremely consumed by Terra intimacy, also."

She paused for another few seconds before asking, "You really think I'm sexy?"

She crossed her hands at her waist, grabbed her shirt, and lifted it over her head. Her smooth, caramel skin contrasted with her white bra as she walked over and took his face in her hands.

"I will not sleep with you out of respect for Elaine," she whispered.

He felt her warm breath on his neck as she gently kissed her way to his ear.

"But I will seduce you."

They shared an unpracticed, yet passionate kiss. For the first time in his life, Pax felt a silken tongue slide against his own. It stimulated him and enticed him to deepen the embrace, until they were both breathless. Aggie broke their contact, stepped back, and awkwardly removed her jeans.

"But I need to take a shower first."

After giving him another kiss, she turned and slowly walked down the hall. Watching her walk away, he noticed the contrast between her young, smooth, Indian skin and her bright white, matching lingerie. He couldn't help but compare her almost-nude body to Elaine and her colored hair and tattooed shoulder that had created his distracting obsession.

Aggie left the bathroom door open. She looked down the hall at a mesmerized Pax and gave him a closed-mouth smile and a tilt of her head. Leaving him standing in the hallway, wide-eyed and flushed, she got into the shower and closed the pebbled, glass door, distorting her figure but still allowing for intimate viewing.

He inched his way closer to the open door and watched the body he had seen naked on many Attal citizens at the station. But none of them had done this. He wondered if seeing him standing in the doorway, confused, yet hypnotized, pleased her. After eight minutes of watching her obscured figure in the shower, he heard the water shut off, and the door opened.

While he watched Aggie dry herself with his yellow, terrycloth towel and noticed how her long, black hair hung down to the middle of her back, Pax got the answer to his question. He should have been eager to join her in her nudity or aroused at the thought of what might come next, but his excitement came from wondering if Elaine would ever come out of his shower. He fantasized about her wet hair, in his favorite shade of red, laying across her shoulders as she dried her paler, shorter body.

Aggie walked over and kissed Pax with twice the passion as before. Hoping he could someday feel Elaine explore his mouth like this, he concentrated on her technique and his reaction. He thought about holding Elaine's face and returning her kisses. He imagined she took her hands from around his back and—

Aggie's hand gently touching his Dockers shocked him back to the present.

Noticing his obviously functional sex organ, she backed away, wrapped herself in his towel, and said, "This is awesome, and I'm thrilled to be successful, but this is as far as I'm willing to go. It just wouldn't feel right."

Pax, embarrassed by his lack of control, took a moment for his excitement to subside, then took her hand and pulled her in for a hug so he didn't have to make eye contact.

"Thank you so much for helping me," he whispered in her ear. "You are beautiful and were very seductive, but I didn't get excited until I thought of her."

"And what are you going to do about those feelings?" she asked, neither surprised nor insulted by his comment.

"Absolutely nothing," he answered. "And neither are you."

"But I was sexy, right?" she asked, showing insecurity was not a Terra-specific trait.

"Very sexy and very Terra," he answered with a kiss on his friend's cheek.

Chapter VI

Eddie became frustrated by his parents' insistence he come home for the weekend and their lack of explanation as to why. He had just seen them a few weeks ago at Jenny's victory party, and he had exams next week. He did not have time to spend six hours driving home and back, not to mention family functions were always planned around his visits.

"Just make it happen. It's extremely important," Gary had said the third and last time Eddie complained about coming home the weekend before exams.

To add to his frustration, he could not leave until after class on Friday and had to fight rush-hour traffic in Columbus. Later, after a 35-minute delay from an accident near Lodi, and less than a mile from home, the check-engine light came on, letting him know his aggravation had only just begun.

Babying his car home and arriving very frustrated, he saw Elaine sitting on the back porch and petting their tuxedo cat,

Gracie, who lay on the picnic table, enjoying the last of the evening sunshine.

"Hey, what's up?" she asked nonchalantly.

"My blood pressure. I thought you were in England with Aggie," Eddie barked as if she had caused his bad day.

"Boy, aren't you just a ray of sunshine? Change of plans," she said. "I'd cheer up before I get to Mom and Dad if I were you."

Eddie, not taking advantage of his sister's advice, headed for the kitchen, complaining loudly, "Well, I finally made it. This better be impor—"

He was shocked into silence by the sight of Pax, Bill, and Aggie standing in the kitchen with his mom and dad.

"It is important, dumbass," Elaine said as she walked in behind him.

Every time Eddie had been with both Bill and Pax, he'd been asked to do something crazy, fun, and on occasion illegal. Even though the last time they were all together he had taken a bullet in his left leg, he was thrilled to see them.

After hugs and hellos, Eddie announced, "This day just got a whole lot better. Is it time for another trip? If my opinion counts, I'm voting for the French Alps and a little snowboarding."

"Not this time, but I'll keep it in mind," Bill said with a chuckle. "We do have another mission, though, and we could use your assistance. It is bigger than anything we've attempted since the Great Revolution. This one is going to take a while and will be extremely dangerous."

"More dangerous than getting shot in the—wait a minute," Eddie interrupted himself. "Revolution? What the…" He started to chuckle and shook his head. "It doesn't really matter. Count me in. Always a good time when you are all together."

"This is different," Gary said with a very serious look. "Pax and Bill think it's time to give you full membership into our little club."

"Hells, yea," Eddie supplemented, as excited as a 16-year-old picking out his first car.

"I'm not convinced you are ready," Gary added. "This is a life changer, and you haven't shown the greatest capacity to follow orders or to do so without showing off."

"He'll be fine," Maria said, not totally convinced but wanting to be supportive. "But Eddie this is the most important decision you have ever made. It will change everything."

She approached him and spoke softly with her hands on his arm.

"Your life will never be the same. You might not be able to be a nurse, you won't be able to tell anyone, and you will never be able to go back. Your life will probably be better, but it will be very different and very dangerous."

"There's no decision to make," Eddie countered. "My fate was decided years ago, and I'm okay with that. I've been waiting to get full initiation since the night in the pub."

After a 45-minute speech from Pax, with occasional interruptions for emphasis, Eddie had no problem believing Pax, Aggie, and Bill were aliens. It certainly helped explain AJ's ability to deal with the police on his behalf and Aggie's ability to heal him after his brush with a wayward bullet.

"I'm glad you are just advanced aliens. I thought you were some kind of magic folk or something. Too much Harry Potter I guess. But I do get my proof, like everyone else got, right?"

"You already believe us," Bill said. "That would just be showing off. But what did you have in mind?"

"I'd like someone to read my mind, and I'd like to see life at the station," he answered.

After a couple of seconds, he amended his request.

"Strike that. I'd like Pax to read my mind. I do not give permission to anyone else. Can Mom, Dad, and Elaine read minds?"

"No," Pax answered. "As of right now, no Terra has those skills."

"Will I learn how to keep people out of my mind?" Eddie asked, suddenly not so thrilled with the idea of three people in this room being able to see his deepest secrets.

"If you like. We also have tools to help keep your thoughts private," Pax said with a smile. "As a matter of fact, that's one benefit of club membership. Are you wearing your Moonlight Trail volunteer necklace?"

"No. I only wear it when volunteering. Why?" Eddie asked, confused about the connection.

"Because we have a new one for you," Pax said, removing a necklace from his pocket. "This one must never be taken off. Unlike the cheap copy you already have, this is an original and very old. It holds the vis we talked about and has Attal technology, allowing you telepathic communication with the other wearers of these necklaces. A group your dad, in his infinite ability to be corny, has named the Pride."

"Who all has one of these necklaces?" Eddie asked the next most logical question.

"Just the people in this room and Ivan, the old man you met in London," Bill answered. "You should know, Ivan, who now resembles a 35-year-old Pax, is the leader at the station. And for the record, our little club is a secret to both your society and ours."

Eddie held out his hand to accept the new, alien-enhanced necklace which gave him membership into the coolest of clubs. Before he could take it, Pax withdrew the gift and clarified the device's abilities.

55

"Once you are wearing this, no one with normal, Earth vis will be able to penetrate your thoughts without your permission. Not even me. You asked me to enter your mind. I can only enter your mind if you are *not* wearing the necklace."

Pax smiled at Eddie and asked, "What would you like me to do while I'm in there?"

"I have a couple ideas," Gary spoke up.

"I've been thinking about a couple things, too," Maria said with a wink.

Pax and Bill then turned toward Elaine, who responded, "Don't look at me. I already know too much about what goes on up there."

Everyone laughed except Eddie, who started to realize the complications accompanying advanced technology.

"I'd like to see the station, and I'd like to experience a mind plant. I think," he said over their laughter. "But I'm losing confidence in my plan."

"Don't worry. What is private will remain private. But you must start trusting all of us unconditionally."

Bill interrupted Pax's explanation and added, "Everyone in this room, plus Ivan and AJ, who is now our home planet delegate, are part of a team that always have each other's best interests at heart. We do not have time, nor should we have to take the time, to explain our actions. When we ask or tell you to do something, you need to do it without question or hesitation. Do you understand?"

Eddie didn't answer, but nodded in agreement.

"So, if Gary calls and says come home for the weekend, you have to trust he knows you have exams, but has a more important need. If your mom says to be here Tuesday at 8:00 p.m. and to wear all black, you have to do it."

"I get it," Eddie answered, his tone showing he didn't appreciate the lecture.

"I don't think you do," Pax said. "Your lack of subordination or delay in action could be the difference in someone's life—including your own."

"We are honored to include you, but to be included means you unconditionally do our bidding," Bill added for emphasis.

When Bill saw Eddie turn and look at Elaine, he answered the question before Eddie could ask it.

"Yes even Elaine. She understands and has accepted the responsibilities that come with membership. But it's not all one sided," Bill said with a tender smile. "For your loyalty, you will have all of us to do your bidding. Trust me; the trade-off will work in your favor many times."

"Of course. I'm sorry," Eddie said, looking at his dad like a little kid who just got caught using his dad's favorite baseball card in the spokes of his bike. "I didn't realize—I didn't—Well, I'm sorry."

"Don't be," Gary said, letting him off the hook. "How could you know? But now you do, and this is of vital importance."

"What is it with that phrase?" Eddie asked, breaking the tension by laughing at his dad. "I'm sorry, but if you don't want people to laugh at you, don't say things like—"

He stood up tall and proper and straightened his invisible tie.

"It is of vital importance."

After a few seconds of laughter in the room, Eddie very seriously said, "I understand the importance, and I accept. I'll try my best."

"We can't ask for any more," Pax said, ending the lecture. "Now, I need a question from you, and I'd like your permission to plant a thought, so you can feel the affect and understand the power."

After a couple of minutes of thought by Eddie and a private conversation between Gary and Pax, everyone was ready.

"You won't feel anything physical," Pax reminded Eddie. "I will guide you through one of my trips to the station, and while I'm in your mind, I will plant a thought and ask your subconscious a question. It might feel like a daydream or a memory you just remembered."

He paused for a second for emphasis.

"Are you ready?"

"Is anyone ever ready for a mind probe and memory extraction? Hell, no, I'm not ready, but let's do this," he answered.

"Spoken like a true Big Cat," Pax said and closed his eyes in concentration. "What question do you have for me?"

"What's the fastest I've ever driven a car?" Eddie asked.

"Wow. Daring request in front of your mom," Pax answered with his eyes still closed but a smile on his face.

Eddie visited Pax's memory of when he had driven him and Bill to his presentation.

When they transported to the station, Eddie said, "Wow. It's spotless, and everyone is naked. I love you guys."

He continued to watch Pax's memory until he left the station. At which point, Pax closed the connection and opened his eyes. Eddie sat opposite Pax with a big grin.

"Way cool."

"Speaking of way cool," Pax said. "I figured the fastest you ever drove would have been in the Mustang on the way to Pittsburgh, but did you and Brandon really get the Evo up to 141 mph on Route 8?"

"She still had a little left in her, but I pussied out," Eddie said with a smile.

To the surprise of everyone in the room except Gary and Pax, Eddie got up and quietly approached his sister.

He gave her a kiss on the check and said, "I'm so sorry I've been such a pain in the ass to you over the years. I'll make you proud as part of this team."

He then got out his wallet and gave Elaine a twenty-dollar bill.

"Buy yourself something nice, and please accept my apology."

Gary walked up to his son, patted him on the back, and handed him a folded-up piece of paper.

"It takes a big man to apologize, Eddie. I'm proud of you."

Unfolding the paper, he read his dad's handwritten note.

You will apologize to your sister for being hard to get along with and give her something for restitution.

"Gee, thanks. I think. Twenty dollars is a cheap price for admission, but give it to Elaine? Really?" Eddie said as he put on his new, antique, Mooncat necklace.

He trained the remainder of the weekend and easily mastered communication and how to open and close his mind. He hated to leave on Sunday, but he had a long drive and an anatomy exam Monday morning.

On his way back home, Eddie felt his Dad's request for communication and accepted.

"We are very proud of you, and we trust you, but as a reminder, tell no one about our friends or your new abilities."

"Yea, how am I going to keep that a secret?" Eddie asked, already concerned about wanting to help or show off for his friends.

"Don't worry about it right now. There's nothing to tell. We will address it later at our next meeting. When in doubt, talk to Elaine. She has experience with keeping the secret from her friends."

"Yeah, and her relationships have worked out so well," Eddie rebutted.

"Because of her personality and her relationships, not because of the Attal," Gary corrected him. *"You are not Elaine. But she can be helpful. It's time to clear your mind and concentrate on school. Good luck on your finals."*

Eddie knew his thoughts were his own again and responded out loud to no one.

"I'm sure I'll do great. I've heard studying for finals is highly overrated."

****

The next morning, Eddie sat in his anatomy class, wishing he had spent more time studying. He had a B- in the class and counted on the final to raise his grade. If he didn't receive at least an 86%, he would have to re-take the class. Without preparation, he resigned himself to relying on his recollection of class discussions and a heavy dose of lucky guessing.

He knew the answer to question six, but the first five answers ranged from educated guesses to an all-out crapshoot. He concentrated on number seven when he got the feeling Aggie needed him. He closed his eyes and opened communication with her.

"Aggie, you caught me right in the middle of my exam. Kinda busy here, but how can I help?"

"There you go, Eddie. Now you are thinking like part of a team," she responded, way too bubbly for Eddie's liking.

"*I'm glad you like my attitude. Again, what can I do for you?*"

"*Nothing,*" she responded. "*You're part of a team now. I'm here to help you. Open your eyes, dumbass, and look at your test.*"

Eddie heard her laughing in his mind. He opened his eyes and read question number eight.

Aggie, who had always excelled in healing Terra bodies, said, "*Eight is C, as in 'cat.'*"

Within thirty minutes, all one hundred questions were answered, including the first six, of which Eddie would have had three correct without his Attal friend. He changed a few answers to make sure he didn't draw attention with a perfect score and thanked Aggie for all the help.

"*Trust the Big Cats. We're here to protect each other,*" she responded. "*I need to head to the airport and pick up your sister. Call any time. See ya soon.*"

"*That's the second time you saved me, Aggie. Thanks.*"

Eddie closed his mind and handed in his test, knowing he would receive a 95%.

Chapter VII

Aggie brought Elaine to her modest, but immaculately clean, two-bedroom apartment, located 12.5 miles south of Northampton. The location gave Aggie quick access to the UK transportation pod and still kept her less than an hour from the outskirts of London. They were unpacking Elaine's bag in the back bedroom when they heard a voice in the living room.

"Aggs, I got your mail again. Good news. It looks like our plan worked. You're officially invited to the Unknown and Unexplained Symposium and Gala at Cambridge. Sorry I opened it, but I just got so exc—Oh, my. I'm sorry. You're not Agrata."

"Very perceptive of you. You must be Robert," Elaine said to the thin, well-dressed Englishman. "Or does Aggs call you Bobby?" she added in a mocking tone, showing her displeasure with his nickname for Aggie.

"I'm English. No one calls me Bobby," he answered, standing as tall as his 5'11" frame would allow.

"Hey, Robert," Aggie said, bouncing into the living room with a big smile. "This is Elaine."

"I should have known from your description," Robert said, looking at Elaine's blue-and-pink-highlighted hair. "It's a pleasure to finally make your acquaintance. Sorry I barged in on your reunion."

"Not at all," Aggie said, excited to have two of her favorite Terra together. "Would you like to join us for a cup of tea?"

"A cup of tea would be lovely," Robert answered as he clasped his hands and bowed his head slightly, a move Elaine would have considered Attal if she didn't know better.

After a few minutes of pleasantries, Elaine sat down in an antique, oak, spindled chair at the kitchen table and said, "Aggie tells me you are a photographer and blogger. What an awesome way to make a living."

"One would think so, but it's not as glamorous as most assume," he answered with a shake of his head. "I spend most of my time explaining my findings and trying to convince financers I'm not some crazy, conspiracy git."

"Just because there's a conspiracy, doesn't make something crazy," Elaine offered.

"From your lips to their ears," Robert answered before pausing to sip from the cup Aggie served him.

"Aggs, I swear you are getting better every day. Another great cup of tea. Soon, England may even claim you as her own."

Aggie awkwardly smiled and turned away to retrieve her own cup. Elaine could tell by her actions and by the way her friend's caramel skin turned the color of her morning mocha, there were more feelings between the two than her friend had revealed.

Changing the subject to help her friend, she asked Robert, "So, what's this Unknown Gala thing, and why is it so important?"

Aggie, in what Elaine felt was an effort to impress Robert, answered instead.

"It's an annual, prestigious, two-day seminar and gathering of the greatest thinkers in Robert's…um…Robert's industry," she struggled to find the right word.

"I would say it's more my circle," Robert corrected her with a sappy smile, demonstrating to Elaine he shared Aggie's hopes of a more intimate relationship. "It's a yearly symposium where the most renowned scholars report their findings and progress in their studies of the unknown or unexplained."

"Like Big Foot or aliens?" Elaine asked, realizing too late her tone sounded condescending.

"Exactly," Robert answered. "But don't be so quick to judge. There are new species discovered on Earth every year, and I would bet my life there is life on another planet somewhere. Just because we don't understand something doesn't make it untrue."

"I'd bet my life on it, too. I didn't mean to sound so American," Elaine said with a friendly smile while fighting the urge to laugh at his comment. "I just named the first two conspiracy theories that came to mind. I believe in aliens and totally agree there are government cover-ups. But how does one make a living studying them?"

"I don't. Hence the financers and photography business."

After a short pause, Robert had an idea.

"Don't take my word. Why don't you come to the event and see for yourself? I'm obligated to get access for my friend, and sometimes partner, Niall, but as luck would have it, Aggs was granted an invitation. All invites come with an 'and one' for curious newcomers or family."

"It's a date. I'd love to spend the evening with my girl learning more about the unknown."

Robert's pale, English skin tone definitely did not hide his blushing cheeks. He only stuttered a little as he explained.

"Brilliant, but I…um…I thought maybe you could—if you don't mind—I hoped you would accompany Niall, while I escort Agrata."

His cheeks turned a deeper pink.

"I hoped to share my work with her and…well…we tend to be geeks. It would look impressive if Niall and I walked in with two beautiful ladies."

"Okay, Bobby. I'll be your friend's plus-one and blind date. When is this shindig? And what am I supposed to wear?"

****

Pax sat in the Moonlight Trail board meeting, attempting unsuccessfully to concentrate on the presentation of their quarterly report. In addition to his important task of choosing a member for the Terra Relations Council and his distracting Terra feelings of intimacy for Elaine, he had been struggling with a troublesome, internal conflict about Bill and AJ's plan ever since the Pride meeting a couple of weeks ago.

He agreed with Bill's priority ranking; stopping Carlos and the Lady was their first priority. But given the fact they had surrounded themselves with an armed militia, he failed to see how they would be successful without harming or negatively affecting any Terra. He had been asked to take actions contrary to things he had been taught his whole life. Things were spinning out of control. He needed to figure out—

"We have to start thinking like a new organization," Pax heard board member Cathy O'Cotter report. "We are no longer a start-up charity looking to sell our idea to a few rich donors."

Pax cleared his head and gave her his undivided attention.

"Although our start-up and growth has been impressive, it is time for us to realize we are now an important, world-wide charity, and with that comes new responsibilities. To properly handle those responsibilities, we need to change. To paraphrase Lee Iacocca, 'One needs to lead, follow, or get out of the way.' And it's time for us to lead."

After her ten-minute presentation, he not only knew she had correctly analyzed the situation facing Moonlight Trail, but found himself impressed with her ability to articulate her position and win over the room. The meeting finished with everyone's promise to read the report and consider voting for what O'Cotter described as aggressive yet necessary changes next month to ensure their long-term stability.

Before they left the room, when only he, Lizzy, and O'Cotter remained, he addressed her, "Mrs. O'Cotter, I enjoyed your presentation and agree with your analysis."

"Thank you, Pax. Your support means a lot. And please, call me Cathy."

"Thank you, Cathy. I'd like to talk to you more about your plans soon. Can you meet with me next Wednesday at 3:00 p.m. to answer a few questions and fine-tune your plan?"

"Of course," she answered eagerly.

"Lizzy, can you block off some time on Tuesday for you and I to discuss any possible changes before the three of us meet again on Wednesday? How about 11:00 a.m.? We can discuss it over lunch."

After confirming Tuesday's lunch appointment, he went to his office, unnecessarily closed his eyes, and requested communication with Gary.

"*Hey. What's up?*" Gary greeted his friend.

"*I'm struggling with a couple things and need a little advice. Ever since our Pride meeting I've been feeling conflicted about what seems to be the necessary breaking of our governing rules. I'm hoping you could give me a Terra perspective on my predicament.*"

"*I'm not surprised. Bill and I have been having an ongoing dialogue about the same subject the last few days,*" Gary said. "*Although I understand the Attal rules as they have been explained to me, I can't tell you how to think like an Attal. But I can tell you—*"

Gary paused to thank a customer and sat back down to concentrate on Pax's conversation.

"*I can tell you Bill is trying to think of the situation as an evolution of Attal rules, not a breaking of the rules. I think it would be best for you to forget about the ideals of your forefathers and concentrate on solving the situations in front of us. You need to create governing rules for the continued co-habitation of the planet. The first step would be to create the Council that you have been instructed to and reminded of many times.*"

"*Is it Ivan's desire to have the Council create a new set of governing rules?*" Pax asked and then had to wait for Gary to retrieve a pack of Marlboro Lights for a customer named Jim.

"*I think that's a question you need to ask Ivan, but it certainly would be logical. I could also see a situation where the Council gives our club a set a new of rules, inspired by but different than either society,*" Gary volunteered as another possibility. "*There have been many times in both of our worlds that rules needed to be changed for the greater good of the

67

society. I think everyone agrees, this is one of those situations. But you asked me for a Terra prospective. I might have a useful suggestion. Of course, there is an equal chance it could just muddy the already cloudy waters."

"I'll take any help I can get," Pax replied.

"It's a slightly unorthodox way for you to study, but I want you to watch a couple science-fiction movies."

"Okay," Pax drug out his answer. "Do you have any suggestions?"

"As a matter of fact, I do. Even though I concede Americans often produce movies to make a profit, they also tend to write about current fears. For example, movies in the 50s and 60s tend to be about America versus the Russians, while in the 70s, they tend to be about war, protesting the government, and drug use. If you look at sci-fi movies over the last decade, you will see some of our fears about what could happen when technology or government becomes corrupt or erroneously evolves—kinda like your rogue Attal citizens. The movies won't tell you what to do, but they may explain the concerns and fears of our masses, which will help you either on the Council or to personally set up an internal set of values."

"Which ones do you recommend?" Pax asked.

"Why don't you watch…" Gary paused in thought for twenty seconds. *"Watch* I, Robot, Divergent, *and* The Hunger Games. I, Robot *is about technology harming people due to an interpretation of rules.* Divergent *might hit a little close to home as it's about the future, when earthlings take a test and have to choose an industry or class to be assigned.* The Hunger Games *is about government control and abuse through lies, fear, and power. These will give you a taste of what fears the Terra live with and possible pitfalls to avoid when creating a set of governing laws."*

"Great," Pax said, appreciative of the guidance. *"Would you like to come over and watch them with me so we can discuss them?"*

"Hell, yes. As long as there's plenty of popcorn and not too much discussion."

Ten hours later, Pax felt Gary could have made his point without watching the three movies, eating snacks, and discussing his choices. But after a long, yet relaxing and enlightening day, he realized the rules as they applied in the past are important but did not pertain to his situation. He had to focus his thoughts and lead this change in both their worlds.

****

During his Tuesday lunch meeting with Lizzy, Pax was pleased she agreed with most of Cathy O'Cotter's suggestions, though not blindly, disagreeing with some aspects of the report. Instead, she offered input where she felt Cathy's analysis lacked intimate knowledge of Moonlight activity. As the meeting wound down, he determined he had to discuss his inevitable change of status at Moonlight Trail.

"Lizzy," Pax said as he got up from his desk and joined her in the chairs on the subordinate side of the desk. "You have done a phenomenal job as the president of Moonlight, but it's time we made a change."

"What?" she asked, confused by the statement and Pax's change of tone.

"With the changes we just discussed, I think we need to transform your office into the newly formed, Development Director's office."

"But, I've given my life to this. I've been here from day one," Lizzy pleaded before she broke down crying, unable to explain how hurt she felt.

"Oh, no. I'm sorry. I think you misunderstood," Pax said, placing his hand on her shoulder. "I think it's time *you* moved into the director's office. I've always been the planning guy, pleased to work behind the scenes, but Moonlight has outgrown me."

"What?" she repeated. "There is no Moonlight Trail without you."

"No," he corrected her. "There wouldn't have been a Moonlight Trail without me. But it is thriving and ready for its next, big transition."

"But we need you even more during the transition," Lizzy argued.

"No, you don't. I have other projects needing my attention, and I'm confident, with you and Cathy running Moonlight, the successes will continue."

Handing Elizabeth an envelope, he said, "The principles in charge of my other project acknowledge the stresses my abrupt absence may cause. Please accept these gifts to lessen the stress and as gratitude for all your hard work."

She opened the envelop and had a true, jaw-dropping moment when she saw a check made out to Moonlight Trail in the amount of $300,000. Her eyes were unable to hold back her tears when she saw a second check, a personal check made out to Elizabeth Summers for $150,000.

Pax, who enjoyed making his chatty friend speechless, kissed her on the cheek and spoke barely over a whisper.

"Thanks, Lizzy. I couldn't have picked or trained a better protégé. I'll leave the furniture and be out next week."

Pax got up to exit the office, but didn't make it to the door before Lizzy got up and chased him across the room. She embraced him so hard she almost knocked him over.

"Thank you. Can I call you when I get stuck?" she asked quietly in his ear.

"Trust yourself, Elizabeth. You won't need me," he hugged her back. "But you can call me anytime. I will check in on you when I'm in town, donating my hours."

He broke the embrace and left Elizabeth in her new office, alone with her thoughts.

Chapter VIII

Elaine and Aggie walked into the boutique on the corner in downtown London. Upon entering Margaret West's, they were greeted by two, middle-aged, immaculately dressed ladies, who escorted them to a thousand-dollar sofa. They sipped tea and were presented dresses much more conservative and considerably more expensive than Elaine ever considered.
With much discussion and more than a little protest from Aggie, she finally brought Elaine to a shop called Mum's Nightmare. Mum's had neon signs, flashing lasers, and music blasting out of twenty-four speakers. They were greeted by a young girl with short, spiky, pink hair.

"'Ello. How's it going? What can Mum do for you?"

"We need a couple dresses for a gala at Cambridge," Aggie answered loudly over the commotion much more reminiscent of a night club than a dress shop.

"And you came to Mum's?" the bubbly, pink haired clerk questioned. "That's me, girls."

They left the store forty-five minutes later with two new dresses and a pair of shoes for Aggie.

"Are you sure this is appropriate for Cambridge?"

"They're perfect," Elaine answered as she turned and waved down a cab. "Most of the attendees are used to studying things they've never seen. What's more elusive to them than girls in sexy dresses? Besides, I got a feeling Bobby's gonna love your dress."

Friday's symposium was business casual. Aggie, dressed in black pants and a buttercup-yellow, button-up blouse, answered the door to find two similarly dressed, but completely different looking men standing at her doorway. Niall's short, stocky, fit physique and well-manicured mustache and beard made the tall, thin, clean-shaven Robert look much more proper than his humble upbringing deserved.

"Right on time," Aggie greeted her friends. "Please, come in. Can I get you a cup of tea?"

"No, thank you," Robert answered.

"A cup of coffee would be brilliant," Niall said with a smile.

"We are going to get along fine," Elaine said, sipping from a large, black mug. "You must be Niall. I'm Elaine."

She lifted her mug by way of introduction.

"Thanks for joining me at the symposium."

He paused for a moment, shamelessly checking out her cotton-candy hair and black, mid-thigh-length knit dress over striped tights.

"Robert didn't exaggerate. You are unique and beautiful. My reputation will be the beneficiary of your style."

"Aw, thanks. But if it's too much I can change into—"

She looked back and forth between Robert and Niall's matching outfits.

"—tan pants and a blue, button-up Oxford if you wish."

"Hell. No," he answered with an uncontrollable smile, like a 14-year-old who just snuck into an R-rated movie. "For the first time in my life, I'm the cool kid."

The symposium's crowd and excitement exceeded Elaine's estimations. She didn't know if it was her knowledge of alien life on Earth or the skill of the presenters, but she easily could have been convinced all the people at this symposium were privy to secret conspiracies hidden to everyone else. Many times throughout the morning, Elaine felt Niall's actions were unpracticed and a little handsy for a first date, but she enjoyed having him and Robert nearby to explain the presentations. Much like watching a magic show with a fellow magician, they easily waded through what Robert called 'the crazy gits' and concentrated on the more serious researchers.

The presentations and information booths were spread throughout several conference rooms, while the premier talks were reserved for the Babbage Lecture Theatre. Niall escorted her into the Babbage with a gentle touch on her back, a little lower than she preferred. She took Niall's hand off her, crooked his arm about chest-level, and smiled. Elaine placed her hand under his arm, allowing him to properly escort her to a fourth-row seat.

"The speaker, Jeffrey Harding, is an American," Robert explained. "Harding is an anomaly at this event. He's not a researcher or studier of the unknown, but rather a retired engineer who accidently uncovered a hidden, government agenda and allowed his curiosity to become an obsession. His background, combined with his relative anonymity in these circles, is probably why his talk is so crowded."

Elaine realized the weakness of her political knowledge when much of Mr. Harding's talk went over her head. Observing the crowd to pass the time, she realized, besides being one of only a couple people dressed with any sense of fun, most of the estimated two hundred and fifty observers were in agreement with Harding's findings. There were many affirmative nods when Harding discussed some of the more well-documented, 'global, governmental secrets,' such as illegal help to Israel by the United States, the use of Canada to broker a deal to punish Russia for acts of aggression, and the brilliance behind Iran's efforts to coax the United States into a war crippling their enemy.

Elaine noticed a guy a row down and few seats over and wondered if they would have enough vegan choices for lunch when she was shocked back to attention by Harding's change of subject.

"Although this is much less documented than the CIA or Mossad's not-quite-secret-enough missions, I'm convinced there is a power attempting to take over all three members of the ABC union in South America. If one group could gain control of Argentina, Brazil, and Chile, then they could easily be the first in the modern era to control an entire continent."

Elaine looked at Aggie, who returned her gaze and asked telepathically, "*Do you think we should tell Pax?*"

"*Hell, yes,*" Elaine quickly answered.

In less than a minute, Elaine allowed Pax to view the presentation through her eyes and communicate with both her and Aggie.

"One could make a case the same group who benefited from the sudden death of the Chilean leader's main adversary is responsible for backing the soon-to-be-successful Argentinean election. If those assumptions are correct, we should see a change in leadership or policy in Brazil's near future."

After about five minutes of supporting his assumptions, Harding moved on to a new twist on the China-Hong Kong relationship.

Niall laid his hand on her knee and whispered, "Pretty cool stuff, huh? Especially for a bunch of crazy geeks."

Looking at the hand on her knee, she heard Pax ask, *"Who's that?"*

"Robert's friend, Niall. He is my touchy escort," she answered. *"He's harmless, but this is the only way Aggie could go with her not-so-secret admirer."*

"Hello. Still here," Aggie interjected. *"Before we get into everyone's social calendar and secret admirers, do you want us to act on this information?"*

Pax paused for a second of reflection and answered, *"Yes. Will there be any time for you to talk to him after his presentation?"*

"After the other presentations, the speaker normally allows questions, and then remains in the room for a few minutes," Aggie explained. *"According to Robert, most, if not all, of the presenters will be at the gala tomorrow. There will be dinner, dancing, and drinks, which should give us a much better opportunity."*

"I agree," Pax said. *"One of you attempt to contact Mr. Harding after the presentation and confirm his attendance at the gala. We will try and get more information from him tomorrow."*

Aggie, in what appeared to Elaine to be a transparent attempt to not leave Robert, offered, *"I will get you away from Niall for a few minutes. I think, with your hair and clothes, you are more likely to make an impression."*

"Yeah," Elaine answered. *"Because there are so many young, pretty, Indian girls here."*

They exited the theater, and Robert made a move to bypass the queue waiting to speak to Harding. Elaine stopped at the end of the line, though.

"My uncle is an engineer and I think he went to the same school as Harding. I'm going to say hey and ask him if they ever met."

Aggie, not missing a beat, took Niall's arm with her left hand and grabbed Robert's with her right. "Well, I'm starving. Come on, boys. You can make me the most special girl in England and both escort me to lunch."

While inching along for fifteen minutes, Elaine decided to play up the ditzy, young girl role when her thirty-second conversation with Harding presented itself.

"I really enjoyed your presentation, Mr. Harding, but I gotta tell ya, if I were dissin' all those governments, I'd be a little scared to sleep at night."

"The thought has crossed my mind," Harding said, chuckling at either her comment or her appearance. "But I always stop short of blaming anyone for specific acts, and I assume I would get a warning to mind my own business before things get too serious. Or, at the very minimum, they might send a young lady with multi-colored hair and striped tights to one of my talks, telling me to back off."

"I guess," she conceded with a playful shrug of her shoulders and a twist of her hair. "Have you had any requests to back off?"

"No shots across my bow, yet," Harding answered.

Although confused by the reference, she continued, "I'm glad. Are you coming to the gala tomorrow night, Mr. Harding?"

"Of course," he answered. "I hear it's the highlight of the event. And, if you don't mind, please call me Jeff."

"Well then, Jeff, I'll move along and let the people behind me say hello, if you promise to save a little time to chat with me tomorrow," Elaine said.

"But how will I ever recognize you in this sea of young ladies with colored hair?" he asked with a smile.

"Right," she said.

"Well, I could always ask for you by name, if I knew it," Jeff suggested.

"Oh, of course. My name is Elaine. Elaine White."

"Well, Elaine White, I'll see you tomorrow. If I can recognize you."

"I'll see you tomorrow, Jeff," she said with a smile as she turned and bounced toward the cafeteria.

****

The next morning, Elaine turned Aggie's kitchen and bathroom into a makeshift beauty salon. After convincing Aggie they needed to make an impression at the gala, Elaine spent the whole morning and the better part of the afternoon coloring their hair and doing their updos, nails, and makeup. After more than twenty conversations about bras, lipstick, nail color, shoes, and jewelry, Elaine finally felt they were ready for the evening. They stood beside each other and looked in the full-length mirror on the back of the door.

"They aren't going to know what hit them," Elaine said. "Robert is going to love your new dress."

"Are you sure it's not too much?" Aggie asked, not convinced she could pull off the look.

"Are you really going to ask a girl with blue and green hair, wearing a long, black evening gown accented with skull jewelry and leather riding boots, if you think your outfit is too much?" Elaine asked.

"Good point. I love my ombre, and my dress is beautiful. I just think it is too much," Aggie persisted.

"You just aren't used to dressing for attention. Tonight, you are Terra. And you look phenomenal."

When Robert and Niall arrived, they confirmed Elaine's assessment. Both men wore black tuxedos. Niall had a black, formal, long tie, while Robert chose the more traditional bow tie. Following Elaine's advice, Robert's tie was the perfect shade of magenta to match Aggie's dress and compliment her skin tone.

"Wow, Aggs," Robert said when she entered the room. "I've never seen you so dressed up. You look brilliant."

This time, Elaine could see her friend's cheeks blush. Robert's comments were supported by Niall.

"I know I usually give you cheek," Naill confessed. "But not today. You really look lovely, Aggie. But have you seen my American, punk rocker date? Bitchin' dress, Elaine. Just brilliant."

"Thank you," Elaine said. "And you guys look like two, perfectly proper, English gentlemen. Shall we go wow the room?"

"Absolutely" Niall said. "I know I'm usually Robert's proper business partner and plus-one, but I'm not too proper today."

He pulled up his pant legs to show black high socks with white skulls, matching Elaine's accessories.

"How did you ever guess," she said with a smile. "Who's bitchin' now?"

At the presentations the day before, men outnumbered women three to one. Tonight, many of the 'conspiracy geeks' brought their wives, creating a ratio much closer to fifty-fifty.

Elaine entered, in awe of the 250-year-old Senate House building. She felt like Hermione Granger going to the Yule Ball in the Great Hall. Although, Hermione wouldn't have mermaid blue and green hair and a black dress with motorcycle riding boots.

When they entered the gala, the host checked Aggie out and gave Robert a nod of approval. She leaned in and whispered in Robert's ear.

"Are you sure I've dressed appropriately? I hoped to impress your colleagues, not embarrass you."

Before he could respond, she nervously added, "Elaine picked out my outfit."

"Then I must tell you I'm slightly disappointed," Robert said, gently pulling her to the side and gazing into her worried eyes. "Now I have to be thankful to someone who keeps calling me Bobby. You are definitely the most beautiful lady in the building, Aggs. You look like an Indian angel, with just the right amount of devil."

He gave her a gentle kiss on her lips and added with a smile, "I've never been more proud or looked more forward to an evening in my life."

As Elaine and Niall made their way through the queue at the entrance, they joined their friends on a search for table number 32.

Elaine heard in her mind, *"Thanks, girl. I owe you."*

"Enjoy being Terra for the night. You guys are so cute. You look like—"

Elaine smiled and stopped her conversation because she realized Aggie's attention was occupied with other things.

The seven-piece band played all night, keeping everyone festive. Even though she had to block a couple of Niall's attempts at intimacy, they found their comfort zone as a couple on a first date, and Elaine enjoyed her evening. Whether due to his persistence or the open bar, her defenses started to wear down. In an attempt to get swept away in the evening and to appreciate the grandeur of the venue, she allowed him to dance more intimately than she would have under normal circumstances.

She glanced over Niall's shoulder and watched a dreamy Aggie and Robert dancing two couples away from her. It would have been a perfect evening if only she could have shared it with—In a panic, she reached out telepathically to Aggie.

"We forgot to get information for Pax! I have to find Harding. I made eye contact a couple times. Damn it, where'd he go?"

"Relax, girl," Aggie said to her friend as she turned Robert to make eye contact with Elaine. *"You've been helping me all weekend. I got your back."*

"I'm sure you do, but—" She looked over and saw an oddly calm Aggie. *"Um...what? Aggie, we need to—"*

Elaine's gaze left her friend as a familiar, thin, blond man in a black, hand-tailored, Italian tux interrupted her dance by tapping Niall on the shoulder.

"Sir, it would make my evening if you would allow me a dance with this beautifully unique lady."

"I've been in your situation many times, mate," Niall said to Pax before turning to address Elaine. "I think I'll get us another drink, luv. I'll see you at the table."

Elaine's smile was accompanied by watery eyes.

"Well, isn't that gentlemanly of him. Although I'm enjoying my evening with Niall, I must admit I was just thinking about you. Get over here and dance with me."

She pulled him in tight and matched his rhythm.

"I believe you referred to me as a beautifully unique lady."

"I was being polite," Pax said with a smile.

She put her head against his expensive suit and had the remainder of the conversation privately.

"*I am so glad you are here,*" she admitted. "*This weekend has been fun, and I've learned a lot, but it felt like something I should have been experiencing with you. I really missed you.*"

"*Since we are being honest, I missed you, too. I could have easily given you or Aggie instructions, but I transported here just so I could see you. You really are the most beautiful, unique girl I know,*" he confessed.

Elaine danced in silence, too intimate for a casual dance with someone she supposedly just met, but she didn't care. This dance, in this historic place, with this partner, combined to make a truly magical moment for her. After the most romantic three minutes of her life, he jerked her back to reality like Cinderella when the clock chimed midnight.

"*Unfortunately, we have some work to do. You better get back to your date, but could you please introduce me to Harding first?*" Pax asked sadly.

"*Let me stay with you. Please. Maybe I can help. You just got here. Dance with me again.*"

"*Nothing would make me happier,*" Pax responded honestly. "*But I need to get some information from Harding, and I get the feeling this is also a memorable evening for Niall, who generously allowed me a dance with the prettiest girl in the room. I need to be gentleman enough to allow him to finish his date.*"

"*But I want to stay with you and I—*" she tried to argue.

"*And that makes all the difference,*" Pax said. "*Now, please introduce me to your friend, Jeff. I believe there is a drink waiting for you at your table.*"

After a few minutes of introductions and pleasantries, Pax convinced his new friend to go for a walk in the courtyard and discuss some of his research. Due to his new, personal set of governing rules, he had no internal dilemma using the fifteen-minute walk to search Harding's mind. During the mind search, Pax opened his own mind to Bill, who guided Pax's search to extract as much information as possible about their South American problem. Afterwards, he planted a thought deep in Harding's mind to visit a Kud researcher who worked for the electrical engineering department at Colorado State University.

Elaine moseyed back toward her table deep in thought. She could not deny the feelings she had when Pax surprised her on the dance floor. Stronger feelings than she had felt in years. Her romantic thoughts monopolized her mind, and she didn't notice the small group standing at her table. She focused back on the present and realized there were two young couples having a debate with a red-cheeked Niall.

"If you didn't come with Robert this year, then where is this awesome date you supposedly have?"

"Your work isn't good enough to get the big sponsors *or* the pretty girls," the heavier of the two men said, pulling his averagely attractive, slightly heavy date in for a side hug and laughing at Niall's expense.

"Another year as Robert's 'and one,' I'm sure. What a git," the second guy added as the laughter increased.

Elaine sauntered her way between the two laughing couples, took the extra drink Niall held, and said loudly for everyone to hear.

"You were right, sweetie. The sponsor you asked me to dance with would love to fund your research. He agreed to sign up for a two-year commitment."

They stopped laughing and looked at Elaine, who took advantage of the silence to help Robert's friend one more time.

"I'm so sorry I left you alone so long. Thanks for the drink, luv."

Niall's "I told you so" smile only lasted a second.

"I'm so proud of you. I hope your friends here get their funding this weekend, too," Elaine said, and in a final act of charity, she turned and kissed Niall on the lips.

Chapter IX

Carlos, dressed in a light gray suit barely concealing his muscles or the scar on his neck, hopped in the back of the taxi driven by his Kud contact and sympathizer.

"ISASP headquarters," he said. "What will be our ETA?"

Without looking at a watch or contacting anyone on the radio, the skinny, black, 35-year-old cabbie answered, "If traffic remains consistent, 1:40 p.m. 1.7 hours from now."

"You really should get used to using minutes," Carlos advised. "And you are certain you will not be needed by the Attal?"

"Certain," the cabbie said without further explanation.

Carlos dialed his cell phone and spoke to his Terra commander on the other end.

"You have final approval. The mission is a go."

****

Three separate missions commenced simultaneously on three different targets: two cargo ships and a shipping port. The international cargo ships were equipped with the latest electronic devices to monitor the seas and alert the captain of any threats from pirates or unfriendly conditions. They might have been capable of fending off all but the most skilled pirates; however, they were no match for a trained and extremely well-financed militia.

Two planes, each flying 20,000 feet over two separate cargo ships, received their final instructions and prepared for an aerial attack. Their targets were the *06* out of Singapore, due to cross into Brazilian waters in nineteen hours, and the *04* out of Hong Kong. The *04* had been in international waters for about two days. Both planes contained a pilot and four paratroopers; each dropped identical packages: four soldiers with three parachutes.

Jumping at over 21,000 feet created difficulties yet ensured anonymity from the ships below. The two single jumpers left the plane after the tandem jumpers and freefell toward their target at the terminal velocity of approximately 120 mph. The tandem jumpers were the first to open their chute. The secondary soldier removed a device resembling a large radar gun from the pack on his chest and pointed it at the control room of the cargo ship.

The effect was immediate. All wireless, satellite, and much of the hardwired communication on the ship immediately became inoperative. The crew, having no reason to feel threatened, assumed the computers just experienced one of their daily 'tech hic-ups' and the system would reset itself in a minute or two.

While the secondary soldier concentrated on keeping a straight line of visual contact with the ship's control room, the primary soldier aimed for the high, flat shipping container close to the tower. Seconds later, two soldiers came screaming past them, pulled their rip cords, and landed on either side of the tower.

Concurrent to the air attacks, a military raft sped toward each ship at 50 mph, with an ETA of three minutes. The four soldiers coordinated their efforts with the paratroopers for a quick, non-violent boarding of both ships.

****

Another team approached at the docks in Sepetiba, Brazil's third largest port, disguised as dock workers. They blended in perfectly, if one didn't notice their ear buds. They easily made their way to ISASP's temporary storage area, where freight waited for clearance from customs, and then to the dock master's office. Their mission went smoothly. No one would know they were there except for the security guard, still alive but having been tased, drugged, tied up, and left under a tarp in a tool shed.

****

The *06* was taken over without any complication or resistance, except for a twisted ankle by the primary paratrooper in the tandem group and the tasing of the captain, who needed confirmation of the seriousness of his situation.

On the *04* things were a little dicier. A security officer and the communication specialist left the tower to check on the radar malfunction and were rewarded with a brief warning of the attack. The security officer's shots missed their target, but successfully slowed down the attack, giving the bridge some warning of the impending danger.

    Carlos' man turned the corner and was immediately met by the communication specialist, who gave him his best Babe Ruth imitation with a massive pipe wrench. But his untrained skills were a little slow. The mercenary jumped back, causing the wrench to crash against his shoulder. He quickly righted himself and hit the sailor so hard his nose shattered.

    When they reached the bridge, it had already been locked down, and they were forced to blow the metal door and frame to gain entry. The whole assault would have taken less than five minutes, if not for the strict order that there were to be no casualties. The end result didn't change, but the mission lasted almost twenty minutes and came with some minor damage.

    Both ships were held for an hour while the teams rounded up the crew, disabled the ships, and contacted their commander.

    Meanwhile, in the Sepetiba dock master's office, the two fake dock workers restrained the DM and attached a sign on the outside of the door: "Out of office—return at 2:00." The team re-programmed his telephone's automated prompting system, sat quietly guarding him, and waited for their cell phone to ring.

****

    The cabbie pulled into ISASP's parking lot at 1:39 p.m. Carlos spoke to him for only the second time during their trip.

    "How much vis were you able to appropriate?"

    "2.3u," he answered, without explanation.

    "Transfer it before we separate," Carlos ordered. He pressed a couple of buttons on his watch, opening his storage device for the transfer, and made his final call to his Terra troop commander, who answered on the first ring.

"Sir?"

"Start the withdraw sequence," Carlos ordered.

"Copy that."

Each mission leader left their target inoperable and without computers or radar, but with a working radio. They left the crew and captain restrained with duct tape and with a very specific message.

"Sir, we are sorry for any inconvenience our visit may have caused. Please continue with your voyage the best you can."

Each leader opened a black, three-inch military knife, stuck it in the wooden desk, and retreated from the ship in their raft. The team at the docks had similar orders with an added instruction to delay their departure by ten minutes.

Mr. Santos's assistant escorted Carlos into his boss's plush, yet modern office at 1:58 pm. Santos came around from behind his large glass top desk and greeted him with an outstretched hand.

"Carlos, it is good to see you again. Although I must admit I question why you requested this meeting. I think I made it clear, I am very confident in my security efforts."

"Mr. Santos, my company did a free security analysis for you, and I'm sorry to report you greatly overestimate your efforts."

"There is no way for you to know about our operations."

"Now, I believe you are underestimating my capabilities," Carlos stated.

"Can we just agree to disagree?" Santos asked. "I'm more concerned about why you are so interested in my company's safety."

"The sooner you learn to not disagree with me, the better it will be for you and your business," Carlos advised. "As I've explained, I need a transparent way to transport my staff and equipment throughout the world, and I need a way to control the undocumented shipments you make for the 'family' I used to work for."

"Now, you listen here," Santos yelled. "We do not, nor will we ever, be involved with any cartel, the shipping of any drugs, or the transportation of your little, pretend army. You have outworn your welcome. It's time for you to leave my office."

"Allow me to give you one more piece of advice," Carlos said calmly. "I don't think that would be your best move right now."

Santos' face turned red, betraying his anger. His stare-down with Carlos ended when his assistant hurried into his office.

"Sir, we have a situation on the *06*."

"Can this wait? I'm obviously busy," Santos barked.

"Um...sir, I...um...sir, they're floating dead."

"What? How in the hell does a twenty-million-dollar ship end up dead in the water? Has anyone talked to the captain?"

"It's the captain who called," the assistant informed his upset boss.

Before the assistant could finish repeating the captain's account of what caused them to be on the ocean without engines or computers, the sudden appearance of security officers shocked him into silence.

Santos' head of security rushed into the office and reported, "Sir, I just got off the radio with the *04*. They are also floating dead and had a small explosion on the bridge. Everyone is okay, but they're requesting instructions and support."

"Jesus Christ! What in the hell is going on? There's no way this can—"

He stopped mid-sentence and looked over to the leather couch where Carlos sat with his arms folded and a straight face.

"I swear to God, if I find out—"

The security officer interrupted, "There's more, sir."

"What?"

"As is protocol, we have attempted to contact every ship and every office. We have not been able to establish communication with the Sepetiba office."

"Get someone over there and find out what is going on! And what the hell happened to my ships? Was it pirates?"

"No, sir," the security officer answered. "They made no demands and stole nothing. It's the weirdest thing I've ever seen."

"It sounds like a security test," Carlos offered. "And if I may be so bold, it sounds like you failed."

The security officer turned on Carlos.

"We are in the middle of a crisis. You have no idea what you are talking about."

"I know it is your job to make sure there are no crises," Carlos calmly replied. "How's your day going?"

"Gentlemen, wait for me outside," Santos instructed his staff.

Once they were alone in the office, Santos took his phone out of his pocket.

"I don't know what you are up to, but as soon as I figure out what is happening in Sepetiba and get my ships running again, someone is going to pay for this. Even if that someone is you. This is costing me millions."

"This could have cost you much more," Carlos responded, totally unfazed by his threats. "Your ships can be functioning in ten minutes. All you need is the computer start-up code. This failure will cost you nothing except a couple of hours and apparently a new door on the *04*. But if you want things to go a little smoother, you are going to have to learn how to follow orders."

"I don't follow orders from you! Who the hell do you think you're screwing with?" Santos yelled so loudly that spit beaded on his glass desk and his tan, Latino skin turned almost purple with rage.

"I know who I'm talking to. Do you? Don't call the office."

"Go to hell, Carlos," he said as he pushed 'send' on his phone.

In his receiver, he heard a computerized female answer his call.

"Mr. Santos, this could have been avoided. I'm sorry for your loss."

The message concluded with a pattern of beeps, increasing in frequency and pitch, and Santos' phone fell silent as the call disconnected.

Simultaneously, the shockwave from an exploding cargo container on the docks in Sepetiba shook buildings a block away. The resulting fire burned for hours.

Chapter X

    Realizing he would never have to work again if he didn't want to made selling Riverside Market to his employees easier for Gary—but just a little. Maria had given her last manicure two days ago and worked with him on their last day at Riverside. They scheduled themselves for the closing shift so they would be available to see as many of the regulars as possible. When asked what they were going to do without two businesses to run, they explained their desire to travel, build their dream house, and hopefully spend a lot of time babysitting and playing with future grandkids.
    The Whites were reminiscing with a bottle of red blend wine at the lottery counter where they were interrupted by five or six customers an hour wanting to say goodbye. Bill entered Riverside around 9:45 p.m. to show his support and try to catch some private time with the Whites. At 10:30 p.m., they locked

the doors, poured another glass of wine, and changed the conversation to Pride activities.

"I know our lives are about to get exciting, hectic, and dangerous," Maria said. "But it sure is nice seeing you all the time again."

"Hear, hear," Gary chimed in, holding up his glass of wine.

"Seeing you guys, the kids, and Pax again is the best thing that has happened to me in years," Bill agreed. "But I'm having a great deal of anxiety, which is rare for an Attal. I'm still apprehensive about putting you in danger and breaking our societal rules."

"We are, too," Gary admitted. "Although I'll deny it if you ever repeat me. And for the record, you are not putting us in danger. We are volunteering to help. Besides, we get a special skill and get to save the world—pretty good reasons to join the cause."

"Also," Maria added. "I'd like to see how this whole Pax-Elaine thing works itself out."

"That just adds to my worries. Pax, Agrata, and I are smashing every known law we have. It's quite disturbing," Bill confessed.

"It is time to grow a pair, Bill," Gary said bluntly. "This mission is *never* going to be successful if you continue to worry about the past laws of the Attal or the Terra. I've already told you, it's time to focus on the task at hand. The Council will give us new rules of conduct. The old rules don't exist. Allow them to be part of you, but move on or fail."

Maria, uncomfortable with Gary's candor, added, "It's like Terra school kids. When they are young, they are taught certain rules: no chewing gum in school, always listen to your teacher, no running with scissors, et cetera. When they become teenagers, the rules change: be home by midnight, finish your homework before you go to bed, et cetera. Then, as adults, the rules change again."

She paused before adding, "You have the same situation, but are struggling to recognize the transition. When you were growing up at the station and competing in your Galtri, you had one set of rules, but now you are a member of the Big Cats. This new membership comes with a new set of rules. Sometimes, as adults, we need to run with scissors."

Bill listened intently to his friends then asked, almost to himself, "How can you guys be so wise and confident when we are so much more advanced?"

"Because we're old," Gary answered honestly. "Well, I am. Maria is still a young kitten."

He gave her a quick kiss on top of her head.

"We are more than halfway through our lifespan. We would love to meet our grandkids, but seeing our kids grow and be happy is the best one could hope for as a Terra. You are only—What?—maybe ten percent done with your life? You are still maturing as an Attal. We have a different mindset."

"Speaking of seeing happy kids," Maria interrupted. "When is your son going to start dating our daughter?"

"His feelings are very strong, but I'm not sure either of them considers dating a good idea right now," Bill answered.

"We'll see," Maria answered with a smirk.

"Isn't it annoying how she acts like she knows everything?" Gary teased with a much larger smile. "Until the Council says otherwise, you may be the most powerful man the earth has seen in thousands of years. Enjoy the freedom and just do what feels right. Otherwise, you'll suffer from 'paralysis by analysis.'"

"I'll try," Bill said, unconvinced.

After a short pause, he added, "I came here secretly hoping you two could help me with a couple of other situations."

"Situations? Okay, AJ. What do you need?" He joked, comparing Bill to his predecessor who often referred to immensely dangerous problems as "situations."

After smacking her husband, Maria said, "Of course, we will help you. If we can."

"You need help naming our yet-to-be-opened headquarters?" Gary asked.

"Will you stop it?" Maria said in a hard whisper and with another smack.

"I have already met with Pax and Agrata and received their input. They have both agreed to allow me to make the final decisions, but I wouldn't feel right deciding without your thoughts."

Bill's hesitation made his internal struggle obvious, and Maria put her hand on his arm and spoke softly.

"We love you and trust you. How can we help?"

Bill took a second to collect himself before he said, "I've agreed to choose the members of the Council from a list the kids compiled, and I have to decide what special skills to give each member of *our* team."

"I wanna fly and have super strength and—"

Bill interrupted Gary's laundry list of powers. "We aren't superheroes."

"Yea, yea, but wouldn't it be cool?" he said.

"If you don't mind, let's first pick the Council," Bill requested. "We went from having no candidates to having too many. After Elaine's trip to the England, they have come up with six people, and I only need to choose two."

"Who are the candidates?" Maria asked.

"Cathy O'Cotter, board member at Moonlight Trail; Jeffrey Harding, engineer and speaker at a symposium; Robert Durham, friend of Agrata and conspiracy researcher; and Niall Phillips, also a friend of Agrata and researcher."

Bill paused as if finished with his list, so Gary spoke up.

"I realize I've had a couple glasses of wine, but I only counted four names, buddy. I thought you said there were six."

"Pax also considered Elaine and Elizabeth," Bill admitted.

"And you don't like them as candidates?" Gary asked.

"I'm very fond of both of them, but we are trying to get a more diverse Council, not all of our friends and family."

"Then it seems like your decision is pretty clear," Gary said. "You pick either Jeffrey or Cathy, and whoever isn't as close to Aggie. Either Niall or Robert."

"It seems easy, but it isn't. Harding comes with a more analytical mind. Without knowing what he has stumbled onto, he has learned a great deal about Seretus' growth in South America. Pax has more experience with Cathy; he likes her leadership skills, and she better represents the upper class. As for our English friends, I like Robert's simple beginnings and methodical personality better, but he is close to Agrata, and we would rather not broadcast our two young Attal's fondness for Terra intimacy."

"Once again, you're tripping over your own feet," Gary stated.

Bill subconsciously looked down. "Pardon me?"

"If you want information from Harding, just go get it," Gary explained. "If someone doesn't like the relationship between two people, let them tell you. It's a new day, Bill. Quit thinking. It's time to act."

"Just do your best and try not to worry. You have a whole team supporting you," Maria said in a much softer tone than her husband.

She got up, gave him a hug from the back, and whispered something in his ear.

Sitting back down, she ended the conversation by asking, "Now, how can we help you with your other *situation*?"

"That one is going a little better," Bill stated as he cheered up and started his report. "Ivan and I have been working relentlessly on new toys and possible, vis-enhanced skills."

"Oooh, now you have my attention," Gary said, sitting up straighter. "I love toys. Do any of them help me fly or smash things?"

"Sure, Gary," Bill answered. "We are going to turn you into Superman, and we thought maybe we'd turn Maria into Spiderwoman."

"Well, now you're just being silly," Gary said. "It was just a request."

"Most of the work has been done," Bill continued. "We are still considering a couple of skills, and there is one more tool in the final testing stage, but the most achievable and advantageous skills have been determined. The task now is to assign each skill and to set a training schedule. Ivan and I have had an interesting conversation about the assignments, but I wanted to get your opinion before I make my decision."

"And you're sure none of them include flying?" Gary asked.

"If they ever do, you're our guy," Bill humored his friend. "I originally leaned toward assigning the skill to the member whose personality best complimented that ability, thus ensuring greater commitment and better success. But Ivan had an interesting perspective. He wanted me to consider assigning the skill opposite of each member's strength, essentially giving them two skillsets."

After a short pause while they contemplated his dilemma, Bill asked, "So, what do you guys think?"

"I agree with Ivan," Gary said. "Let's get as many different skills as we can."

"I hate to muddy the waters, but I agree with you, Bill," Maria said. "I would have more confidence using an enhanced skill if it were something I've already had some success with."

"Well, I guess we didn't help much," Gary admitted.

"On the contrary, you confirmed exactly what Ivan and I had concluded: It depends on the individual in question."

"In that case, you know what the opposite of walking is, right?" Gary asked.

"Yes," Bill quickly answered. "Sitting out and watching from the sidelines."

"I was going a different direction, but technically, you might be right."

"Bill," Maria said softly. "I'm glad you wanted to discuss this, and I will respect your decisions, regardless of your choices, but I do have a couple of requests and concerns about Eddie and Elaine."

"I thought you might," Bill said. "Let's discuss those now."

Chapter XI

    Bill had planned for this day with his friends for over a year. For dramatic effect, he kept all his conclusions to himself and sent a message to the Pride to meet at the Whites' house for a mandatory meeting, Saturday at 9:00 a.m. Everyone gathered in the kitchen, laughing, with their juice and coffee when Elaine arrived at 9:04. He watched her wish a few good mornings on her way to the cupboard to retrieve a coffee mug.

    "Thank you all for coming," Bill said, quieting down the conversation. "I'm sure you're excited to find out my conclusions, but first, I'd like to update you on some changes our members have made. Gary, Maria, Pax, and Aggie have quit their jobs to concentrate on their training. Eddie has agreed to leave Wright State and will be finishing his nursing program at Walsh University so he can be closer to headquarters; the transition will be smooth because the department head is a Kud. Gary and Maria will be selling this house. And, because of my formal, but erroneous status as a resident of our home planet, I'm unable to transport or visit our Pacific station without revealing myself. Thus, I will be a temporary resident at the Whites' new house."

Pax interrupted Bill, "I still think you should move in with me."

"As explained, the Whites may need my help with their training, and being a young man, you may want your privacy at times."

No one observed the barely noticeable, closed-mouth smile on Maria for her insistence that Pax may want to privately entertain someone in the near future. But Elaine certainly had a new-found interest in her cup of coffee.

"Besides, I think you will be satisfied with our proximity," Bill said. "Before we go to the new surface station, I need all of your Mooncat necklaces."

Gary couldn't help but notice the change in Bill's demeanor. He led the meeting with efficiency and confidence. Any insecurity or indecision seemed to be replaced with purpose and certainty.

Gary, being the last to place his necklace in the red bag, said, "Elizabeth is going to be pissed when she loses—" He did a quick count of the room. "—seven cats from Moonlight Trail."

Bill put the red bag in the backpack at his feet and pulled out a green bag. He handed Gary a new necklace, apparently identical to his forfeited necklace.

"Not only will she not lose any members, she won't even notice the change."

Bill then gave Gary a thin, platinum-and-gold watch with diamond accents. When he accepted the gift, he recognized a similar watch on Bill's left wrist.

Everyone in the group received an identical necklace and a personalized watch. Maria and Aggie were each given a classic, slightly enlarged, gold, lady's watch, Pax an expensive, European-style, slim, self-winding sports watch, and Eddie a diver's watch. Bill approached Elaine, who sat at the kitchen table sipping her coffee.

"You were a little more challenging."

He handed her a necklace identical to the others, then pulled a gold ring out of his bag. The ring featured a gold coin, similar in size to a U.S. nickel. Stamped on the face of the antique coin was an ancient warship, flying a Jolly Roger flag used by pirates to warn and strike fear in their enemies.

"You sure know what a girl likes," Elaine said. "I love it."

Bill gave her a wink before addressing the group, "I'm sure you all assume this, but your jewelry is enhanced with technology and should be worn at all times. Now, if everyone would please follow me, I think it's time for show and tell."

"Nice," Gary said with a slow affirmative shake of his head. "Love the Terra reference. There may be hope for you yet, Bill."

Following Bill, the Whites pulled into their new, winding, 200-meter driveway. It continued up a wooded hill to a modest-looking, but deceptively large, brick ranch. As they walked through the three-car garage, Gary noticed an abnormally high number of interior doors.

The interior had three high-security doors on the back wall and two low-security doors on the outside wall on the right. They entered through the high-security door on the left and passed through a mud room before entering a family room.

The large kitchen on the left featured a modern decor with light, hardwood floors and stainless-steel, commercial-grade appliances. It opened to the great room with a vaulted ceiling, featuring a wall of windows which showed off a spectacular view of a pond a couple hundred yards away and a barn almost hidden in the distance through the trees.

After the tour of the two bedrooms on the east side of the kitchen and the master suite on the west side, Maria pointed to a door off the family room.

"Where does that lead?"

"I believe you call it a mother-in-law suite," Bill explained. "It's an extra bedroom, bathroom, kitchenette, and sitting area. It even comes with its own entrance from the garage. I thought it might come in handy for either an aging parent or a single child who wants to be close but also have some privacy. In the immediate future, however, I hoped it could serve as an alien-friend suite."

"For as long as you need," Maria answered with a gentle touch on his arm.

"I think you should slap a mailbox on the outside and make it a permanent residence," Gary added.

Both Elaine and Eddie were outwardly impressed to a level just short of jealousy.

"It figures," Eddie said. "You guys get this house *after* we move out."

"Yeah, we had a life-long, detailed plan set," Gary said sarcastically. "Work our asses off, become intimate with an alien race living on Earth, risk our lives and the lives of our kids, so some day we might get new a house out of the deal."

"Wow. Over-reach much?" Eddie said as he joined Pax and Elaine, who were looking out the back window.

Pax, more thinking out loud than complaining, said, "I understand the design and topography, and I can appreciate the security, but I'm surprised you picked a place with another house so close."

He nodded southeast, where, about a hundred yards away and hidden by a small grove of pine trees and a mammoth oak, he could see a small, brick ranch.

"Really," Bill said with a smile, "I am surprised you haven't already figured out my plan. I must admit, I find myself a little disappointed."

Pax raised his eyebrows and turned to face Bill, who tossed him a key ring.

"Welcome to the neighborhood," Bill said. "This property, which incidentally covers 212 acres and is owned by the Whites, has four visible buildings: this residence, Pax's residence, a barn for maintenance machinery, and an office building on the far end of the property that allows public access to the grounds. All four of these buildings, plus two underground, undetectable buildings are connected by a highly secured tunnel system. They have been set up with the Attal's most advanced security options. Any audio or visual eavesdropping is impossible with current technology—even ours. If you are within this property, everything you do and say is secure."

"Jesus, Bill," Gary said, clearly surprised and impressed with his briefing. "How did you do all this in a month?"

"We didn't," Bill answered with a sheepish smile. "AJ designed and ordered this project before he left Earth. We've been working on this for years. It is problematic to allow Terra on the Pacific station. He predicted, as we moved forward, we would need a location with easier access for the Attal and Terra to work together. Even though it is technically underground, we refer to this as the surface station."

"Well, that isn't nearly cool enough. After a proper tour, I'm sure I'll be able to do better," Gary proclaimed with total confidence while his teammates made no effort to hide their smiles.

Ignoring Gary's promise, Bill turned toward the flat-screen TV mounted over the mantle, and it automatically lit up.

"The entire property is set up to operate telepathically, assuming you are wearing your watch or ring. Every appliance can be operated manually, but with time and a little practice, you will be able to work them mentally."

"I love you guys," Eddie said as he sat on the leather couch.

Bill showed everyone the schematics of the property on the flat screen.

"Immediately beneath the barn is a 4,500-square-foot lab and technical center. Sixty feet underground, between the Whites' house and Pax's house, is the surface station, which is the size of an average elementary school. All the buildings are connected by a tunnel system. Although it may be time-consuming with security and inefficient backtracking, it's possible to reach all buildings while remaining underground.

"In the barn's loft, there is a security office. Two Attal are responsible for all security and maintenance or repairs assigned to this property. They will not be permitted access to either residence without the presence of one of the Pride's watches. They will follow your orders unconditionally and have been instructed to make your safety their number-one priority. You will meet them in a couple of days, but I should warn you, they are not as practiced or comfortable dealing with Terra as you are accustomed."

After a thirty-minute presentation, Bill concluded, "I think I've told you everything I can from here. The best way to become familiar with the property is to experience it. Your watch or ring will gain you access to every building except the security office in the barn loft, because it is also the main residence for the two Attal assigned to the property. They will allow access if asked, but please give them a little privacy until they are more comfortable with 24/7, Terra interaction. There are three four-wheelers in storage behind the garage. You can access it from the outside of the house or through the unsecured door on the left in the main garage. Go, have a little fun and learn the lay of the land. We will meet back here in two hours."

Gary and Maria took a camouflage four-wheeler and headed toward the office to familiarize themselves with the street view of their new property. Eddie and Aggie toured on a red four-wheeler, speeding off toward the barn to look for new toys, while Pax and Elaine slowly headed toward his new house on a black four-wheeler.

With so much to see and so much space between buildings, each group used all of the allotted time and arrived back at the main house within minutes of each other. They put away their new toys and entered the living room, laughing.

"Welcome back," Bill greeted them. "Did you guys learn anything?"

"Yes. When we complete our mission, you have given us the dream location to retire in. Thank you, Bill," Maria answered on her way to the kitchen to quench her wind-blown thirst.

"This property is so impressive, we're going to need more than a couple hours to study it properly," Pax said.

"Only if you are riding with Grandpa Jones here," Elaine said sarcastically with a tilt of her head in Pax's direction.

"I learned Eddie likes speed a little too much and what it feels like to be airborne in a four-wheeler. We had time to check all the above ground buildings," Aggie said.

"Unfortunately," Eddie countered, "I learned Aggie isn't a fan of horsepower. I also now know what it feels like to have a girl dig her fingernails into your ribs."

They were all gathered in the kitchen, sipping water and laughing about the different approaches of explorations when Bill spoke up.

"Well, I'm glad you all learned something, but I hope you saved some energy for our training after lunch."

Excited to see the station and learn of their new abilities, the group ate quickly. Within thirty minutes of returning from their exploration of the property, they were in the basement, standing in front of a thick, black, metal door in the back of the storage room.

"There is a similar door to this in Pax's basement and in the barn," Bill explained. "They all lead to the tunnel system, which connects all the buildings, plus gives one access to the research lab and the station. It can only be opened with Attal security. You must be wearing one of our necklaces, which incidentally, Ivan also wears, and as an additional security measure, there is a telepathic password."

"Well, aren't we fancy smancy," Eddie said. "What's the alien, high-tech, security password? Do we need to learn a whole new language?

"In a temporary lapse of judgment, I agreed to let Gary pick the phrase," Bill admitted.

"Oh, God. Why would you do that?" Eddie asked.

"Let me guess," Elaine interrupted. "*Alohomora*, the Harry Potter spell for opens locks."

"No, but good guess. I considered that," Gary said with raised eyebrows and a goofy grin.

"You mean it's even cornier?" Elaine asked.

"Gary, why must you be so—well, be so *you*?" Maria asked, rolling her eyes.

"Can't ask water not to be wet, Bun," he offered.

"The phrase our infamous, walking thesaurus chose is—"

Bill spoke the word telepathically, "*Abracadabra.*"

The nine-inch-thick, black door opened to expose a surprisingly clean, well-lit hallway.

"Even though we have taken all precautions against eavesdropping, don't ever speak the password verbally," Bill said.

"Can we speak verbally what a dumbass Dad is?" Eddie asked.

"Of course. No security issues there," Bill said.

As they continued down the hallway, Bill started the briefing everyone anxiously anticipated.

"After much discussion, it has been decided, due to the unprecedented nature of this mission and our—for lack of better word—club, we will have a great deal of flexibility formalizing the guidelines which govern our group. But we will have oversight. We will be monitored by both Ivan, who is representing our society, and the newly formed, Terra Relations Council. By accepting our technology and our invitation to join our society, you concede to our leadership's authority over this mission. Does everyone understand?"

After everyone accepted Bill's terms, he continued, "Ivan has agreed, with regular updates, he would allow the Council to oversee our daily activities. The Council has been set and will meet independently of our activities on a monthly schedule, with the ability to call emergency meetings. We have attempted to create the checks and balances we lacked in the past."

"And you think that will work?" Gary asked. "Our government has been trying for decades, and we still have corruption."

"Now that we are aware of the abuse and making efforts to avoid it, I think we will be more successful than your government, which still sees tremendous, personal gain from corruption. When creating the Council, we were very careful," Bill explained. "The majority of the members are Attal, but there are three Terra members. The majority are mature adults, but it includes three young members. The majority is not represented by the Pride, yet it has three group members. Our two, non-Pride, Attal members are from two different classes, and our three Terra members are from three different income brackets. And finally, we have given each member the ability to protect themselves and expose our secret if they feel we are endangering the Terra or abusing our technology."

"Doesn't that put your existence at risk?" Maria questioned.

"We are exposed like never before," Bill answered. "But we are pleased with our Council selections and feel it is the only way to continue with the co-habitation efforts and gain the trust of the Terra."

"I guess time will tell," Gary said. "I hope your leadership is more successful than our government. Is the committee going to be present at our meetings?"

"No," Bill answered as the elevator stopped. "They will meet with us today and then get regular updates from Pax, Aggie, and Gary, who are part of both groups."

"So, when do we meet the Council?" Pax asked.

"Right now," Bill answered as the elevator doors opened.

"Robert! I'm so glad Bill chose you," Aggie said on her way over to hug her beau.

"Hey, Bobby," Elaine said, using the nickname she knew he hated. "Looks like you're not a conspiracy git after all."

Chapter XII

    Pax approached Cathy O'Cotter and welcomed her to the Council. Pax and Aggie recognized the other members of their race and made proper introductions. One of the Attal citizens worked in research, and the other as a vis-production supervisor. After introductions were made, all eleven of them were given a tour of the station. Bill saved the most intriguing and secretive room for last—the transport room.

    After viewing the room, Bill asked, "Would you like to see it work?"

    "Yea!" Eddie said excitedly.

    Bill went behind the small control booth and pressed a couple of buttons. The Terra watched in amazement as the white, horizontal, tubular machine created a body. The process was amazingly quick. They saw at least three bright lights and something like steam, and heard the sound of a tremendous amount of pressurized gases being released. Twenty seconds later, the machine flashed an almost-blinding red light, followed by a yellow, gaseous substance covering the machine. The red light turned off, letting the controller know that the signature had been transferred. After the yellow gas had been vented, Ivan's naked torso sat up in the cylinder-shaped machine, and he addressed the crowd.

"Although I'm not the humblest person on your planet, since I share a body style with Pax, please give me a minute to get dressed, and I will join you shortly in the research room."

Everyone moved to the research room, where the Attal citizens were trying to explain the feeling of transporting to the amazed Terra, when Ivan, wearing a cream-colored robe, entered the room and immediately took control of the meeting.

"I would like to again thank all of you for your service to our society. It is my hope our efforts will make this planet a safer place for all of us to live. The Terra Relations Council will meet monthly. After each meeting, I will get two separate updates. One from my assignee," Ivan said, pointing to the Attal member he had assigned from research, "and one from Mrs. O'Cotter. I'm going to ask each of you to not discuss what you plan on reporting with each other. I value both of your opinions and prefer to get them untainted.

"I personally vouch for every member of this team. But if any of the Council thinks they have been penetrated, controlled, or manipulated by any team member or Attal citizen, you may seek asylum at this station, and we will easily be able to conclude what happened to you and by whom.

"I have met with the non-Pride members of this Council, concerning our plans to share our technology and skills. They agree our rogue members need to be apprehended and understand we are in uncharted territory. The full Council will be responsible for the setting of future guidelines and any disciplinary actions for rule violation by this team. The daily decisions of the Pride, though, will operate under Bill's authority. The Council will receive monthly updates, but they will not have daily interaction or individual authority over the team. Does everyone understand this separation of responsibilities?"

After another ten minutes of instructions, the Pride all left and made their way toward the research lab under the barn. During the three-minute walk, they discussed the Council, Ivan's role in their team, and how far Bill's authority reached.

When they arrived at another black door, Bill said, "This is an Attal working lab. Please remember these people aren't used to seeing or sharing with Terra. They are aware of our plans and are informed of your presence. There is bound to be an adjustment period. Please respect their culture and their ignorance of your culture."

When the black door swung open, they saw five people at work on different machines. Its' purpose didn't resemble any one Terra building. It appeared to be part garage and part lab. It had a medical center and what seemed to be a learning center. Except, it appeared too clean for a garage, too open for a lab, too small for a medical center, and there wasn't any teaching taking place. A tandem-seat cage sat in the corner and something resembling a golf cart without wheels stood off to their right. There were also a row of benches, where three workers were concentrating over small components, and a couple of empty beds. Although impressive, it seemed too quiet and too sterile to be effective. A middle-aged black man carrying an IDC approached the group, faced Bill, and then walked away.

"Our room is ready," Bill announced.

They entered an office in the corner of the room. The large, immaculately clean, well-lit office came equipped with lab equipment along one wall and a desk with an extra chair along the adjacent back wall. In the middle of the room was a conference table, designed to seat four. Extra chairs were brought in, and everyone sat down when Bill motioned to the chairs.

"Well, show-and-tell time is over," Bill said. "Let's get down to business."

"Two awesome references in the same day," Gary said. "You have been working hard on your Terra pop culture and mannerisms."

"You have no idea," Bill answered with a smile. "We have known for quite some time the Seretus Ligare would be much stronger than just two rogue runaways. This property was AJ's brainchild, but Ivan's and my first priority for more than a year. This is more than a little club of misfits getting skills to bring down a bad guy. This is the first, Attal-Terra effort to use all means at our disposal to create a working partnership as equals. It will ultimately lead to the discovery of our existence, but by that time, it is our hope we will be integrated, understood, and peacefully working together for the betterment of the planet while still advancing both our needs. For the record, this is the first time we have chosen to work with, instead of hide from, our unknowing hosts.

"Now, let's discuss the talents and skills we hope to give you to assist you with your role in our mission."

"That's what I'm talking about," Eddie said as he sat up tall in his chair.

"Before we go over each person's skill, we need to go over some new, Pride rules. First, with the exception of Aggie, none of you should use your skills against any other member of our team. Unannounced use of your new abilities is authorized, but you are never to use your talents out of anger, revenge, boastfulness, or dishonorable motives. If you do, there will be disciplinary consequences."

"Aggie is allowed to read my mind?" Eddie asked, doubting the wisdom in Bill's decision.

"No. Let's go over each skill," Bill suggested. "Then we can see how they are interconnected and complimentary. Some of us are going to have surgery, and all of us are going to have personal, Attal trainers. Be patient and give your skill time to develop. With the exception of Gary, your new capabilities will help you long after this mission. Trust me, and embrace these gifts."

"What the hell?" Gary blurted. "I don't get to keep my skill?"

"The skill—yes," Bill said. "But the toys and technology—maybe not. We haven't decided yet."

He could see the disappointment in his friend's face, so he added with a wink, "Don't despair. I saved the coolest trick for my best friend."

"You mean, I get to fl—"

"No, you will not get to fly."

"Here is what I came up with. The leadership has worked hard with me, both physically and mentally, to increase my already-impressive memory. I have learned to access and plant large amounts of information quickly. I have the ability to use my mind similar to a backup, computer hard drive; only, I can do it with a Terra brain. With my memory and abilities, I'll be able to plant enormous amounts of information in each of your minds or plant a thought in a large number of people at once. I will work as the command center, gathering information from many sources while leading and instructing the team."

Everyone nodded in understanding; although, if they were honest, Gary and Eddie were underwhelmed with Bill's power.

As if reading their minds, he added, "In time, it will look more impressive than it sounds.

"Aggie, we have decided to aggressively and substantially increase your skills of controlling Terra health. Of course, you, and anyone else in this room," Bill said, looking in Pax's direction, "will have the ability to do any Attal skills you have already learned. But we want all of your training to be on analyzing, repairing, and hopefully controlling the Terra body."

"What do you mean by controlling?" she asked.

"Besides keeping our group healthy," Bill explained, "we are hoping you will be able to determine if someone is being honest, increase someone's heart rate, and possibly give them blurred vision or nausea, et cetera."

Turning his attention to his son, he said, "Pax, I would like you to concentrate your efforts on Terra technology. We have given you some of our latest technology in your watch, but we are hoping in time, besides knowing how to hack complex security firewalls and control most computer-assisted devices, you will be able to search any Terra system without direct access and capture information transmitted wirelessly."

He then turned his attention to the White women.

"Maria, Elaine—I'm going to ask you both to have a simple surgery to increase some normal, Terra functions to greater levels."

Maria didn't look as understanding as Pax and Aggie had, and the color of Elaine's complexion immediately paled.

"Have you not heard about my fear of needles?" Elaine asked. "I'm pretty sure it is very well documented."

"We are not Terra, Elaine. We won't need needles," Bill explained. "Aggie will make sure you are pain free and will be with you the whole time. We are just going to make some simple changes to your larynx and your digestive system. You are going to be our communication and social specialist. You will be fluent in almost every Terra language, able to mimic speech patterns and pitches, and capable of eating and drinking almost anything without too much effect on your body. This last adjustment has the added benefit of making you immune to most known poisons. Hopefully, with training and practice, you will be able to imitate any Terra voice and, with a little vis assistance, easily convince people to do your bidding."

Elaine, although not convinced Attal surgery was much better than Terra needles, got her color back in her cheeks and seemed to be pleased with her future abilities. Bill gave her a few moments to process all the information and consider what she might be able to achieve before turning to address Maria.

"You have always been the glue keeping our group and your family together. I don't want to change you or your role," he said. "To help you and this team, I've decided to reverse the aging of your senses and improve them to undocumented levels. You will have the best hearing of any animal on Earth, able to smell from miles away, and have perfect vision at both close-up and great distances. With the enhancements from your watch, your optic range will include infrared and night vision. Your new skills will take some time to master, and you will most likely suffer from sensory overload. It can be overwhelming and painful—both physically and emotionally—to hear and see too much, but we hope you will learn how to ignore non-critical information and help us see, hear, and smell our enemy from a safe distance."

Eddie still sat on the edge of his chair, nervously shaking his knee when Bill addressed him.

"Eddie, due to your lack of experience with our culture and energy, I have decided to give you skills that do not require vis."

Eddie's disappointment manifested so quickly and strongly, one could have easily described him as pissed, so Bill rushed to explain further.

"We will use Attal technology to increase your skills. We plan on making you Agrata's back-up on team health and first response in case of injury, but it is our hope you never have to use those skills. More importantly, you will be our mechanical expert."

Loosening his pursed lips, Eddie asked, "What does 'mechanical expert' mean?"

"I've seen how you operate a car under great stress," Bill said, referring to Eddie's high-speed assistance years ago on a multi-state race to Pax's Galtri presentation. "You will be responsible for all transportation, weapons, machines, and toys."

"You mean, I—"

Bill smiled and interrupted the youngest member of the team, "You will design and operate all of our vehicles and machinery. I will implant in you the knowledge of how to build, fix, and operate everything from a supercar to a helicopter, from a Terra gun to Attal surveillance equipment. You will have to study hard and practice around the clock."

"When do we start?" he responded with the largest smile Gary or Maria have ever seen.

"He gets to fly helicopters and play with guns, and she—" Gary said with a tilt of his head towards his wife, "—gets eagle eyes and bat ears. And you said you kept the best for me? I can't wait to see what I get!"

Unable to control his anticipation, he stood up and started to pace.

"What do I get, Bill?"

"You get to be our superhero," Bill said with a smile he tried unsuccessfully to hide. "We don't have the technology to make you fly yet, but we do have this."

Bill took a device off the desk and tossed it toward him.

Catching it, Gary looked up at his friend and asked, "What the hell is it?"

"It's a cloaking device similar to what we use on our ships. It's much easier to use in space, due to the vacuum and distance between objects, but we've been working on a portable version designed to bend the light on the surface," Bill answered.

"I'm a little confused," Gary admitted. "I get to work on a portable device?"

"No, we have recently mastered the technology," Bill informed him. "Everything you need is in your watch."

"Everything I need for what?"

"You get to be the Invisible Man," Bill answered.

Chapter XIII

    Juanita sat on the terrace, studying her information device, when she heard Carlos's unannounced entry to her hotel room. His lecture started ten feet before the door.

    "There are at least a couple Attal with damn near limitless vis hunting for us. It's reckless to sit in the open air totally unprotected."

    "I'm never unprotected," she countered. "I have you looking out for me. What have you found out about our search party?"

    "I still haven't confirmed Bill's location, but I have confirmed Pax has left his job and apartment. Our station sympathizer failed in his attempt to contact him. It appears they have doubled their efforts to hunt us down. And I'm still bothered because I don't know how he made it to his Phase-II presentation," Carlos added to himself as a side note. "He will be a worthy opponent."

"I think there is still value with my being at the bank. Do you think it is safe for me to go to work, or should I relocate to the compound?" Juanita asked.

"I don't think it's necessary to relocate you, yet, but the time may be coming soon. I think you should start the process of moving money. And you do need to be more aware of your exposure," he added as he nodded his head toward the balcony railing, reinforcing his dislike for her preference for the unprotected outdoors.

"Also, I think we should be on the lookout for someone investigating our movements. We might get lucky and find Bill and Pax before they find us. I already have two men on a seek-and-destroy mission, but I'm going to add another team."

After a short pause, she conceded, "Okay. I'll make an effort to remain inside and put some Terra tracking devices on our computers at the bank so we can see if anyone is monitoring things a little too closely. How are things going with ISASP?"

"Very well," Carlos reported. "Now that Santos realizes what can happen to his financing and security by not following orders, he has been very cooperative. We currently have men in six ports and on eight ships and are continuing to expand. My latest projections show we could be ready for a test in North America in approximately a month."

"If things go right with the Terra cartel, we should have enough money to supplement what I've been skimming from the bank and move on to the next stage of our plan. I'll be happy when we conclude our dealings with the drug lord and I can leave the bank," she admitted.

"Assuming he keeps his word," Carlos said.

"After the well-publicized repercussions Mr. Santos received for ignoring our advice, I can't imagine anyone would break their word to us," Juanita countered.

"I hope you are right. I don't fear going to battle with his family, but it would be violent and we would lose some of our much-needed troops," he said, closing the subject.

"And our vis level?" she inquired.

"We have no chance of taking control of North America without considerably more. We are still dangerously low, but we haven't used any since our last meeting."

"After a successful, small-scale test in North America, I will start our plan to acquire the reserves needed. I'm sure the leadership will expect us to attack the station or transport pods, but not even Ivan could predict my vis-procurement plan. Soon, brother, we should have all we need to move forward."

"Maybe," he responded, not sharing Juanita's confidence in her plan. "The amount of vis, money, and personnel needed to gain control of North America is massive. And our room for error is small."

"Then let's not have any errors. You just make sure we have men available at all the world's ports," she advised.

"And you think that will be easier than one attack on the station?" Carlos asked for the fifth time.

"I don't think they will ever underestimate our disregard for the Attal's anti-violence rules again. I have considered thousands of variables, and this plan has the best probability of success. The only other option with a higher potential for long-term returns is our going into hiding. Which do you prefer?"

"If I'm going to have to be looking over my shoulder, let it be because of action rather than inaction," Carlos conceded.

****

Lying on the bed in the underground research lab, Eddie nervously asked, "Explain to me why I'm the first for a memory binge-and-puke?"

"A what?" Bill asked.

"Isn't that what you do?" Eddie said. "Binge on someone's memories and then puke them into me."

"I guess," Bill conceded. "You Whites and your nicknames…"

He chuckled for a few seconds then answered Eddie's question.

"I've chosen you first for a couple of reasons. First, you're getting the largest memory download ever attempted."

"That doesn't sound good," Eddie interrupted.

"I'm 94.3% sure it's totally safe. But if I successfully transfer all the memories to you, then we can be confident the other, smaller downloads will be problem free."

"You don't think it would be better to work your way up to me?" Eddie offered, suddenly not happy with feeling like a lab rat.

"No. If your download is successful, then there should be no danger to any other member," Bill answered. "More importantly, even I have limited brain capacity. It has taken me months to capture and store all the memories I am downloading into you. I have very little remaining space. I need to insert these memories then clear my mind so I can extract information for the others."

"For the record, what are you inserting?" Eddie asked.

"I've extracted information about logic and problem-solving from the most intuitive thinkers in a variety of fields: a fire chief with extensive, emergency medical experience, a mechanical engineer, an electrical engineer, and a U.S. Army weapons and combat specialist. Using their skills and thought processes, I've created a logic algorithm to take over your problem-solving approach when you are faced with a challenge. The algorithm will be inserted into the decision-making section of your brain. Also, I've extracted a massive amount of information from over two hundred sources and ranging from your nursing professor at Walsh to a NASCAR pit crew chief, from a helicopter pilot to a NASA engineer.

"Lastly, I took some information from Ivan about our technology and the recent weapons and tools he's created. If my efforts are successful, you will have a wealth of information available to you and the logic to access and implement the information quickly."

"Jesus," was all Eddie could come up with before adding, "I thought you were just going to teach me to drive and fix things."

"If that's all we needed, we could have hired a driver. I told you, you will be a mechanical expert."

"I just didn't realize you were being so thorough," Eddie responded. "Are you sure it's going to fit?"

"Theoretically"

"Great. It might fit, and there's a 6% chance I could end up with scrambled eggs for brains. You sure have a hell of a bedside manner," Eddie said.

Just then, Gary, Maria, and a smiling Aggie came into the room.

"No worries," Gary chimed in. "I've already told Bill: If anyone gets to scramble your brain, it's me."

"I'll be right beside you the whole time," Aggie assured him.

"Me, too," Pax said, entering the lab. "I'll monitor your brain activity while she monitors your vitals. At the first sign of danger, I'll kick Bill out and restore your unscrambled brain."

Maria, without saying a word, sat in the chair beside Eddie and held his hand.

Gripping her hand, he said, "I doubt it gets any better than this. Let's start the binge-and-puke before I'm the one who pukes."

Bill's results in the procedure were not able to be confirmed. After eleven hours of deep concentration, he collapsed. They both slept through the night and were still lying motionless when Elaine entered at 7:00 a.m. with two cups of Columbian-blend coffees.

Handing one to her dad, she asked, "How are they doing?"

"Don't know. Pax thinks it went well, but both of them and your mother passed out from exhaustion hours ago."

"I did not," Maria responded without lifting her head. "Just because I don't pace and talk to myself all night doesn't mean I'm not awake."

"I'm awake, as well," Bill added quietly and without opening his eyes.

"How are you, Bill?" Maria asked, sitting up, awake and alert.

"I'm fine," he replied, still remaining motionless. "I'm removing all the information I had stored for Eddie. The process will take a couple more hours. I need to concentrate. But I'm fine."

"Thank God," Maria said and squeezed Eddie's hand.

"So, what's going on with the maintenance man here?" Elaine asked Pax. "Is he going to be all right?"

"I honestly don't know," he answered softly. "Aggie reports he is okay physically, and I've checked his brain activity every couple of hours. It is working very hard to make sense of all the new information it just received. I assume he's struggling with the decision-making algorithm, but I can't tell."

Elaine's concerns for her brother were temporarily replaced by personal fears.

"Is my brain going to struggle also? Could I end up with Swiss cheese?" she asked, pointing to her temple.

"Unlikely," he answered without looking up. "He's the only one scheduled to have changes to his reasoning skills. His brain needs to learn to analyze and solve problems in a completely new way. It's very complicated. I'm surprised Bill attempted it, but he's confident in the theory behind his decision and in his skills."

"Eddie's always been smarter than me—although I'll deny it if you ever repeat that," Elaine said. "If he can't handle the download, I don't stand a chance."

"Your download is much simpler," Pax said nonchalantly. "Your only risk is the surgery, which technically comes with a very low risk factor."

"Gee, thanks. Now I feel much better."

"I'm sorry," Pax said as he shook his head back to the present. "I'm exhausted from monitoring Eddie. To be honest, I'm a little worried his brain hasn't sorted everything out yet. I didn't mean to downplay your anxiety."

"That's okay. I'm worried for him, too," she replied, gently clasping Pax's hand and silently standing over her troubled brother.

Although certainly concerned for Eddie, she was much more troubled about the risk in her surgery. No matter how low the probability, her body would still be dramatically altered.

It took a great deal of convincing from Gary and a repeated promise from Aggie before Maria would agree to undergo an alien surgery while her son still lay unconscious.

"And you are sure my procedures will only take a couple hours?" she asked.

For the third time, Aggie answered, "All three surgeries will take no longer than two hours. They really are simple procedures with our technology. One of the seven Attal we chose to include in our mission is our top medical member. With her and me, you will be in safe hands and back at Eddie's side in a short time. We've spent a considerable amount of effort to get her here for the day, and she needs four hours for Elaine's procedures."

Maria woke up one hour and fifty-three minutes after her surgery. She sat up, very confused. Whether a dream or a side effect of the alien anesthesia, everything seemed fuzzy and somehow chaotic.

"You did great, Maria," she heard Aggie in her mind. *"I have blocked your vision and plugged your ears and nose. We are trying to combat what we are sure will be overstimulation. Eddie is still asleep and lying beside you on your right. Elaine is now in surgery."*

Gary interrupted Aggie in Maria's mind. *"Bun, I'm right here. You did great. Try and get some sleep. I won't go anywhere until you and the kids are awake."*

"Wake me up when either of them wake up. You promise?" Maria asked.

"Of course," Maria heard Gary promise before dozing back into unconsciousness.

****

The next morning, Bill walked over and touched a sleeping Gary's shoulder, startling him back to consciousness. After his heart rate approached a semi-normal level, Gary addressed his friend.

"I got to tell you, I'm a little concerned about all the improvements you've made to my family. Maria woke up twice with massive migraines. Elaine has thrown up three times and can't talk. Eddie's still in a coma. If their conditions don't show any improvement soon, you might wish *you* were invisible."

"I share your concerns for Eddie," Bill conceded in an uncharacteristically melancholy tone. "I expected his new reasoning skills to take over long before now."

Trying to convince himself, he added, "Admittedly, we have never tried to alter a Terra brain before, but my theory is sound."

"I don't give a shit about your theories. I want my son and his mind back. He was fine before your so-called improvements."

"I agree, and I'm sorry. I tried to give him a more efficient way to access all the information I inserted. He really does have a lot to sort out. Maybe I should have downloaded it in two sessions," Bill said, more as a personal criticism than part of the conversation.

"Or maybe not at all," Gary said, using what Maria referred to as his 'Daddy voice.' "And what about Maria and Elaine?"

The Attal in the room were not used to insubordination or confrontation. They all turned toward the heated conversation. Surprised by Gary's displeasure with their results, they intently waited for Bill's response.

As calmly as he could, Bill said. "I'm pleased to announce the girls are progressing right on schedule. Eddie is the only surprise to us. Elaine will be fine once her swelling goes down, and we predicted Maria's struggles until she learns to be more selective with her enhanced senses. Right now, she is hearing, seeing, and smelling too much. I'm surprised she isn't nauseated from her hyper-sensitive smelling. The headaches will lessen as she learns to focus her hearing and vision."

"You're sure they will be fine?" Gary asked, dropping some of the anger out of his voice but not sure Bill should be so calm.

"Positive," Bill responded. "And although we are not happy with Eddie's progress, let me assure you he is in no long-term danger."

****

During the next two days, Elaine, Pax, and Aggie all went through large information downloads, and true to Bill's word, they were all able to use the data within a couple of hours. Elaine still needed a great deal of training with her new voice box and still struggled with the variety of textures and tastes they served her at every meal. Although she understood almost every major language, she needed to improve on controlling her cracking voice that reminded Gary of when he went through puberty.

Pax spent a great deal of his time in the corner office, sitting in front of a computer screen and scrolling through information at an alarming rate. He came out every once in a while to check on Maria and Eddie, but mostly kept to himself.

Aggie accepted her download, but chose to sit deep in concentration over Eddie instead of training with her Attal mentor. Gary's frustration grew, and his refusal to undergo any training until Eddie showed improvement added to the friction between him and Bill.

****

After five days in a self-created coma and with no warning, Eddie abruptly sat up, shocked, confused, and breathing heavily. He blinked many times, attempting to adjust to the light, and looked back and forth to make sense of his surroundings. Without saying a word, he closed his eyes again, curled up in a fetal position, and fell back asleep.

He woke and assessed his situation four times over the next seven hours. With Aggie deep in concentration over her friend and Maria running her hand through his hair, he finally woke up and spoke for the first time in nearly 130 hours.

"Jesus, I'm exhausted," he said barely over a whisper. "Who's next for their binge-and-puke? I think I need a nap."

Chapter XIV

Two days later, Gary entered the lab for what Eddie would have bet had to be the hundredth time.

"How are you feeling, Cubby?" he asked his son, who had occupied the same bed in the lab for almost a week.

"I couldn't wake up for days and now I can't sleep. I have a constant headache and weird music stuck in my head. I got a lot of new shit up here," Eddie said, pointing to his temple. "And I'm tired of lying around. I just need to start practicing."

After seeing the look on his Dad's face, he added, "Really, I'm fine. I just want everyone to quit asking me how I feel and start treating me normal. And why do you feel the need to call me Cubby?"

Trying to explain his feelings on the matter, Gary said, "We thought we scrambled your brain and were a little worried you weren't coming back. We were all pretty scared. Mom and Aggie barely left your side for days, and I'm a week late on my own training. Just give it some time, and things will get back to normal. Well, normal for a bunch of altered people working with aliens to save the world."

He patted his son's leg and stood up.

"And you will quit calling me Cubby?" Eddie asked.

"Oh—hell, no. You are still the youngest in the Pride," Gary answered with a wink. "But I learn how to be the Invisible Man today, so I'll be too busy to check on ya. I agree it's time for you to get up and play a little. So rest up, Cubby. The pampering ends today, for tomorrow, you start your training."

Gary turned and walked out of the lab.

"Thank God," Cubby responded to no one.

****

True to his word, Gary informed Bill the Whites were ready to start their Attal training. The next morning, they all started an intense schedule. During the next ten days, they worked mostly independent for fourteen hours a day. With the help of consultants, Attal trainers, nearly perfect training conditions, and unlimited vis at their disposable, they all made enormous strides in their individual areas of specialization.

Eddie worked longer than anyone, secretly hoping to exhaust himself to sleep, but he still woke up confused and angry the few times he actually went into REM sleep. Following Pax's advice, he used vis to supplement his sleep and hoped the internal conflict in his brain would find its harmony.

As Bill predicted, Gary had the most trouble mastering his new skill.

"You have to think like an Attal to operate the cloaking device at peak efficiency. Concentrate on remaining hidden," his tutor advised Gary for the twentieth time.

After two fourteen-hour days, Gary could sit in a room totally undetected, but he tended to leave what he described as a shadow or ghost image when he attempted to move too fast or had a break in concentration. No one could see him, but obviously someone or something moved in the room.

Bill remained reassuring and supportive during Gary's training, while the rest of the team used his struggles to poke fun and point out his failures. One morning, after a hard day of training, Elaine entered the lab and walked over to a supposedly invisible man snooping around the lab.

"Morning, Dad," she said as she set down a cup of hot coffee on the desk beside him.

Bill had reminded him the Pride would always be able to see him when wearing their jewelry, but Gary still didn't feel his results matched the rest of the team's progress.

Two evenings later, Gary worked with his Attal training partner, who attempted to distract him during a simulated mission. Eddie sat beside them and practiced mantling and dismantling weapons blindfolded while listening and singing along to Billy Joel's, "Prelude/Angry Young Man."

He overheard the trainer report, "Better, but I saw a ghost of your movements when the simulated gunshot sounded."

"Nice try, Casper," Eddie bellowed to his frustrated dad.

From that day forward, even though he thought of himself as the patriarch of the Pride and wanted his nickname to be Mufasa, the Pride called him Casper whenever he struggled.

Bill increased the challenges during the next week, and they took turns training with their fellow Big Cats. Gary attempted to stay concealed as he held on for dear life while Eddie drove him at full speed through the woods on his four-wheeler. Eddie gave Pax a ride on the back of a motorcycle while he tried to use a handheld IDC to hack into the public library and erase Maria's overdue book fee. This would have been easier if he didn't have to dodge trees at over 60 mph. Later, with Aggie's not-so-appreciated help, Eddie had to diagnose, fix, and drive a broken-down Ford F-150 pick-up while throwing up his lunch and dealing with a heart rate artificially increased to anxiety-attack levels.

Maria mastered shutting out distracting stimulants, but she still had to concentrate when focusing on more than one enhanced sense at a time. During one of her missions, she had to read a random code, so small it could have been printed on a grain of rice, in low light and relay the code to Bill telepathically. He used the code and tested his multitasking memory by mentally monitoring all thirty-two of the surveillance devices placed on the property simultaneously. Maria then had to focus on Eddie, driving Elaine at full throttle a quarter mile away, and estimate his speed while also listening to Elaine quote by memory the proper etiquette for greeting the leaders of foreign countries in their native language. To make the test more difficult for Elaine, she had to maintain the world leader's voice patterns while many times bouncing four inches off her seat.

The White family switched partners and attempted similar mini-missions three or four times a day. Elaine loved Bill's creativity in designing the missions, but she felt under-trained in her main responsibility of manipulating non-Pride members.

During her latest mission with Pax, he attempted to hack into the CIA, Mossad, and the British Secret Service's interrogation surveillance cameras throughout the world while suffering from debilitating migraine and cold sweats. Elaine then had to translate the interviews to English in real-time, using each interviewee's specific voice patterns. After seventy successful minutes, she had translated and copied three male and two female voices perfectly. During a pause, she proudly looked over to Pax. Instead of returning her look of confidence and happiness, she saw only pain and concentration on his face. She asked Aggie to stop the headache, bringing him instant relief. Elaine brought him a glass of water, wiped his damp forehead, and kissed his neck from behind.

"You okay?"

"I was fine," he responded, intellectually knowing he could have continued with the exercise, but very happy to be rid of what he would have described as the world's worst headache. "But I'm much better now," he added as he raised his right hand and gently caressed the back of her hair as she gave him two more butterfly kisses.

She blew across the moisture on his neck, sending chills all the way to his toes.

"Thank God Bill didn't choose you as my distraction. I wouldn't have been able to hack Eddie's email."

The training continued with similar, but increasingly difficult simulated missions for another week. Bill, who meticulously monitored results and individual skills, noticed the team's abilities peaked, and they often turned to attempted sabotage and trickery as an escape from boredom. Everyone laughed when, for two days, the Pride all squirted Gary with water pistols every time he attempted invisibility. Another bit of fun had at the Invisible Man's expense, which Bill thought to be in poor taste, happened when Gary attempted to climb a flight of stairs without being seen or heard. He had allowed a ghost to give away his position, when he reached the top of the stairs to find Maria standing in nothing but a wide-open, white bathrobe.

Bill knew he had to cancel the training missions when Elaine, mimicking Bill's voice, instructed Gary to break into the surface station and attempt to dismantle the transporter pod and Pax hacked the computer in Eddie's truck in an attempt to keep him from achieving his goal. The latter of which resulted in

Eddie completing his mission on time by speeding up the driveway with Van Halen's "Runnin' With the Devil" blaring from the radio of a SWAT truck he had commandeered.

"Okay, it's clear you guys are bored with these exercises," Bill said at the emergency Pride meeting he had called.

"How was I to know it wasn't you who sent me to the Cat Cave?" Gary argued, using his Bat Man-inspired name for the surface station.

"Hey, don't blame me. Computer boy shouldn't have f—"

"That's enough," Bill interrupted in a rare show of emotion. "I take responsibility for your shenanigans. I should have known, with such advances, you would get bored. Let's take a break for a day or two. Get some rest. I will design a full-team, final training mission. Afterwards, it will be time to get serious about stopping the Seretus Ligare. Any comments or questions before you are dismissed?"

Bill had assumed incorrectly he would be questioned about the team's final mission.

"Thank God," Maria said. "We could use a break."

"Shenanigans?" Gary asked, impressed with the word choice. "Nice!"

"Don't mess with my shit, and there won't be no shit," Eddie mumbled.

"Is the transporter okay?" a much more serious Pax asked.

"I wonder what Robert's up to?" Aggie wondered out loud.

Chapter XV

  Juanita, driven by Carlos' South American, Kud driver, entered the compound just as fifteen mercenaries returned in perfect formation from their morning, six-mile run. She had been much more reserved and respectful of Carlos' efforts since their last meeting. She entered Carlos' office and greeted him with the proper, efficient, Attal mannerisms.
  "Are we still on schedule for tomorrow?"
  "Yes," he answered.
  "And what about our research on Pax?" she asked.
  "We have learned Pax has allowed himself to get close to two Terra females. My men have reported he is close to Elizabeth Summers, the president of Moonlight Trail, and a friend of hers, Elaine White."
  "Do you think he will be in contact with one of them in the near future?" she asked.

"Definitely. Rumor has it, he checks in with Elizabeth about Moonlight activities every week. His relationship with Elaine is more personal but much less predictable."

"Do we have enough personnel to handle that situation with the test tomorrow?" she asked.

"With men to spare," Carlos answered proudly.

"Do you think a couple of those spare men can help me with a snooping situation I uncovered at the bank?" she asked.

"This is lining up to be a pivotal week," Carlos stated. "Did you find Bill or Pax? I'll be happy to arrange for them to have an unannounced visit from a couple of friends."

"No, but I found someone researching our actions in South America."

"That could be problematic."

"Hence the request," she admitted.

"Who's the snooper?" Carlos asked. "Does he have any connection to the Attal? And where do I need to send a team?"

"I couldn't come up with any connection," she answered. "His name is Jeffery Harding, and he lives in Colorado."

****

They planned all night and assigned their available soldiers. Four recent recruits were headed to Colorado to convince Harding to visit their recently opened, North American compound for an informative and likely unpleasant visit. The teams hunting down Bill and Pax were headed to Moonlight headquarters to escort Ms. Summers to the same compound.

Two teams of four soldiers were leaving their ports in southern Louisiana and Houston and heading toward their respective business districts. The remaining soldiers not on ISASP ships or monitoring harbors were split between the North

American compound in the United States and the South American compound in Brazil.

In the South American compound, Carlos and Juanita met with the leader of South America's largest drug cartel and monitored their North America test. Pedro Ramirez, true to his reputation, dressed in an imported suit, Italian leather shoes, and a $200 tie as he questioned Carlos and Juniata.

"And you are sure this will not be traced back to me or my operations in any way?"

Changing her demeanor back to a power-hungry woman who enjoyed using her body to manipulate men to do her bidding, Juanita walked across the room in her thin, cotton dress with two buttons intentionally undone. She showed entirely too much of her chest when she bent over to sit down beside the drug lord.

"My dear Pedro, I personally witnessed my employee discover and report Lima's money-laundering activities to the authorities and hired an unknown stranger to anonymously tip off the DEA on their shipments intercepted last week. Not only has your only true competitor lost his most important men, but the U.S. government seized many of his accounts and confiscated more than two hundred million U.S. dollars' worth of drugs. After our campaign today, you will be the only family from South America with any type of infrastructure in the U.S."

"And my most skilled man personally shot your rival's son with a government-issued Glock, during the biggest drug bust in U.S. history," Carlos added. "He is totally professional and would not allow his connection to me be known even if tortured to death. If, for some unforeseeable reason, they learned about his connection to me, he has no knowledge about my relationship with you. More importantly, after today, the U.S. government will hold the Lima family responsible for the death of approximately fifty government officials and the demolition of two buildings."

"We have much invested in our relationship with your family," Juanita said while placing her hand on his leg. "After today's missions, two things are going to happen."

She paused long enough to smile and push her hair behind her ear.

"The Lima Cartel will have the entire U.S. government looking for them and our families' business dealings will be finished."

"Let's not forget the twenty-five million dollars and small armory you'll receive for your services," Ramirez added to her list of outcomes as he took her hand and kissed it.

"A small price to pay for exclusivity to the U.S. market," she countered as she got up and poured their guest a glass of Don Julio tequila.

At the same time as Ramirez sipped his tequila, a generic man of average height and features gave a kid a hundred dollars to go into a coffee shop and use a public computer to send the same e-mail to two different DEA offices in the United States.

"You are responsible for the death of my son and the embarrassment of my family. Those actions have repercussions. May God show you more mercy than you showed my son."

-Hector Lima

Exactly two hours later, at 4:35 p.m., mayhem unleashed. Within fourteen seconds of each other, the local DEA offices in downtown Houston and New Orleans exploded with enough force to send shattered glass flying almost one hundred feet. Shock waves caused alarms from both buildings and multiple cars in nearby parking lots to scream over the sound of the approaching sirens. The explosions were expertly placed and detonated to create maximum fire and physical damage to the buildings. They were successful in creating a chaotic emergency situation, sure to be on every television in the world for days.

Thirty minutes later, Carlos received confirmation of the successful results of their North America test. Without any detection, they had set off simultaneous explosions in two federal buildings and framed the second largest cartel in South America. Later numbers would show ninety-eight people had died, eighty-seven of which were government employees. The total number of deceased almost doubled their pre-mission estimate of fifty. The explosions created a diversion sure to monopolize much of United States' efforts while concurrently making the Lima family the world's most wanted criminals.

****

Elizabeth sat in the comfortable, well-lit, large, windowless room, scared and confused about why she would have been abducted. She had no idea where she was or who her captives were. Trying to guess her location, she estimated her blindfolded drive had lasted six hours, although stress and fear certainly affected her guess.

"What do you want from me? And where the hell am I?" she demanded of the man dressed in all black who opened the only door in her two-room jail.

He placed a tray carrying a sandwich, an apple, and a bottle of water on the table closest to the door. He smiled almost apologetically, then silently backed out of the room and locked the door. She sat back down in the wingback chair on the wall opposite the door, pulled her knees into her chest, and rocked back and forth.

She couldn't cry any more if she wanted to. She had cried for two solid hours while blindfolded and hooded and restrained in the back of the van. She didn't know what action, if any, she should take, but she knew she had shed her last tears because of those assholes.

Intellectually, she understood the theory of shock, but she had never experienced it firsthand. Not knowing how to improve her situation, she returned to the calming motion of rocking back and forth in her chair and staring at nothing except the way the light created shadows on the wall.

****

Jeff could almost distinguish between light and dark, but he could see nothing else through his blindfold and hood as he was humanely, but aggressively escorted from the back of the van and onto a waiting plane. His senses picked up on very little traffic of any kind along the way, so he guessed he and his captors were taking off from a small, possibly remote airport.

Based on the noise level in the vessel, his proximity to the pilot, and the turbulence of the flight, he also surmised they flew in a small, four-to-eight-seat, prop plane. He couldn't guess in which direction they flew, but he estimated they traveled for about three hours before landing, refueling, and taking another, slightly longer flight.

After landing the second time, his captors escorted him to another van for a forty-five-minute trip before apparently arriving at their final destination. Still blind to his surroundings, he concentrated on his other senses in an effort to determine his location.

The interior of the building felt old and spacious. It seemed damp for this time of year, and most sounds were accompanied by a faint echo, which reminded him of a large, unoccupied gymnasium. Jeff dragged his feet and felt them slide over a thin, but noticeable coating of dust and debris as he climbed the cement steps. The man controlling his pace and direction pulled on his arm and repeated the same word sixteen times.

"Step…Step…" he heard two more times in a deep, strong voice that made Jeff envision a large, black man.

At the top of the steps, he heard his captor press a four-digit code into a panel and open a door. The stranger removed Jeff's hood, which made things brighter, but he still couldn't see through the thin, black, elastic blindfold. His captor cut the plastic restraints from his wrists and gently pushed him into the room before leaving and locking the door behind him.

Jeff removed his blindfold and blinked many times before he saw the blurry young lady standing in front of him.

"Are you okay?" she asked.

"I'm fine," he calmly answered as he continued to blink. "My name is Jeff. May I ask who you are?"

"I'm Elizabeth. Do you know why we are here?"

Still blinking and focusing on the girl who could have been very pretty if she combed her hair and cleaned her smudged makeup, he said, "I have an idea why I'm here, but I have no idea what enemy we share. The good news is, if they wanted to harm us, they wouldn't have brought us here. We should be okay if we stay calm and work together."

Uncharacteristic of his analytical personality, but in response to sensing her shock, he slowly approached her and gave her a friendly, gentle hug.

He felt her cling to him like letting go would cost her, her last breath, clearly relieved to have a friendly companion. Trying to calm his new roommate, he spoke softly.

"They obviously want something from us. I can only assume time will reveal their need. Try to relax, and we will get through this together."

He broke their embrace, and guided her back to the chair. He nodded toward the lunch tray and added, "You need to eat and drink. I'm sure the food is fine. They don't need to drug us. We are already their captives."

Elizabeth retrieved the stale sandwich and bottle of water and picked off bite-sized pieces of the turkey sandwich. She ate a couple of bites and stared at the floor.

After a quick glance at his surroundings, Jeff wondered why their captors would spend so much money and effort to set up this room. He confirmed their actions were being monitored by four cameras, and noticed that, although there were no windows, there were curtains to create the illusion of a window. A round, oak, kitchen table with two chairs sat in the corner, and another bed could fit into the space if someone wanted to add one. Due to the contents in the drawers and the bathroom cupboard, he concluded no more roommates would be added and Elizabeth would be the only other prisoner.

He spent the next twenty minutes completely searching the main room and averagely sized bathroom. He checked every piece of furniture and every drawer. He looked under the corners of the carpet and examined every power outlet. He looked in the vents and studied the door hinges. His observations gave him some useful but confusing intel. He turned toward his new friend.

"Elizabeth, I have good news and bad news."

"I'm not sure I can handle any more bad news," she responded.

"Well, the bad news is they plan on us staying a while. They gave us each a change of clothes and basic toiletries."

He saw her hunched shoulders drop even more and heard the air deflate from her lungs.

"But the good news is," he quickly added, "they don't plan on harming either of us. They've given us a spacious room, separate beds, healthy food, and a clean, working bathroom. They want to keep us here and keep us hidden, but for some reason, they care about our comfort."

He put his hands on her shoulders, bent down to look in her eyes, and repeated his impressions.

"Elizabeth, they want us comfortable and safe."

"Well, if we are going to be here for a while, why don't you call me Lizzy?" she said before sitting back in her chair.

Chapter XVI

    The Pride had different ideas on how to spend a relaxing evening. Bill, used to working without breaks, planned on using the uninterrupted time without the other Cats to finalize some details for their last practice mission. Gary and Maria were going out for dinner and then to Lucy's for a slice of pie and to check in on Maria's mom, before coming home to a hopefully empty house for a little of what Gary referred to as "cuddle time." Eddie wanted to get to bed early to try a new sleep plan he and Pax had designed, but first wanted to work the bugs out of a couple Attal toys without the pressure of a mission. Elaine and Aggie were planning to pull what they were sure would be a protesting Pax along for a night of loud music and crowded clubs.

    Aggie headed to the barn to give Eddie his weekly check-up. She could hear the music long before she reached the barn. "Born to Be Wild" by Steppenwolf played too loud to have a conversation. Eddie sang along while simultaneously controlling two flying, remote-control devices Gary had nicknamed Frick and Frack. Aggie was ten feet inside the barn before Eddie noticed he had a visitor.

He turned the volume down telepathically and without looking at her said, "Put your hands out."

She stopped in her tracks and got ready to receive a package from Frack, the two-foot-long, quad-propeller, silent drone flying overhead.

First, he flew Frick, the miniature, surveillance robot resembling a common housefly, to within three feet of her and kept it hovering just over head. The drone then swooped down and made two figure eights as if it were dancing to the music. It slowed when it approached Aggie and paused just long enough to allow a delivery. Dropping a .357 revolver into her waiting hands, it flew off and made a perfect landing on the workbench at the far side of the barn.

"Thanks, Cubby, but my job is to save lives, not take them."

"The only way you're going to take a life with that gun is to club someone over the head with it. It's not loaded and there's no firing pin," he responded as he took off the special glasses he needed to control his toys and turned the music down again.

"Good job on the drop, though," she complimented him.

"Thanks. So, do you give everyone a check-up every week?" he asked, wondering if he was still being babied by the Pride.

"Yep. Except for Elaine and your mom," she answered. "They get one every other day because of their surgeries. But I'm about to reduce their visits to once a week."

After about two minutes of silently monitoring Eddie, Aggie reported, "As fit as a fiddle. Did I say that right?"

"As right as rain," he answered with a forced smile.

"Are you still waking up confused and upset?" she asked.

"Only when I fall asleep," Eddie joked.

"Can I ask you something out of curiosity? I promise it won't go in my report."

"I have no secrets from you. Shoot," he responded.

"I can't," she said, starting to laugh. "You said it's not lo—load. It's not loaded."

She tried a witty comeback, but only got to the word "not" before she laughed too hard to understand, pointing the gun at him anyway.

"You used to be so reserved and polite. You really should consider spending less time with Elaine and Dad. You're becoming more like them every day," he observed.

"Maybe, but I would consider that a huge compliment," she said.

She paused for a couple of seconds until her laughing stopped.

"Not to change the subject, but why all the old music lately?" she asked.

"It's classic rock," he corrected her. "And I have no idea. Pax asked me the same thing. He thinks it has something to do with the logic algorithm Bill downloaded into me. Possibly one of the donors loved classic rock? But I can't get enough of it, and surprisingly, I already know all the words."

"Doesn't it distract you?" she wondered.

"No, the exact opposite. It blocks outside distractions and helps me focus. Does it bother you? I can turn it down, but for some reason, my music and whatever magic you do up there," he said, pointing to his temples, "seem to be the only things controlling the headaches."

"I don't know about the others," she said with a sympathetic smile, "but I like it. Besides, if it helps you, then it helps the whole Pride."

She proved he might be right about spending too much time with Elaine by holding up her hand, extending just her pointer and little fingers, and shaking her hand.

"Keep rocking, Cubby. I'd love to stay and rock with you, but I need to go give Bill his check-up. He expected me at noon, and I'm already three minutes late."

She started to leave, but turned to face Eddie again.

"Hey, Elaine told me you plan on staying here tonight. Why don't you come with us? Maybe we can find a place playing some *classic rock*," she suggested, emphasizing his music choice was not the oldies.

"No, thanks. I want to get to bed early. Besides, I heard Robert might be coming, and I'd feel like a third wheel. Another time, maybe," he answered.

"Nonsense," she said immediately. "He knows we're all stuck together until the conclusion of this mission."

"Kinda my point. I don't want to make anyone stuck with me," Eddie said.

"That's not what I meant," she said, suddenly quiet and curious about what her shoes looked like. "The last few weeks have been the best of my life. I love your whole family."

After a short pause, she added, "It's been different with Robert. Well, it's just—I mean—well, Robert has been a little weird since he learned I can, you know, control his body and read his mind."

"In his defense, it's hard to understand if you are on the outside looking in," Eddie responded, understanding Robert's struggles.

"I guess. I hope he can make the transition. He likes being part of the inner-circle, but he is used to being the smartest one in the room and feels lied to and betrayed."

"He'll learn to accept it. I'm never the smartest one in the room, and I love hanging out with you guys."

"You seem very smart to me. Besides, you know all the cool songs," she added with a wink as she turned around and walked toward the door leading to the lab.

Exiting through the back door, she yelled before he could turn the music back up.

"Think about coming with us so I can check out your dance moves."

At 12:15 p.m., Gary sat down to watch a re-run of *M*A*S*H* he'd only seen four times. Halfway through, he was interrupted by someone at the door. Pausing the TV so he didn't miss the best line of the episode, he went to greet Robert, whose arrival had been announced two minutes ago, compliments of their Attal-enhanced security system.

"Hello, Robert. Come on in."

"Thank you, sir. I thought Agrata might be here this afternoon," Robert formally announced his intentions.

"Please don't call me sir. You gotta get used to calling me Gary, or if you prefer, you can call me Mufasa."

"Rumor has it I should call you Casper, but I consider that disrespectful and down-right un-English of me—sir."

"You can call me whatever you like, Bobby," Gary said with a smile. "Please make yourself comfortable. Can I get you something to drink?"

"A cup of tea would be brilliant," he answered.

"A cup of tea it is, but I don't know how brilliant it will be," Gary said on his way to the kitchen.

"Is Aggs around?" Robert asked.

"She's in the Den," Gary answered. "I already told her you are here. She said she'll be up in about five minutes."

"It's awesome but a little creepy how you communicate," Robert responded, concerning Gary's telepathic conversation with Aggie. "Where's the Den?"

"Oh, that's just my little name for the lab," Gary said as he put the water on to boil.

"And you Americans say we talk funny," Robert said with a chuckle on his way to the kitchen table.

In an attempt to make conversation, Gary asked, "So, how's the Moonlight European Trail office going?"

"It's going well, although it reminds me how much I miss seeing Aggs every day. And we certainly miss Pax's leadership, but numbers are still increasing slightly."

"There is no replacing Pax, but I'm sure Elizabeth and Cathy will figure things out," Gary responded.

"They are doing fine." he agreed. "Although, I left a message with Elizabeth's assistant yesterday, and she never returned my call, which is out of character for her."

"She is probably just busy trying to fill those big old, floppy shoes of Pax's," Gary suggested.

"Yea, probably."

"Probably what?" Aggie asked as she came bouncing up the steps and almost knocked Robert over with her hug.

"You are probably going to be the prettiest girl in the club tonight," Robert said, returning her embrace and kissing her cheek.

"Probably? You couldn't come up with a better compliment for your date?" she kidded.

"If you dress half as well as when we went to Cambridge, then you will be the prettiest girl in all of America," he quickly recovered.

"Well, now there's a challenge."

****

By 5:30 p.m., Gary and Maria were halfway through their first glass of wine. He ordered a steak and commented on how long it had been since his last dinner alone with his wife.

Aggie and Robert went shopping and agreed on a dress not as fancy as her Cambridge dress, but had a short hem length, much to his delight. Robert picked the dress, so Aggie got to pick the restaurant. They were laughing and getting caught up on their way to one of the area's premier, vegan restaurants, for a much-needed, long, romantic dinner before a night at the club.

Pax and Elaine were walking hand-in-hand around the pond and enjoying the late-day sun. Although they had yet to have any "cuddle time," they enjoyed being intimate and the apparent approval they received from the Pride.

All the Big Cats received Bill's urgent message at 5:34 p.m.

"Sorry, guys, but your night off has been cancelled. This is not a training mission. Emergency meeting at the Whites' in thirty minutes."

"Are you kidding me?" Aggie said out loud to a surprised Robert.

"What?" he asked, totally confused by her outburst.

"Turn around. We have to go back to the house. Bill just called a meeting."

Robert, who already felt like an uncomfortable outsider without the ability to communicate with the Pride, allowed his misplaced frustration to show.

"Of course, he did. Yet another advantage to dating an alien."

Gary flagged down the waitress, cancelled his order, and gave her twenty dollars. He and Maria were the last to arrive back home.

"Our final training mission has been cancelled. It's time to go to work," Bill announced to the Pride and Robert, who were all sitting in the Whites' living room. "Robert, we are going to miss tomorrow's Council meeting, so please stay, take some notes, and report our findings to the Council in our absence."

As Bill started his briefing, the TV over the mantle came on and displayed pictures to support his claims.

"There has been quite of bit of questionable activity in South America recently. My research confirmed our friends on the run are responsible for most, if not all, of the suspicious activity. I'm sure you all heard about the explosions in the DEA buildings. Although Hector Lima is blamed for the blast, we doubt he planted those bombs. They were too similar to the bomb which exploded on the docks in Sepetiba, Brazil. We have yet to uncover their motives, but we are 98% certain the Seretus Ligare is responsible for both acts of violence."

Behind him, the Pride saw pictures of the demolished buildings and many of the innocent, dead Terra.

"Confirmation of these acts alone would be enough to call us to action, but we have just received some additional, disturbing news."

Gary and Pax both sat up straighter and leaned forward.

"It appears they are coming after us."

"How do you figure?" Eddie interrupted.

"After Elaine's and Pax's encounters with Jeffery Harding at Cambridge, we had him fitted with a chip and instructed him to check in every day with our Kud professor at Colorado State University. Not only has he not checked in, but he hasn't been to the office in two days. A search of his assistant's mind revealed his research of South America's political climate led him to Carlos."

As a reminder, the latest pictures of Carlos and Jeffery Harding showed above his head.

"Ivan also reported a Kud taxi driver has fallen off the grid, and we have confirmation he's been asking questions about Pax at the Pacific station.

"We have to assume they know I'm still on the planet and Pax is working with me. I doubt they know about the Whites or this station, but it would be easy to learn about Pax's relationships with Moonlight and Elaine."

Pax put his arm around Elaine to confirm his fondness and assure her he would protect her.

"Although not confirmed, we believe his connection to Moonlight has cost Elizabeth Summers her freedom. Elizabeth has also been missing since yesterday"

Elaine and Maria both gasped as a picture of Elizabeth appeared on the Whites' TV.

Bill said, "We have made every attempt to contact her and have failed. Her car is at Moonlight headquarters, but she has disappeared."

Within twenty minutes, Aggie said goodbye to a frustrated Robert, who secretly wondered if, as the newly appointed director of Moonlight European Trail and boyfriend of Aggs, he might be the next to disappear. She grabbed the pre-packed bag she kept in the lab and was ready to leave within minutes of her awkward goodbye.

Eddie, with all his toys and equipment, finished last. He grabbed a large, black, leather duffle bag and threw it over his shoulder. He looked up at his waiting team, picked up another large bag by the handles, and led them out the door.

"It's time to rock and roll," he announced.

Chapter XVII

Having a private plane had its advantages. Forty-five minutes after leaving the Den, Eddie finished his final checklist and was cleared for take-off from the Canton/Akron Airport.

"Not that I don't trust him, or Bill's binge-and-puke," Elaine said quietly to Pax as she held his hand and got ready for the G-force of instant acceleration, "but it's going to be hard getting used to having my little brother fly me around in a jet."

Just then, Eddie spoke in all their minds telepathically.

"Ladies and gentleman, please be seated and return your seats and tray tables to their upright positions. We are cleared for take-off. As always, thank you for flying Attal Airline and enjoy the flight."

Simultaneous to hearing the word "flight" in their minds, they also heard, over the plane's speakers, the guitar-solo prelude to the Steve Miller Band's classic, "Jet Airliner."

Eddie taxied the 2007 Gulfstream IV to the east end of the runway. The volume of the music increased to a louder, but not uncomfortable level. Elaine gripped Pax's hand as the plane accelerated to Eddie's singing along with Steve Miller about going through Hell before he can get to Heaven.

They landed at Detroit International Airport and, according to Bill's information, were only fifteen minutes away from the Attal tracking chip secretly installed in Jeff Harding's right arm. A half hour after parking the Gulfstream in a hanger they had rented for the week, they were at the car rental booth, choosing their transportation.

Eddie left in a Cadillac CTS coupe, with Elaine in the passenger seat and Aggie cramped in the back seat, designed more for a bag of groceries than for comfortable seating. Bill drove the rest of the team in a white, Chevy van with three rows of seating.

Eddie dropped the girls off at a coffee shop for Elaine's evening meeting with Mr. Suzuki, which she had set up through his assistant while on the plane. He promised to return in an hour to pick them up and went to Suzuki's building to check on the delivery of the toys he had left on the plane.

Once in the coffee shop, Aggie sat two tables away, sipping a decaf café mocha and pretending to look through her phone. Elaine dressed uncharacteristically conservative and whose hair was a depressingly normal shade of dark blond, approached the waiting, 57-year-old, Japanese businessman.

She spoke in perfect Japanese; avoided eye contacted, and greeted him with a low, respectful bow which she held until she heard his response.

Although Aggie could have used vis to ensure Suzuki's cooperation, Elaine felt she could get more information than a simple mind sweep. Aggie instead monitored his vitals and telepathically informed Elaine whether he answered honestly or not. Although she could easily recognize dishonesty, she found determining whether he exaggerated the truth or told a bold-faced lie tended to be more of an art than a science.

Elaine, with her natural abilities and enhanced skills, was an artist. Within twenty minutes, she had negotiated a contract and telepathically informed Bill and Pax which office numbers Suzuki had agreed to rent to the Pride.

After thirty-five more minutes and two cups of tea, ordered and served perfectly by Elaine, Suzuki was impressed with the young, pretty, American girl who had a surprising grasp of his culture and language. In the time it took Eddie to return, Elaine had signed a rare, one-week rental agreement for two office spaces and access to the roof for satellite communication, received a complete history of the building and its tenets, knew the general layout of the town, and received a job offer if her make-believe boss ever undervalued her skills. She smiled shyly and politely asked Suzuki to be dismissed.

"Oh, my God," Elaine exclaimed after the van door slid shut. "That was amazing."

Talking with three times the volume and twice as fast as she had with Suzuki, she confessed, "I had no idea the value of the gift Bill gave me. The voice thing is cool, but I had the guy eating out of my hand. What a rush!"

"You got more than I could have with vis," Aggie confirmed. "You were awesome."

"Or Bill was," Eddie added, predictably giving his sister little credit.

"I'm sure Bill would be awesome at batting his eyes and getting his way," Elaine rebutted. "With vis, you get facts, but with conversation, you get opinions, stories, and useful tidbits."

After she explained her success and informed Eddie of his unlimited access to the roof, he admitted, "Good work. Thanks."

Both of the girls were amazed at the progress the Pride had made during their absence. In the conference room, Pax had three monitors, each displaying nine cameras. The first showed a four-story building, its entrances, parking lot, and adjacent property on all four sides. The second monitor showed cameras on the inside of the building. It displayed hallways, training rooms, a cafeteria, and sleeping quarters. The last one displayed the inside of two different apartments. One appeared to be dark and empty, but the other showed two very familiar residents.

As Elaine leaned in closer to confirm the girl sitting on the chair and rocking back and forth was her friend Elizabeth, she heard Pax entered the room.

"Welcome to Shepard Industries."

"What's Shepard Industries?" Elaine asked, not taking her eyes off her friend.

"A bankrupt company that owns the building. They ran a fabrication and assembly plant there for over forty years during Detroit's heydays," Pax explained. "They closed up shop fifteen years ago. I've been searching every record I can find. Officially, it's still an empty building owned by the heirs of Shepard Industries."

"It doesn't look empty," Elaine said, finally looking up from the third monitor. "Where is it? Have we been able to contact Lizzy or Jeff, yet?"

A few hours later, and a little more than a quarter of a mile away, Bill and Maria held hands and slowly strolled toward the Shepard Industries building. Behind them, invisible to anyone not wearing the Attal-enhanced jewelry, Gary made sure no one bothered the couple who had apparently made an uninformed, bad decision to take a walk after dark in this abandoned neighborhood.

Before the building even came into full view, Maria went to work. Speaking telepathically to Gary, Bill, and, most importantly, Pax, she used her night vision, infrared vision, smell, and hearing to describe what would normally take a team of experts with obvious equipment to discover.

"...and I see motion detectors on each corner of the building," Maria continued. "Although I cannot see the back, I assume there are eight."

"Okay. Got them," Pax answered, making note of them on his computer model of the building. "Any obvious holes in their coverage?"

"They've done a good job, however, a small person or device at the northwest corner, at exactly a 135-degree angle, would stand the best chance. Something could also be dropped from above, within eight feet of the building and halfway between each corner," she answered.

"Can you see the roof?" he asked.

"Yes. I can hear the buzz of a floodlight on the northeast corner by the fire escape, but I don't detect any monitoring. Hold on," she said, closing her eyes in concentration.

Trusting Bill to guide her, she focused on her non-visual senses. They were past the building and had turned to head back when she opened her eyes.

"A couple of the guards apparently take a smoke break by the shipping and receiving doors. The taller one speaks with a Middle Eastern accent and smokes menthols. The shorter one sounds military. He is smoking a cigar and is in desperate need of a shower. He speaks English very well, but may have a slight Latino accent. I'm not sure. That's more of an Elaine thing. The Middle Eastern guy just got off work and is asking the other one to join him later at Johnny's. Oh, shit."

"What?" Gary asked, looking in every direction.

"I just heard commands on a radio behind us, and now I hear footsteps. He is about forty yards behind, but has just *picked up his pace. He's getting instructions to find out who we are and persuade us to stay away by any means,"* Maria said.

"I'm sure a vis-enhanced conversation will get us out of this," Bill reassured a nervous Gary, who looked in every direction but saw no one. *"Just to be sure, fall back and allow him to pass you. Be ready to act quickly if I can't control him. But only as a last resort. Maria, just tell him we are traveling through. We stopped after a long drive and needed to stretch our legs. Be sweet and I'll do the rest."*

Although unnoticeable to most, Maria could hear Gary put some distance between them and concentrated on the stranger's steps, sounds, and smell.

"Any second now," she informed Bill.

By the time the guard confronted the couple walking down the dangerous street considerably later than they should, Bill had entered his mind and assured him they meant no harm and weren't a threat.

"Excuse me, but can I help you?" the stranger asked.

When Maria and Bill turned around, they saw a tall, white man with broad shoulders and a square jaw covered by at least two days' worth of stubble. His matching black pants and jacket informed any strangers of his seriousness, even without his belt, which held an array of tools and weapons.

"We're going on vacation in Canada and just stopped after fourteen hours on the road," Maria answered with a smile and slight tilt of her head. "We were tired of sitting, so we decided on a walk. Nice night for a walk, don't ya think?"

"It's a fine night, ma'am, but this isn't a nice neighborhood. Can I assume you're visit is only for a night?"

"Oh, yes. We're on our way back to the hotel now and then heading north after breakfast tomorrow," she answered.

"I recommend you hurry back," the stranger said in a tone resembling a command much more than it did a suggestion.

"Absolutely," Bill said. "Thank you for the advice. Have a good evening."

As they turned and walked off, Maria could hear instructions coming from his earbud.

"Drop back twenty yards, but make sure they don't get lost on their way back."

The stranger did as he had been told and followed them for two blocks before informing his superior all was well and heading back to the base.

They returned to the Suzuki building, and Maria finished telling Pax about her intel, while Bill briefed everyone else about the information he had acquired from the unaware guard while he was visiting his mind. The Whites were familiar with the efficiency of the Attal, but Maria, who helped Elaine get ready for her night out, continued to be amazed with the team's progress.

"I swear, it looks like we have been here a week," she said before adjusting the hijab Elaine wore to cover the majority of her hair.

"I know. Watching him is impressive when he is focused on something," Elaine answered, nodding toward Pax.

Even though Maria assumed the organizational skills were mostly Bill's doing, she allowed Elaine's comment.

"Are you sure you have your scarf on properly?" she asked.

"Of course. Let's see if he is ready for a little bar hopping," Elaine answered.

They could have guessed Eddie's concentration level before entering the conference room. He had his special glasses on, sang along to Warren Zevon's greatest hit, "Werewolves Of London" a little out of tune, half-swaying, half-dancing to the music as he maneuvered the remote control, communication device through the ductwork of the Shepard building. Maria and

Elaine walked into the room and saw Frick traveling in a dark air duct while Eddie continued his chorus and moved to the beat.

Elaine, dressed in a floor-length dress, no makeup, and a perfectly worn Hijab, gently took Pax by his hand and whispered in his ear, "Let Eddie do his thing. We have our own monster to catch."

Pax entered Johnny's first, occupied one of the two empty seats at the bar, and ordered a beer. Two minutes later, Elaine came in and sat alone at a small table against the wall, counting on the fact a lady in a hijab alone in a bar at this hour would be too much of a target to ignore. Johnny's was a stereotypical, neighborhood bar, right down to the uneven tables and torn, black, vinyl seats. An AC/DC song played in the background, reminding her of her brother, but the twenty-plus patrons easily drowned out the words. Most of the crowd gathered at the bar or around one of the two pool tables in the middle of the poorly lit, working-man's paradise.

By her quick count, there were only three women in the bar, although admittedly she wasn't positive about a couple of them. Detroit had a larger-than-average Arab population, so a young lady wearing traditional, Middle Eastern garments certainly wouldn't be a spectacle. She had assumed correctly, though, that a lady in Arab dress, sitting alone an hour before closing time, would be too tempting for the overworked, liquored-up guard to ignore. From Maria's description of his uniform, accent, and preference for menthol cigarettes, she knew immediately she had caught the right guy when he came up to the table.

Playing right into her hand, he aggressively said, "It's disgraceful for a young lady to be alone in a bar. Where is your husband? Does he know you are here?"

"I do not have a husband," she answered in English while not breaking eye contact. "And although it's none of your business, my ex-fiancé does not know I'm here, even though he is the reason."

Disgusted by her insubordination, he replied in Arabic, "He's a lucky man to rid himself of a filthy, American wannabe."

As he turned to leave, she shocked him when she rebutted in perfect Arabic.

"He wasn't even man enough to please a woman. He couldn't hold a job or his liquor."

He turned around to face her, leaned in, and continued the conversation in Arabic.

"Maybe the behavior of his woman disgusted him."

She allowed him to have dominance by breaking eye contact and replied, "I have no problem playing the dutiful woman. I did it for three years. But he has to be man enough to keep a job, hold his liquor, and, for god's sake, please his woman."

"Maybe you have not met the right man, yet?" he suggested, sitting down at her table.

"I'm sure I haven't," she replied. "But I hope that will change soon. Do you have a job?"

Elaine proceeded to test her Attal surgery to its limits. After two drinks at Johnny's, she took a taxi with her new friend, Mohamad, to a private, after-hours bar with no name. Two spicy appetizers and six drinks later, Mohamad slurred his words, staggered on his way to the bathroom, and bragged about his high-security job to the young, American girl that could speak perfect Arabic and drink as much as he could.

Elaine could tell she had consumed alcohol, but she remained in total control of her functions and mind. Although appreciative of her new talents, she missed the buzz normally accompanying a night of drinking. She also grew tired of reassuring Pax every five minutes that her surgery had worked perfectly.

The air had a definite crispness as Pax waited in the van and watched everything play out through Elaine's eyes. Finally, he heard the phrase he had hoped to hear hours ago.

"I think it's time to call it a night before it's time to say good morning." Elaine said to a couple of her new friends, who again commented on her ability to remain coherent after so much liquor.

"Don't let the hijab fool you," she responded, touching the scarf covering her hair. "I come from generations of hard-working, Irish drinkers."

"I'm going to call Mo a cab," the red-headed pub owner said. "You want one, too?"

"Thanks, but I already called my brother. He'll be here in a couple minutes. We'll give Mo a ride home. It's the least I can do for all the drinks and company."

On the way back to the Suzuki building, Pax stopped by Johnny's to retrieve Mo's car. Elaine drove his black Honda Accord while Pax followed closely behind in the van with the unconscious soldier of fortune beside him.

Chapter XVIII

  The combined efforts of the team to gather information, supplemented greatly by Pax's hacking into every security system within a mile of Shepard Industries, surpassed Bill's expectations and gave him ample knowledge of the building. But even with their superior information, Bill felt unhappy with the danger of his plan and disappointed they could not verify Carlos had ever been at the base. He continued discussing mission options with Pax and ran multiple success probabilities in search of lower risk alternatives. After a final mind search on Mo, he abandoned one more option that gave Gary more safety, but greatly increased Maria's risk. Realizing he would never be entirely pleased with any plan, he concluded it was time to implement his rescue mission and retrieve Elizabeth and Jeff.

  "Elaine," Bill called out as he pointed at Aggie. "I need you to make her look like him."

  He pointed to the unconscious Mo.

"What?" Elaine asked, not understanding.

"She has dark skin, black hair, and we are going to need her skills on the inside," Bill informed the girls.

They both stared at him with a "there is no way this is going to work" look on their faces.

"It only has to work for eight minutes and at a distance," he added, assuming incorrectly that he had cleared up any confusion.

"Just do your best," he finally said in defeat.

After an hour and a half, two haircuts, and some impressive makeup, Elaine felt Aggie could easily pass for Mo's younger brother, with some bulky clothes and a little bit of distance.

"I know it's kinda the point, but eww. She looks like a dude," Eddie said, confirming their costuming success.

Aggie promised Mo would not be coherent for a couple of hours, but he would certainly recover by lunch. Pax made a copy of his radio and pass card, memory planted specific orders for him to follow, made sure he would not have any memories from his night after he left the private bar, and took him home on his way to a 24-hour Walmart.

The next morning at 7:30 a.m., Jeff Harding woke up from yet another night of worrisome tossing and turning. He had resigned himself to remaining clueless about his future until his captors chose to reveal their intentions, yet he still had not given up hope of escape or rescue. He lay in bed and started working on his new favorite pastime: planning his escape. Even though unlikely to succeed, he kept coming back to the same two choices. He needed to either overpower one of the soldiers during food delivery and fight his way out or come up with a way to communicate to someone on the outside. He assumed it would be by theft or engineering. Although certain Lizzy would follow his lead, he thought maybe he should get her opinion about any possible plan.

He stared into the darkness and contemplated how to include Lizzy, when out of the corner of his eye he thought he caught a barely visible, tiny, green flash. Looking around and finding no noticeable light source, he used the backlight option on his black, waterproof sports watch to examine the spot where he thought he had seen the green light. On his sheet, almost hidden under his pillow, sat a housefly, just slightly larger than normal. When the glow of his watch illuminated the insect, it jumped a quarter of an inch to the right and then back to its original position. As soon as his watch went dark, the small eyes blinked green.

For the first time since arriving, Jeff had something to get excited about. This obviously wasn't a housefly. There would be no reason for his captors to go to this much trouble to monitor or communicate with him—it had to be friendly. But still, he had four cameras watching his every move twenty-four hours a day. Trying to slow down his heart rate and make sure he didn't draw any unnecessary attention to himself, he came up with a plan to test his new friend.

Assuming there would be very little monitoring this early in the morning, he pulled his cover over his head, like a kid trying to read a comic late at night. He lit up his watch again and watched as the fly jumped to the right a quarter of an inch and then jumped back. Jeff tapped his pillow two times with his free hand and became excited when the fly blinked its eyes twice.

Eddie, who stood in the conference room wearing his control glasses, called for Bill.

"We've successfully made contact," he reported. "What do you want me to do?"

"I've been impressed with Jeff so far," Bill answered. "Let's follow his lead."

Bill sat in a chair next to Eddie and waited for the next move. Three minutes later, under the covers, Jeff turned on his watch light and spoke barely above a whisper.

"Can you hear me?"

After he saw the fly blink again, Jeff instructed, "Get into my hand."

He felt the gentle landing of the tiny, RC communicator on his left palm. He closed his fist, retrieved his glasses from the night stand, and went to the only place in the small apartment not monitored.

The bathroom did contain a surveillance camera, but in an effort to give them a shred of privacy, their guards had made a mistake Jeff noticed on his first of many sweeps of their space. They had left a dead space which he could use to communicate with someone on the outside.

After about six questions, to which Eddie and Bill answered with one blink for yes and two blinks for no, Jeff finally asked the question Bill had been waiting patiently to hear.

"You can see, fly, hear, and hop. It only makes sense you can speak. Can I hear you?"

After blinking its eyes once, Eddie landed Frick in Jeff's hand. Holding it to within millimeters of his ear, he heard Bill's voice projected out of the fly at a level barely audible.

Bill methodically explained much of his rescue plan to Jeff, avoiding unnecessary details or anything concerning aliens or otherworldly technology. Within half an hour, Jeff knew the layout of the building, the approximate time of the rescue attempt, and that his "friends" were monitoring him using Shepard's cameras. Bill informed him they would not be in constant communication, but instructed him to keep the RC fly with him at all times, in case of emergencies and as a way to relay crucial information. Having devised a way to signal each other, Bill wished him luck and left the excited engineer alone again in his apartment jail.

****

Pax returned and tossed a Walmart bag at Aggie.

"This will help with the disguise."

She put on two layers of clothes to add bulk and then a black jacket and matching pants. Her height could not be helped, but as long as she didn't stand next to anyone, she might pass. Now wearing the extra clothes, boots, and a hat, she certainly appreciated her skills in controlling her body temperature, because she knew she would overheat otherwise.

"Gary, are you ready?" Bill asked. "You are next. Even though it's early, get ready to get into position soon."

Although no one could witness it, Gary left the Suzuki building, slowly walked a couple of blocks, and waited outside an accountant's office. Maria, wearing her Pride jewelry, could see her invisible husband standing nervously on the curb and turning his head right and left like a guy watching a tennis match.

"Stop being so nervous," she said in her husband's mind. *"I can hear the truck, and it's still about a block away."*

"You aren't supposed to be here," Gary said. *"What if the same guard from last night sees you?"*

"I'm sure his shift is over. Besides, I'm not going to follow you after your ride comes. It's a female carrier, and either I'm concentrating too hard, or she really needs to cut down on the amount of hairspray she uses. Do I ever smell that strong?"

"The next time I get super smelling, I'll let you know. Thanks for coming."

"Just be safe and you can thank me later. She's two stops away. She has her headphones on, but the music isn't very loud. Focus."

The blue and white mail truck stopped in front the building were Maria stood pretending to change the music station on her smart phone. She focused on the package on the front seat and read the label: "James Levin, Levin & Associates."

"They are getting a package at Levin's," she informed her husband. *"Wait for her to get out of the truck. Good luck. I love you."*

"Love you more. See ya soon."

The mail truck stopped in front of the Levin & Associates office. The carrier gathered a couple of magazines and letters, grabbed the package off of the front seat, hopped out, and headed toward the front door. Gary quietly climbed onto the back bumper, grabbed the handrail, and unnecessarily squatted down so he wouldn't be seen. Two deliveries later, the truck pulled right up to the front door of the Shepard building.

The guard smiled at the carrier.

"Hey, Martha," he said as he held the door open, unknowingly allowing the most polite breech of security possible when Gary walked through and smiled at the oblivious doorman.

Once inside, Gary stood in the corner and became increasingly nervous with every passing minute. The quiet waiting bothered him more than anything.

After eighteen anxious minutes, he finally received a break. A short, muscular, white man, dressed like all the other soldiers and carrying a bag from Home Depot, came in the front door.

"Hey, John. Buzz me in."

After a loud buzz followed by a click, the short man opened the door and went through, tailed by a middle-aged, invisible man.

"I'm in," Gary told Bill before backing himself into a corner and waiting for instructions.

"Understood. Stand ready," Bill responded. "Pax, tell us when you are ready."

"I'm ready now. Starting in ten seconds," Pax answered.

Bill told Gary, *"Get ready to come around the corner in—"* He paused for two seconds. *"—3…2…1. Now."*

Just before Bill finished the count, Pax froze Shepard's surveillance camera that monitored the empty hallway where Gary hid. He recorded the live feed and saved it on his hard drive.

At the word "now," Gary pressed a button on his watch and became completely visible. He came around the corner and looked back and forth, avoiding the cameras. He still ducked around windows and doors, despite Pax assuring him the rooms were empty. He kept moving until he ran into a security door requiring a swipe card to open. He retrieved a gray compound that reminded him of Silly Putty, jammed it in the crack as close to the lock as possible, and added a hardener to seal the door. He pressed a button on his watch and reported.

"Casper is back and waiting to exit."

Twenty minutes later, he left the building and carefully made his way to the emergency exit on the other side of the rigged door and waited for Bill's command.

"Taping again in 3…2…1. Now."

Gary pressed the button on his watch again and ran away from the corner of the building, toward the empty lot adjacent to the Shepard building. As he crossed the space, Eddie came speeding down the side road in a black Cadillac with no license plates. He tested the Caddy's anti-lock brakes and allowed Gary only a couple of seconds before he squealed his tires and headed south—the opposite direction of the Suzuki building. Two seconds later, all the cameras were working perfectly as Gary traveled safely back to the Suzuki building to keep his promise to Maria.

Chapter XIX

The whole Pride sat nervously waiting to start their mission. They were going to synchronize it with the fourth security sweep of the third shift. Although completely unnecessary, Pax went over the layout of the building one more time so it would be committed to memory.

"Remember, we are going to be working on the west side of the building and creating a diversion on the east side. Once you are inside, don't forget, due to the cranes and machinery once used in this building, the second floor only covers the west side of the structure. There's a two-story rappelling and climbing station on the east side. The second story is the most secure, and you must access it from the elevators or central stairs. Also as a reminder, we want to avoid the third floor if at all possible. The third floor houses the headquarters, the main security offices, the conference rooms, and the officers' sleeping quarters. There are very few cameras up there, so we are less familiar with the area. It also has little to do with our mission. Just avoid it if at all possible. The fourth floor—"

"We know," Eddie interrupted. "The fourth floor is empty, and the shipping docks and main entrance are on the first floor."

"The fourth floor is made up of the abandoned offices of Shepard Industries," Pax continued. "The Seretus might use some of it for storage, but we believe they ignore the space. The emergency exit on the northwest side of the building is our primary escape path."

Pax continued to irritate everyone with his relentless regurgitation of the building's design and the mission's timeline until almost midnight. Finally, Bill came to their rescue.

"Pax, I think we all know the details of our mission. Excellent briefing. Guys, if Pax is right—and he almost always is—we have one hour until we start our mission. Do whatever you need to do to relax, and we will meet again in the conference room in forty-five minutes."

As the team left the conference room, Pax had to smile at Elaine's attempt to defend him to the others.

He heard her explaining to Aggie, "He means well. He just—Well, he's just Pax."

He couldn't help but remember when Maria had learned about Gary's secret password to the tunnels and sassily asked him, "Why must you be so—well, be so *you*?"

Eddie went to the roof for a final check of his modified, Air Création, ultralight trike. The hang glider-style, tandem, two-seater, whose manufacturer boasted could take off and land in less than one hundred feet, was built to support a little over half a ton. That didn't stop Maria's uncertainty when she joined Eddie on the roof.

"Are you sure this will carry us both?" she asked, touching the black, nylon wing, which felt like a parachute and made Maria think about falling. "Will we have enough space to take off?"

She looked back and forth on the roof of the Suzuki building.

"Probably," Eddie answered as he stopped his mental checklist and turned to face his mother. "What did you have for dinner?"

At 12:40 a.m., Elaine and Pax, walking hand-in-hand, entered the conference room as Bill handed out last-minute instructions.

"Eddie, Maria—it's time to go. Aggie, you and Gary need to leave in an hour."

Rather than sitting helplessly while waiting to join the mission, Pax and Elaine used the time to pack up everything except Pax's main computer and monitors.

Eddie and his mom, dressed in all black, buckled themselves into his ultralight as he taxied to the east end of the building.

"Are you sure this is safe?" Maria asked nervously. "I'm not so sure the terms 'ultralight' and 'safe flight' deserve to be in the same sentence."

"Safer than your mother's arms," Eddie answered with a smile as he telepathically turned on his music.

He did a U-turn and headed straight for the three-foot wall on the west side of the building 150 feet away. Maria clenched her teeth and white-knuckled the handles on both sides of her seat. When the trike got to within thirty feet of the wall, Eddie pulled up and easily cleared the ledge by at least three feet. Even if the glider wasn't Attal enhanced, it would have been quiet enough to go unnoticed. With the modifications, it was quieter than an average box fan as it flew above the buildings.

Although unnoticeable to anyone else, Maria could easily hear Styx playing from Eddie's earbuds. The glider seemed so light and smooth in the air that she couldn't help but appreciate Eddie's choice of music. In an attempt to not think about the distance between her and the pavement below, she concentrated on his earbuds and listened to Styx sing about sailing away in a starship.

Thankfully, the Shepard building had a larger footprint than the Suzuki building. Eddie had no problem landing the ultralight on the 180-foot roof. His military binge-and-puke immediately took over. After a gentle landing, he aggressively continued to the northwest corner of the building. He turned the trike around and came to an abrupt stop. He hopped out seconds later and pointed a weapon Maria had never seen at the barely noticeable shadows and staircases.

"Do you see or hear anything?" he asked telepathically.

Maria used a combination of her night and infrared vision to scan their rooftop airport.

"No, but be quiet and don't move."

Eddie turned off his music and, despite having only a tenth of Maria's superior vision, scanned the rooftop in both directions, looking for any sign their arrival had been noticed. Maria listened for anything unusual, also scanned the area, and attempted to note if the smell of any human seemed to be getting stronger. She had to concentrate hard to cancel out the buzzing of the security light, the road traffic, the conversation taking place from two people taking a smoke break, and Mo, scuffing his feet as he made his first perimeter sweep.

After three minutes of deep concentration from the girl with the best senses on the planet, Maria confirmed their arrival remained undetected. Immediately after receiving the "all clear" and checking with Pax to verify no cameras or door alarms were going to surprise him, Eddie went to work. He picked the lock on the rooftop door, pried it open, and installed a specially designed device on the door to allow anyone wearing a Pride necklace to open the door. Although much more advanced, the device operated similarly to recent model cars that unlocked whenever the owner was near the vehicle. He then did a quick check of the rooftop, moving some chain, a couple of forgotten tools, and some sheet metal. After ensuring a safe runway, he gave his mom a hug before leaving her on the roof and heading back to the Suzuki building.

"See you soon."

"I'll see you first," she responded with a smile before returning to her work.

Maria fed Bill a constant stream of information from her observations. She mainly relayed things Pax's hack into the Shepard building's security couldn't report. She told him about the road traffic, which soldiers were taking a smoke break most often, if anyone strayed off camera, if she sensed an increase in security, and, although she thought it unimportant, when the kitchen and showers were in use. Most importantly, however, she studied and reported every move Mo made when making his second and third perimeter sweeps, which included a six-minute timeframe when his actions were out of camera range. Even though they were hidden to everyone else, Maria could see and smell Aggie and a cloaked Gary waiting for Mo as he made his fourth round.

"He lit a cigarette and called a friend on a cell phone. He is speaking Arabic, so I don't know what he is saying, but he'll be at your location in about three minutes."

Bill, with his advanced memory, monitored all twenty-seven cameras and the view through Aggie's eyes, while communicating telepathically with Maria. When Aggie received Maria's report that Mo traveled to within sixty feet of her hidden location, she entered his mind and suggested he hang up the phone as he headed to the key-card checkpoint. After scanning his security card, he suddenly had the urge to retie his left boot.

    Bent down and concentrating on his combat boot, Mo became an easy target for the invisible Gary to surprise. Mo barely felt the prick on the side of his neck from the needle inserted before he became unconscious. Maria hoped no one with night vision goggles watched Mo's rounds. Even the dimmest of mercenaries would recognize a problem if they saw the impossibility of a sleeping soldier dragging himself by his heels to hide behind the half-dead bushes at the back of the adjacent property.

    As soon as Gary hid Mo behind the neglected barberry bush, Aggie removed his ID card, grabbed his keys and radio, and continued on his rounds to the southwest corner of the Shepard property. Maria wanted to talk to Aggie, but followed protocol and reported to Bill that she needed to slow down. According to Pax's computer records, Maria was right; Aggie reached the last checkpoint two minutes faster than Mo's best time.

    Aggie already thought she moved slower than a ninety-year-old going to bingo, but she pretended to check her cell phone, stopped to light a cigarette—almost causing a coughing fit—and slowed her pace. Gary finished securing Mo in the bushes and hustled to the southwest entrance to catch up with Aggie, while still moving slow enough to not leave a ghost.

    "Eddie, it's time. ETA five minutes," Bill said to Eddie, who drove Elaine in the Caddy and had just finished verifying a safe escape route from the Shepard building to the expressway.

    Eddie pulled over two blocks away from the Shepard building, removed the license plates from the Caddy, put his RC control glasses on, and looked through the eyes of Frick. Seeing Jeff sitting at the table and playing gin rummy with Elizabeth at this late hour assured him he and Elizabeth were on board with their role in the escape plan. Eddie made the fly jump twice and fluttered its wings.

Recognizing the signal, Jeff looked straight at his pet housefly and blinked twice. Eddie responded by blinking the fly's green eyes three times. He took off his glasses, started the Caddy, and reported to Bill.

"Jeff received and understood the message. Heading to Shepard now."

"The mission has started. We are past the point of return. Good luck, everyone. Repeat, the mission is a go," Bill said as he added the views from Eddie's and the housefly's eyes to the list of things he monitored in his mind.

Jeff signaled to Lizzy, who intellectually understood what she needed to do, yet felt insecure and uncomfortable about her role, which Jeff had apologetically explained to her this morning.

During the last hour of their card game, the prisoners laughed for the first time in days. Lizzy flirted with the much older Jeff, laughing at pretend jokes, flipping her hair, and tilting her head with a smile. After getting his signal, she arched her back and started to rub her neck as if she had just sat through a four-hour college exam. Jeff got up from his chair, circled around, and stood behind her, starting to rub her neck and shoulders. The staged back rub had its desired effect.

The security supervisor on the third floor poked his co-worker and said, "See, I told you it would happen sooner or later. You owe me twenty bucks."

"Not until they make out or hook up, I don't," the younger, much bigger man responded as he rolled his desk chair over to watch the events in Apartment 1.

Similarly, the large, black security guard manning the booth leading to the apartments couldn't take his eyes off the smiling Elizabeth as she rolled her neck from side to side under Jeff's fingers.

About two minutes into the back rub, Aggie pulled her uniform cap down, threw her shoulders back in an unsuccessful effort to make her upper body look broader, and opened the northeast entrance door to Shepard Industries. After Gary entered, she moseyed over to the security checkpoint and scanned Mo's card.

At about the same time Eddie, driving too fast but not out of control, pulled into the northeast entrance and quickly pulled up to the building. He instructed Elaine to sit back and shot something across her body and out of the passenger window with a quiet, long-barreled gun, easily confused for a harpoon gun. The gray substance Eddie had created matched the brick of the building perfectly and reminded Elaine of a golf ball-sized spit wad from high school. Eddie traveled another twenty feet before Bill reported to them.

"They're on their way outside in 5...4...3..."

Eddie shot another of his spit wads onto the side of the building and continued toward the front door. He covered up the gun a second before it would have been visible to the guard. Elaine, wearing a sundress with cowboy boots and borderline too much makeup, opened the car door and addressed the man.

"Hello, sugar," she said in a sweet, South Carolinian accent. "We got all turned around, and y'all are the only ones with the lights on. Do you think y'all could help us? We seem to be lost. Please be a darlin' and point us back to 75."

Instead of using a cell phone or GPS, Elaine opened the map on her lap and smiled at the guard who looked perturbed by the interruption.

"It's back about three miles to the south," he said.

"Is this little old spot here us?" she asked, smiling helplessly and pointing to a location thirty miles away from where they were.

"Mark, the Caddy is just lost. I'll be right back," the guard reported on his radio to the other front-door guard.

"Copy that," came the response.

"No, ma' am," the guard said, unable to resist Elaine's sweet, helpless smile. "You are right here."

He leaned halfway into the car, pointed to their current location on the map, and barely felt the prick on his neck before falling unconscious onto Elaine's lap. Eddie and Elaine pulled him as far into the car as they could before Eddie pulled out his gun and shot a spit wad three inches from the front door.

While Eddie and Elaine were talking to the front guard, two things were happening simultaneously. Aggie, looking like a perfectly dressed, yet admittedly short soldier, moved totally unnoticed to the next station, and Elizabeth, who seemed to be enjoying her massage, added to her role in the escape.

In a pre-planned move to draw the guards' attention, Elizabeth undid two buttons of her shirt and pulled it off her shoulders, showing she intended to allow the massage to continue. Jeff leaned down, acting as if he planned to take advantage of her move by nibbling on her neck and get a better view of her breasts. Instead, he closed his eyes out of respect and whispered in her ear.

"You're doing great. I'm so sorry, but I'll be a gentleman. You just be ready to get dressed and run out of here at a second's notice."

On the third floor, where all twenty-seven cameras were monitored, the two guards were mesmerized by the goings-on in Apartment 1 and eager to find out who would win the bet. On the second floor, the apartment guard, who had nine cameras on his monitor, also focused on Elizabeth and her much older, suddenly intimate friend and his more-than-friendly massage.

The elevator arrived at the second floor. Aggie, with an invisible Gary close behind, made a double turn to her right and waited at the door behind the elevator. Without looking up at the camera, she nonchalantly waved to the unknown soldier at the guard station. Due to habit, distraction, and carelessness, he buzzed open the security door, getting her through the first layer of the second story's high-security defense. Unfortunately, she would not be able to pass any more levels with just her disguise.

****

Eddie and Elaine pulled the guard into the car and drove off the property.

"What's going on, John?" came from the radio connected to the unconscious guard lying on Elaine's lap.

Elaine took a radio Pax had copied from Mo, pressed the talk button, and in a perfect imitation of John, she responded, "I'm going to make sure these dumbasses get off the property. Pick me up in two minutes at the corner."

"I don't have clearance. I'll check upstairs," Mark responded.

Chapter XX

Aggie pulled out a black, plastic, conical device, designed to copy sound and repeat it digitally without background noise or static, and placed it over the receiver of her radio. She bent her torso in an unnatural way to avoid any recognition from Mo's colleague while still placing the radio close to the security microphone in the locked cage. She and Elaine, still in the Caddy with Eddie, stood by to receive Bill's instructions.

"We need Mo's verbal passcode in 5…4…3…"

When Bill finished the countdown, Elaine spoke out of Aggie's radio and through the device held up to the receiver, her voice sounding exactly like Mo's.

"Security pass 218. Mohamad."

The bulletproof glass door slid open like the doors at a supermarket. Aggie immediately started concentrating on the large, black guard's vitals.

"Mo, you got to come see this," he said without looking up from the intimate massage taking place in Apartment 1.

While crossing the thirty feet to the raised guard's station, Aggie focused on inducing nausea in the man until he broke into a cold sweat.

"Watch the booth, Mo," he said as he ran across the hall to the bathroom, breaking protocol and leaving behind his radio.

Gary removed some of the putty-like substance from his pocket and spread it into the door jamb. He quickly added the hardening substance and held the door for ten seconds. When he turned, he saw a smiling Aggie.

"Here's the code. I'm going to the other side."

"Are you sure we have time?" Gary asked.

"We need to take away their weapons and draw the attention of the local police. Go save our friends."

Aggie, moving faster than she had all night, approached the other security cage on the west side of the elevator, waved to the oblivious soldier, and told Bill she needed Elaine's help again.

****

Eddie gently left the sleeping guard in an empty lot around the corner, hurried back to the Suzuki building, parked the Caddy, and reported to Bill that "show time" would start in five minutes. He jumped into the driver's seat of the waiting van while Elaine got in the back with Pax, who remained deep in concentration monitoring his computer. With everything packed except Eddie's ultralight, which he would send for later, they headed toward the Shepard building.

****

With Elaine's help, Aggie easily got through the other second-floor security checkpoint. Using the same technique as she had with the apartment's guard, she easily sent the large, rough-looking, Latino guard running for the bathroom. Unlike his counterpart, however, he followed protocol and took his radio with him as he emptied the contents of his stomach. Applying the putty and hardener to the door guaranteed he wouldn't bother her, but he had a radio so she had to think and act quickly.

****

Jeff ran out of ideas. He felt confident the guards would be enjoying their little show and understood the strategy his unknown rescuer had explained, but he had taken his little charade with Lizzy about as far as his conscience allowed. He may be a prisoner, but he was still a gentleman.

Leaning over her in another pretend show of affection, he whispered, "I thought we would have some resolution by now and I'm not going to let the guards see any more of you. Pretend to get mad at me for my advances and slap my face. The fight will keep them entertained."

She lifted her right hand and placed it around his neck and responded, "I could never fight with you. Meeting you is the only thing good to come from this place. Follow my lead."

****

Aggie entered the security booth guarding the back room and retrieved the daily code to the secure, reinforced room used as the armory. She pressed in the four-digit code and used Mo's card to enter the 1200-square-foot space. The lights came on upon her entrance, and she saw rows of guns, explosives, ammunition, electronics, and uniforms. Nervous about her shortened timeframe and her lack of experience in destroying anything, she placed a device on the first two dangerous items she saw, a case of bullets and a box marked "EXPLOSIVE." She set the manual timers for twenty minutes and hustled out of the armory. Whether she lived or not, this room would be destroyed and the explosion would certainly draw the attention of the local police creating an investigation into the activities in this old assembly plant.

From the back of the van, one minute before entering the perimeter of the property, Pax took over the security cameras of the Shepard Building and disabled all of the door alarms. As soon as she got the okay from Bill, Maria came through the rooftop door that unlocked automatically, thanks to Eddie's device, and hurried down to the second floor emergency exit. The door opened with help from her smiling husband, who blew her a kiss before leaving her at the exit.

As soon as Pax informed Bill the emergency door was open, Bill communicated with the whole team.

"Everyone needs to be out of the building in less than two minutes."

Pax played his pre-recorded security footage on all the security monitors. The guards in the third floor security station could tell immediately something was not right. They were watching the camera in Apartment 1 as the young, pretty hostage took the skinny, middle-aged man by the hand. Wearing only her bra and jeans, she escorted him to her bed and got under the covers. Suddenly, the camera blinked, and she sat in her favorite chair while the man read a book at the table.

The guards were confused for a second, but were immediately shocked into action by the view on another camera, where they watched as a middle-aged, almost-bald guy in a red shirt creeped down the hall and toward the southeast emergency door.

While the footage played for the guards, Gary used Mo's copied security card, typed in the four-digit code, and entered Apartment 1. Forgetting about his invisibility, he saw Lizzy and Jeff jump up from the bed and look back and forth for the person who had opened their door. Lizzy grabbed her shirt and put it on while Jeff grabbed the shiv he had made out of a fork and stood in front of Lizzy in an inefficient but chivalrous attempt to shield her from any danger. During the confusion, Gary pressed a button on his watch and appeared in the doorway, propping open the only exit from their prison.

"Mr. White?" Elizabeth said at the sight of Elaine's dad. "What in the—"

"No time, honey," he interrupted. "I'll explain later. All hell is about to break loose. This way. Quick!"

From the second floor, the explosion of Eddie's first spit wad sounded like a bolt of lightning striking very close to the building. The white van pulled up to the northwest emergency exit right as the second spit wad exploded. The armory guard locked in the bathroom got on the radio, reported the intrusion, and admitted his embarrassing situation. Confused about how the first-floor intruder overtook the second-story, armory guard, the security supervisor ordered the whole building into an emergency shutdown. He also sent all available personnel to the southwest emergency exit, where the door alarm sounded as the intruder ran through the empty lot.

"What about the white van?" the front-door guard asked, just as the third spit wad exploded.

"What the hell?" the frustrated security officer said. "Bob, check out the van. Everyone else to Exit 3. I want the intruder caught."

Gary half-escorted, half-shoved Jeff and Liz toward the emergency exit where Maria stood holding the door.

"Mrs. White? But—"

"Hurry, honey. We have to go," Maria instructed.

Unfortunately, the emergency shutdown system had a separate power source and a self-contained control system. Pax could not affect the shutdown procedures, but he did throw a wrench into the process by blinking on and off all the cameras and door alarms and starting a self-made malware program to jam all cellular technology, except his, of course. He called the local police and reported the explosions and intrusion.

Gary, still visible, was the last to exit the northwest emergency door and get in the van. As soon as he shut the sliding door, the front guard came around the corner, yelling commands. Eddie floored the accelerator which caused the tires to squeal, gravel to pepper the guard, and an unprepared Gary to be thrown to the floor of the van.

"What about Aggie?" Gary asked as they sped toward the alley.

"The building's on lockdown," Bill reported. "She can't get out any of the doors except the ones we had propped open. She can take care of herself. She has plenty of vis, and the police are on the way."

"Oh, hell, no," Eddie responded as he turned north, away from the expressway, and sped down the alley. "The armory is going to blow in fourteen minutes. I am *not* leaving her behind."

"Eddie, there's no time," Bill responded. "I've contacted Aggie. She's searching for a secure spot to protect herself from the explosion. There will be dozens of police and firefighters there within thirty minutes. Go to the airport."

"Thirty minutes? She could be dead in thirteen," he responded.

Ignoring Bill's commands, Eddie contacted Aggie as he traveled at seventy miles an hour on a city street.

"How you doing, Aggie?"

"I've been better, but I think I'll be fine. I found a spot that should withstand the blast. I'll catch up with you soon."

The van came to a screeching stop in front of the Suzuki building. Eddie turned and yelled, "Bill, get everyone to the airport. Pax, pull up the blueprints for Shepard and help Aggie."

He jumped out of the van and ran up the steps two at a time, searching for his keycard as he informed Aggie of his plan.

"Change of plan. Contact Pax and get your ass to the roof."

"What? No! The north side might give way under the blast."

"Then I may need some emergency medical assistance, cuz I plan on being up there. GET YOUR ASS TO THE ROOF!"

Realizing too late the video of Gary running through the vacant lot occurred during daylight and thrown off by the loud, but so far non-damaging explosions, the security supervisor did what he should have done ten minutes ago. He ordered his troops to take emergency Defense Pattern Alpha 3.

Pax conceded he had no choice but to work with Eddie's ad lib rescue plan. He informed Aggie that due to the lockdown, their only options were fire escapes and maintenance access. He quickly devised a plan he felt too risky, but in his opinion her only chance of making it to the roof in—He looked down at his watch—nine minutes. Aggie ran to the elevator on the second floor with the doors froze open. She climbed onto the handrail and shoved up the emergency door in the ceiling. Once she stood on top of the elevator, she had to jump six feet to a maintenance ladder running the length of the elevator shaft. The jump would have been a no-brainer if a failed attempt did not mean falling far enough to leave her too injured to heal her own body.

She overestimated the distance and underestimated her adrenaline, causing her to hit the ladder way too hard. She bounced back, but caught herself awkwardly with only her right foot and left hand. She corrected herself, took a deep breath, and headed up the ladder.

Eddie didn't have time for a pre-flight checklist. He jumped into his ultralight and took off toward the far corner of the Suzuki building while still connecting his seatbelt. Forgoing stealth, he barely climbed high enough to clear the downtown buildings as he headed straight toward the glowing Shepard building.

Bill and the others in the van traveled ninety-five miles an hour down the expressway toward the private hangar at the airport, without their pilot. Maria watched for any highway patrol hoping to catch any late-night speeders, while Pax tracked the police on his computer and kept Aggie moving toward the roof. Lizzy, while grateful to be saved, commented that she felt more scared, confused, and out of control than she had in days. She sat in the middle row of seats, rocking back and forth in Jeff's arms.

Aggie made it to the rooftop entrance of the elevator shaft, only to find the maintenance door locked. An unsurprised Pax reported he would have it unlocked in a second. He hacked into the security system and set off the fire alarm, which added to the confusion at the Shepard building and would unlock any door not on the shutdown list for emergency personnel access. Thankfully, anything above the third floor did not make the list.

Her excitement about making it to the roof was short-lived. When she walked through the door Pax had cleverly unlocked, she met a soldier who pointed an assault rifle at her head.

He blurted out conflicting commands, "Don't move. Get on your knees and put your hands behind your head."

After getting on her knees, Aggie put both hands behind her head and pressed a button on her watch. Using some of her stored vis, she easily convinced the soldier she was friendly and he should lay down his rifle. Unfortunately, she didn't have time to do a proper mind search, or she might have discovered that Defense Pattern Alpha 3 called for two men to secure the roof.

Eddie was twenty feet above and ninety-five feet north of the Shepard building. He slowed down for a landing when he saw Aggie by the door with a soldier lying face down on the roof beside her. He also saw a second soldier, hidden to Aggie, making his way toward her.

His downloaded military training took over as he informed her telepathically, *"There's a second guy at your ten o'clock, heading your way."*

In an effort to draw the second soldier's attention away from Aggie, Eddie telepathically switched his music from his headphones to the speakers he had installed last week. The sudden sound coming from above made the man stop in his tracks. He took a defensive stance and turned to find the source of the noise. Before he could get his bearings, Eddie made an emergency landing twenty-five feet behind him. The soldier dove to his right to avoid being crushed by what sounded like a flying jukebox. Eddie slammed on the brakes and removed a modified gun from a holster mounted to the frame of his trike, resembling a cowboy drawing his Winchester from the saddle of his horse. Eddie fired six shots. The first two missed. The next two bounced off the soldier's chest, protected by a Kevlar vest. His fifth shot struck the man's forearm, and the sixth got the back of his right hand as he made a feeble attempt to protect his face.

Before the soldier passed out from the drug delivered by Eddie's miniature darts, he got off two shots at the flying jukebox. Although one could clearly make out the sound of the gunshots, they were muffled by Steven Tyler singing about a dude who really looked like a lady.

Eddie continued to the far end of the roof, made a U-turn, and came to a brief stop. It only took eighteen seconds for a sprinting Aggie to climb into the back seat of the ultralight that had Aerosmith blaring from its speakers. As soon as her feet left the roof, Eddie headed toward the far wall at full speed.

The first soldier gathered his wits and realized the little guy dressed in one of their uniforms had climbed on what looked like a black hang glider. Aggie's vis-enhanced suggestion was not specific enough to stop his aggression. Although he followed her orders, he proved to be a well-trained soldier by pulling out his handgun and emptying his clip at the imposter that kind of looked like a lady.

Seven seconds after clearing the Shepard building, the shockwave from the explosion shook the little two-seater.

"Thanks, Eddie, but you shouldn't have come back."

After thinking about his heroic, yet defiant moves, Aggie chuckled and added, *"I'm glad you did, but Bill is going to be pissed."*

Eddie took a second to right the glider then said, *"Dad always says there's no use being stupid unless you are willing to prove it. And shame on them for—Well, there's no way I—um..."*

After a short pause to collect his thoughts, he said, *"I will always come back for you."*

"Well, thanks, Cubby. I owe you," she said as she ran her hand through her pilot's windblown hair.

Verbally, knowing he would never hear her over the music she added, "You make me feel like a Terra princess."

"Well, I may need to collect on your debt sooner than you think," Eddie said. *"One of those bastards nicked me."*

The bullet had barely grazed Eddie's left bicep. It did enough damage to create a bloody mess on his shirt and get some sympathy for his heroics, but not enough to require anything more than a couple stiches if he didn't have one of the world's best healthcare providers with alien abilities sitting behind him. Aggie easily stopped the bleeding before the ultralight landed on a city-owned baseball field a quarter of a mile from the protected airspace of the airport. Within fifteen minutes, the team picked up Eddie, Aggie, and the ultralight and were heading back to the private hangar housing the Gulfstream.

It took a little persuasion at this late hour, but less than forty-five minutes after his narrow escape from the rooftop, Eddie taxied down the runway and gave a brief speech.

> "Ladies and gentlemen, please take your seats.
> We are about to take off and fly with the birds,
> but first let me leave you with the following words.
> It's best after a mission that's dangerous and long
> to be thankful you survived and
> to always end with a song.
> Enjoy the flight."

He turned up the Meatloaf song playing over the Gulfstream's speakers. As the plane accelerated down the runway, he sang outload about leaving this place like a bat out of hell.

"Is your brother really going to fly us home?" Lizzy asked as she lay her head on Elaine's shoulder. "I thought being kidnapped would be the craziest thing to ever happen to me. Girl, we really need to talk."

Chapter XXI

Carlos and Juanita had planned to move into the third floor of the North American compound next week. After the update from the soon-to-be ex-commander concerning the captives' escape and the demolition of their building and armory, however, they booked the first flight available to Detroit International Airport. One member of the militia had lost his life, four of them had to be transported to the hospital, and the damage to the Shepard building, while not insurmountable, certainly was extensive.

It took Carlos two days and almost 5u's of vis to get the situation under control. After convincing the local authorities the Shepard Building operated as a training center and all the personnel were either trainees or educators for a personal protection company, Juanita and Carlos explained the explosions as a gas leak accidently ignited. After finishing with the local authorities and using way too much vis, they turned their attention to their Seretus Ligare plans.

"I don't think you understand," Carlos explained to her. "I'm not saying we are going to have to make changes to our plan. I'm saying Bill and Pax wrecked our plan."

"Are you suggesting we activate our escape plan?" Juanita asked.

"I think we should consider it. But we have a couple of details we need to address first," he responded.

****

The Pride, along with their two, newly freed friends, arrived back at the Whites' property, exhausted. After Elizabeth and Jeff laid down for a much-needed nap, Bill contacted Ivan and asked him to attend a post-mission meeting and scheduled an emergency Terra Relations Council meeting for the day after tomorrow. Sitting in the meeting room of the Cat Cave, Bill meticulously reported the many successes of their missions and his pleasure with the rescue of Jeff and Elizabeth.

"There were only three situations where I feel we failed as a team," Bill reported.

"Here it comes," Eddie whispered under his breath.

"Pax," Bill said to everyone's surprise.

"Yes," he said, sitting up at attention.

"You did a great job learning about the building's layout and the security patterns, but we shouldn't have been surprised by their emergency plan and the two soldiers on the roof. Even though we shouldn't have been there, we should have known about the procedure and the presence of a second, armed guard."

Pax didn't answer, but nodded his head in understanding and agreement.

"Aggie," Bill continued, "when Eddie reported the timeframe had been shortened, you should never have attempted to blow the armory. I give all of you room to act independently and expect you to make tough decisions under stressful situations, but we agreed if anything changed we would rescue the prisoners and get out safely. In the future, we must stay on plan."

"Eddie," Bill said, looking at the youngest member of the Pride, "same thing goes for you. You performed admirably, but you have to follow orders and protocol. During any mission, I have much more information than any of you. We can't have seven people with seven agendas. You must follow orders.

"Now, if there aren't any more questions or comments, I'd like Ivan to stay afterwards to discuss our new Terra friends."

"I have a comment," Eddie spoke up.

"Go ahead, Eddie. What is it?" Bill asked.

"I got a major issue with you leaving Aggie in the Shepard building to die or get captured. And for the record, I would do the same thing again in the same situation. I will follow orders to a point, but if you ever plan on asking me to leave a teammate behind, then we have a problem."

"Then we have a problem," Bill answered calmly, proceeding to explain his logic. "Aggie had a 58% chance of surviving the blast without any injury and an 89% chance of survival. With her medical skills, the percentages of her survival chances might even have been in the ninetieth percentile. Your rescue plan had a 14% chance of success, without calculating the effect of a second guard. As I stated earlier, I have more information, and you must learn to trust my lead. You traded a 90% plan for a 10% one. A very foolish move."

"It wasn't foolish. It was Terra. I would have risked my life for a 3% chance to save Aggie's. You not comprehending my actions is why I have a problem. You should have picked a less heroic soldier than me," he said, folding his arms in a defiant, aggressive stance.

After a moment of silence, Bill said, "Thank you for your honesty. I understand your feelings and will speak to Ivan and the Council about your concerns."

Bill ended the meeting and stayed to speak to Ivan.

As they walked through the tunnels, Aggie took Eddie's arm.

"Only three percent? You wouldn't have come for two?"

"My mind doesn't think that way. You have always looked out for me, and I will always *look out for you,"* Eddie answered. *"I would have come even if Bill said I had no chance."*

She pulled on his arm to stop him, stood on her tiptoes, kissed him on his cheek and said, "I know you would have."

She let go of him and ran to catch up with Elaine and Pax, who were walking hand-in-hand down the tunnel. Gary and Maria caught up with Eddie, who moseyed ahead of them deep in thought. Gary gently punched his arm.

"Ahhh, the fruits of your labor. Well done, G.I. Joe."

Gary got smacked for his comment as they passed him in the tunnel, and Maria said, *"We are very proud of you."*

After his meeting with Ivan, Bill reported they were waiting to speak to the Council about Eddie's concerns and insubordination. They also decided, for the time being, they would tell Elizabeth and Jeff the same lie they had told many times. Even though they didn't expect them to believe their "technological company working on special projects" story, they only needed to buy enough time until they could meet with the Council. As a precaution, they also thought it might be prudent to bring Elizabeth, Jeff, and the Whites' immediate family to the property to have the protection of the Pride and the Attal.

****

"I don't think it's time to escape, yet," Juanita said after a short pause. "But I think our friends are a little too close and too organized. We need a new plan."

"Agreed. They have succeeded in stopping us from taking over the Pacific station," Carlos conceded. "Probably too lofty of a goal, anyway. Our new priorities should be to gather as much money and vis as possible so we can disappear properly, create havoc by exposing the Attal, and kill Bill and Pax."

"So you still want to activate our escape plan, but at a later time?" Juanita asked. "If so, your last two goals conflict with disappearing and melting into a Terra existence."

"If the station is being investigated by the Terra and the Attal are detained or imprisoned by the government, we would have the only usable vis, which would make it easy to evade capture," he rebutted.

"Possibly," Juanita admitted. "But if they know about our existence, we could have the entire population looking for us, making blending almost impossible."

"Maybe, but I won't be able to blend and relax if Bill and Pax are still running around, enjoying vis-related benefits, and searching for us," Carlos said. "Besides, they need to pay for their disrespect."

"Our superiority over the Terra diminishes if we start thinking and acting like them," Juanita pointed out. "They rescued their friends like you hoped. They were just quicker and better organized than you estimated."

After a short pause to let it sink in, Juanita added, "I really don't want to be apprehended because of your vengeful, Terra feelings. After our vis and money acquisition plan is complete, it will be time to part ways. You can hunt down and destroy any Attal you want, but I'm going to take my half and disappear somewhere where young, Terra men rub lotion on my body as I sit by the pool, drinking mineral water and enjoying the surface sunshine."

****

After easily convincing Ed and Michele, Gary's parents, to come stay at their new property and visit for a while, Maria and Gary went to Lucy's for a piece of pie and to talk to her mother, who they had unsuccessfully tried multiple times to convince to retire.

"Mom, please," Maria pleaded for the third time. "Not only might you be in danger, but you shouldn't have to work this hard anymore."

"I love working here," she argued. "Besides, there really isn't much of a Lucy's if there isn't a Lucy."

"Yea," Gary said, unable to help himself from poking fun. "Because McDonald's only sells hamburgers when the funny-looking clown is in the store. Man, does that guy get around."

"Very funny," Lucy said before she smacked him on his shoulder and walked back to the kitchen.

"Is it me or is smacking me hereditary?" Gary asked his wife.

"It's you," she said with a gentle smack to the back of his head on her way to the kitchen to convince her mom to stay with them for a little while.

During the next couple of days, there were many changes made to the Whites' and Pax's houses. Even though they had an enormous property, its design did not include the ability to become a commune or refuge for so many people. Elaine, Elizabeth, and her sister Jenny moved into Pax's house. Bill and Aggie moved into an extra room in the surface station. Eddie turned the office in the lab into a makeshift bedroom. Jeff's family of four moved into the Whites' basement. Mike and Kathy Summers moved into the in-law suite, while Lucy took over Elaine's room and Gary's parents moved into Eddie's room.

There were way too many people and too many secrets. All told, not counting non-Pride members of the Attal, there were twenty people running around the property when Cathy and Robert arrived for the emergency Council meeting.

Per Gary's request and after a lesson on what is meant by a white lie, Bill called a meeting to half-explain and half-cover up why everyone had just uprooted their lives. With the open-concept floor plan, people could walk into the kitchen and dining room and still see and hear Bill, who stood in front of the fireplace with the TV behind him, showing pictures and videos to support his story.

"Bill tested his skill of mind planting multiple people at once and continued his far-fetched explanation. "For some time now, the Whites have been working with Pax and me on special projects for the company we represent. For security reasons, it's hard to explain what we do. In an effort to simplify a complicated situation, we consult in high-end technology and security for many governments and multi-national businesses.

"We sometimes upset people who are caught doing things they would rather keep secret and have been known to occasionally bend rules for the greater good. These situations unfortunately sometimes put our lives and those of our friends in danger. The recent abductions of Jeff and Elizabeth prove our safety and the safety our friends should be taken more seriously."

After another thirty minutes and a couple vis enhanced suggestions, Bill convinced everyone to take a little vacation at the Whites' and to make themselves comfortable anywhere except the barn. He simply told them the barn was off limits for security reasons.

Later that evening after the Council meeting, the members came through the lab on their way to the elevator leading to the barn entrance to the property. They passed Eddie who worked diligently on one of his pet projects at his personal work bench. Gary approached his son.

"You are going to have a choice, and it's a tough one. We love you and support you, regardless what you choose. If you need to talk—" Gary squeezed Eddie's arm and shook his head.

Eddie didn't respond, but nodded in understanding.

Aggie stood in the doorway, very interested in her shoes and the floor of the lab, while Eddie talked to his parents. When alone again, Aggie took Eddie's hand and led him to his makeshift bedroom.

They sat down beside each other on the bed, and she said, "Ivan is going to talk to you after his update."

"Should I be scared? Am I going to be punished? Just what is an Attal punishment?" Eddie asked in rapid order and without waiting for a response.

"Don't worry," she assured him. "You're a hero."

With renewed interest in the floor, she corrected herself, "You're my hero."

"Then what's the problem? What's going on?" he continued questioning.

"It's not my place to say," she said, making eye contact again, "but please do whatever you can to stay on the team."

She laid her hand on top of his.

"I feel better with you in my life and even better with you close by."

"And I love being here," he responded, taking her hand in both of his. "But I can't condone leaving you behind."

They sat holding hands for a few seconds before Eddie tried to lighten the mood by saying, "I'll try and hold onto my ethics while staying on the team. We need to stop the Seretus Ligare, but we need to leave enough time to do something about your haircut, Butch."

Chapter XXII

Ivan contacted Eddie after his updates and reinforced there would be no punishment.

"I do, however, request a day or two for research and reflection before speaking to you," he said.

"All things being equal, I would rather speak now," Eddie said.

"All things are not equal. You made your feelings clear, and I know where you stand. I, on the other hand, need to consider your potential actions, the team's feelings, the mission, future missions, the Council, the entire Terra population, and the Attal population. You are extremely important to me and even more important to the team, but we will meet in a couple days."

In an effort to lower his high level of anxiety and reduce his throbbing headache, Eddie took advantage of the beautiful day and trained outside. He tried to occupy his mind by getting lost in his music and concentrating on the simple task of maneuvering his RC devices Frick and Frack. In a half-meditative state, he set his music on repeat and, for the third time, sang along to Dobie Gray's song "Drift Away."

He concentrated on improving his high-speed maneuvers with his housefly Frick, when he saw Jeff wandering around the grounds deep in thought. Eddie brought Frick to within a couple inches of Jeff's face, who swatted at his miniature savior twice before he realized it was not part of the wildlife. He put his hand out, palm up, and gave Eddie a proper landing pad.

"Hello, my little friend."

Frick hopped twice and blinked under the expert control of its designer. It flew around Jeff a couple of times before it led him toward the barn. He could not help but smile when he saw Eddie sitting on the bench, bobbing his head and singing along to the music coming out of the barn about drifting away and getting lost in his music.

As Jeff approached, Eddie cut the volume of the music in half. The RC fly landed on the bench, and Eddie lifted his glasses and rested them on his head.

"How ya doing?"

"Confused, but happy to be safe and with my family," he responded. "How are you?"

"I'm okay-ish," Eddie answered. "I'm under review for some of my actions during your escape. So I'm a little confused, too, but happy you are all safe."

Jeff, careful not to crush his little friend, sat down beside Eddie and let his own thoughts wander until Eddie broke his concentration.

"Hey, you want to learn how to control your little buddy here?"

"Why not?"

After about fifteen minutes of explanation, Eddie allowed him to take control. He went into the barn and retrieved an extra pair of specialty glasses, leaving his on so he could control the device if Jeff struggled. Jeff's skills were dwarfed by Eddie's, and he had many crash landings before he learned the controls, but it didn't take him long before he could take off and head in the proper direction. He did pretty well as long as he did not have to land. After his third crash, Eddie telepathically changed the music coming from the barn. Jeff's fourth crash was so synchronized to the music one would swear they worked the choreography out in advance. Just as AC/DC sang about how long the road to the top was if he wanted to rock and roll, Jeff neglected to stop in time and crashed into the side of the barn. By the end of the song, though, he had made three successful takeoffs and landings.

"I think I got it. Give me a challenge," Jeff requested.

Elaine and Aggie finally got away for what they considered an extremely important discussion. They were sitting on a blanket by the pond, trying to solve each other's romantic troubles.

"Your hair looks so stinking cute. How does Robert like your new pixie cut?" Elaine asked.

"He seems indifferent about it," Aggie admitted as she unconsciously played with the short hair behind her right ear.

"Really?" Elaine said, a little surprised. "You look cute with short hair. It's such a drastic change. He has to have an opinion."

"Not one he is willing to share," she said. "But Eddie makes fun of it every chance he gets."

"Yea, but that's just Eddie being a pain in the ass. He made fun of my half-pink hair just this morning," Elaine said with a toss of her hair. "His track record for liking long hair is well documented, but it's Eddie. Who cares?"

"I do," Aggie said quietly focusing on the long grass next to the pond.

"Really?" Elaine said, before she started singing. "Aggie and Cubby sitting in a tree—"

"What?" Aggie asked, making eye contact with her best friend again. "We've never been in a tree."

"Forget it. It's a teenage, Terra thing. So, you like Eddie?"

"I like all of you."

"That's not what I asked," Elaine said, unable to control her smile.

"I'm not supposed to talk about this, but at the Council meeting—" Aggie started to say before being interrupted by Maria inside her mind.

"If you're not supposed to talk about it, then maybe you shouldn't talk about it. If our trip to the Shepard building taught you anything, it should have taught you that you never know who's listening."

Maria paused for a couple seconds, and then apologized. *"I'm sorry to eavesdrop, but it's hard to keep me out at times. And for the record, Eddie likes you, too."*

"What?" Elaine asked, confused by Aggie's sudden quietness. "What happened at the Council meeting? And why are you blushing? I've only ever seen you blush once, and that's when—"

She stopped and looked around for any sign of Eddie or Robert.

"It's not them," Aggie reported. "Your mom eavesdropped on our conversation and gave me a little advice."

"Oh, come on, Mom! Really?" Elaine said, looking toward the main house. "You're not playing fair or nice."

"Sorry," Maria said in her daughter's mind. *"But I've told you for years, you talk too loud."*

Before Elaine could articulate her frustration with her Mom's invasion, Maria added, "*I am sorry, honey. Trust me; it can be a curse as much as a gift.*"

Elaine sensed the sincerity in her mom's thoughts and let her off the hook, but decided to have the rest of the conversation with Aggie telepathically.

"*So what happened at the meeting?*"

"*The Attal researcher felt Eddie wasn't justified in coming back to save me. I don't blame him. He's never been with the Terra, and insubordination is rare in our world,*" Aggie explained. "*But as soon as I explained how heroic Eddie's actions were, Robert started having a problem with him. How can I be with a person who would argue against coming back for me?*"

"*I don't think he's against the team coming back for you. I think he's against Eddie saving his girlfriend,*" Elaine pointed out. "*It fueled his already jealous feelings concerning my family being included in your world and given special abilities.*"

"*He's got to get over those feelings. I can't help who Bill picked. And his actions proved Bill picked well.*"

"*So, Eddie?*" Elaine said telepathically but couldn't hold back the smile on her face.

"*Shut up!*" Aggie responded, lying on the blanket with her eyes closed and enjoying the summer sun with a smile on her face. "*So what's going on with you and Pax? I haven't seen much of him since our mission.*"

"*Wow, what a seamless transition,*" Elaine joked. "*He has been working hard watching, tracking, and searching for something. I'm not really sure what it is, but it has certainly consumed him. I think it's kinda like Eddie's music. His work takes his mind off dealing with all the people around and gives him an excuse to not deal with his feelings about a certain, colorful, Terra girl.*"

"*I know he wants to deal with a certain, colorful, Terra girl. Just give him time. We—well, at least Pax and I—tend to be confident with our intelligence but insecure with feelings of intimacy.*"

"*I don't need him to psychoanalyze me. I just want him to kiss me. I couldn't be more patient. Trust me, I've never been this patient,*" Elaine said. "*If it wasn't for the team and this mission I—*"

"*And he wants to kiss you, too. Just give him time,*" Aggie interrupted.

"*Then tell him to piss or get off the pot, because he's had more than enough time.*"

"*But you don't understand how scared and anxious he is of intimate acts. It's not the kind of thing one can learn from a book,*" Aggie tried to explain.

"*He's the smartest man I know. Why would he be insecure?*"

Elaine thought for a second then added as an afterthought almost to herself, "*I mean, it's just a kiss. I'm sure he is a fine kisser.*"

"*He is,*" Aggie answered before realized what she said.

"*You know, I mean all you have to do is*—Hold on a minute," Elaine interrupted herself verbally. "What did you just say?"

"What? I said I'm sure he's a fine kisser," Aggie answered.

"No. You said he *is* a fine kisser," she corrected her friend. "Aggie, have you ever kissed Pax?"

"Um…we weren't…um…he just thought—ah—well…yes," she finally conceded. "But you have to understand, it wasn't sexual. Well, it kind of was, but it wasn't like—"

"Is he a good kisser?" Elaine asked, knowing her friend well enough to not be threatened, yet enjoying her struggles and feeling she deserved them.

"We were both curious," Aggie tried to explain. "It would be like if you were one of only two Terra dealing with—"

"So you think I should make out with Robert because we are both dating Attal," she suggested.

"That's not the same thing," she argued intellectually. "You already know what it feels like to kiss. But if you both wanted to experience…um…let's say transporting, or a pleasure vis hub, or something like that, you may be insecure about how to act."

"I didn't ask why you kissed him," Elaine corrected her friend. "I just wanted to know…"

She paused to hold onto her torture for just a moment and repeated, "Is he a good kisser?"

"He did fine," Aggie said before blushing for the second time during this conversation. "Truthfully, I concentrated on my abilities, and he said I did very well. Although he doesn't have anything to compare it against."

"Aggie, sit up and put out your hand," she heard Eddie say in her mind.

Halting her awkward explanation, she did what he said and opened her hand, palm up.

Elaine asked, "What's going on?"

"Don't know. It's an Eddie thing," Aggie answered.

"Well, hell, if it's an Eddie thing then let's stop our conversation and see what our hero wants," Elaine said with a smile and a roll of her eyes.

Frick circled a few times before attempting to land on her hand. He missed his target and had to circle around before sloppily landing in Aggie's palm.

"Not your best landing, but what's up, Cubby?" Aggie asked, looking down at the little RC fly.

"How did she know I was coming?" Jeff asked over AC/DC reminding him that it's a long way to the top.

"A beacon in the fly contacts all team members when it's close," Eddie lied.

"Nice addition, but here is where the sound projection enhancement we discussed would come in handy," Jeff suggested.

"I agree, but I couldn't come up with any additional projection small enough to fit in the disguised frame of the fly," Eddie admitted.

"Not using traditional speakers and electrical power. Have you considered alternative power?"

Aggie interrupted their technology discussion and asked Eddie telepathically *"Do you need something, Cubby, or are you just practicing?"*

Elaine also contacted her brother telepathically, *"We were kinda in the middle of something here. Go bug someone else."*

Chuckling at her pun, she lay back down and closed her eyes.

Eddie told both Aggie and Elaine, *"Jeff's playing with Frick, so I gave him you guys as a target. You look real busy. I didn't mean to cut into your important 'lying in the sun by the pond' time. Or are you trying to figure out a way to cut Aggie's hair a little shorter."*

"No, we were just talking about what a dick my brother is and how cute her new pixie cut looks," Elaine rebutted.

"Aggie, you are without a doubt the cutest guy I've ever seen," Eddie proclaimed before leaving their minds.

"Do you really hate it?" Aggie asked Frick.

"I don't hate it. You look fine, but I did love your long hair," Eddie answered in only Aggie's mind.

"Do we really hate what?" Jeff asked

"Who knows with them two?" Eddie answered. "Why don't you bring him home and we'll play with his brother Frack."

After Frick flew away, Elaine said to her friend, "He really does think you're cute. Guys will sometimes give you a hard time to flirt with you. They assume you know they are kidding and are too stupid to realize we are insecure about almost everything. Or he's just being a dick."

"I hope he's just kidding and nervous about his talk with Ivan. I don't want Ivan to think—" Aggie stopped mid-sentence.

"What's wrong?" Elaine asked, seeing the distressed look on her friend's face.

Aggie stood up.

"Ivan gets a Council update from the Attal guy who's against Eddie's heroism, and I saw him talking to Robert after the meeting. Both have problems with Eddie. He's going to get the wrong impression. I've got to talk to Ivan."

"Just call him," Elaine suggested, touching her Mooncat necklace.

"I thought…um…by going to—It's just—No," Aggie finally said, clearly holding something back. "I think I'll go see him at the station."

She hustled up to the barn and quickly walked past Jeff sitting on the bench by himself.

"Good job with Frick," she said without stopping.

She passed Eddie in the barn. He had his drone delivery helicopter Frack with him.

"What's wrong?" he asked. "You look upset. Can I help?"

"I'm fine," she responded with a forced smile. "I just thought of something I really need to do. I'll be right back."

"Okey-dokey. Let me know if I can help," he offered.

Almost an hour later, Jeff stood outside of the barn with Eddie while AC/DC continued to play a little too loud. He attempted another delivery with the much-more-complicated Frack, when Eddie noticed Aggie coming out of the barn. Coming from the dark barn into the bright sun, he had to wait a few seconds before confirming what he thought he saw. With a shake of her head and a smile that warmed his heart, he realized Aggie must have transported. She wasn't "Butch" anymore, as he had been calling her, but an exotic, Indian beauty again.

With nothing more than a thought from Eddie, the music coming out of the barn changed. Eddie thought his gesture bordered on corny, but Aggie seemed to appreciate it as the drum and guitar prelude started. Her smile got even bigger as she approached the boys, and her walk became more of a strut as Roy Orbison's "Oh, Pretty Woman" played out of the barn's external speakers.

Jeff looked up to see what had caused the change in music and was penalized for his lack of concentration. Eddie didn't even notice Frack smashing into the side of the barn. He watched Aggie walking away from him and turned up the music even louder.

Chapter XXIII

  Carlos and Juanita agreed she would transfer as many Terra holdings into cash as possible over the next week at the bank before she mysteriously stopped coming to work and apparently just disappeared. Concurrently, they would use the time to relocate their Terra army for what would be their last mission. A synchronized blitz should acquire enough vis for them to disappear for at least a couple of hundred Terra years, since they no longer planned to overtake the Pacific station. One morning early in the week, Carlos entered Santos' ISASP shipping office for an unscheduled meeting.
  "I need you to change a couple of your routes," Carlos demanded.
  "I can't just change shipping routes without filing paperwork, contacting the authorities, or explaining things to my captains. They will arrest me first and lock me up as crazy second," Santos complained.

"I don't care if they hang you from the gallows," Carlos exclaimed. "I need these ships to go to these ports."

He passed a report across the large, glass desk.

"I couldn't make this many changes without serious, unwanted attention, large bribes, and risk to my crew," Santos said, starting to feel his temper rise. "What's so important about these cities?"

"Nothing you need to worry about, but I can tell you this will be the last communication we'll ever have. After this, our business will be terminated."

"What?" Santos asked.

"After these shipments are completed, my men will no longer be security officers on your ships and you will never see me again. As an added incentive, you will receive two million U.S. dollars in your account for your time and trouble when the last ship has docked."

"And our dealings will be done?" Santos stressed for clarification.

"Done," Carlos said.

At the same time as Carlos and Mr. Santos were going over his shipping needs, Juanita worked in her office, using her personal laptop and company computers to set up an alias, create new bank accounts, rent safety deposit boxes, and move money. Before lunch, she had safety deposit boxes rented in South America, North America, and Europe. She set up accounts in the Cayman Islands and Switzerland and created an alias, Megan Patrick.

Megan had a birth certificate, social security number, and a Pennsylvania driver's license. The best thing about Megan was that Carlos did not know she existed, but she had access to all of their joint accounts and a couple of individual accounts. Tomorrow, Juanita would order a passport with all of her documentation. She felt confident she could create the proper incentive to have her legal documents filed and printed within forty-eight hours.

****

Pax sat at his desk, staring at his enhanced laptop like he had done for the majority of the time since returning from their mission. Elaine came in to take a shower and clean up before what Gary had promised would be the mother of all cookouts. She rubbed his shoulders for a few seconds before leaning down and kissing his cheek.

"Are you going to be able to make it to dinner tonight? The self-proclaimed world's best griller is serving chicken and steaks. But he's going to roast corn for his vegan friends and Grandma White promised the largest fruit salad this side of the Mississippi."

"Of course," he said without looking up. "Gary has been bragging about his grilling for two days."

"Okay, I'm going to take a shower. Try and wrap things up soon so you can buy me a beer out of Dad's fridge before dinner."

"Okey-dokey," he responded in the grill master's honor.

Elaine was drying herself off and applying some lotion when she heard Pax yelling in the other room.

"I got you! Finally! I knew it."

She wrapped herself in a towel and came out to see what had caused Pax's outburst. She saw an uncharacteristically excited Pax standing up and yelling at his computer.

"I knew it. I knew you couldn't resist. I finally got you!"

He looked over and saw Elaine in the doorway, wearing nothing but a towel. This was the scene he had dreamt about hundreds of times since his exploratory evening with Aggie, but he found himself grossly unprepared for what he considered the scariest moment of his life.

"Um…I found her—I—ah—We finally—Well, I've been trying to…um…and…I…"

Realizing he needed to slow his mind and control his emotions, he paused for a few seconds.

"You look really nice," he finally said, forgetting about his recent success.

"What? This old thing?" she asked with a smile.

He approached her, put his hand on her neck, pulled her wet head toward him, and gave her the long, passionate kiss he had been thinking about for weeks.

"That was even better than my dreams," he whispered in her ear.

Elaine allowed her towel to drop to the floor while pulling him in for another kiss. Almost two minutes passed before she gently pulled away. She bent over to retrieve her towel and rewrapped herself.

"I don't want to sound condescending," she whispered with a gentle smile, "but I hear you were worried about your kissing skills. You can brag to all your friends—you are an excellent kisser."

After a short pause, she put her head down and stared up at him with penetrating green eyes and an accusatory expression. "But it's obvious you lied to me."

"What? I've never lied to you."

"You said Terra nudity doesn't excite you. Liar."

She gave him a flirty smile before gently pushing the blushing alien out of the bathroom and shutting the door in his face.

******

Twenty people had gathered in the Whites' backyard, grilling, eating, listening to music, and chatting, when Lucy leaned in toward her daughter. She nodded her head toward the hill and asked.

"Does Pax have a brother?"

Maria looked at the man walking toward the house with the demeanor of someone without a care in the world.

"Oh. That's Ivan. He's…um…Bill and Pax's boss at work."

"Is he related to Pax?" she asked.

"Not directly," Maria answered as she got up and took her mom's hand. "But I think they share an uncle. I hear them refer to an Uncle AJ all the time. Come on. I'll introduce you. He's a very powerful and important man."

After dinner, drinks, and some much-needed laughter, Ivan approached Eddie.

"You want to take a walk with me? Maybe talk about a few things?" he asked with a kind smile.

As they aimlessly walked away from the barbeque, Ivan attempted to make small talk until they had a little privacy.

"AJ and Bill really outdid themselves creating this property. I wish I had had a place this nice during my forty years in hiding," he added more as a thought to himself than a comment to Eddie.

"Ivan, I love Bill, but I can't condone his decision to leave Aggie behind," Eddie said, getting right to the point.

"For the record," Ivan responded, "Bill came to your defense and is your strongest supporter. He understands and respects your actions and very much wants you to stay on the team."

After a short pause, he said, "But that doesn't change the necessity to follow orders absolutely."

"I understand you come from a completely different culture," Eddie said, "but no one should *ever* follow orders absolutely in every situation. If you want to see the ramifications of mindlessly following orders, research the Terra Holocaust in Europe during World War II."

"Eddie, I'm a very old man," Ivan responded. "I lived during the Holocaust."

Eddie picked a wild daisy and started removing its petals one at a time before saying, "I forgot. I'm sorry."

"That's okay," Ivan said kindly. "But for Bill to run operations properly, certain rules must be followed."

"My military binge-and-puke came from a soldier who appreciates the chain of command and understands there are consequences for breaking the chain," Eddie said. "I accept any punishment the Attal assign. But the same download also gave me a strong feeling of loyalty to my unit, or in this case, my team. I would voluntarily give my life to save anyone on our team. Even our station leader."

"I know you would, and that is the Terra attitude and commitment we were hoping for when we created this team," Ivan admitted.

"Then you'll allow things to remain the same?" Eddie asked, excited about the direction the conversation seemed to be going.

"No," Ivan said with no explanation.

"But you said—"

"I said we love your Terra attitude," Ivan interrupted. "And if I planned a mission, I would want you with me. But we cannot allow someone to be openly insubordinate."

In an effort to explain his position, he added, "When planning a mission, Bill can't worry about what six different people think about his plan and who may or may not follow orders."

"So I'm out?" Eddie asked, feeling defeated.

"You're never out, son," Ivan said absolutely. "The Pride, I think your Dad calls our group, will always protect its own. You just can't stay in your current capacity."

"Okay," Eddie said slowly, showing some hope, yet very confused. "What did you have in mind?"

"I'd like Bill to do another eat and dump, but this time, you'd be eaten not dumped."

After letting it sink in for a few seconds, Ivan said, "I know Pax has a Pride meeting scheduled for ten o'clock tonight. I've already talked to Bill, but I'd like to talk to you and your parents before the meeting." Without raising his voice, he added, "Maria, can you and Gary meet us in the Cat Cave, please?"

"You're a funny man," Maria answered in Ivan's mind. *"Wouldn't it been easier to just invite one of us on your little walk?"*

"What fun would that be? I don't get to interact with the Terra much anymore," he answered. "Don't deprive an old man his simple pleasures. We'll see you in fifteen minutes."

He turned to Eddie and said, "You may not get everything you want, but I think you will be happy after we talk. Trust the Pride, Eddie."

"Okay, and Ivan, for the record, it's a binge-and-puke."

At 10:03 p.m., Elaine entered the lab for the Pride meeting and got a little surprise. Ivan and Aggie's friend Robert sat at the table waiting for Elaine, the last Pride member to arrive.

"What's going on? Why are they here?" she asked Aggie as she sat.

"No idea," Aggie answered. *"But I'd bet it has to do with Ivan's talk with Eddie."*

"Now that we are all here," Ivan said with a smile in Elaine's direction, "I would like to update you on a few changes. As we stressed when we created the first ever co-op between our two worlds, we might find it necessary to make adjustments along the way. After our first, successful mission, we are going to make the following changes to continue our development and success. Robert, who has been requesting a more significant role, will become our transportation expert. Bill will copy some of Eddie's knowledge about machinery and operations and insert those memories into Robert. Bill will not change his reasoning or decision-making, just his knowledge base. He will have to move to Ohio and, in an effort to keep our Council neutral, he will have to resign from the Terra Relations Council.

"Well, there's an interesting turn of events," Elaine said to Aggie. *"Obviously, Ivan and Bill aren't experienced in intimacy either."*

Aggie didn't answer, so Elaine took one more shot at her friend and had to turn her head to not give away her smile.

"What to do. What to do. So many men and all so close."

Unaware of Elaine's secret jabs at Aggie's love life, Ivan continued his update.

"Eddie, who has been an important part of this team, will use his skills in a different capacity. His designs of weaponry and communication devices have been impressive. He is going to concentrate on those skills as the leader of our development labs, while concurrently heading up special projects for me. He will design and provide all your tools, weapons, and training. As a member of the team, he will be expected to attend all Pride meetings, but he will report directly to me and will not be part of your team during live missions.

"Although we have not spoken to him yet, it is our hope that Jeff Harding will work with Eddie as the only other Terra in our labs. We also plan on asking Elizabeth to be the newest member of the Terra Relations Council. Bill thinks, and I agree, they both deserve to know the truth and should be given the opportunity to join our efforts should they feel inclined."

"That just turned your love life into a messed-up triangle," Elaine stated the obvious to her best friend while trying unsuccessfully to keep a straight face.

"As an Attal, I am happy to have another member on our team. I trust Ivan and Bill's decisions and like Robert very much. He's an intelligent and sensitive person," Aggie responded.

"Yea, sure. But how does my best friend, who tells me everything, feel about having Eddie and Robert working together?" Elaine asked.

"I wanna know what the hell Ivan is thinking," Aggie answered. *"I mean,* come on. *Really?"*

"In his defense," Elaine said, *"he only had about two billion people to choose from."*

This time, neither girl could hide her expression.

"If we are intruding on your fun, ladies, we could schedule this meeting for another time," Ivan said, interrupting his own update.

"Sorry," Elaine said, lying just a bit. "Just continuing a conversation we were having at the picnic."

"Is the conversation over?" he asked.

"Of course," Aggie promised for both of them.

After Ivan's report of the personnel changes, Pax reported his discovery from earlier.

"I put a couple of well-hidden keystroke recorders on the Shepard's computers before we left and have been tracking them since we departed. I also have been monitoring the movements of all of the world's largest banks, with special concentration on those in South America." He smiled and added, "I figured they would have to make a mistake sooner or later."

"And did they?" Gary asked.

"Oh, yea. They allowed greed and arrogance to overcome their logic and security."

"Have we figured out who Barry has become?" Bill asked.

"Yes. He assumed the identity of Juanita Hernandez. But even better," Pax said, "we know where Hernandez keeps all their money."

"And can we get to the money?" Gary asked with a mischievous smile and raised eyebrows.

"Yes, but I want to give her a couple of days to move the money. As of this afternoon, I have found seventeen accounts, totaling more than thirty million U.S. dollars. I assume she is going to consolidate her funds, change her identity, and lay low. All signs point to that happening soon in South America.

"So what's our plan?" Gary asked.

"I will monitor her movements and get a feel for her overall plan. Bill will work out the Pride's timetable and mission, but I would assume we have at least five days before we need react. Maybe longer."

"We'll meet again in three days at 7:00 p.m.," Bill announced. "That will give me time to do a memory transplant on our new Pride member, allow us to talk with Elizabeth and Jeff, and let Pax learn more about Juanita."

"*And Aggie time to figure out her love life,*" Elaine added in her friend's mind.

Chapter XXIV

Aggie, in an effort to avoid Ivan, Robert, and Eddie, hurried to exit the Cat Cave's conference room. Assuming most of the team would return to their houses, she quickly headed down the tunnel toward the lab. She wasn't fast enough.

"Aggs, wait up."

She heard Robert's winded voice from behind her and considered running through the Den's door and sprinting toward the barn. Instead, she stopped.

"Oh, hey. What's up?"

"I think we should talk about the meeting."

He paused to catch his breath.

"And my new appointment."

"I think Ivan said everything," she said, sounding colder than she felt.

"Well? What do you think about it?" he asked.

Aggie entered the Den without a destination, hoping something might present itself and possibly delay this conversation.

"I think the time to ask my opinion was before you requested a bigger role."

"That's not fair," he said, following her into the lab. "You never asked—"

She turned on him and interrupted him loudly enough to draw the attention of most of the lab workers.

"Fair? How about blindsiding me at a meeting. How is that fair? I was born into this. You apparently begged for it. And you did it without talking to the one person in your life who would understand."

"You don't know what it's like to watch you and the Whites at your meetings then have to listen to all your training and mission stories. Now I get to be part of the fun," he attempted to explain.

"It is a responsibility and a necessity and many times dangerous, but it most certainly is not fun," she said, entering the elevator.

"You talk about it like there is no place you would rather be. I was tired of not being included," he rebutted and then sighed. "That didn't come out quite right."

"No, I think it did. I talked about my mission so you would understand what I've been through, so you might learn to like and embrace the Whites instead of being—Well, I hoped you would get closer to Eddie and Elaine."

"Well, now I'm their equal," Robert said, unconsciously standing up taller. "And now we can be teammates, too."

"I didn't need another teammate. I needed someone who was proud to be my boyfriend and accepted my situation."

She entered the barn and started walking with her head down and softly said, "Now you're just another teammate."

"Exactly. I don't think we should cloud up the team with titles and expectations. I think we should just work on our training and the missions," he said to her back.

She turned on him for the second time. "What do you mean titles and ex—Wait a minute. Are you breaking up with me?"

"It's just, I need to train and learn, and I have to treat everyone equal, and I—"

"No, Robert. You just can't stand being with someone who is smarter than you."

He tried to respond, but she stopped him by raising her hand. She stood in silence while tears gathered in her eyes.

"Welcome to the team," she finally said as she turned and left him in the barn.

Aggie walked in solitude for about an hour before she had the feeling Ivan wished to communicate with her.

"Agrata, could you please come to the station? We could use your assistance with Bill's memory dump, and I'd like to speak to you about a personal matter."

"Of course. I've wandered to the far side of the property. It will take me a few minutes, but I'll be there shortly."

Less than a minute later, long before she could see anything, she heard a four-wheeler approaching.

Eddie pulled up beside her, removed his headphones, and asked over Billy Joel's "Prelude/Angry Young Man" playing too loudly, "You need a ride from an angry young man?"

"Sure, Cubby, but I'm not ready to face everyone just yet."

She paused for a bit then admitted, "Robert just broke up with me, you're off the team, and Ivan wants to have a private conversation, which can't be good. I'm just a little overwhelmed right now."

"You're getting really good at being Terra. You sound just like Elaine," he said.

After a moment of silence, she asked, "Is that a bad thing?"

"She is insecure and worries too much," he responded. "Although, I must admit, she is better since her binge-and-puke."

"It's just, we are halfway through an important mission, and now everything is changing," she offered as a possible explanation.

"Not really," he said. "I bet Ivan just needs your skills. Robert is finally where he wants to be, and I'm just using my engineering binge-and-puke more than my soldier one. I'll still be around."

"I know, but Robert is all about—well, all about Robert. He'll never look out for me like—Well, I mean—With the team changing—I just…"

"What did I promise you?" he asked, taking her hand and looking into her deep brown eyes. "What did I promise you?"

"You promised you will always come back for me," she said with a little, girlish smile. "But—"

"No buts, Aggie. You just concentrate on Bill's plans. I'll concentrate on watching your back," he said with a smile. "I mean, who knew you needed a lift?"

Realizing he actually gave her two lifts, she hopped on the back of the red four-wheeler.

"Thanks, Cubby. Let's go see what Ivan needs."

"You know, you can call me Eddie," he said.

"I know, and don't get me wrong, Eddie is a great guy." She put her arms around his waist and laid her head against his back then added, *"But Cubby's my hero."*

Aggie monitored and controlled Eddie's, Bill's, and Robert's vitals during the two-hour binge-and-puke. After verifying everyone's health, she contacted Ivan.

"We have successfully completed the memory extraction and transplant. Everyone is healthy and safe. Did you want to discuss something?"

"Yes, I'll meet you in room three in six minutes."

Eddie woke up suddenly in a cold sweat.

"How you feeling?" Aggie asked, standing over him with her hand on his forehead.

"Like shit," he answered, sitting up. "But my guess would be it has more to do with bad dreams and no sleep than it does Bill's binge. How are the others doing?"

"Sleeping soundly," she said. "Sorry."

"That's okay. Good for them. Actually, I'm glad I'm up," he lied. "I need to have a conversation with Jeff and get to work, anyway. I'm working on some pretty cool toys."

"Anything you can share?" she asked, glad to have her friend awake again.

"Not until they're tested and cleared through me he can't," Ivan interrupted from behind them.

"Oh. Hey, Ivan," she said, hoping her Indian skin would hide the blood rushing to her cheeks.

Once in the privacy of the separate room, Ivan quickly changed demeanor and became very serious with Aggie.

"I want you to do me a couple of unofficial, undocumented favors, if you don't mind."

"Of course. What do you need?" she asked.

"Please don't question my motives or methods, but I need some monitoring and health adjustments to some of our friends."

"What adjustments…and which friends?" she asked with skepticism.

"We made many quick, unplanned changes to our numbers lately. I think they were all necessary and important, but I'm not sure everyone is coping as well as planned. I'm a little worried about Elizabeth. Could you please check on her daily and make sure she is doing well? Occasionally, also check on Robert. And on Jeff, after he speaks with Eddie. Make sure they are healthy, but also check to make sure they are—let's say properly motivated to be part of our long-term success and have all intentions of keeping our secrets. And lastly, I hoped you could—well, if you would—It's kind of personal, but could you relieve Lucy of some of her aging discomfort?"

"Elaine's grandma?" she asked with a smile.

"We've been talking a lot lately. We've lived through many of the same things, you know," Ivan offered as an explanation to his actions. "It's just, I know what it's like to live in a seventy-year-old Terra body, and we were talking the other day, and she—"

"Of course I can help," she said, letting him off the hook. "I'll check all the Terra and help them a little with their aging pain."

"Thanks, Agrata. Feel free to keep this between you and me."

"It will be our little secret."

She smiled at his uncomfortableness and left the meeting room.

Meanwhile, Jeff, used to keeping his mind active with research, was getting bored just sitting around the Whites' house. Realizing his conspiracy-snooping days were probably behind him, he resorted to the mindless task of pulling weeds as he tried to figure out where his future would take him. He considered coming out of retirement and working in some research labs currently recruiting, possibly going back to his roots in electrical engineering and computer design with a

Colorado company, or maybe even continuing to investigate the unexplained. He had admitted to himself that, even though he loved the challenge of explaining the "yet to be explained," if he continued to research the unknown, he would have to change fields away from government conspiracies. He was so deep in thought, he didn't notice Frack, the duel-propeller delivery helicopter, until it landed beside him.

"Hello, Eddie," Jeff said. Noticing a note attached to the delivery tray, Jeff retrieved and read the slip of paper.

If you are done pulling weeds and are ready for a little excitement, come up to the barn!

--Eddie

Assuming he would hear Eddie's music, Jeff was startled when he turned the corner and saw Eddie sitting on the bench outside the barn and waiting for him.

"Hey, Jeff. I wanted to chat with ya and thought the barn would give us a little more privacy," Eddie said, getting right to the point. "I know you're too smart to believe Bill's bullshit story he told everyone the other day, and I wanted a chance to fill in some of the gaps."

"I must admit I'm still confused about you and your group," Jeff responded, sitting down beside his young friend.

"Well, I've been impressed with your ideas about Frick and Frack. The powers that be were very impressed with your research on government secrets."

Eddie cupped his hand in front of his mouth to simulate a whisper, and then spoke out of the corner of his mouth.

"And your calm, logical demeanor during our little escape mission."

"Honestly, I think my getting out of trouble had a lot more to do with you and your friends than my demeanor," he proclaimed. "But thanks anyway for the kind words."

"Well, I'm glad to hear you say that, because me and my friends would like to offer you a position in our organization."

"Seriously? Your organization hasn't even been honest about who they are or what they do," Jeff responded.

He paused for a couple of seconds, debating about how honest and aggressive he wanted to be.

"It's incredibly presumptuous for one to lie, cheat, and kill to get their way, yet assume I would want to drop everything to join your 'Pride,' I think you call yourselves. I'm not sure what it is your organization really does, but I'm quite sure you have a ton of money, break a lot of rules, and are quite dangerous. Frankly, I can only think of a few organizations who operate like that, and they all scare me."

"Probably because you have never heard of one like ours," Eddie said with confidence. "Would you at least give me time to explain who we really are and what we really do before you make your decision?"

"I owe you that much for the rescue. Besides, truth be known," he added with a smile, "I'm dying to know what's really going on with you and your friends."

"Follow me. I have a long, complicated story to tell you."

Eddie got up and escorted Jeff through the barn and into the lab. He stopped in his office/bedroom and talked for almost an hour. Afterwards, he and Jeff went to the surface station, where they met with Ivan. He talked to both of them for twenty minutes about the hierarchy of the Attal leadership and the position they were offering Jeff.

"You will be a special consultant to Eddie," Ivan said.

When he saw the doubting expression Jeff couldn't conceal, he added, "Don't let one's physical age or appearance make you underestimate his intellectual abilities. I look like a 35-year-old Russian, yet I'm over 250 years old and am the most powerful person on your planet. Eddie has more knowledge in his young mind than a whole team of engineers. Please think about our offer."

Ivan clasped his hands at his waist, bowed slightly, and tipped his head down and to the right.

Returning his gesture, Jeff announced, "I will consider it."

As they left the station, Eddie stressed, "Although we are proud to bring you to the Cat Cave, we are asking you not to tell anyone about the Cave or the Den."

"For the record, what will happen if I turn your offer down?" Jeff asked.

"That's a better question for Ivan, but you and your family will be protected and rewarded financially, regardless of your decision."

Jeff had easily believed Eddie's story; it helped to explain many unknown details about his rescue and the Whites' actions. They walked the rest of the way in silence as Jeff reflected on everything he had just learned.

"Thank you for allowing me to explain everything. I hope you choose to join me in our efforts. Do you have more questions?" Eddie asked when they got to the barn.

After a short pause, Jeff answered. "Only two at this time. Why all the corny nicknames, and what's with all the music?"

Chapter XXV

  After sitting in front of his computer for ten straight hours, Pax's back told him his break was two hours late. Assuming correctly that Eddie would still be awake, he entered the Den and approached his work bench. Being the only one in the lab allowed Eddie the freedom to be selfish with the volume of his music. He howled away at Warren Zevon's "Werewolves of London" when Pax touched his shoulder. He jumped so high off his chair he would have landed on the floor if Pax hadn't anticipated his reaction. Gathering his bearings, he turned down the music and stood up.

  "What the hell! Isn't that getting old, yet?"

  "Sorry, but with the music so loud, it's inevitable," Pax claimed as a weak defense of his fourth late-night fright test.

  "Yea, I'm sure the smartest guy I know could never blink the lights, inform me telepathically, or turn down my music. Whatcha need, asshole?"

Pax pulled up a chair and sat beside Eddie. "I was on the computer—"

"Really?" Eddie interrupted sarcastically.

"I was on the computer," he repeated with a proud grin, "and I found them."

"What? You mean the big *them*—as in, the pissed-off, alien terrorists *them*?" Eddie asked, sitting up excited.

"I was going to say the fugitives, but yes."

"Well, let's fire-bomb the place and be done with it," Eddie said.

"You know our rules forbid us from harming the Terra. I would think the pre-meditated murdering of hundreds would be outside those laws. We don't even know if the militia are all in control of their own minds," Pax said, shocked at the seriousness of Eddie's suggestion.

"Remember? I've been kicked off the team for not following rules, so I'm clearly not the guy to give advice," Eddie told him. "But they know all of your rules and are using them against you. You're always going to find yourself bringing a stick and a good set of morals to a gun fight with a bunch of the pissed-off, alien, soulless, terrorist bastards."

"Then we need to learn to win with a stick," Pax proclaimed before changing the subject. "Do you need any help with your—What is it you are doing?"

"Naw, I'm okay. This is just a little idea I had. I work on it when I can't sleep. So where are our *fugitives* hiding out?" Eddie asked, covering his work with a white sheet and awkwardly changing the subject again.

"I haven't visually confirmed that the—I think you called them—the pissed-off, alien, soulless, terrorist bastards live there yet, but their compound is just east of Campo Verde in Mato Grosso, Brazil."

"What are we going to do now?" Eddie asked. "Are we still going to go after their wallet, or are we going to concentrate on the compound?"

"That's a question for Bill. But if any of these toys," Pax said, waving his hand over Eddies work bench. "Help in the fields of Brazil, it might be time to start testing them."

"I'll have a few tricks ready by then," Eddie said with a sheepish smile.

As they normally did during their late-night breaks, they went for a walk to stretch their legs and enjoy the cool, night air.

"Have you considered my idea about your sleeping?" Pax asked.

"I just keep hoping things will fix themselves. I know I'm tired and angry a lot, but I've been feeling better lately, and I really don't like the idea of being totally defenseless. Especially with all the conflict surrounding us lately."

"Makes sense," Pax agreed. "But you can't supplement sleep forever. We have found, after about ten days, your body and mind will start punishing you. You need sleep, Eddie. I will help you anytime and keep it confidential. I'm sure Bill or Aggie would offer the same."

"I know. I had hoped by giving control of my brain to my engineer side instead of my soldier side that this piece of shit would find a little harmony," Eddie said, pointing to his temple.

"It could happen, but the offer still stands. If you want a dreamless night of sleep, just let me know. Or you can tell Aggie during your secret, pre-dawn meetings, which should be starting in about an hour."

"You're a funny man," Eddie said.

"Remember who my Terra influences are," Pax pointed out.

"Yea, but how 'bout a little more Mom influence and a little less Dad?"

"No promises, Cubby," Pax said as he turned and headed down the trail back to his house. "See ya tomorrow."

"I don't know. I gotta start working with Bobby the British Wonder."

Pax stopped and turned to face Eddie.

"You shouldn't be making fun of him. You should be thanking him."

"The man gets his first girlfriend ever, and now he's giving me relationship advice," Eddie turned and headed toward the barn. "See you tomorrow, Dr. Phil."

A few hours later, Pax entered Elaine's bedroom and found her sitting on the bed, petting Buddy and gazing out of the window.

Clearing his throat so he didn't startle her, he asked, "Are you ready to go talk to Lizzy?"

"Yea," she said, not breaking her stare at a blue jay yet to catch Buddy's attention. "Do you think we will ever have a normal life?"

"I don't know how normal your life can be when you are dating an alien, but my goal has always been to be happy. And I am," he answered honestly.

"I'm sorry," she said, shaking her head back to the present. "I am, too. So happy. It just seems like every day we are having life-changing or life-ending decisions. I sometimes miss my biggest problem being a broken-down car or a bad hair day."

"I can mess up your hair and have Eddie sabotage your car if you want," Pax suggested, proving anyone can be a Terra smartass if they spend enough time with Gary White.

"I'll be fine," she said with a forced smile at his effort to make her feel better. "Sometimes I would rather be behind the chair, worrying about a haircut, instead of hurting friends and hiding from terrorists, you know?"

"Would you like me to talk to Lizzy by myself? I don't mind," he added.

"No. I'm good," she said as she got up and ran a brush through her hair.

Elaine, as her more customary, loud, bubbly self, and Pax were an hour deep into their conversation with Elizabeth when they started to hear Eddie in the distance. The closer he got, the better they could make out the Steppenwolf song "Born to be wild." As the music got louder, they finally searched the skies and saw Eddie and Robert doing a fly-by in his ultralight trike with the music blaring. Eddie dove to within twenty feet of the trio and gave a playful tip of his wings as they passed over his friends.

"And Eddie," Elaine said for emphasis as the trike disappeared in the horizon, "you may have guessed from your flight away from the Shepard building, has been appointed as our mechanical and weapons specialist."

They continued their strolling confession of the Attal, the Whites, and their current global missions until they were sure Lizzy understood everything.

"With Robert's addition to the Pride, we find ourselves one person short on the Terra Relations Council. You are under no obligation to help us, but we would be honored if you joined our Council."

"Would I still be able to work at Moonlight Trail?" Lizzy asked.

"Of course," Pax gently assured her. "You will be in charge at Moonlight until the day you decide to pass it off to the next leader."

As Pax explained the Council's responsibilities, Elaine thought about the turn her day had taken. Earlier, when staring out the window and contemplating her day, she had thought her already-fragile friend would be overwhelmed with yet another life-changing day. She couldn't have been more wrong. She considered her error in judgment during Pax's continued explanation and had to use a great deal of self-control to stop from smiling when she used her vast knowledge of customs and cultures to quote the Christian Bible in her mind in the affected voice of a southern preacher.

"As we read in John 8:32, 'And you will *know* the truth, and the *truth* will set you free'."

Apparently, knowing the truth helped Elizabeth piece together many inconsistencies about Pax, his relationship with the Whites, his ability to work endlessly, her kidnapping, her escape, and why her family had been brought to the property. Elizabeth seemed so relieved to make sense of things, Elaine thought she saw a spring in her step as she got on her tiptoes and gave Pax a big hug.

"Thanks for including me. I don't know about the Council, but for the first time in weeks, I feel safe here. Can I think about it for a couple of days?" she asked.

"Take as long as you like," Pax said.

"Girl, it's good to have you aboard. I hated lying to you," Elaine said as she gave Lizzy a big hug, which helped her more than Elizabeth.

Shortly before noon, Aggie took a four-wheeler and headed toward the barn. As soon as she turned off the engine, she heard what she assumed was Eddie's music. She assumed wrong. AC/DC sang out to Robert and Jeff about how long it was to the top if they ever wanted to rock and roll.

"I'm glad I caught you. It's time for your check-up," she said loudly over the music.

"My what?" Robert yelled as Frack slammed into the side of the barn. "This noise is bloody maddening."

"Turn it down," she suggested.

"I can't. The git locked it!" he yelled.

"Hey," Aggie asked Eddie telepathically. *"Can you please turn down the Def Leppard while I talk to Robert and give him his physical?"*

"No, because there isn't any Leppard playing. Nice try, though."

No one could see Eddie smiling to himself at his work bench, but the music's volume suddenly cut down by about seventy-five percent.

"Why do I need a physical?" Robert asked in a snooty tone.

Aggie allowed his rudeness due to his hectic training schedule and recent failure with Frack.

"If I were you, I'd be nicer to me," Aggie responded as she closed her eyes for extra concentration. "A bad health report to Bill, and our new fly-boy will be grounded."

She finished her physical on Robert in about two minutes, but pretended to stand over him in concentration for a few more minutes, during which time she did a mind search on both of them and scanned Jeff's vitals.

"All done. Fit and ready to fly."

"Sorry," Robert said, realizing he had let too many emotions show with his outburst.

"Understandable. You must have a ton on your mind," she said with a smile. "I'm sure you'll do great."

She turned and headed back to Pax's house. When she got about ten steps away, she sent Eddie a message.

"I can't hear you."

She laughed out loud when the barn immediately sounded like the second row of an AC/DC concert. She bounced her head back and forth, enjoying the music and her role in the joke, but her ears were very glad she headed farther away.

237

Halfway back to Pax's house, Aggie saw Lucy and Ivan sitting at the picnic table and having a snack in the Whites' backyard.

"How have all your check-ups gone?" Ivan asked telepathically while waving to her in the distance.

"Everyone is pretty normal," she reported while keeping her hands on the handlebars of her four-wheeler. *"Robert's heart rate was a little elevated, but he had a lot going on. I think Elizabeth is doing much better, and I've cured a few minor ailments for Gary's parents and Jeff's son Andrew."*

"And the other things I asked you about?" Ivan inquired.

"Jeff is going to join Eddie, but is conflicted about what it might do to his family to relocate. Robert is definitely struggling with something, but I couldn't tell without a more in-depth search if his feelings were about me, anger at Eddie, or insecurity at his progress. I'll know more after a second search when I have information to compare it to."

"Thank you, Agrata," Ivan said. *"I'll have Bill offer to help with Jeff's family. Keep an eye on everyone. Things are getting close."*

"I will," Aggie promised.

She was glad Ivan didn't have Maria's vision, because she could not hide her smile when she asked, *"And how's your new friend feeling after three adjustments?"*

An hour before dawn the next day, Aggie entered the Den to find Eddie looking like a chemist. He stirred a liquid of his own design so dark it looked black. It had no odor, but he wore protective gloves and goggles.

"Hey, Cubby," she quietly said as she entered the lab. "Is it safe to come over?"

"Hey. Oh, sure. I needed these for an earlier step. It's stable now," Eddie answered, taking off his protective gear.

"I hope you don't mind, but Pax and I were talking about your sleep, or lack thereof, and—Wait a minute. It's too quiet in here. Where's your music?" she interrupted herself.

"After getting the shit scared out of me every other day by Pax and spending twenty hours a day in the lab, I decided to run a few tests. My assumptions were confirmed. The guy who puked my love for classic rock is the soldier. I still can't sleep and prefer the music when I'm doing high-risk maneuvers, but I seem to be okay when I'm doing first aid or R&D."

"That's a step in the right direction, but I'm still worried about your sleep," she admitted.

"Me, too. I'm so tired and so angry all the time. Don't tell him, but I find myself needing to quote Dad in my mind. I remind myself a hundred times a day: Just be nice."

"I think you're awesome," she offered.

"That feeling is very mutual, but I wouldn't ask Bobby, Bill, or Elaine what their opinions are. They think I'm a dick, and I kinda get where they're coming from. But they don't understand the conflict I'm fighting every day."

"Bill does. And Elaine loves you very much. She even told me how worried she is about your sleep," Aggie said.

"I'm hoping my new assignment to R&D might help. Speaking of," he said, "I want to test something on you."

"Oh, yeah? What?" she asked.

"I'd like to give you a—Well, I don't know what to call it. It's not a tattoo, and it's not a branding. Let's call it a mark."

"Why?" she asked skeptically. "What does it do?"

"Does it matter?" he answered with a devious smile. "You know you are going to say yes. It's an idea I had, and I need to test it on one Terra and one Attal."

"Who's the Terra?"

He didn't have to say the obvious answer. He gave her a closed-mouth smile, raised his shoulders, and tilted his head. Eddie handed her a small bottle of clear liquid.

"This removes the mark, but I'm asking you to not use it except for cases of emergency. It's something I plan on using in the future. I just wanted to test it first. I hoped to make it inconspicuous, so I made it look like a tattoo." Eddie blushed before asking, "Would you like it to be in a discreet place?"

"You still didn't tell me what it does?" she said, pulling down her jean shorts and exposing her caramel-colored hip.

"I would rather not tell you. I want an untainted report about how it affects you, if it affects you at all. If you do feel different, I'd like to know how long the feeling lasts."

"I feel different already. I'm standing here in my underwear," she replied.

Chapter XXVI

Elaine showed up two minutes early for the Pride meeting, but still arrived last. She was glad to see Jeff and Lizzy sitting at the table in the meeting room.

"We have a couple of changes to go over before I explain our next mission," Bill announced as soon as Elaine sat down. "First, as luck would have it, Jeff's wife Anna received an excellent job offer with a company in Canton. They even offered her a large signing bonus. The family is looking forward to a fresh start in Ohio. So I'm very pleased to announce Jeff has agreed to sign on as Eddie's partner."

"Consultant," Eddie stated for clarification.

"Elizabeth has graciously declined our invitation to join the Council. She's decided to leave all the 'hiding in the shadows' and 'saving the world stuff' to the Pride and return to her rewarding life as the president of Moonlight Trail."

Elaine nodded in agreement with her friend's difficult decision. Bill picked up a black, velvet bag.

"Pax and I, with the approval from the remaining Council, have decided to allow her to return to Moonlight with our secrets and a little bit of our technology."

He retrieved three Mooncat necklaces from the bag.

"These will allow us to locate and protect all three of our friends from Attal activity as they interact with the Terra," he explained as he handed Jeff, Elizabeth, and Robert each a necklace. "Jeff has been granted access to the lab and communication with Eddie and me. Elizabeth does not have any access, but has been granted communication with Elaine and Pax."

"Perfect," Elaine said.

"Robert has been given full Pride security and abilities. All we ask in trade is none of you ever removes your necklace without informing one of us in this room."

After getting a confirming nod from all three proud, new owners of an Attal necklace, Bill continued.

"Jeff and Elizabeth will not be part of any other Pride or Council meetings. I granted them access today to increase their understanding of our goals. I've already experienced trying to keep things from you. You are all too skilled and too close to have many secrets. So, I'm sure you're all aware Pax has located the fugitives' South American compound, which is disguised as a cattle ranch in southern Brazil, just outside of Campo Verde."

As he continued his report, a map displaying the ranch just to the east of the small town showed on the monitor behind Bill.

"We are now able to track their money and their compound."

"Are we going after the compound?" Gary asked the question everyone wondered.

"Not yet, but soon," Bill reported. "I want to give Robert a little more training time before we put ourselves in a high-risk situation. Also, I have already planned out the mission to financially cripple their efforts, and I'm hoping they will dismiss some of their paid mercenary squad. As such, we will conduct our mission to deplete their funds while I start planning for what I hope is our final mission to shut down their compound and the Seretus Ligare."

"It seems they have learned a few lessons since the Shepard building," Pax intervened. "They are not using the internet or any wireless, closed-circuit cameras that showed up on my exhaustive search. All of my surveillance is from satellites. They tend to be high security, unpredictable, and of poor quality. Any chance we can get some eyes on their camp, Eddie? We need a lot more information before we attempt a mission."

"Get me the coordinates and I'll get you live feed in about twelve to fourteen hours," he answered.

After another hour, Bill concluded by saying, "We will leave together at 8:30 a.m. tomorrow morning. Robert, work with Pax and Agrata to master communication before then. Elaine, I need you to make your appearance match Juanita's as much as possible. I expect you to show up at the station at 7:00 a.m. for final inspection and adjustments."

Aggie felt an unfamiliar and disproportionate amount of anger during the Pride meeting. She wished to bring the fugitives to justice, but certainly did not feel any hatred toward either of them. Although she felt it unfair to be dumped by Robert, it gave her the freedom to accept the advances of another teammate and eliminated even the smallest chance of guilty feelings. As a member of the Attal and a student of the

Terra body, she had always been excellent at controlling her vitals. Yet she felt the need to repress her anger and fought an increased heart rate. If she didn't know any better, she would also report being jealous. But of what, she had no idea.

Thirty minutes after the meeting, Eddie launched one of his modified toys. It resembled a Terra rocket, but used Attal technology, giving it many more capabilities. The vis-powered device would not leave a heat signature and had radar-blocking technology. It measured just under thirty-nine inches tall and traveled so fast and so high, its trip would be unimpeded and untraceable, even if someone knew its whereabouts.

Knowing he had over an hour before his rocket delivered its ten miniature, mechanical houseflies and one RC helicopter to the South American compound, he headed outside to assist in Robert's training. Before entering the barn, Aggie met up with him.

"Can we talk for a minute?"

"Sure. I thought I'd go help Bobby with his training, but I have an hour before I really need to do anything. What's up?"

She subconsciously rubbed her right hip while saying, "I'd like to talk about the tattoo you gave me."

"It's technically not a tattoo," he said.

"Does it have any side effects," she asked.

"You mean besides being a beautiful piece of art? The only side effect I've noticed on mine is a little irritation, but I easily controlled it with the simplest of thoughts."

"Yes, I had some irritation, too. What I'm talking about is more mental. I've been very—let me say, emotional since its application."

"Oh, ye of little faith," he said. "That isn't a side effect."

Still not understanding, she asked, "You made a tattoo that deliberately upsets the wearer?"

"Yea. I made a rage-tattoo, because not enough tattooed Terra have anger issues."

After watching her unsuccessfully try to analyze his invention, he gave an explanation.

"It's designed to track one's location and emotions. It works with someone who's marked from the same batch. I call it Link-Ink."

"So those emotions—" she said, finally understanding.

"Are mine," he admitted with a blush. "Sorry, but I needed an Attal and a Terra for my test, and I—Well, I would've picked you to be linked with even if you weren't the perfect test subject."

Embarrassed by his admission, he quickly added, "It can't read minds or plant thoughts. I had to make it simple so it wouldn't be noticed by any Attal scanning for penetration. It just shares the linked person's general mood and location. It also doesn't send a continuous stream of information, just a quick burst lasting less than a hundred jiffies. I didn't even know a jiffy was an actual measure of time until I studied our necklaces. Anyways, they warn us when vis is used in our presence. The threshold used is set to warn of any use lasting longer than one hundred jiffies, or the amount of time it takes light to travel one meter in space. To get a signal out faster than that took some serious—"

"Pretty slick," she admitted. "Let's see what you feel now."

She gave him a kiss on the cheek and left him with a warm feeling in his heart.

"You know, there is a mission-related function for—" he tried to explain in her mind before she interrupted him again.

"You don't have to explain yourself to me. I've always desired to know what it feels like to be Terra. Sharing emotions

with a Terra is the most wonderful of gifts. Especially my hero's."

"*Your life-long goal is to feel like an angry young man?*" he asked before leaving her mind.

****

At 6:55 a.m., Elaine, looking as much like Juanita as possible, walked into the Den. She had jet-black, straightened hair and, through a combination of a spray-on tan and expert makeup, looked very much like a young, native South American. Dressed in a thin, but professionally conservative, dark blue dress, she sat down and waited for her Attal trainer. The lady sitting opposite Elaine had higher cheekbones and slightly thicker lips, but she could easily pass for a relative. Assuming Juanita hadn't had surgery to change her voice box, the Attal woman would have Juanita's exact voice patterns.

"Bom dia," the stranger said, continuing in perfect Portuguese. "I prefer my other body, but even this beats the aches and pains of a seventy-year-old hiding with the Terra."

Despite the flawless Portuguese, Elaine laughed so hard she became almost incoherent.

"Iv—Ivan—Oh, man—That's—That's awesome!"

"I have no idea who you are talking about. My name is Juanita," Ivan responded.

In very little time, Elaine felt confident she could replicate not only the voice, but the arrogant mannerisms of an alien Pat-wannabe. She entered the mission briefing in character.

"Wow, quite the disguise. Well done," Aggie said after seeing her friend.

Ignoring the compliment, she gave her friend a blank look as if she were no more important than the chair she sat on.

"Get me a coffee, black."

After a thirty-minute briefing, everyone understood the plan. In an effort to steal most of their money before it could be moved, while avoiding a confrontation with an armed militia, Bill had decided to go after all of her bank funds and two of her safety deposit boxes in a simultaneous attack. This led to a serious challenge. Both the Cayman and Swiss accounts were set up so any changes over one million dollars had to be made in person. True to their reputation, both banks had the highest security in the industry. For the largest of accounts, this included a separate, on-site computer system, disconnected from the internet, which could only be accessed from internal bank terminals. The feature made transferring money or making changes to an account tedious and expensive, but it also made it hack-proof unless one had access to the on-site terminals for a substantial amount of time.

According to the plan, Ivan and Bill were going to transport to Florida and visit a beauty salon so Ivan, still using the female body from his recent transformation, could have a makeover to address all the changes in Juanita's appearance since her last transport. After looking like Juanita from the most recent video Pax had recorded through her work's security cameras, Ivan and Bill will pick up Maria and Gary from the airport in Miami. They'll travel together to the Cayman Islands and wait to coordinate with Pax's team. Pax, Aggie, and Elaine will fly to Switzerland with Robert. After changing ownership of the accounts, both teams will travel to a nearby bank and attempt to clean out the safety deposit boxes. Bill's team will go to the box rented in South Florida, while Pax's team traveled to London. Robert will then fly to Florida, pick up Bill's team, and head home with a very expensive payload.

Pax, Elaine, and Aggie waited on the Gulfstream at the Canton Akron Airport.

"Where's Bobby?" Elaine asked.

Aggie just shrugged with a "how should I know" expression. Pax contacted him telepathically. After a twenty-second pause, Pax saw through Robert's eyes. Looking down at a carrier full of drinks, he saw Robert's feet walking quickly across the hangar.

After he climbed aboard, Robert said, "I don't know what the protocol is for one's first flight, but things might get hectic later, so I thought we should start off properly."

He handed Elaine, who looked like a snobby, Latino bitch, a cup of black coffee and passed a cup of tea to both Pax and Aggie.

Keeping one cup for himself, he held it up and said, "Here's to a quiet mission. Cheers!"

Elaine broke character and smiled while saying, "Now that's service. To Switzerland, please, dear Bobby."

Robert tipped his head to her and asked, "Good enough service to call me Robert?"

"No pastries. Sorry, Bobby."

They sat in silence as Robert went over his pre-flight checklist. Aggie exhaled and had to make a conscious effort to lower her heart rate. She wondered why she felt so lonely and anxious when they had not even left the ground. It only took her a couple of seconds to realize those were Eddie's feelings. She loved the connection to Eddie, but conceded feeling his emotions would be a huge distraction during her mission.

She thought about using the removal cream Eddie had given her, but before she could locate his formula, she had a better, extremely dangerous idea. She closed her eyes and pressed a button on her watch, releasing some vis. She knew the theory, but to her knowledge it had never been done. Taking a second to admit to herself the recklessness of her plan to experiment with a Terra brain minutes before a mission, she started the most irresponsible thing she had done.

Impressed with Eddie's effort to hide his bug, it took her more than ten minutes to find the affected section of her brain. Once she located the command the Link-Ink had created, she moved it to a secured section of her mind. Having separated a portion of her memory and put it behind a mental barrier, she hoped it would still be accessible at will while not allowing involuntarily access.

After the twenty-minute process, she opened her eyes and did a quick inventory of her senses. She took a sip of tea and performed a brief body scan of Elaine, testing to make sure the procedure had not affected her mind's normal functions. Pleased with her success, she proceeded to access Eddie's emotions and then closed them, accessed them again, and again closed them off. She continued toggling between monitoring Eddie's emotions and blocking them off, when she felt him in her conscience mind.

"*Hey, Link. How's it going?*"

"*Hey, what?*" she asked.

"*Link. You're my Link cuz you've been inked,*" Eddie answered in a sing-song response.

"*I'm fine. Just getting ready to take off. I miss the other pilot we had, though this one did serve me a cup of tea.*"

"*Well, la-di-da,*" he responded before getting serious. "*I wanted to chat quickly before you get too far away. I've been having some problems with my Link-Ink. I can still track you, but your emotions have been—Well, this isn't going to make sense—but they've kinda been blinking on and off. Maybe I didn't make it strong enough.*"

"*No, your formula's fine. I just made a few, internal adjustments,*" she confessed.

After a five-minute conversation explaining what she had done, she promised Eddie she would test his Link-Ink when they were thousands of miles apart.

"Please sit down, everyone. We've been cleared for take-off," Robert announced as he started taxiing down the runway.

Aggie took a sip from her cold cup of tea, sat back, and quietly enjoyed the happiness Eddie felt at her desire to stay connected. She didn't smile, but the ends of her lips definitely turned up as the drum prelude to Foreigner's "Juke Box Hero" played over the plane's speakers.

Elaine gave her friend a mischievous smile and tilted her head.

From the cockpit, the passengers heard, "The bloke isn't even here, and I still have to deal with his bloody noise."

As the Gulfstream raced down the runway, Aggie turned up the volume. Eddie could feel the satisfaction and love coming from her and accepted her request to join in her thoughts. They enjoyed the rest of the song together.

As the song neared its end, she said, *"I'd love to freeze time right here, jukebox hero, but I gotta go make some money."*

"Just keep rocking, Link, and get home safe," he said before returning his mind to the Den.

Chapter XXVII

Ivan, who looked like a plain version of the rich and fancy Juanita, entered the high-end beauty solon in South Florida with his pretend husband Bill. Even though they didn't have an appointment, they threw around enough money for immediate service. Three hours later, with more than enough time to meet the Whites at the airport, he left the salon looking almost identical to the picture of Juanita Pax had hacked from the bank's security cameras.

****

The rest of the flight to Switzerland, including Robert's first-ever landing, was uneventful. They rented an Audi A6 at the airport and headed to a hotel three blocks away from the bank. The next day, at 2:15 p.m. local time, they were all sitting in the parked Audi, waiting for Bill's command. Pax typed furiously on his Attal-enhanced laptop.

"It's time to get ready, guys. Bill wants to hit the banks after Juanita checks her accounts in the morning, which she does at 8:30 a.m. The time change gives us a very short window to get the money here and get to the safety deposit box before the bank closes in England. Robert, make sure we are cleared to take off as quickly as possible. It won't take Juanita long to figure out what's going on, and I want to cripple them as much as possible before they catch on and move their money."

At 8:45 a.m. EST, Bill contacted Pax. *"We are at the bank and ready to go. We will enter at 9:05."*

"We are a go, guys," Pax reported. "We are going to enter the bank at 3:05 and hopefully be in London by 4:30. Be in character and ready to go in ten minutes."

Everyone except Pax, who continued typing furiously on his laptop, tried to relax and visualize their roll.

At 3:00 p.m., he announced, "I've done everything I can do. I'm pretty sure once we get the money it will be untraceable. It will go through three screenings, in an effort to clean any possible tracking software, and will be transferred twenty times. Then it will float around in cyber space for two days before being cleaned again and deposited in a safe account."

After a final check with Bill, all eyes were on Pax.

"Once again, we find ourselves at the point of no return," he announced as he pressed the enter button on his computer. "Let's go get the rest."

Pax and Robert remained in the Audi as Aggie entered the bank to gather information about opening an account. Elaine, speaking the specific but non-traditional dialect of German most common in Switzerland, entered a couple of minutes later as the arrogant Juanita look-a-like and informed the greeter she was pressed for time but needed to make changes to her priority account.

****

Simultaneously, in the Cayman Islands, Ivan's security guard and pretend boyfriend Bill, held the bank door open for a middle-aged, American woman and her invisible husband.

"I would like some information about opening a secured account," Maria said to the gentleman.

He politely escorted her to a waiting area and handed her a brochure.

"A banking representative will be with you shortly," he said with a kind smile before returning to Ivan and Bill.

"I have a preferred account and wish to make some changes to it," Ivan said, speaking perfect Spanish.

The gentleman escorted them to a small, but plush, private office.

"An account specialist will be with you shortly. May I get you a beverage while you wait?"

"No," Ivan said without making eye contact.

****

Pax, temporarily operating as mission leader, simultaneously monitored the two missions. Unlike Bill, Pax struggled to balance the overload of information as he continually replaced bank security system cameras on his monitor with the bank transfer information, only to be replaced by traffic cams from outside both banks. He concentrated so hard he wasn't sure what he saw, but Robert appeared to be texting someone. Using a skill he'd been working hard to master, he concentrated on Robert's cell phone number and viewed the text sent wirelessly as if it were sent to him. He saw Robert had texted: "…London to Miami."

Pax monitored too many things to make sense of the message and questioned why he even cared.

"Robert, I need some help with the monitoring. And who did you text London and Miami to?

"Pardon? Of course. What can I do to help?" he asked.

"Could you please monitor the bank transfers and security cameras in the Caymans on this?" Pax asked as he passed an IDC to the front seat. "I only need to know if anything shows up red on the bank transfers or if anything looks out of character in the bank. I'm in communication with Bill, and I'll monitor our team. Who were you texting?"

"Pardon?" Robert asked, clearly trying to figure out what his monitoring responsibilities were.

"The text, 'London to Miami,'" Pax said. "Who did you send it to and why?"

"Oh, I had to check and see if I could obtain emergency clearance with short notice to take off from England and fly to Miami in a couple of hours."

"Were you given clearance?"

"Yes," Robert said. "But I had to make a small donation to get bumped to priority status. Two thousand British pounds ensured it could be done."

"Excellent. What about the flight to England?" Pax asked before stopping Robert's answer. "Quiet. Everything is happening now."

Both of the banks' electricity blinked for a moment. When the cameras came back on, the live security feed showed footage Pax had borrowed from the archives of last week's customers.

****

"Buenos dias, Ms. Hernandez," the well-dressed man said as he entered the private room and sat down opposite Ivan and Bill behind a large, antique, cherry desk. "I hear you would like to make some changes to your account."

"Yes. I need to open a new account and transfer much of the money from my current account into the new one," Ivan corrected him

"Of course. A simple change, but per your request, we need to go through a couple of unique security steps. Before we can go any further, what is the main password associated with the account?" the bank manager asked.

"$ e R e T u $," Ivan replied easily, thanks to Pax's computer spying.

"Gracias. Now, if you and your…um…friend could please step through the door, we will be done in just a couple of seconds."

As Ivan and Bill stood up, the manager took a familiar watch out of the drawer and put it on his wrist. Using the included instructions, he pressed a specific set of buttons which, unknown to him, blocked anyone from using vis in his proximity. Holding a note in his hand, he opened the door to the soundproof, windowless room no bigger than a large closet. Once they were inside, his gentle voice came over a hidden speaker.

"Please stare into the retina scanner on the east wall and repeat the on-site password when you are ready, Ms. Hernandez."

****

"That's correct, Ms. Hernandez," the proper, Swedish gentleman told Elaine after she repeated the account password.

"Now, per your specific security requests, I need you to go through two more steps before we can make any changes to your account."

He picked up his phone and, speaking Romansh, Switzerland's native, almost-dead language, asked the person on the other end to bring her the security box associated with account number 61-188-055.

"It's nice to hear people use the regional languages," Elaine said in perfect Romansh.

"Very impressive, Ms. Hernandez," the bank manager admitted. "Few foreigners speak our true language, and almost all of them live in Europe."

Confident about her dialect, she smiled.

"Thank you. I find it insulting when one wants to do business in my country, yet doesn't take the time to learn our language. I would never wish to insult the people who take such good care of my money. Am I conjugating all the verbs correctly?"

"If I didn't know better, I would think you were a local," he responded with a smile.

****

The woman who helped Aggie with her new account broke into a cold sweat and her temperature rose to a feverish level.

Giving a smile to Aggie that took all her energy, she said, "Would you please excuse me for just a moment. I'll be right back."

After the woman had staggered toward the restroom, Aggie took a small notecard and matching envelop from the pile beside her computer monitor. She retrieved a black pen from her purse, wrote a message on the notecard, and sealed it inside the envelope.

Concurrently, the bank manager's assistant delivered a dovetailed wooden box to her boss.

He set the box on top of his desk and entered a four-digit code on the keypad that protected the contents. He took a moment to read the note and its specific instructions.

"I see a lot of different requests in an effort to keep money secure, but I must admit, this one is most unique."

He retrieved a black watch and placed it on his wrist, when a bad taste developed in the back of his throat. He took a deep breath and finished attaching the watch to his wrist as his forehead beaded with sweat and he became nauseated.

"My dear Ms. Hernandez, please excuse me for a brief moment."

The last two words were spoken from the doorway as he hurried down the hall. After confirmation from Pax that the cameras were somehow malfunctioning, Elaine quickly removed a small, white envelop from the box and put it in her purse. Standing in the doorway, she easily took the envelope from Aggie without any notice. Placing the new envelop in the box, she sat down and waited for the kind bank manager to return, knowing he would be feeling better any minute now.

****

Ivan knew his retina would be an exact match for Juanita's, so without hesitation he allowed the scanner access to his right eye while, in the other room, the account specialist opened the sealed envelope containing the security phrase. As he read the phrase, he did not understand the terminology, but the invisible Gary, standing behind him, knew exactly what it meant.

Gary slowly and silently moved a few feet away. Standing in the corner of the room, he spoke quietly enough so one could only hear it if they were sitting directly beside him.

"Win your Galtri and you're a Pat, but a Terra will always be a Terra."

Inside the soundproof room, Ivan and Bill heard the banker's voice out of a small speaker. "The retina scan is a match. Please repeat the security phrase, and we will be done with these cumbersome security checks."

With a little telepathic communication from Maria, who remained far enough away to be unaffected by the Attal watch but could easily hear her whispering husband, Ivan easily repeated the password. After all of the security checks were passed, it only took twenty minutes to set up a new account and enact the transfer. The balance of just over ten million dollars dropped by nine and a half million, which made its way to the alternate account, with a whole new set of passwords and security checks.

****

"I am so sorry," the bank manager said to Elaine as he returned to his office and sat down. "Please forgive me for my unprofessionalism."

"Sometimes things come up. It's fine," Elaine said with a smile and a flirty tilt of her head.

The move was out of character for an evil, rogue alien, but she thought it would be more useful than snobbery toward the bank manager, with whom she felt a connection, like almost everyone since her surgery. She figured she could use her rapport and charisma if Pax's skills did not deliver on his promise.

"Please look into the scanner with your right eye, Ms. Hernandez, and repeat the on-site security phrase for me."

"Pax, I'm about to get scanned," Elaine said, looking for some last-minute reassurance.

"I'm ready," he answered, not nearly reassuring enough for Elaine.

Pax had already explained to her that, even though the bank's computer system was self-contained and un-hackable from anywhere other than one of the bank's secured terminals, the retina scanner was monitored and maintained by an external company via an outside network for updates and database storage. He had hacked into their software in nine minutes, despite their impeccable track record and state-of-the-art technology, and downloaded a copy of Juanita's retina to send after he blocked Elaine's scan.

She heard the bank manager say, "Thank you, Ma'am. Now the security phrase?"

Elaine let out a sigh of relief and felt a little guilty for doubting Pax. The guilt was quickly taken over by humor as she repeated Aggie's message to the bank manager.

"It's not bubble gum. It's cotton candy, bitch," Elaine said, remembering the telepathic conversation she had with her friend a lifetime ago.

"Again, one of the more unique security steps and phrases I have encountered," the bank manager said with a chuckle. "Usually, people use a line from a children's book or a list of their grandkids—but correct, nevertheless. How may I help you Ms. Hernandez?"

Elaine transferred eleven million dollars to a new account, leaving a balance of a little over two hundred and eighty thousand U.S. dollars.

****

Juanita monitored her computer screen while talking to Carlos on his Terra cell phone.

"The bastards cleaned us out. They've left less than one million in the bank, plus what's in the boxes."

"Can they get to those?" Carlos asked. "And how much do we have in them?"

"I've just emptied the one here. Its contents are with me. The boxes will be easier to get to than the twenty million they just stole," she answered honestly. "How close to Miami and London do you have soldiers?"

"I can get a team to Miami in about an hour. I don't have anyone close enough to London to make a difference."

"We don't want any bloodshed in London, anyway. Send everyone you can to Miami," she instructed.

Chapter XXVIII

Robert completed all the necessary arrangements, both legal and questionable, allowing them to take off within minutes of returning to the airport. Elaine and Aggie entered the London bank twenty minutes before closing and requested access to their safety deposit box. Elaine fiddled with the fake key in her pocket, designed by Eddie as she contacted her brother.

"I'm about ready to use the key. Are you sure it's going to work?"

"Pretty sure," he answered. *"I tested it on every kind of lock I could find."*

"Good afternoon, Ms. Hernandez, ma'am," the bank manager interrupted the conversation he could neither hear nor see. "We have an interesting situation concerning your safety deposit box."

Elaine smiled, subtly flipped her black, straight hair, and gently touched the gentleman's arm.

"I'm sure you do. I bet my sister called, upset, and tried to lock me out of my box."

"Um…exactly," he confirmed. "She—ah—she said a thief would come in posing as her to clean out her belongings. She requested we restrict access."

"Did my dear sister tell you she's in South America?" she leaned in and added in a slow, airy whisper. "And did she inform you about the new love and the two thousand pounds a day it costs her to keep her habit?"

"The lady on the phone claimed to be Juanita Hernandez, and yes, she did inform me she lived in South America."

Taking out the passport Bill had given her, she winked at the manager and said, "That's why they give us passports and these silly, little keys for our boxes. I apologize for the situation my family has caused. I assure you, today is the last time you will hear from her. Now, if you could please escort me and my friend to my family's box, I would certainly appreciate it, luv."

With a little vis-assisted encouragement from Aggie, the bank manager did not notice the unusual key Elaine inserted into the lock. After pressing the unmarked, black button on the back of the key, she inserted the small, metal rod into the lock. The key scanned the mechanism, expanded to the exact shape, and opened the box as if it had been designed by the bank.

"I apologize for any confusion and wish you the best of luck with your sister, Ms. Hernandez. The bank officially closes in twenty minutes, but we will gladly allow you as much time as you need. Let me know if I can be of any further assistance," the manager said before leaving Elaine and Aggie alone with Juanita's safety deposit box.

****

Maria and an invisible Gary were in the lobby of the Miami bank, surveying the area and getting in position to provide backup if needed. Ivan and Bill were walking toward the front door, when Ivan's necklace became warm on his chest and he got the feeling a non-Pride member of the Attal wanted to communicate with him. Even though he accepted the communication from Juanita, he pictured and addressed her as Barry.

"Hello, Ivan. I hear Bill is still on the planet. I assume he is going to attempt to empty the contents of my South Florida safety deposit box in the very near future. I highly recommend you have him make other plans."

"After all this time, you only contact me when you are about to lose your Terra money," Ivan responded. *"I must admit, I find myself disappointed."*

"Money does allow for certain, enjoyable comforts on the surface. Unlike us, the Terra have chosen not to limit one's social status for their entire lives due to the results of a corrupt competition; but that's a conversation for another day. Between your actions in Michigan and the cleaning out of our accounts this morning, we have been forced to change our motives."

"Interesting commentary, Barry. I'd love to have a conversation about it with you someday, but it may be more prudent to ask what your current motivations are," Ivan asked.

Separately and concurrently, he told Gary and Maria, *"We are fine, but need to delay. Stall operation. I'll update soon."*

"My dear brother Carlos and I have decided to part ways soon," she said. *"We have found ourselves desiring different things of late. I have grown accustomed to the pleasures money, intelligence, and a little vis can create here. I no longer wish to make a statement, punish the Attal for their obviously flawed leadership, or harm any Terra."*

"And Wendy?" Ivan asked.

Choosing the truth again, she answered, "He still very much wants to punish the Attal. Well, technically only three Attal, but he has no qualms about hurting any Terra or Attal to achieve his goals."

"And why should this knowledge stop us from going after your stashed cash and valuables?" Ivan asked.

"It could save many lives, including those of your friends," she responded with no emotion.

"I hear nothing except empty threats, Barry. If you truly want to save lives, I'll make you a deal. Turn yourself in to the Attal, and I will give you my word your life will be spared. You obviously can't stay on Earth, but I'll transfer you to another planet where you will work your remaining days as a Nish."

"I can't agree to those terms. I will agree to helping you catch Carlos, if you promise to leave me and my money alone. I will disappear and live out my natural life peacefully on this planet."

"You know there is no way I can agree to your terms. Any information you give me about Wendy will help you when you are disciplined by the Council, but there have been too many innocent Terra killed and injured by your actions. You cannot go unpunished."

"I'm sorry to hear that, Ivan. I've always liked you, but if Bill and Pax go after the remainder of my—I think the Terra call it—nest egg, then I will have no choice but to join my brother's final campaign."

"By issuing a threat, you have already told me everything I need to know," Ivan said. "Enjoy poverty."

Juanita looked over at the muscle-bound Carlos and said, "I bought you about five minutes. Let's hope that is enough."

"They are twelve minutes away. It will be close."

****

Ivan knew Wendy had an ulterior motive for her communication, but he decided to analyze the conversation later. When he and Bill entered the bank, they were met with the same situation Elaine had experienced. Once it became obvious they were going to be allowed private access to the box, Maria finished her inquiry and headed outside to monitor activity. Gary, still invisible, waited in the lobby in case Bill and Ivan ran into any unforeseen interference in the bank.

Maria sat on the steps of the office building across the street from the bank, when she heard the squeal of tires. Approximately six hundred yards down the divided road, an SUV headed toward her as fast as the congested road would allow. By weaving through traffic and going through a couple of lights that had already turned red, they were quickly navigating the midday traffic on the busy, Miami streets. Even through the tinted windows, Maria could make out at least three people.

Contacting Bill, she reported, *"We may have a situation out here. Are you guys almost finished?"*

"We will be out in three minutes," Bill reported.

"I think we will have company by then," she responded. *"There is an SUV approaching in a hurry. If they are coming for us, I predict you have less than two minutes."*

Bill immediately started giving commands.

"Maria, stay where you are and continue to report any activity. Gary, head outside the entrance and attempt to slow down anyone looking questionable. Ivan, we have to move. It appears they have sent some troops to impede out efforts. I have a plan to handle this, but it's probability is greatly increased from a more defensive position."

The bank manager was not even completely out of the vault before Ivan opened Juanita's box. Without checking the contents, he dumped them into the black, leather satchel, replaced the box in the only empty slot, and exited the vault less than a minute after the manager. Bill recalled the bank's schematics he had memorized last week and guided Ivan to an unoccupied office at the far end of the lobby. The top half of the walls were glass, which offered minimal protection but optimal viewing. Ivan clumsily crouched behind the desk in the floral, summer dress he had chosen to best imitate Juanita. He retrieved a hair tie out of his satchel and created a practical ponytail out of his long hair. Bill positioned himself behind the desk in an effort to blend in as a bank employee and prepared himself to test the limits of his skills.

"Three men got out of the SUV with masks pulled over their faces. They are either here for us, or we have really bad timing and they are here to rob the bank," Maria updated the team.

"I see the men. They are going to enter in twenty seconds. Do you need me to slow them down?" Gary asked.

"No. Let them enter. It's time for me to test one of my new talents," Bill answered.

"The driver didn't park, but pulled away. Instructions?" Maria asked.

"Keep monitoring the entrance for any activity. Gary, enter with our friends in case my plan doesn't work."

As soon as Bill saw the strangers enter the bank, he knew they were Seretus Ligare supporters. They wore the same black, military uniforms as the men at the Shepard building, complete with combat boots and bulletproof vests. They had the hand gestures and quick, sharp movements of a well-trained military team. Sitting low behind his desk, Bill waited for the three masked men to make their first move before he acted.

One guard, with an invisible Gary standing beside him, stayed close to the entrance, his automatic gun drawn as he slowly, predatorily scanned the lobby. The other two soldiers headed through the crowd of about twenty customers and employees until they were almost to the counter. They spread out to form a triangular defense pattern, once again displaying their military training. The soldier closest to the office Bill and Ivan occupied made an announcement in a deep, loud voice with just a hint of a South American accent.

"This is a robbery. Everybody place your hands where we can see them and don't move a muscle, or you'll be shot where you stand."

He then fired two rounds from his M4 into the ceiling to reinforce the seriousness of his message.

Bill pressed two buttons on his watch, closed his eyes, and concentrated harder than he ever had in his life. Obviously knowing how to plant a memory, he concentrated on the distance and strength of his command. The effects of the command rolled away from the corner office like an invisible fog. Approximately a second or two apart, each person, starting with the one closest to the corner office, laid whatever they were holding on the ground in front of them, got on their knees, and closed their eyes. Within twenty seconds, everyone in the bank not wearing a Pride necklace knelt on the floor with their eyes closed.

"Wow," Gary exclaimed as he picked up the rifle from the masked gunman beside him.

He removed the man's mask before making his way to the next soldier.

"Impressive. I thought the memory thing was cool, but kind of wimpy. This is the coolest thing I've ever seen. Consider me a huge fan."

"I hate to break things up, boys, but the driver is back, and I hear sirens in the distance. I think your party is about to have some crashers."

Bill contacted Pax, who sat in the back seat of the rental car on the way to the airport.

"Are you monitoring our bank?"

"Of course. It looks like you had some complications. How can I help?" Pax answered.

"Although we didn't steal anything or injure anyone, Gary and my actions might be hard to explain to someone watching the security footage. The authorities would likely be concentrating on the gunmen, but it would still be helpful if the cameras weren't working."

"I will erase everything since the last upload as soon as your team is out of sight. Anything else?" Pax asked.

"Not now. Stay ready."

Thirty seconds later, three M4 assault rifles floated through the air and landed on the floor of the corner office, from which a middle-aged man and an attractive, Latina woman were making a hasty retreat. As soon as Maria saw them in the entrance, she started to make her way down the steps. She never heard the gunshot, but she saw Bill fall to the ground. Seconds after Bill's fall, Ivan dropped to the ground, bleeding from his belly.

Realizing there must be another gunman, Gary took immediate action.

"Ivan, Bill—grab my leg."

Bill lay on the cement sidewalk, bleeding from his shoulder, while Ivan knelt beside him with blood covering his dress. Shocked and injured, neither understood Gary's request. Not having time to explain the extension of his skills he and Eddie had been working on, Gary pressed a couple of buttons on his cloaking device and dove on top of his bloody friends.

"*Bun, get the car. Quick!*" he yelled to his wife.

The driver of the black SUV and the sniper he had dropped off as he circled the building both stared in disbelief. Where the two targets stood bleeding a second ago, they now saw nothing except a wavy mirage, like heat reflecting off a hot road in the summer time. The couple bleeding at the bank entrance had disappeared quicker than a Las Vegas magic act.

Hearing the sirens become louder, the driver radioed his comrades and headed around the block to pick up the confused sniper at the side entrance, away from the bank building. In the time it took the driver to leave the scene, the invisible Bill and Ivan had switched places. Bill knelt over the more seriously injured Ivan, who lay unconscious on the sidewalk. Bill still attempted to hold everyone in the bank frozen on their knees while telepathically asking Agrata for advice on how to control Ivan's bleeding.

Maria drove up onto the sidewalk and parked within two feet of her friends. She slammed the car into park, jumped out, and opened the back, passenger door.

"We really need to hurry. We have about two minutes before we are arrested."

"We could damage Ivan if we move him," Gary exclaimed.

"It doesn't matter," Bill quietly interrupted with a scratchy throat. "I'm barely keeping him alive. Get him in the car."

Gary lost his ability to concentrate upon hearing the severity of Ivan's condition and, for the first time in weeks, could not stay invisible. He picked up Ivan and quickly laid him in the back seat. Not even noticing the blood on his hands, arms, and shirt, he ran to the driver's side and spun the tires as he left the curb and sped down NW 11th Street.

Maria leaned over the front seat and applied pressure to Bill's shoulder wound as he still focused on trying to slow Ivan's heart rate. Knowing he had to leave the area, Gary subconsciously headed toward I-95. Not sure if he should go to the hospital or to the airport and seeing Bill deep in concentration and pain, he contacted the smartest person he knew, even though he was in another country.

"We have a situation here," Gary informed Pax. "Ivan and Bill have both been shot. Bill seems semi-stable, but he's struggling to keep Ivan alive. I'm on NW 11th Street, heading toward 95. Should I go to the hospital or drive past it to the airport?"

"I have your location on my computer. Aggie is trying to help Bill. Do not get on 95. I need you to turn around and head west. You are going to turn north on NW 4th," Pax instructed.

"Any chance I could get a little help with the traffic? And where the hell am I going?" he asked.

"I can't do anything about the traffic, but I'm in control of the lights. They will be green the rest of the way. You are looking for Flagler Street, a couple miles north. You are going to turn left, heading west on Flagler. We have to get them to the office on Flagler. And Gary, not to add to your stress, but time is of the essence. You have to drive a little—"

"Oh, really? You think?" Gary interrupted him as he swerved at the last second to cut off a Toyota Camry that had the nerve to only be driving fourteen miles per hour over the speed limit.

Chapter XXIX

    Carlos picked up his Terra cell phone on the first ring and listened with disbelief as the mission commander gave his report.

    "What do you mean they disappeared?" he yelled. "Go back to your camp and wait for instructions."

    He threw the phone against the stone wall and turned toward Juanita.

    "Bill and Pax are becoming a real pain in my ass."

    "One of us has certainly devolved into a Terra madman," she retorted.

    "There is nothing wrong with showing emotion every now and then. It's cleansing," he responded. "Although a little expensive. I think I'm going to need a new cell phone."

    "What's your plan now?" Juanita asked.

    "It's time to get our vis and separate. How much longer can we pay our men?" he asked.

Juanita, who had a little more than four million U.S. dollars in the Megan Patrick account Pax had left alone, looked up at the ceiling as she ran calculations in her head.

"If I combine what I removed from our local security box with the money Bill left in all our accounts, we have a little over two million in cash and approximately one million in diamonds. With our current payroll and expenses at both compounds, we could last about six weeks if we didn't make any additional money or take any for personal use."

When he didn't respond, she added. "You can stay and fight as long as you wish, but I need at least one million to start a new life."

"I too have plans that require funds," Carlos said with a mischievous smile. "And I'm more determined than ever. We will execute our final mission this Friday. By Saturday evening, we will have enough vis to last each of us a Terra lifetime if we use it sparingly."

"I will split the money into two new accounts and try to erase any evidence we were ever here. On Sunday, I'll take my half of the vis and leave the compound for the last time," she announced.

"Fair enough," he said.

Quietly and more as a personal thought than a request for Juanita's opinion, he added to himself, "Should I wait here for Bill or go on the run and hunt him down?"

He looked down at the floor and chewed the inside of his cheek for a few seconds before he headed toward the hallway and his office.

"Hmm. Either could work."

****

With Pax's traffic control assistance and Gary's uncharacteristic, aggressive driving, they came to a screeching stop outside of the Flagler Street office in just under eleven minutes. Ivan had stopped breathing a mile and a half ago, but Maria had jumped into the back seat, sat on him, and gave him chest compressions while communicating with Eddie. Bill, in constant contact with Aggie, used all his remaining strength to stay conscience and keep Ivan's brain functioning, even though he had lost almost two pints of blood in the back seat of the rented Lexus.

Two people emerged from the office and opened the rear door before Gary could even get out of the car. He knew immediately they were Attal. The middle-aged, black man looked identical to the lab manager in the Den, and the Indian woman who accompanied him showed Gary exactly what Aggie will look like when she takes her thirty-year-old body in a couple more years. The black man half-carried, half-drug Ivan into the red brick building marked with nothing except the number "268" and a "No Solicitation" sign. Maria followed behind, while Gary helped the Indian girl get Bill inside.

Once in the building, the black man said, "No, ma'am, you must stay out here. We will take care of her in our inner office."

Maria knew she could help with Ivan's and Bill's bodies, but the explanation and possible resulting shock the Attal could experience at discovering two Terra knew their secret would waste more time than taking a subordinate position would.

"Of course," she said. "Let me know how she does."

After Gary got the same story from the Indian lady, he sat beside his wife in the lobby of the small office designed to resemble a Terra accounting firm.

A secure, soundproof door camouflaged as an oak office door protected the back room. Even with Maria's enhanced hearing, she had to concentrate very hard to identify the familiar noise of the transport machine.

"I hope we made it in time," she heard the Attal man say. "Now, what do we do with the Terra in the office?"

"I have no idea," his partner answered. "I would normally ask Ivan, but considering the current situation, I don't know who to ask."

"Come on, bun," Maria said. "We've done everything we can here, and we are complicating these guys' sense of simplistic harmony."

"Yeah, I guess," Gary said, looking down at himself and then over at Maria. "I imagine having two blood-covered Terra sitting in the office of your secret transport station could constitute a stressful situation. Let's go find a place to clean up."

As he opened the front door for Maria, he asked, "Do you know anyone who wants to buy a slightly used Lexus?"

They were less than a mile away from the building when the whole Pride received a communication from Bill.

"I am at the surface station and one hundred percent repaired."

"Oh, thank God," Maria commented with her eyes closed in a quick moment of gratitude.

"But Ivan didn't fare as well," Bill added to his report. *"He is here and is alive. Eddie, Agrata, and I were attempting something a little unorthodox during Gary's efforts to get us here. For now, the official report is he is fine and resting at the surface station. I will keep you informed. Continue with your mission, and we will meet again soon at the property."*

Before he could answer any questions, Bill closed his mind, returned to Eddie's office that doubled as his bedroom, and stood over an unconscious Ivan lying on the bed.

****

After Gary had cleaned himself and the car and negotiated the price of a new back seat and full detail for the rental, he barely made it to the airport before Robert landed and taxied down the runway. While Robert refueled and added two people to his manifest for the flight back to Ohio, Gary and Maria stored their two carry-on bags, gave hugs and kisses to the other team, and got Gary a large cup of coffee. There was not a quiet moment on the plane as they updated each other about their missions, discussed the confrontation with the Seretus, and questioned the health and secrecy surrounding Ivan. Aggie, whose mission responsibilities were over, opened the previously locked section of her mind linked to Eddie by her hidden tattoo. As she sat on the tan leather couch listening to Gary brag about his driving skills, she felt both pride and defiance.

****

"You never said I couldn't experiment with the transport process," Eddie corrected Ivan. "You said Attal laws forbid *you* from altering the procedures. I thought you meant you *wanted* me to look into them."

"Why would I want you to break one of our laws for me?" Ivan said, louder than he intended. "Eddie, those laws are in place for a reason. Of all people, you should understand the dangers and possible complications when someone attempts to alter one's DNA or, more importantly, their mind."

Ivan lifted his head and leaned on his elbows. He pivoted to address Bill.

"What were you thinking? As much as I don't believe Eddie's little tap dance around the truth, I know you know the risks and illegality of having two concurrent signatures."

"I had no idea. I had a request from a team member to copy your memories since your last transport. I didn't question why," Bill rebutted.

"But you know better than to modify any part of the transportation process," Ivan stated.

"If my memory serves me right, and my memory almost always does, we agreed during this confusing time in our history that we may have to set aside traditional rules until this mission was complete. To quote one of the sweetest Terra I know, 'Sometimes, as adults, you need to run with scissors.'"

"You know what?" Eddie interrupted. "Let's just call it a lack of communication. How about, instead of yelling at me for a questionable experiment, you just say thanks for saving your life."

"The success of your experiment is not the point. We are tracking the Scrctus Ligare because they thought our laws were meaningless rules standing in the way of their goal. We must capture and punish their actions, but we must do it according to Attal statutes."

"You mean remaining hidden from the Terra and never revealing ourselves or communicating with them," Bill pointed out. "Ivan, I love the Attal society and respect its rules, but it is too late to stand by those principles. I, too, struggled with this concept. Gary and Maria helped me come to terms with what might be necessary to defeat Wendy and Barry and their barbaric lack of regulations. With your blessing, we created a Council to let us know when we exceeded our expanded freedoms from some of our laws."

Bill turned slightly so Ivan could not see his face and winked at Eddie, who had to work hard not to smile.

"Maybe you should call a Council meeting and inform them of Eddie's slightly out-of-bounds experiment, or maybe you should talk to Gary and Maria about rules and scissors.

Either way, we are headed toward a showdown with our friends, and we are going to need to know where our leader stands."

Ivan sat up on Eddie's bed and remained deep in thought for a few minutes.

Eyes down, he softly said, "This is not an insult of your obviously impressive engineering skills, but I assume you had to have some help with the transporter to copy and store my last signature before I went to Miami."

He looked up at Eddie.

"Can I assume this is a byproduct of your late-night strolls with Pax?"

"I, and I alone, have been experimenting with the transporter," Eddie answered. "I may of had a couple questions about the system's technical capabilities and may or may not have asked a really smart friend of mine about the feasibility of hypothetically hiding a dual signature of certain Attal members in case they were mortally injured. Maybe."

"That is the worst answer in Attal history—and we are a very old culture." Ivan said, standing up. "If, hypothetically, the Attal leader told you having two signatures of anyone is an unbreakable rule that must be followed, could one assume it would be possible to remove those signatures and any evidence they existed from the system?"

"Absolutely," Eddie said. "But to be clear, not knowing the importance of certain rules, I acted alone in this. And allow me to stress, it was a very successful experiment."

"Okay, Eddie. Unknown to you, there was a time in our past when a group cloned and copied signatures without destroying the originals. It created a rather ugly situation. To put it in Terra terms, that is why we cut and paste the signature, never copy and keep."

"I got it," Eddie assured him. "Remove the copies and *never, ever* have dual copies of anyone or their signature."

Ivan was not completely confident Eddie understood or that he had a desire to follow Attal rules, but he had to admit he was glad he had allowed Eddie to remain part of the team and thrilled to be alive. He made a personal promise to spend some of his illegally acquired, extended life educating his young friend about the history of Attal culture and laws. After another minute of silent contemplation, he stood up.

"Come on, Bill. We have a debriefing to go over."

As he headed out of Eddie's room, he turned to face him, clasped his hands together, bowed his head down and slightly to the right, and said, "Thank you."

****

Exhaustion overtook Aggie. She slouched so far down in her seat that she appeared to be lying in it. She casually listened to the conversation about what the Pride should do with all of the money confiscated from Juanita and allowed the hum of the plane to lull her into a state of relaxation. The Link-Ink she had come to love so much transferred his feelings of happiness and pride to her.

Robert gave his team a smooth and quiet flight back to the Canton/Akron Airport and pulled into the Whites' driveway just under an hour after they had touched down. Elaine and Pax had to wait for Maria to finish lecturing Bill before they could give him a hug.

With a harder-than-necessary smack on Bill's arm, Maria concluded, "…and that's for scaring me to death."

After she felt Bill understood the seriousness of her points, Maria approached Ivan.

With a less exaggerated, but sincere hug, she said softly in his ear, "I'm so glad you are okay. You guys need to quit with the close calls."

"I'm glad our team is okay, too. And although I'll deny it if you ever repeat it, I owe my life to Eddie and his propensity for rule-breaking."

"Well, then thank God he takes after his father," she responded with a kiss on the leader's cheek.

Chapter XXX

After the debriefing, Michele White, Anna Harding, and Kathy Summers treated everyone to a delicious, relaxing, festive cookout. They all sat under the clear, autumn sky and enjoyed burgers, dogs, and plenty of salads and fruits. As the evening wound down, Eddie took Aggie by the hand.
"Come with me, Link. I want to show you something."
Escorting her through his parents' house, he brought her into the garage where his red four-wheeler waited. He helped her onto the back and started it up, and they were immediately serenaded by Foreigner's "Juke Box Hero."
"So, where are you taking me, Link?"
"Somewhere a little less crowded to show you a couple of my newest toys," Eddie answered as he circled around the house and headed toward the pond.

Eddie turned down the volume and drove slowly so he would not draw attention to their escape. But he underestimated the skills of his team and their capacity for shenanigans.

Maria nudged Gary and pointed toward the couple heading up the hill without headlights. Noticing her mom's actions, Elaine, who had joined Pax in a large, lounging deck chair, also pointed out Eddie's attempted escape. Both couples decided to let Eddie know his departure had not gone unnoticed. As soon as the red vehicle reached the top of the hill, Gary telepathically turned on the floodlights of the barn, temporarily blinding Eddie. Before the younger White could figure out what had happened, Pax and Elaine changed his music to one of Eddie's earlier and infinitely less romantic favorites—Van Halen's "Running with the Devil."

Eddie stopped the four-wheeler, telepathically turned off the barn lights, and switched the music back to Foreigner before contacting everyone.

"Really? Help a guy out."

Heading toward the pond, Eddie pulled off the path and drove to higher ground until he reached a wide, flat overlook that had been recently mowed. He parked next to a large, plastic storage bin with small, solar lights on either side, which doubled as insect repellents.

"Stay here for a second," Eddie told Aggie as he left her sitting on the back of the four-wheeler.

The music changed to Styx's "Come Sail Away" as he started to unpack the bin. He spread the blanket and pillows on the ground and poured some lemonade, working slowly enough to allow the music to reach just the right spot. While Styx sang about angels appearing and allowing him to climb aboard their starship, Eddie escorted Aggie to the bed under the stars.

"Aggie, wherever your starship takes you, I'd like to go there with you."

"Thanks, Link, but I thought you knew. I was created here. I've never been on one of our ships."

"Your so damn cute," Eddie said over his chuckle.

"What?" she asked with a confused smile.

"I attempted, obviously unsuccessfully, to be symbolic," Eddie said. "What I tried to say is, I can't stop thinking about you and I like it. I don't know how a relationship with an infinitely smarter alien will work, but you make me both calm and excited at the same time. So, wherever this symbolic star-ride takes us, I'd love to head into the unknown, uncharted sky with you."

"Why didn't you just say that?" she asked, giggling.

After a short pause, she held his hand with interlocking fingers and said, "Earlier this year I had feelings for Robert."

"Gee, thanks. Would you like me to call him over?" Eddie interrupted, showing he also lacked experience and patience with intimate situations.

"Let me finish," she said. "I will always remember Robert fondly, and he is a close friend. But it wasn't Robert I desired. I desperately wanted to sense intimacy, acceptance, and belonging. With you and your family, I have those feelings. What I dream about is being with you. Sharing and learning with you."

Despite their combined inexperience, there was no mistaking her intent when she turned slightly toward him and held both his hands in hers.

"If we take the next step in our relationship, I can't promise you I'll be a perfect girlfriend. I'm quite sure I won't always get your symbolism, nor many of your family's jokes, but you already monopolize my thoughts. I would love to promise you my loyalty and all my efforts to become more Terra."

"There are billions of Terra women on this planet," Eddie said. "I don't want them. I don't love them. You just keep being you, and I will just keep loving you."

Her hug knocked him over onto the pile of pillows.

"I love you, too."

After five minutes of hugging, mixed with some passionate kissing, Eddie sat up and repositioned the pillows.

"We are too exposed, and I don't trust my family. Let's take a break and pick up this conversation at a later time. Do you want to see my latest invention?"

"Not yet. Can we just relax for a few minutes? Between my mission, missing you, and your actions tonight, I've had a wonderful but exhausting twenty-four hours. Can we just look at the stars for a while and enjoy the moment?"

"We will look at the stars then watch the stars," Eddie answered as she laid her head on his lap.

They listened to Eddie's playlist of romantic 70s songs and gazed at the stars.

"See?" Aggie said. "I'm already lost on your symbolism."

"I wasn't being symbolic," Eddie admitted. "Just punny."

After sitting in silence and gently caressing her hair and forehead for twenty minutes, Eddie said, "The stars are beautiful. Now, let's quit looking at them and watch them."

He pressed a button on his watch, and the barn lit up like a movie screen at a drive-in theater.

They lay under the stars in each other's embrace for the next two hours, eating fruit, drinking lemonade, and watching *Pretty Woman* displayed on the side of the barn.

After escorting her home, they stood at Pax's door and hugged for a moment.

"Thanks for the movie. I loved how two people overcame completely different pasts to eventually find love, and the title song made me smile."

"See? You understand symbolism. You're becoming more Terra every day."

Eddie gave her a kiss and returned to his bedroom in his lab. That night, he got four hours of peaceful sleep before he woke up in a cold sweat. The most he had had in months.

****

With less complaining than expected, Elaine went inside to help Maria clean up from their late-night dinner party. Pax approached Bill to discuss a rare, personal request concerning the contents of the safety deposit boxes they had emptied from Juanita's banks.

"I understand it's not yours to give away, but you do understand my request and see the symbolic value of using it, don't you?"

"Yes. Let me say for the record, I'm thrilled with your plan, but if we just take what's not ours, we become the same as her," Bill answered. "Also, what about everyone else on the team? If I grant your request, what about the next request?"

"I think you analyze each situation as it presents itself," Pax argued. "Has anyone else ever asked for anything of value?"

"Do any of the Whites know about your plan?" Bill asked.

"Not yet," he answered.

"Then I'll tell you what," Bill compromised. "I'll let Gary authorize it for his family, and Ivan will authorize it for us. If they agree, then I'll go along with it."

"If I agree with what?" Ivan asked, joining the conversation. "I agree you two should be punished for helping Eddie illegally manipulate our transportation system. Is that what you were wondering?"

"I wouldn't say we helped him," Pax replied.

"Oh, I'm sorry. I should punish you for maybe allowing him to possibly, or possibly not, manipulate the transporter, maybe."

"I was going to say enabling, but I like your explanation better," Pax said with a smile.

It took the better part of the night, but after three separate conversations and a predictably hard time from Gary, Pax got permission to keep some of Seretus Ligare's safety deposit stash.

Even though Eddie and Aggie did not officially announce the change in their status, it became obvious they had begun a committed relationship, or at least a more public one. If Eddie was not in the lab, they were always together, holding hands and performing other such public displays of affection. Making fun of those moments had become a favorite pastime of the Pride over the past two days, excepting Robert.

Pax took advantage of finding Aggie alone Thursday after dinner. Seeing her walking up the path to visit Eddie, he hustled to catch up with her.

"Hey, Aggie. Hold up a second."

"Hey. What's up?" she asked, waiting for him.

"I wanted to run something past you," he said. "I've noticed throughout Terra history, before every war, there's a huge spike in marriages and, about a year later, births."

"Okay. Kind of random, but thanks for the Terra population trivia," Aggie said.

"Elaine often asks me about our home planet, technology, or our natural form, et cetera," Pax said as he stopped walking.

"I know. Eddie does, too. I guess it's natural. We certainly ask about their culture a lot," Aggie said.

"Well, given the danger of our mission and the apparent showdown looming, I contemplated a—Well, I considered—I want to create a pleasure vis hub with Elaine. What do you—"

"Yes! Absolutely! That would be amazing. Elaine would love it. But do you think the leadership will let you?"

"Eddie had to break at least three laws just to save Ivan, and Elaine risked her life doing the same thing. So, I thought last night would be a good time to ask."

"You mean you already asked?" she squealed, unable to contain her excitement.

"Yes, and I've been cleared to do a hub tomorrow morning," he answered.

"I'm so jealous," Aggie said.

"Don't be. I'm inviting you and Eddie to join us."

"Are you kidding? Oh, thank you. I haven't been in a hub in almost two years. Oh, wait until I tell Eddie. Oh, thank you—Wait. What about—Are you sure?"

With the last question, she almost dropped Eddie's dinner giving Pax a hug.

"Of course. You are my and Elaine's best friend, and Eddie is already like a brother to me. We might as well let them experience it together. Besides," he added with a smile, "I have no secrets from you."

"Nor I from you," she conceded, proving once again that Indian skin could blush. "But I wouldn't assume the same thing with Eddie and Elaine. I accept your invitation and assume Eddie will, too, but I need to explain the ramifications to him first and let him decide."

"I'm sure you will explain everything properly, and I'm equally sure he will want to experience it. As the host, I will go over everything again tomorrow before I create the hub. Being Terra, I assume they will have a hard time comprehending a pleasure hub. Make sure he understands it's a subconscious exploration, not a night full of sex and partying."

"I will, but with Elaine's subconscious, are you sure I should make that promise?" she said with a smile before turning around and running toward the barn. "Thanks again. I can't wait."

Thursday morning, Eddie entered his parents' house through the tunnel door in their basement. After a quick breakfast, he and Aggie walked hand-in-hand to Pax's house, arriving ten minutes earlier than planned. They were greeted by an obviously thrilled Elaine, who escorted them to the living room and could barely contain her excitement as she offered them something to drink. Pax came out of the bedroom a couple of minutes later and moved an antique chair with hand-carved, wooden arms over to the sofa and loveseat to form a makeshift circle.

After adjusting his chair to ensure he could make eye contact with Aggie and Eddie sitting on the couch and Elaine sitting on the loveseat, he started his Terra explanation of a very Attal activity.

"I don't know, and I don't want to know all you've experienced in life, but if you continue forward with Aggie and me, I promise you an experience beyond your comprehension."

"I'm in," Eddie said.

"Satan himself couldn't make me say no," Elaine added.

"I doubt that's true, but you need to let me finish. This is an awesome experience and one I'm glad Ivan has agreed to let me share with you, but it has many side effects."

"You said it's safe," Elaine argued.

"I assume with this group we won't have any problems or I wouldn't have created it," Pax explained. "But let me get through everything, and then I will give you one more chance to ask questions. Once you are in the hub, anything can happen. Normal rules and laws don't exist, even the laws of physics."

"I've always thought of it as a dream, except you get to consciously control it and remember it when it's over," Aggie added.

"I would agree with Aggie, but add it is also being controlled by everyone else in the hub. So, it's more accurately like being transported to a fantasy land where the four of us can control everything, including things like the weather, the laws of physics, species roaming the streets, languages, and so on."

Elaine couldn't contain her excitement and sat on the edge of her seat, uncontrollably bouncing her leg as fast as humanly possible.

"But there are things I can't control," Pax said as he leaned forward and put his hand on her leg in a futile effort to calm her. "Just like when you are dreaming, all—and I want to stress *all*—of your thoughts, fantasies, fears, and secrets could possibly be revealed. This is why some Attal refuse this activity. Certainly, any Attal wishing to join the Seretus Ligare would never accept an invitation to a hub. If you dream about killing someone, we will all see you commit the murder. If you have a fantasy about running around naked, then, well—"

"Elaine, you gotta keep your pants on. I really don't want to see that much of you," Eddie interrupted, laughing at his own humor.

"No promises, Cubby," Elaine answered, unfazed. "I've said for years that you don't want to see what goes on inside my head. Well, here is your chance to back out."

"Oh, hell no," Eddie defiantly stated.

"This procedure is more bonding than any intimate act you've experienced as a Terra. Well, at least any Terra acts I've experienced. It also creates an unsurpassable utopian feeling. The biggest side effect is what the exposure can do to relationships, both romantic and platonic. For the duration of the hub, we will be in a semi-trance-like state where we will be physically unaware of our true surroundings. And, although it is biologically non-addicting, you will definitely want to spend more time in the hub, which is why they are illegal to create without leadership authorization."

It appeared the Whites were not taking his warnings seriously.

"I mean it, guys. Hubs like this have ruined lives and, one could argue, created revolutions. The good is great, but the bad can be devastating," Pax added for emphasis. "If you still want to experience it, why don't you go to the bathroom, get a drink of water, sit down, and relax. We will start in a few minutes. I need to inform Bill, so they can protect our bodies and give him the code for entering the hub."

"Is he going to join us?" Elaine asked.

"No, but even for an experienced host, it is very easy to lose track of time once inside. In case something happens in the real world or our allotted time is about to expire, he will send a predetermined image into the hub. As the host, I will recognize we are needed in the real world or that our connection will close in a little more than sixteen minutes. It is always preferred to ease out of the hub if possible."

"What kind of image?" Eddie asked.

"It can be anything, but one is instructed to pick something normal enough so it doesn't shock us back to reality, but unique enough to not be misunderstood."

"What did you choose?" Elaine asked.

"That's not important. You just enjoy the experience and leave the rules up to me."

After everyone agreed to continue, Pax explained how the process would begin.

"Here is what is going to happen. When my living room is filled with vis and I start the hub, you are going to feel warm, happy, and free, but very tired. Allow yourself to relax, and you will start a personal dream. After what seems like a few seconds or maybe an eternity, Aggie and I will enter your dream. We will use our experience to help bring your subconscious forward in an effort to increase your exploration, while hopefully keeping the hub platonic and moving along to maximize everyone's excitement."

He spoke to both of the Whites but held Elaine's hand and gazed into her eyes.

"You guys just enjoy it. We will guide you and keep you safe. Keep in mind, Aggie and I can't turn away from our true feelings either. You may not get what you expect, but you will get the truth. Now, close your eyes, relax, and enjoy the freedom of the hub."

.

Chapter XXXI

    Pax had not exaggerated. Elaine and Eddie felt as happy and as excited as children on Christmas morning, while concurrently experiencing warmth and relaxation. Within five minutes of starting the hub, both of the Whites started their dream and were totally unaware of their surroundings. Following Pax's directions, they allowed their deepest desires to come to the surface in hopes of freely expressing themselves. With Pax's guidance and an enormous consumption of vis, they were in a relaxed state that would have made even Sigmund Freud envious.

    While Pax and Aggie viewed the cooperative efforts of Eddie's and Elaine's dreams, Pax's living room started to change. A warm fog fell over the space, reminding Elaine of a steam room, yet without any moisture. When the fog cleared, the room had transformed into what appeared to be the owner's loge in a football stadium. The loge was decorated with leather furniture, a ten-foot-long buffet, and enough seating for approximately one hundred people.

After another fog cleared, Elaine stood in a room full of people, apparently attending a pre-event party. She wore a black dress and had tequila-sunrise hair that blended purple on the top through red and orange tones to its yellow ends. Along the far wall, guests were offered a complete open bar with two recognizable bartenders: Conan O'Brien and Ellen DeGeneres. Mixed in with Elaine's high school, beauty shop, and Moonlight Trail friends were many more famous people. Over by the buffet, Marshall Mathers (better known as Eminem) enjoyed some fancy appetizers and laughed with Kat Von D and Elizabeth Summers. At a stand-up bar, Elaine's high school friend Haley chatted with Joel Zimmerman, who was not as recognizable without his Deadmau5 head. Approaching her with their hands full of drinks were social media star Jenna Marbles and actor Charlie Hunnam, who handed her one of the glasses.

The whole room buzzed with activity, except for a guy on the black, leather couch against the wall in the corner, beside the buffet. Even though he appeared to be passed out, he did not draw any more attention from the crowd than the serving spoon in the clam dip. After what seemed like hours of laughing, drinking, and people thanking Elaine for the tremendous party, Jeremy Clarkson, a British star from the popular BBC show *Top Gear*, approached the hostess.

"Pardon the interruption," Clarkson said, "but I am here by invitation of Eddie White, yet I can't seem to find him. Am I at the right place? It wouldn't be the first time I crashed the wrong party."

"Yes, this the right place. Help yourself to a drink. When I see him, I'll let him know you are here."

All the commotion in the room created a white noise, allowing Eddie to fall into a deep sleep. Ironically, in a place that allowed for unbounded, creative thinking, his deepest desire was for stress-free sleep. While enjoying his peaceful slumber on the oversized, black, leather couch, Eddie dreamed he was a guest at Elaine's party, which created a second Eddie. This deeper subconscious version of Eddie was enjoying the chance for responsibility-free observation of Elaine's party while the first version remained asleep in the corner. He took an unofficial inventory of the celebrity guests while checking out how the "other half" lived, or at least how Elaine perceived them to live. He turned when he heard an agitated Elaine loudly disagreeing with someone behind him, someone who turned out to be Billy Joel.

"Why would I ask you to entertain at my party? No disrespect, Mr. Joel, but look at me. Do I look like your average fan? I mean, you're great and all, but your music really isn't my genre."

"All I know is I'm supposed to come here and play," Billy said.

"Yo, Billy. How 'bout I help out?" Eminem interrupted. "You hit the ivory, and I'll cover some classics—MM style. Do a little old school, free rapp'n."

Without waiting for an answer from Billy or Elaine, Eminem turned toward a high-top table on the other side of the loge.

"Hey, Dead, we need a beat."

Leaving the luxurious suite, the trio headed down to the field, where a stage had been set up on the home team's end zone, and played for a sold-out crowd. Their combined efforts resulted in an amazingly creative, somewhat enjoyable, extremely confusing genre of music. Deadmau5's EDM beat sped up Billy's normal tempo, but after cracking his knuckles and adjusting the bench, Billy started the long piano solo to "Prelude/Angry Young Man." He played so fast Eddie could barely see his fingers hit the keys on the jumbotron. Instead of Billy Joel singing, Eminem rapped an altered story.

After a couple of verses and without any forewarning, Eminem transitioned to an angry and bloody cover of AC/DC's "It's a Long Way to the Top (If You Wanna Rock 'n' Roll)." The seamless transition took everyone by surprise except Deadmau5, who easily kept up with the switch. After a few minutes, he tested the other musicians by switching the beat to an EDM remake of Meatloaf's "Bat Out of Hell." Just as the crowd seemed to recognize the vulgar, rocking, elecro-rap cover, Billy joined the game and changed the song.

The morphing of three so distinctly different genres, combined with continual, angry lyrics and constantly changing songs, gave Eddie quite a headache. After trying a couple of times to adjust to all the chaos, he sat down in one of the outside, padded seats and closed his eyes in an effort to ignore the music and clear his head. After falling asleep, he dreamt a third, deeper version of his subconscious returned to the loge and realized Elaine had apparently also been bothered by the concert, because she had changed the scene dramatically.

Although the room and set-up were the same and the trio continued to play their improvised music outside, someone had lowered the volume to less than half of its earlier level. The crowd had dwindled to only about a dozen guests, who were all young men in their mid-twenties.

They stood in a semi-circle around Elaine and argued with her in different languages. It appeared the group had two things in common: They were all upset at Elaine, and they were all ex-boyfriends. Most of them were yelling over top of each other, and the others seemed to be on the verge of violence.

Eddie watched as, unable to handle the chaos, Elaine tried to quiet them one at a time, her efforts doing nothing for his worsening headache. Without warning, Deadmau5 changed the beat to a house version of Steppenwolf's "Born to Be Wild." Hearing Eminem's angry rap and his sister's fruitless battle with her exes, Eddie needed a break and turned to check on the sleeping version of himself on the black couch.

The sight froze him in place. Pulling on his right arm, as hard as his sixty-year-old body would allow, stood a fire chief in his blue, work uniform. He lectured about safety first.

"You need to avoid trouble and come with me."

Pulling harder on his left arm, Eddie saw one of the toughest people he had ever seen. The Navy Seal, dressed in fatigues and black combat boots, also yelled commands at Eddie.

"Forget these pansies and get your ass in line, soldier!"

Pulling on each leg and apparently not as comfortable with physical labor, were engineers in white lab coats. They had united their efforts and told him confidently that they could help him create a tool to get him out of any situation.

Eddie ran to the tormented, unconscious version of himself on the couch. Holding his head in pain, he tried desperately to convince the demanding group to calm down and begged them to leave him alone.

In the midst of his struggles to stop the fighting over his sleeping body, or more accurately his mind, he heard a familiar voice behind him.

"Hey, Link," Aggie said, showing neither surprise nor excitement at the scene.

She kissed him on the cheek and continued, "I see why you struggle to sleep. How could you not be angry all the time with those assholes yelling at you all day?"

"The music dulls the fighting," Eddie said, trying to defend his lack of success in controlling his own mind.

"This is going to stop right now."

As she approached him, Eddie noticed she was not dressed for the party. She wore a pair of jeans and a button-up, striped blouse over a yellow tank top. Her ankle-high, brown, leather boots clicked on the hardwood floor as she made her way to the couch. When she got within a few feet of it, she stopped and closed her eyes in concentration. A couple of seconds later, she opened them and addressed the characters pulling on her boyfriend.

"Hi, boys. I'm a friend of Eddie's. This wonderful new feeling I'm sharing with you is what happens to people who cause him pain."

The result could not have been any more immediate. All four of the men pulling on the sleeping Eddie grabbed a bucket that had appeared at their feet and started to violently vomit. The fire chief took his own pulse, and the soldier pulled his sidearm, but neither could stop the sick from flowing uncontrollably.

"Now, here's what we are going to do," Aggie instructed. "Firefighter, you are going to take a back seat. Eddie has me to monitor his health. He will call on you if he or someone else is hurt. Right now, you are killing him with stress and sleep deprivation. Is that good, medical practice?"

Eddie noticed she did not wait for a response before addressing the engineers pulling on his feet.

"When he is working in the lab or needs to modify something, please assist his logic, but you need to let him make mistakes in everyday life. It's humbling, not to mention kind of fun, to be wrong every now and then. And, sir," she said, addressing the soldier, "you've got to ease up. Not everything is a death-defying adventure. When things get a little dicey, Eddie will need you to jump in and help, but he's a good man—he needs to call the shots. And by the way, thanks for the music, but really, man, bring it down a notch or two. Lastly, and most importantly, all of you need to leave his subconscious alone when he is trying to sleep. Do I make myself clear?"

Three of them started to complain at the same time.

"Yea, but there is no way he—" the soldier started to yell.

"But you don't understand. He has—" an engineer protested.

"That sounds good, but how can he—" the fire chief interrupted.

Aggie closed her eyes again, and they all hit the floor and held their heads, pained expressions on their faces. They broke into a cold sweat and grabbed their hearts in a pointless effort to slow them down.

"I can't believe I didn't make myself clear," Aggie yelled. "I wasn't giving you a suggestion. I've learned how to cordon off sections of the brain and move memories. If you don't learn to get along, I'll put you behind so many damn firewalls you will never see conscious brain activity again. Either figure it out, or I'll kill you. Is that clearer?"

She gently addressed the version of Eddie standing beside the couch.

"Retrieve the other dream Eddies that created you, take these guys somewhere in your subconscious, and explain to them what your needs are and when you want help. I'm going to wash up. When I return, I better find him—" She pointed to the Eddie lying on the couch. "—sleeping peacefully."

A casually dressed Aggie came out of the bathroom, wearing just her yellow tank top and a pair of jeans. While she had been cleaning up in the bathroom, the Eddie from the couch woke up with the quietest mind he had experienced in a long time. Realizing restful sleep was now obtainable, all of the versions of him came together to create a much happier Eddie.

"Thank you, *so much*," he said to Aggie, unable to stress just how much he appreciated the peace and quiet he felt in his mind.

"Anything for my juke box hero," she responded with a gentle caress to his right cheek. "Why don't you lie down and take a proper nap? After you are rested, we'll have a little fun."

"Rested—what is that?" Eddie joked.

She guided him back to the couch, sat down, and allowed him to use her lap as a pillow while she caressed his forehead and ran her fingers through his hair. He concentrated on the words Heart sang about a dream world he did not fear for the first time in months.

He was almost asleep when he asked, "What happened to your boots and shirt? And I'm not complaining, but where's your bra?"

"How would I know?" Aggie answered. "This is the outfit you imagined. Although not what I would have picked, I decided to keep it on for you. Now, go to sleep, Link."

"Well, I did a great job," he complimented himself right before he fell asleep.

Sitting on the couch with Eddie peacefully using her lap for a pillow, Aggie watched Elaine work through her problems on the other side of the loge.

Elaine continually lost ground in her attempt to keep any sense of order. Her dozen ex-boyfriends would not listen to a word she said. They were firing questions at her faster than she could comprehend.

She sat down, put her head in her lap, and yelled to no one, "It's not my fault. I didn't ask for all of this."

She started to cry and said to herself, "I would've stayed with any of you if you were just more like—just a little more—"

Elaine's efforts to explain her actions were interrupted by a warm, gentle breeze blowing in another blinding fog. She opened her tear-filled eyes and stared into the haze.

"It's okay, Lainey," she heard her mother's voice from behind her.

"Mommy?" Elaine asked, even though she hadn't called Maria that in almost twenty years.

"The puff balls won't hurt you," a younger, less-lined, and too thin Maria said to her crying little girl.

Even though Elaine knew she had entered the hub as a 23-year-old, she couldn't help but continue the scene as the three-year-old, curly-haired Lainey. The fog cleared and revealed a playground twenty yards away. The traditional sliding boards, swings, and monkey bars were overshadowed by the twenty kittens that used the area as their personal playground.

"I want a kitten, Mommy."

"Then go get them, honey," Maria said, digging in her purse.

"No, Mommy. Puffs..." the three-year-old said, pointing at the twenty-yard lawn filled with dandelions gone to seed, one of the little girl's fears.

Elaine stretched up her hands, and Maria picked her up and placed her daughter on her lap.

"It's okay. I brought your socks, honey."

Although her socks helped, Elaine stood frozen on the sidewalk and contemplated whether the protective value of the socks would be enough for such a large field of puff balls. As she did, a blond, seven-year-old boy appeared out of nowhere. He crouched in the grass in front of Elaine.

"Hop on. I'll give you a piggy-back ride over to the playground."

Elaine and the helpful, blond boy laughed and played with the kittens for what felt like hours. She went down the yellow, corkscrew slide with a kitten in each arm, but by the time her feet touched the ground, a warm fog had covered the playground. She was not scared, but looked back for her mother when she heard her speaking from behind.

"Lainey, you will be fine. Just wear your headphones or talk to someone. Maybe make a new friend."

When the fog cleared, an eleven-year-old girl stood on the sidewalk with Maria as a yellow school bus turned the corner. A familiar argument played out between Elaine and her mother.

"I'm not a baby. Quit calling me Lainey. I need to pee. Can you wait for me to go the bathroom and drive me to school?" she pleaded.

"You just went, Elaine," Maria reminded her, gently but firmly. "You will be fine, honey. I'll see you right here after school."

"But, mom—"

"Listen to your headphones. If you are lonely or scared, look out the window, honey. That always helps you."

She reluctantly got on the bus, but could not find a window seat. A boy who looked big enough to be a freshman saw her struggling and seemed to somehow understand her dilemma.

"Would you like a seat by the window? You can sit with me."

"Okay," she said as she waited for him to stand up and scooted in toward the window. "Thanks. Do I know you?"

"I don't think so," he answered.

"What's your name?" Elaine asked.

"My name is Pax. It's Roman for 'peace,'" he said, quickly adding the explanation for his unusual name.

"What's Roman?" the young Elaine asked, thinking being called Pax could not be as bad as being called Lainey.

He gave a fifth-grade summary of where Italy was and promised to save her a window seat again tomorrow.

Staring out the window, she blushed slightly as she proclaimed to her new friend, "Well, I like the name Pax."

She pressed play on her CD player and for some reason did not think it odd at all when the slow, romantic song "These Dreams" by Heart came out of the headphones.

As the bus drove through the underpass of the expressway, a rolling fog enveloped it. Once the fog lifted, Elaine realized she was now the only passenger. She looked out of the window and did not recognize her surroundings. Still, she obeyed the friendly bus driver, who pulled over, stopped the bus, and opened the door.

"Here we are, honey. He's waiting for you in the owner's loge."

The blue-and-green-haired, 23-year-old Elaine had exited the bus when the driver stopped her.

"Don't forget this," he said as he handed her a fishing pole.

When the elevator opened, she entered the owner's loge where her dream had started. "These Dreams" played as she entered the room and saw Aggie in her yellow T-shirt and jeans, smiling and waving to her with Eddie asleep on her lap. She continued toward the door leading to the outside seating area of the stadium. With the concert over, the stadium was completely empty—kind of. It had filled with water, all the way to the upper deck.

Gary sat in the owner's seat, smoking a cigar and casting his line into the new pond. Elaine sat down beside him.

"Hey, Dad."

After a short pause, she asked, "Here's a question I thought I'd never have to ask: What are you doing fishing in a football stadium?"

"I find fishing helps me think," Gary answered and chuckled. "I have no idea why I'm doing it here, but when I feel overwhelmed, it is usually a good idea to slow down and take some time to think."

Elaine helped herself to a worm in the blue, plastic container at Gary's feet and baited her hook.

"That's all I do is think," Elaine countered. "There's no more room up there."

"You can't think too much."

He cast his line back into the stadium-pond.

"But you can *worry* too much, and you are very good at worrying," he said as he took a puff on his cigar and watched the smoke disappear in the breeze. "There's beer in the cooler."

After about a half hour of fishing, Elaine said, "You know, sometimes I just wish I didn't know what I know. I never wanted to save people. I just wanted to color and cut their hair."

"Because you didn't know then what you know now. When you were three, you didn't even know how to read and write, and you were convinced dandelions were part of an evil plot to rid the world of little kids."

"Yes, but my brain wasn't developed then. Everything scared me, except you and Mom."

"And we are at a similar point with our knowledge of the Attal," Gary pointed out. "Once we are more familiar with their culture, things will get much easier for you. I'm sorry you and Eddie got roped in when you were so young, but it couldn't be helped. What could I do? I couldn't stand by and not help Bill and Pax?"

"Of course not. But I'm not sure I'm ready to save the world," Elaine admitted.

"Me either," Gary agreed as he paused to cast his line into the pond again. "But someone has to catch these assholes. Besides, I'd rather die trying than be an unwitting victim of one of their Seretus games."

"I guess," she conceded. "But I'm not in a big hurry to die saving anyone."

"The puff balls won't get you, honey. Just wear your socks," Gary chuckled out loud.

"What?"

"You are surrounded by people who love and want to protect you," Gary offered.

"I do like some of those people," she said, unable to contain her smile.

"Really? I hadn't noticed," he kidded. "Besides the big, goofy guy, there are a lot of people watching your back who love you very much. In a couple of months, I think this will all be behind us. Then we'll have all the time in the world to fish."

"In a football stadium?"

"I wondered the same thing," he said, puffing on his cigar. "I'm just glad you included me. It's nice to have a little alone time with you. It's been too long."

After two beers and an hour and a half of fishing, Elaine asked, "So…um…what're your thoughts about…um…me and Pax."

"I think you're a short, colorful, very loud girl with a huge heart. Pax—he's a tall guy with an enormous brain who is kinda awkward in Terra social situations."

"You can't make anything easy, can you?" Elaine asked. "What do you think about us as a couple?"

"It doesn't matter what I think. What do *you* think?"

"I love being with him. He makes me happy, and I feel safe by his side."

Gary said nothing for a couple of minutes. He reeled his rod in, placed it on the chair beside him, and stood up.

"It's time for me to go check on your mom. Give your dad a hug."

During their long hug, Gary spoke just over a whisper.

"You've always been unique, honey. If you want long-lasting happiness, find someone who wants to be your friend first and your lover second. Find someone who loves you for your uniqueness, not someone hoping to change it. Speaking of unique," he chuckled and broke off their hug, "both of my kids are dating aliens."

His chuckle grew into a laugh, and he walked away with one last word of advice.

"No matter what happens, two things will remain constant. Your mother and I will love you unconditionally, and you are going to have tough decisions to make throughout your life."

Elaine turned toward her fleeting dad.

"What's that supposed to mean?"

"It means you need more fishin'."

Chapter XXXII

  Elaine continued fishing for another hour, during which time she enjoyed the most worry-free period of self-reflection she had ever experienced. She placed her pole beside her dad's and headed back to the loge. When she entered, Pax sat at a high-top table in an empty room, except for Aggie and the sleeping Eddie.
  "Hey. Whatcha doin'?" she asked, seeing Pax smile at her.
  "Technically, I'm watching Eddie sleep and you fish," he answered. "But actually, I wanted to wait for you two to experience the hub and learn how to use the freedom inside before I joined you."
  "It's been pretty weird and kinda helpful, but—Well, I— I just—Oh, never mind."
  "What's wrong?" he asked, inviting her to sit down by patting the seat next to him.

"I wish you wouldn't have let me waste hours just reliving my nightmares and fishing with Dad. It's really cool how things keep changing, and I feel much better about—Well, I've worked a few things out up here," she said, pointing to her temple. "But I'd hoped for some special time with you."

"Many times, especially for beginners, one has to work through some issues before they are free to explore their subconscious."

"I guess that makes sense," she conceded after a few moments of thought. "I just wish Eddie and I didn't spend most of our time sleeping and fishing. I mean, I'm sure you didn't go to all this trouble just to watch me fish."

"I wanted to get to know you better, learn how to help you, and bond with you. It has been intimate and quality time for me. It sounds like you are nervous about wasting the day. How long do you think you've been in the hub?"

"I'm not sure, but I went to the crazy party, the weird concert, the awful fight, plus a couple of childhood memories," she said, turning away from Pax. "Then fishing with Dad and now talking to you. I'd say eight to ten hours. Since we are in a hub, I'd guess about an hour—maybe two?"

"Elaine," he said with a chuckle and then kissed her cheek. "You're so cute. I'd gladly sit and watch you fish for days if it made you feel better, but you've only been in the hub for seven minutes."

"What?"

"Pretty cool, huh?"

Just then, Eddie and Aggie came over, hand-in-hand, and joined the conversation.

"God, I haven't felt this good in a long time," Eddie said. "I can't remember the last time I slept for eight hours straight."

Pax and Elaine looked at each other and started laughing loudly.

"What?"

"Nothing, Cubby," Elaine said, her speech disrupted by laughter. "You just need to learn the reality of the hu—hub."

"What do you say we stop wasting all this good vis and show them a thing or two," Aggie suggested.

The song "These Dreams" stopped playing in the background and the music switched to the electronic, upbeat "Sweet Dreams (Are Made of This)" by Eurythmics. Aggie bounced back and forth to the beat, unable to control her enthusiasm about the remainder of the hub.

Pax took control of the group by explaining, "In the hub, we can and will experience different things simultaneously, like Eddie's nap while Elaine traveled through time. But the hub will break up, limiting our time, if we venture too far away from each other during our stay. In an effort to maximize the experience for you both, I'm going to alternate whose dream path we follow. Try and stay close to the team controlling the dream. Understand?"

"What about your and Aggie's dreams?" Elaine asked. "I want to experience them, too."

"Thank you," Pax said, squeezing her hand. "Aggie and I have already achieved our main goal by sharing the hub with you and helping each of you with some internal issues. In time, our dreams and thoughts will become clear. Now, the party and the majority of its guest belonged to Elaine, so we will start the fun with you, Eddie. Elaine and I are going to enjoy a romantic, hot air balloon ride to Pittsburgh International Airport. Let's see if you are as good as you think you are. Think you can get there before us?"

Pax took Elaine's hand and escorted her to the football field that had been drained of water and to the beautiful hot air balloon in the shape of a smiling, black cat. As they walked down toward center field, the music played over the stadium PA system and became louder.

The couples' trips to Pittsburgh could not have been any different. Elaine and Pax barely had enough room in their balloon basket, due to the packed lunch, portable speakers, warm blankets, and two tiger cubs. After exhausting the cubs, Elaine backed into Pax's waiting arms, swayed to the music, sipped champagne, and surveyed the land below in search of Eddie.

"Is this more what you had in mind?" Pax whispered in her ear.

According to Aggie's estimate, Eddie's Bugatti had finally pulled ahead of the huge cat-balloon they were chasing. Once he made it to the expressway, the advantage of the car of his dreams became apparent. At two hundred miles an hour, he passed cars as if they were standing still and made great time, until he noticed the police roadblock ahead, no doubt Pax's attempt to ruin his chances of winning the race. Eddie summoned the soldier from his subconscious.

"You better hold on to something. This is gonna get dicey," he said to Aggie.

Slamming on the brakes, he slid through the berm and median sideways at well over one hundred miles an hour. They kicked up a cloud of dust, dirt, rubber, and smoke large enough to fill the stadium they had just left. The radio that had been singing about a dream world changed to Foreigner's familiar song about a young, juke box hero who would keep on rocking and never stop.

"Aw, you're playing our song," Aggie said as she looked over to Eddie, who raised his eyebrows and gave her a look that should have warned her about her near future.

Eddie slid more than two hundred yards before he regained control, made a U-turn, and punched the accelerator, driving through the clouds the skidding Bugatti had just created. Coming out of the dust, Eddie sped the other way on the expressway on a Ducati motorcycle with Aggie in a black, leather jacket sitting behind him and holding on to his waist.

"I love this hub thing!" he shouted over the music coming from their helmets.

Eddie avoided the police, but out of necessity ended up traveling in an indirect path on side streets with too many turns. Despite the amazing maneuverability and acceleration of the Ducati, he lost ground. As he and Aggie turned the corner, they could see the airport about a mile away. The hot air balloon floated gently over the runway, more than two hundred feet in the air. Aggie pointed it out, somewhat dismayed, but Eddie dismissed Pax's advantage.

"Yea, but he still has to land the thing," he said.

"You're thinking like a Terra," Aggie informed him, and then pointed up the road. "See the hill there?"

"Yea?" Eddie said, not understanding her plan.

"Hit it with everything you've got and hold my hand."

"Are you sure?" he asked.

Instead of a yes or no answer, she summarized the message of the music streaming into her helmet, "You gotta rock it all the way to the top."

Eddie hit the bank at 167 mph, and they both went airborne. Aggie grabbed his outstretched hand. With her leading the way, they flew the last mile to the airport and landed three seconds before Pax and Elaine, who had jumped out of the basket. Elaine and Eddie's adrenaline had them yelling at each other about what they just done.

"Holy shit," Eddie screamed. "Did you see that? We flew here!"

"We just jumped from two hundred feet. No parachute. We just jumped!" she countered.

"Did I mention we flew here?" he yelled.

In what should have taken the better part of a week in real time, they continued their bonding adventure. They ate lunch in Italy, swam with whales in Alaska, explored an Egyptian tomb, and floated down the Nile. Their outfits, the weather, and the languages changed as needed, and every thought materialized in front of them. After a sushi dinner in Japan, everyone got ready for another of Eddie's dreams.

Much to Aggie's liking, Pax and Elaine opted to stay in Chamonix's warm, exclusive lodge instead of snowboarding down Mont Blanc in the French Alps. Eddie and Aggie cuddled in the enclosed ski lift while traveling to the top of the picturesque mountain, and on their second trip, opened their minds to each other completely in the intimate Attal tradition of mind-sharing. They boarded down the Alps three times, becoming lost each time and resting on a private cliff or among the evergreens for what quickly became Aggie's favorite part of snowboarding. After a while, they took a break and sat on a bench in a café just on the low side of the tree line, sipping on hot chocolate.

They were discussing taking Aggie snowboarding sometime without the assistance of a physics-free hub, when a midget walked up to her and asked in perfect English, "Pardon me, but would you happen to have the time?"

Sitting by the antique, brick fireplace in a large, overstuffed chair, Elaine and Pax sipped warm brandy and basked in the warmth of the amazingly intimate mind-share they had just experienced. Pax wiped a tear from her smiling face as he contemplated his next move.

His thoughts were interrupted by a midget, who approached the couple and asked in perfect English, "Pardon me, but would you happen to have the time?"

Both Aggie and Pax knew they had just received Bill's warning. Aggie gave Eddie a big public display of affection.

"Last time down, Cubby. That was Bill's signal," she announced.

Bill's timing certainly perturbed Pax. He stood up and took Elaine's hand.

"Bill just signaled us. We have to head home soon."

"I hoped this day would never end, but I knew it had to," Elaine responded. "This has been amazing. A little funky—but amazing."

"I agree. It's been an almost perfect day and by far my best hub," Pax said. "I had hoped to make it even better."

"I can't imagine that's possible, but let's make that our goal for our next hub," she suggested.

He grabbed her other hand, looked deep into her hazel-green eyes, and said, "No, it needs to be this one. I don't know if you are becoming more Attal or I am becoming more Terra, but my already wonderful existence would be perfect if you would honor me by being the first of hopefully many who choose to be a mixed-species couple."

"What?" she asked, a little confused. "I thought we sorta already were a couple."

"What I had in mind is something a little more permanent. We've just experienced the most intimate thing my culture offers. I hoped to join you in one of your culture's intimate rituals."

"You want to have sex?" Elaine asked. "Definitely…but not in here. Not with Eddie flying around."

"No. Well, yes, but—um—no—Oh, my," Pax finally said. "I practiced this thousands of times in my head, and I couldn't even get it right in the hub."

"Get what right?" Elaine asked, showing a little frustration.

"Try getting on one knee, you big goof," Eddie said from behind him.

"Of course," Pax said, more to himself then to anyone else. "I was so nervous I forgot the most important part."

Holding both of Elaine's hands, he knelt on one knee and looked up at her.

"Elaine, would you do me the honor of being my wife?"

"Oh, my god!" Aggie squealed in delight.

"Atta boy. Now, was that so hard?" Eddie added.

The accolades from behind proved he had at least got his message right this time. Staring at the most uniquely wonderful person he had ever met, he waited for what felt like an eternity for an answer. Elaine did not speak for fifteen seconds, but a tear traced down her cheek.

Trying to look as good as she could with water-filled eyes, she said, "You are the reason I have been unhappy with all of my boyfriends."

She saw the confused look on Pax's face and realized she was not being clear.

"I've been waiting for you, because you are perfect for me."

Elaine closed her eyes and shook her head, causing her hair to turn into Pax's favorite color, fire-engine red. She could not contain herself any longer and lunged at Pax in an enthusiastic hug. Since he balanced on one knee, the force of her move knocked him to the expensive area rug, and she lay on top of him as they celebrated their engagement. After watching them kissing for ten seconds, Eddie had had enough.

"If I have to watch any more of this, your special moment is going to be ruined. I may throw up on you two."

Elaine ended their kiss and whispered in Pax's ear, "You've just made the hub so much better."

As soon as she stood up, Aggie almost knocked her back over with one of her own eager hugs.

"If we weren't in a hub, my face would be sore from smiling so much today," Aggie stated.

As the two couples walked out of the lodge, they were greeted by a warm fog. After the mist cleared, they boarded the Pride's Gulfstream waiting for them. Without conversation, Eddie and Aggie headed toward the cockpit while Pax and Elaine shared more physically intimate time on one of the leather couches.

Eddie patted Aggie on the bottom on her way to the cockpit and asked, "Since we are in the hub, do you want to fly 'er home?"

"No. I like you taking care of me," she answered.

Eddie unnecessarily pressed a couple of buttons and the Gulfstream started up as the Steve Miller Band started singing "Jet Airliner" over the speakers. Eddie looked over at Aggie, who smiled at him with a love-dazed expression on her face.

"Always, Link."

Chapter XXXIII

 Elaine and Eddie woke up on Pax's couch, extremely relaxed, yet excited and totally infatuated with the hub. Wondering when they would be permitted another trip into the hub and if they would remember the "ultimate high" they had experienced were just two of the many questions they asked, faster than a kindergartener waiting for his first day of school. After Pax and Aggie answered all of their questions, the two Attal both professed this had been their best hub experience ever. Eddie and Elaine easily understood Pax's earlier warning about the problems the Attal had faced in the past with people attempting to never leave the hub.

 "Between the binge-and-pukes, instant transports, and now the hub, I can see why you searched for other planets to manufacture more vis," Eddie admitted. "I've experienced it less than a year, and I'm already sold on its merits."

"The discovery of vis is what has allowed the growth and success of our people, but it hasn't always been peaceful growth," Pax said.

"I bet not," Eddie agreed. "I'd fight for more—"

"Before we digress back to discussing politics or the rogue fugitives we are chasing, I still have a little hub business to finish," Pax interrupted Eddie.

Turning to Elaine, he admitted, "I took advantage of the utopian sense inside the hub to ask you a life-changing question. Now that you are not under the influence of vis, do you still wish to honor me with your hand in marriage?"

"More than I have ever wanted anything in my life," she answered.

"Then do me one more honor, please?" Pax requested. "With the approval of Ivan and your dad, I thought it appropriately symbolic to commandeer these from our latest mission to cripple the Seretus. Would you please wear this?"

From an antique end table, he retrieved a ring box and opened it. Kneeling on his right knee, he presented her with an emerald-cut, two-carat, black diamond in a platinum band with smaller, black diamonds channel-set around the entire band.

"Classic black and stolen with love while saving the world. How did you ever guess?" she asked, before forcing Eddie and Aggie out of the house by aggressively and shamelessly hugging and kissing her fiancé.

Although they could never match the high experienced in the hub, the two young couples' excitement and recollection of their events were improving the moods of almost everyone at the property. Gary knew Maria had anticipated Elaine's announcement longer than anyone, but he had difficulty choosing who was more excited between Maria and Bill. After the third comment on how his son was the first Attal who chose to partake in the ultimate Terra ritual, Gary had to give the edge to Bill.

Eddie stayed up all night working in his lab on Thursday, but for the first time since his binge-and-puke, he stayed up due to excitement and a desire to finish his project not out of fear of his subconscious. With the much-appreciated assistance from Aggie, he finally had control of all the experts Bill had downloaded in his brain. Due to his increased focus and separation of duties, the engineers inside his mind were making changes at twice the normal speed. He concentrated so hard as he almost cleared what he thought would be the last hurdle to his latest invention, he again became startled in the middle of the night when Pax appeared.

"Really?" Eddie asked after jumping an inch off the ground and gasping for air. "I thought that after our time in the hub and you being family, this might stop."

"Apparently not," Pax answered with a smile. Looking over Eddie's shoulder, he asked, "Do I want to know what your project is?"

"Not if you want plausible deniability," Eddie answered with no apologies.

"Are you ever going to learn to follow our rules?" Pax asked half-sarcastically, but certainly concerned.

"Apparently not," Eddie answered, covering up his latest invention.

Friday morning during breakfast, Bill announced he and Ivan had agreed, due to the financial and emotional crippling of the Seretus, they needed to attack soon before Juanita and Carlos separated and disappeared. He told the Pride they would depart on Monday, as he still needed some last-minute information. He requested a noon meeting with Eddie and Pax to go over recent activity at the Brazilian compound and their inability to monitor the inside of the main house. He informed everyone there would be a full Pride meeting at three o'clock. Although Elaine was appropriately nervous after hearing about the upcoming mission, she seemed more relaxed and controlled following her time in the hub.

Gary sat on the porch, contemplating the upcoming mission over his second cup of coffee, when Elaine came to the back door with a thermos, tackle box, and two fishing poles.

"Come on, Dad. Let's see if our alien friends were smart enough to stock the pond."

"You're not going to ruin a good test of our pond as an excuse to reveal some problem or talk about wedding plans are you? Gary asked.

"No way. I just thought we could have a cup of coffee and waste a couple hours." Elaine answered.

"Never a waste. I'm in," Gary said.

Thankfully, and not surprisingly, Bill and AJ had not overlooked this detail of the property. Elaine caught and released her second fish (or maybe the same fish twice), recast her newly baited hook, and said something Gary had always considered an urban legend told by other parents.

"Thanks, Dad."

"You're welcome," he replied, pausing long enough to cast, "but thanks for what?"

"For including me in all this bullshit, for loving mom, and for being a pain in the ass. Basically—well, thanks for—Just, thanks," she summarized with a smile.

"You are most welcome, but I can't—"

The interruption came from an uncharacteristically anxious Bill in all of the Pride's minds simultaneously.

"Everyone to the station. Now."

Gary and Elaine dropped their poles and ran to the barn. They arrived two minutes before an out-of-breath Maria, who came in last.

"Sorry. You caught me in the shower," she said, water dripping from her hair as she sat down beside Gary.

"We have a horrible situation requiring immediate action," Bill stated. "We now know how the Seretus planned to acquire their much-needed vis—and it's horrible. No, it's deplorable. The means they used to acquire enough vis to enable their disappearance is indefensible. We thought they might use an insider to steal some of our reserve or maybe attack a transport station. Instead, they have systematically and concurrently attacked Kuds and stolen their storage watches. Of the 145 members of the Attal carrying a reserve of vis on the surface, ninety-two were attacked; and of those, forty-one are dead."

"The bastards pulled them from their taxis and their classrooms. They surprised them at work and at home. These Kuds would have peacefully handed over their watches…" Bill trailed off in rare moment of speechlessness.

After approximately two minutes, Bill announced, "This mass killing, combined with the DEA bombings and a few other documented deaths, brings the Seretus Ligare's recent actions to a total of more than 140 Attal and Terra. The need for swift action from both of our worlds has never been greater. Even though we could use some time to mourn our losses and reflect on our next move, we need to confront and apprehend the Seretus before all the vis they brutally acquired is delivered to them and they disappear again, ensuring another bloody campaign in the future."

Gary, Bill, and all of the women were wiping tears from their eyes when Eddie suggested, "This may sound a little un-Attal, but we know where they are. Why not just bomb the shit out of the compound and then go clean up the mess?"

"I'm embarrassed to admit I have considered that scenario already," Bill said. "But we couldn't be sure a bombing would kill both Juanita and Carlos, And we must avoid any unnecessary, further harm to the Terra. Additionally, it would be extremely advantageous to complete a mind sweep with the stronger, homeland vis before either of their minds were damaged. This would allow us to ensure no factions of their secret society remain."

After twenty minutes of questions and answers, Bill concluded, "Thank you all for your input. We leave for South America in three hours. Robert, please make sure the Gulfstream is ready to go. Although I doubt the Seretus has any knowledge of this property or the Pride's involvement, it would be a logical precaution if the flight plan to Mato Grosso didn't exist."

As everyone started to leave the room, Eddie realized his protest and multiple requests to accompany the Pride to South America would not be granted.

He said to Aggie telepathically, *"Please stay after everyone leaves."*

She nodded to him before approaching Elaine with a question on her way out of the room.

Bill approached him before leaving to prepare for the mission. Putting a hand on both of his shoulders, he looked Eddie in the eye and softly stated, "I would love to have you on this mission, Cubby, but it's not my call. Only Ivan can reverse his original ruling. Please understand."

"I do, Bill," he responded. "Where is Ivan?"

"As you can imagine, he has a crisis on the Pacific station. He has called all remaining Kuds home. He has to deal with our bloodiest day in centuries."

"Take care of everyone, Bill, and bring them all home safe."

"Besides stopping the Seretus, that's my top goal," Bill responded before clasping his hands and bowing to Eddie with his head tilted slightly to the right.

After Bill left the room, Eddie took Aggie's hand and said telepathically, *"I need some help. Come with me, please."*

"Link, you know I love you," Aggie responded. *"But I can't help you with Ivan. Respecting his command is one of our top laws."*

"I know, but I need a favor before you leave," Eddie said.

"You know I can tell when a Terra is lying, right? Especially the one's I'm linked to," she said as she walked past him.

****

The team spent the next hour in a flurry of activity and private conversations. Elaine gave a condensed update of the situation to Lizzy before packing her travel bag and returning to the Den for a private meeting with Bill.

"Are you sure you don't need to listen to their voices again?" Bill asked, making sure she could correctly mimic the voices perfectly.

"You've already played the recording three times. Their mothers wouldn't be able to tell the difference," Elaine responded and then smiled. "I'll make three copies. Use whichever one you like best, but they will all be spot on."

****

After some help from Aggie and some specific instructions to Jeff, Eddie anxiously ended his meeting with Ivan, who had already had a meeting with Pax, a debriefing from his assistant at the Pacific station, and a hurried talk with Lucy to cancel their weekly dinner date.

"Trust me. I understand and I'll be ready." Eddie repeated, slightly louder the second time. "But I really need to see Dad before he leaves."

"Why?" Ivan asked. "This doesn't concern him."

"I've made a few updates to Casper's costume," Eddie answered with raised eyebrows and a proud, yet devious, closed-mouth smile. "I need to get it to him and test it before he leaves."

"Your advances have been impressive the last few days," Ivan admitted. "Even by Attal standards."

"Gee, thanks, I guess," Eddie said, obviously insulted. He stood up and started to leave the room.

"One more thing," Ivan said to Eddie's back as he exited the room. "I would prefer if this conv—"

"I know. I know," he interrupted without stopping or looking back.

A few minutes later, Eddie and Gary met in the barn. After a brief explanation, they were walking down the path toward the main house.

"Are you sure this is going to work?" Gary asked.

"I'm not sure," Eddie admitted. *"I didn't have time for proper tests. Most importantly, I need to make sure the invisibility still works before you leave."*

Lucy greeted him at the back door and asked, "What's going on, Eddie?"

"What do you mean, Mema?" he answered, using his and Elaine's chosen name for their grandmother.

"Elaine just came in, just to give me a hug, Ivan cancelled our dinner plans, and your mom and dad were here earlier telling me they love me," she reported.

"All I know is Bill and Ivan's company has a big problem and the family is all going to South America to help. Well, not all of us. They won't let me go with them," he answered honestly. "Speaking of Mom and Dad, do you know where they are? I have to give Dad something before they leave for their big meeting."

Proving Eddie's adjustments had not altered his dad's cloaking abilities, she answered, "I haven't seen them in about half an hour. Last I heard, they were heading to the basement for something. It looks like we are both going to be left without dinner plans. Do you want to join me?"

"Sorry, Mema, I have plans. But soon," he promised as he hurried down the steps to the basement with an invisible Gary close behind him.

Gary gave his son a hug as they parted ways.

"Thanks, Eddie. I'm sorry you can't come with us."

"Me, too. Just bring everyone home safe."

As they broke their embrace and headed in different directions, Eddie turned and reminded his dad, "Don't forget to put the new Frick I gave you under one of the seats on the plane. It's *vita*l to our plan."

Gary chuckled at Eddie's choice of words and hustled down the tunnel toward the barn.

Aggie, who had received last-minute, telepathic advice and goodbyes from Eddie, arrived to the Den last.

"I promise," she repeated. *"I'll store and block our link as soon as the Gulfstream takes off. You're going to keep the link primary, though, right?"*

"Of course. I had you section off a part of my brain for something else," Eddie reassured her. *"If you need me, call, but I need you to focus and concentrate. Shut me out and come back safe—please."*

"I will, but I still wish you were here to say goodbye," Aggie said, wiping a tear from under her eye.

"Me, too, but I have a couple more things to set up for your mission. Let me know when you are on the plane, Link, and be careful."

Not knowing how to respond, she chose not to. She concentrated on how she would say goodbye on the plane before closing off their connection, when she realized she had just proved his point by only catching the very end of Maria's conversation with Bill.

"I'm just not sure I trust him," she said barely over a whisper. "I know I shouldn't eavesdrop, but I keep hearing things I can't make sense of."

"If you are talking about Robert," Aggie interrupted, "he has been dishonest recently. I get the feeling he is hiding something, but I contributed to his uncomfortableness with Eddie and me."

"I appreciate your candor," Bill responded. "We cannot waste energy second-guessing ourselves. I will take it under consideration, but you both need to concentrate on *your* part of the mission."

He then turned and announced to the rest of the Pride, "I just heard from Robert. The plane is ready, and we are scheduled to take off in forty-five minutes. With our best effort, hopefully this whole situation will be diffused and behind us in the near future. Now, let's go catch us some bad guys."

He winked to Gary, who could not conceal his grin at Bill's awesome Terra reference during such a high-stress situation.

Chapter XXXIV

After a small bribe and a short delay, the Gulfstream sped down the runway without a flight plan or known destination. As soon as the back wheels left the asphalt, the popular Beatles song "With a Little Help from My Friends" started playing over the speakers.

"Oh, bloody hell," came Robert's frustrated voice from the cockpit.

Most of the Pride enjoyed Eddie's little joke, easing the tension as they began their most dangerous mission so far. Halfway through the song, Maria heard something that shocked her to attention. In a frequency so high it would not even bother a dog, she heard Eddie's message.

"Mom, I need you and Dad to do me a favor, but you can't tell the Pride."

Unlike many of the Pride's flights, the team was busy planning or meditating on this trip. Pax communicated with

Eddie, who controlled the miniature insect monitoring system at the compound and tracked a steady stream of helicopter landings. Pax assumed, due to their worldwide attack on the Kuds, the compound would be thinly defended with only a dozen men. Unfortunately, sixteen additional men had already landed and joined the group inside the main house. Elaine scheduled a surprise, yet important meeting with Mr. Lima. It took some serious negotiations to gain enough trust to allow a face-to-face meeting since he had recently become "America's Most Wanted." Besides flying the plane, Robert promised he would have transportation waiting when they landed. All the while, Maria and Gary were having a private conversation about a hidden message in the Beatles' song.

True to his word, Robert had three vehicles waiting for the Pride upon their arrival: a white, windowless delivery van that hid the high-tech surveillance equipment, a black limo, and a taxi. The Pride grabbed their gear, wished each other luck, and started their mission.

Aggie telepathically said her last good-bye to Eddie before getting in the back of the surveillance van with Pax and Bill. Gary, with his backpack, and Maria, dressed like a hiker or bird watcher, jumped in the back of the taxi as Elaine tipped her head to the driver of the limo, who opened the back door and greeted his client.

"Nice to meet you, Ms. White. Please make yourself comfortable and let me know if you need anything."

"I'll be fine, James."

"Ma'am, my name is Mathew."

"Don't you watch American movies?" She asked with a smile. "The driver is always James."

Bill made it to his position first. Thanks to Pax's hacking of satellite images and Eddie's remote control cameras, he had an intimate, working knowledge of the compound and surrounding terrain. Although hacked records estimated the cattle ranch and acreage Carlos and Juanita controlled to be more than two miles in diameter, the Pride concentrated its efforts on the airfield and main house. Bill parked the van off to the side of the road about a half a mile away under a couple of large trees and turned on the cloaking device Eddie had apologetically admitted would only keep Bill hidden when the van was not moving. Retreating to the back of the van, he monitored all of Pax's equipment and contacted Gary and Maria.

"We are in position, and everything is quiet. Proceed with the plan and good luck."

"I'm sure everything is hunky-dory in the nice, comfortable van and in the back of the Elaine's limo, but we still have a two-mile walk before we even get to the hilltop," Gary answered.

****

After a twenty-minute drive which, per Lima's instructions, included two trips around the block, the driver pulled Elaine's limo into the parking lot of a coffee house.

"Ma'am, would you like me to wait with you in case your associate doesn't show up?" the driver asked over the intercom.

Elaine, who had been in uninterrupted communication with Pax, knew about Lima's "associate" sitting at a window table and reading a paper, about the two "associates" in the black SUV parked at the restaurant across the street, and about Lima's limo roughly a mile away circling around town to make sure no one followed him.

"No, thank you, James. My meeting has been confirmed. But headquarters might need a little more help. Please stay close and available."

The driver opened the door for her and said, "Have a wonderful day, Ms. White. I hope your stay in Brazil is a pleasant one."

She reached into her small, black purse when the driver held up a hand.

"That's not necessary, ma'am. Robert has generously prepaid for any service you might need," he told her as he handed her a card. "I will leave you here, but I will stay less than five minutes away for the next two hours. Call if your plans change."

****

Maria and her invisible husband were sitting on a log sixty feet inside the tree line. Hiding under the cover of the woods, they waited until sundown to continue their part in the mission.

"I am not happy with Elaine's being alone with those thugs," Maria repeated for the third time in the last two hours.

"It's out of our hands now," Gary reminder her yet again. "I doubt she's alone, though. I would bet my superhero costume Pax and Bill are in her mind, helping her. We just have to let her do her job and concentrate on ours."

"Yea, sure," she rebutted. "I'll handle the tough task of sitting here on this log while Lainey is negotiating with a South American drug lord by herself."

****

Halfway through her cup of coffee and forty-five seconds before Lima's lookout heard from his boss, Elaine received an update from Bill.

"Lima's limo is about two blocks away," Bill reported. *"If we are a go, then we will soon be past the point of no return. Elaine, everything looks as expected, and we have a green light from Pax, but it's your call."*

Without responding, she stood up and surprised the well-dressed, dark-skinned, Brazilian lookout. In perfect Portuguese, she said, "Come on, Lookout Boy. Your boss will be here in a minute."

Less than two minutes later, Elaine and her escort were joining the perfectly groomed Mr. Lima, two other guards, and what appeared to be an assistant in the back of a Cadillac Escalade stretch limousine.

"Good evening, Ms. White," Lima said in English. "Do you mind if I ask how you found me or how you gathered the information you claim to have?"

"I don't mind what you ask," she answered in Portuguese before switching to Spanish, "as long as you don't expect an answer."

Lima took a sip from his lowball without offering Elaine a drink.

"Your grasp of our languages is impressive for someone your age, but do not play games with me. We are not friends or partners, Ms. White. This meeting, and possibly your life, will be cut short if you don't answer my questions to my satisfaction," Lima said as he gently brushed the unnoticeable moisture from the corner of his mouth and groomed his thick, black mustache.

"I work with some very smart, very powerful people. As luck would have it," she continued, "we are in need of your services. I have been authorized to offer you something rather valuable to you, but of little importance to us for your services."

"Okay, Ms. White, I'll bite," he responded. "What is it you can offer my family that is so valuable?"

Elaine smiled at the drug lord and handed him a flash drive.

"I can deliver you the people who worked with Santos to set you up."

After a pause to let her comment sink in, she added, "We have an unedited file proving your family's innocence. As a bonus, we will throw in all the money and diamonds these people keep at their compound. Simply put, Mr. Lima, I am offering you your life back."

"In my business, one is never offered such a prize out of charity. What is it you expect from me in return?"

"Well, of course, we would expect some sort of payment for our efforts."

****

Even though the night sky made it dark enough to be almost impassable with normal vision, Maria would not start the mission until she had heard from Elaine. Thirty-five minutes after their scheduled start time, she and Gary made their way through the open field between the woods and the hill leading to the compound. They slowly continued down the semi-exposed hill toward the house. With Maria in the lead, they easily avoided the trees and bushes in the narrow paths of mostly uncleared thicket. Even Gary, who could not see sixteen feet in front of his face, could see the small, personal airstrip lit up about thirteen hundred feet to their left. The Seretus' efforts to camouflage the runway were apparently non-existent. If the lights and lack of brush, water, fences, and cattle was not enough to make one question the property's use as a cattle ranch, certainly the helicopters landing every hour or so would give it away. Off to the Whites' right, there were more than three hundred acers of pasture, with approximately twenty-five head of cattle grazing to provide at least some sort of disguise.

Directly in front of them lay ninety-eight feet of thicket leading to a spacious, well-manicured front lawn with decorative gardens around the house. The large, four-bedroom, two-story white building featured an enormous front porch and a three-car garage. In the fields just beyond the house, there were two noticeable other buildings. Maria estimated the large, white barn dwarfing the house in size stood one hundred and thirty feet beyond it and appeared to be in need of maintenance. She guessed the smaller, but newer equipment barn to be approximately three hundred and thirty feet northeast of the cattle barn. Even with Gary slowing down Maria's progress, in two hours' time, the superhero couple made their way through the thicket along the electric fence that protected the airfield and flanked the house, while avoiding all security cameras on the way to the main barn.

****

"Before I agree that your price is worth the risk to my organization, answer me this," Lima said. "What's stopping me from taking your flash drive, keeping you as a hostage, and selling you back to your secret organization you say is so powerful and resourceful?"

"Now, Mr. Lima, that makes you sound downright mean. Is that any way to treat a new friend?"

"I have enough friends."

"Fair enough. So, before we part as acquaintances, answer me this," Elaine said with a smile. "Even though we found you with minimal effort and shared a copy of the flash drive that could clear your name, you still sound a little—shall we say—cocky. Are you underestimating my organization's abilities or overestimating your security?"

"I have hundreds of people trying to kill me every day, yet here I am with you. My security is airtight. I'm not used to dealing with children. To be honest, Ms. White, you're lucky to be alive."

"Yet here I am," she responded with an unfazed smile and tilt of her head. "Today is just your lucky day, then."

"And why is that?" he asked.

"Because *we* are not one of the hundreds of people who want you dead."

"I think this meeting and your freedom have both come to an end," he said as he looked at the large, muscular man dressed in all black seated beside Elaine and nodded his head.

"Why does it always come to this?" Elaine asked Lima before she contacted Bill telepathically. *"Have Pax start in 10...9..."*

She leaned forward toward Lima and tilted her head down and to the side.

Looking up at him, she said, "Tell muscle dude here to calm down. You might want computer boy to check his laptop and—Oh, yea. Do you know a good mechanic?"

Lima held up his hand to his security guard and nodded to his assistant, who opened his laptop and entered the code just as the car lost power. As the car came to a stop on the dusty berm, the assistant turned the screen to face Lima, and the bodyguard waited for orders. None of them noticed the miniature RC housefly make its way to a hiding place under the back seat. Lima looked at the split screen on his assistant's laptop. The right side displayed two sections. The top half showed his bank balance—400 BRL, or roughly $100. The bottom half gave a warning: "All access to this computer and any account this computer has accessed has been locked until we confirm the safe return of Elaine White." The left half of the screen played a video on a continuous loop. The video showed a full-color replay of the conversation in the back of Lima's limo, specifically the part where the drug lord had boasted about his airtight security.

After almost five minutes of being stranded on the side of the road and searching the limo for the camera that had taped their conversation, Lima looked up at his assistant.

"Stop that damn recording and find my money."

"Sir, I can't," he reported. "I'm sure in time…"

He trailed off as he furiously typed to no avail.

"Once again, you underestimate me," Elaine interrupted. "If I wanted your money or any of your information I would have taken it. All I want is your undivided attention and a little muscle. I would never steal from a friend. If you want the recording to stop, just ask nicely."

"Would you please stop the video?" Lima asked.

"Of course," Elaine answered with a smile.

Pax, who monitored the situation through Elaine's eyes, stopped the video and changed the screen so it only displayed the warning.

"Who are you, lady?" the not-so-scary and substantially less confident drug lord asked.

"As I tried to explain to you on the phone, I am part of a peaceful, powerful, private organization, and we need your help. In exchange for your assistance and my continued safety, we have the power to punish Mr. Santos for the innocent slaughtering of those DEA agents, clear you of those crimes, and deposit large sums of money into your bank accounts."

"I assumed you were part of some US plot to set me up again," Lima admitted. "I'm still convinced you are not being completely honest, but you have sold me on one fact. I would be dead if you wanted it. Maybe we should go back to my compound and discuss the possibility of a partnership. As soon as our cell phones and car start working again, I'll make the arrangements."

As if on cue, a shiny, black limo pulled up next to Lima's. The driver opened the door and showed a great deal of grace under pressure when greeted by two 9mm handguns, compliments of Lima's men.

"Ma'am. Rumor has it you may be having some engine problems. May I offer you a ride?"

"Thanks, James," Elaine said as she took the chauffer's hand and exited the car. "Mr. Lima, are you coming?"

"Do I have any choice?" he asked.

"Of course," she responded. "One always has a choice."

Chapter XXXV

On the way back to the protection of the bushes and trees, Gary and Maria were almost spotted by the guard posted on the roof of the house's garage. Pausing just long enough to shoot one more of Eddie's special spit wad-looking explosives into a tree on Carlos' front lawn, they scampered into the bushes to debrief Bill, continue to monitor from the safety of cover, and await orders. Using Maria's enhanced senses, Pax's skills, and Eddie's toys, they were able to finally get a good feel for the security at the Seretus' compound. Carlos and Juanita had corrected some of their mistakes from the Detroit compound and were prepared for an attack from the Attal, so the Pride faced a formidable defense. Bill remained extremely uneasy about their lack of information about the interior of the house.

"We know there're only five guards posted outside the house," Bill summarized to the team. *"Two at the airstrip, one each on the roof and front porch, and one who makes rounds to*

each building every hour. We now know the reason Pax couldn't hack any wireless communication; they don't use any. They smartly hardwired twenty-seven cameras and communication stations to what Pax assumes is a security office in the house. Also, the Seretus cautiously and shrewdly decided to use some of their precious vis to establish an anti-hub in the main building."

"That sounds bad," Gary interrupted. *"What's an anti-hub?"*

"It creates an atmosphere where no vis is usable. It's what we do at the station during Galtri presentations," Bill explained. *"It's also how the Mooncat necklaces block use from any unauthorized member. But an anti-hub is more absolute. No vis use of any kind within its borders. It's our society's greatest equalizer."*

"So no mind reads, memory plants, or body adjustments?" Maria asked.

"No. Also, Gary's cloaking won't work, nor will any of Eddie's toys using vis, which certainly explains why we lost two RC bugs."

"Then I need to get in or nearer to the house," Maria offered. *"They don't even know about Supergirl's upgraded Terra senses."*

"That would be ideal," Bill admitted. *"But you wouldn't be able to use telepathic communication to tell us what you know. Not to mention the sheer number of potential guards. Pax is concerned about the lack of visible defenses around the grounds. By his count, there have been twenty deliveries made since the Kud massacres and no departures. Those men, combined with the dozen or so recent habitants of the compound, comes to thirty-two people. With the five we see roaming the grounds, there's likely a small army of thirty-eight*

335

armed killers inside the house. That's too much for Supergirl, no matter how good her senses."

After some discussion, Bill decided they had no choice but to try and apprehend Carlos and Juanita that night. They had to stop the Seretus, regardless of the risk. Maria army-crawled slowly, with Gary bear-crawling over top of her so she remained invisible—a move he inappropriately announced would be quite fun under different circumstances. They successfully made their way to a garden just thirty-two feet from the house. Lying still behind a clump of ornamental pampas grass with her invisible husband crouched over her, Maria concentrated with all her effort. Pax and Aggie, who assumed they would have to enter the house at some point and thought their skills would be helpful with any guards on the grounds, left the van and started their hike across the pastures. Reporting what she heard, smelled, and saw to Bill, Maria focused so hard she lost track of her immediate surroundings, as if in a trance or a dream. Her heart rate slowed, and she seemed to be outside her body, making her way around the compound and trying to allow her senses to penetrate their defenses.

"The man on the porch smokes cigars, but not cigarettes. He has a slight limp on his right side and sighs often as a stress-coping method. The roof guard is fighting exhaustion. He is a non-smoker and dozes off often. There is some movement in the house, but it sounds and smells like a much smaller group than Pax described. I can hear some faint movements and the hint of a conversation, but I'm sad to report I can't confirm a meeting or a large gathering. The guard making rounds just shut the door to the equipment barn and is slowly walking to the back of the house. He drinks on the job. Whiskey, I think. There is a helicopter approaching in the distance. I think they are getting another delivery."

Maria kept the reports coming as a constant stream of semi-conscious observations. In fifteen minutes, the helicopter landed at the south end of the airstrip just long enough to drop off one male passenger then took off. Maria continued her report.

"The man had a brief conversation in Portuguese, which I didn't comprehend. In retrospect, that may have been a flaw in my training. The new arrival stands tall and walks heavy. He is a non-smoker and chews spearmint gum. He's walking unescorted and briskly to the house."

Maria heard Elaine request access to her senses.

"Hey, Mom. I'm safe and able to concentrate. Bill wants me to try and listen with you so I can translate. Can you let me mind-share? I'm heading your way, but things are loud here. I'll try to try to block them out."

"I'm glad you are safe," Maria said before she quit her report and concentrated on sharing her senses with Elaine.

"How was your trip?" Elaine interpreted the conversation of the porch guard and the new guest to the Pride.

"Too loud and too long. Anything going on here?"

"Same old here, except for all the deliveries."

"It took me so long. Am I the last?" the new soldier asked.

"That's above my paygrade," the guard reported. *"But the boss is expecting you. Best not to keep him waiting."*

"No man scares me," he bragged. *"But the bitch makes me a little nervous."*

The guard just smiled and nodded toward the door, granting him access to the house.

"Brigado," the new visitor said as he headed through the door to greet Carlos and Juanita.

"I think there might be another delivery coming. I hear another helicopter in the distance," Maria reported.

In the six seconds the front door was open, Maria blocked out everything she could and concentrated on the sounds and smells so hard she gave herself a headache. After the door shut, Maria relayed everything to Bill.

"I would never discount Pax's intelligence gathering, but I really don't get the feeling there is a large group in the house. There's an offensive smell I don't recognize. It reminded me of maybe a sewage backup someone tried to cover up with a room deodorizer. But it disappeared when the door shut. The porch guard looks really stressed he—Oh, my God. A gun just went off in the house."

The front door opened again, and the smell of covered sewage returned. Maria heard someone dragging something across a floor, and she could only assume it was the body of the guest. The guard inside the door spoke up.

"That's the last one. We will be leaving in a couple hours."

"Thank God," his comrade responded.

Maria heard a latch being released inside the house, followed by a large spring and the faint thud of a body landing from a fall. The scent of death and decay intensified after the impact and overwhelmed her. Her concentration broke too late to allow her to block her body's response, and she threw up the energy bars and water she had consumed in the woods earlier. The noise of her wrenching drew the attention of the two guards on the porch.

"Get up, bun," Gary ordered. *"We need to head back to the bushes. Now."*

He grabbed the back of her jacket and pulled her to her knees as he tried to lead her to safety and keep her invisible at the same time. Before they moved ten yards, the guards were already in the flower garden with their flashlights confirming someone or something had thrown up something. One of the guards abruptly shined the flashlight toward Gary and Maria.

"There is something over there," he reported in and accented English. "Go report—"

He stopped his command mid-sentence and looked over toward the airstrip.

"We aren't expecting another delivery. Scratch my last command. Check the landing pad. I'm going to find out what that noise is."

Gary used the distraction of the helicopter to change his plan.

"Run for cover."

He pushed Maria toward the bushes only seven yards in front of her. The guard looked over just in time to see her disappear into the shrubs. Turning off his flashlight, he quickly gave chase in the darkness.

One could hear the sound of a gunshot over the helicopter blades. The first guard at the airstrip fell dead before he knew what hit him. The second, however, returned fire while retreating toward a more defensible position. Twenty seconds after the helicopter landed, eight commandos, dressed in all black and armed with AK-47s, jumped out of the helicopter and ran toward Carlos' overwhelmed guard. As they secured the airstrip, three more people exited the copter: Lima and the bodyguard from his limo with his left arm around Elaine's neck and a pistol pointed at her head.

"If I'm not back in twenty minutes, shoot her and take off. I'll meet you at the safe house," Lima ordered the man.

"Really?" Elaine said, sounding confident, but secretly scared to death. "You think it's a good idea to end this friendship?"

"We were never friends, and I don't take orders."

"Yet here we are," Elaine said.

"Shut up! You know, my men are right. You really can be an annoying bitch."

"Funny, my family tells me the same thing," she replied. "I hope you meet them someday."

She watched Lima follow his troops before she contacted Bill.

"I have a desperate situation that needs to be addressed in less than twenty minutes."

Chapter XXXVI

In the chaos following the shootout at the airstrip, many things happened simultaneously. Six armed men exited the house to defend the grounds from the unknown attackers. Maria continued to play hide-and-seek with Carlos' main guard in the thicket. Elaine tried to convince the bodyguard to let her go, and Pax and Aggie decided to use the pandemonium to enter the house and search for Carlos and Juanita.

If all that was not enough for a mission leader to keep straight, Bill announced, *"Things are about to get interesting. It's time for plan B. Maria, get to the hilltop. Gary, we could use those distractions."*

Lima's helicopter pilot received a warning from an anonymous source about what was coming his way. Seeing the lights of the approaching aircraft in the distance, the pilot assumed Bill's warning came from a friendly source. Starting the blades, he waited until the last minute before lifting off.

Robert knew the length and terrain of the grass-covered runway would make for a bumpy landing. He came in low and slammed on the brakes seconds after hitting turf. The Gulfstream threw up dust, bounced at least two feet off the ground, and skidded across the airstrip designed for small prop planes and helicopters. He slid to a stop eight feet from the tree line just as the helicopter pilot flew away, leaving Lima's men to fend for themselves. Taxiing around the flat, grassy runway so he would be positioned to take off, Robert did the hardest thing he had ever done. He listened to the mayhem below and waited for the meeting he had scheduled.

****

In her haste to make it to the clearing at the top of the hill, Maria accidently allowed herself to be spotted by her pursuer. He yelled something in Portuguese Maria did not understand since Elaine was busy with her own problems but did not need help translating. She knew if she did not stop, she would die. Turning slowly, with her hands raised in the universal sign of surrender, she smiled at the guard.

"Sorry for the confusion. Do you speak English?"

His answer never came. The blow to the back of his head from the retractable baton Gary had retrieved from his tool belt knocked him out immediately.

"Is he dead?" Maria asked.

"I don't know and don't care. He pulled a gun on my bun."

Even with guns blasting in the background, Gary could not help chuckling at his rhyme.

"Now, go to the hilltop. I have some confusion to create."

****

Aggie gave the guard on the roof such a bloody nose and headache he thought he had just had a seizure. Pax planted the idea he should come down from the garage roof and surrender his weapon. After disarming him and stealing his key card to the house, they zip-tied him to the porch pillar. Awkwardly, the two peaceful, yet extremely unprepared, Attal entered the house with Terra guns drawn. Searching the house, Pax had a mild sense of relief at not being greeted by dozens of armed, angry militia, but he felt his anxiety continue to climb at the silence. They both tried to communicate with each other telepathically, but Carlos' anti-hub worked perfectly. Relying on hand signals and a slow, careful search, they agreed the house seemed empty. Trying to decide if Carlos and Juanita had managed to get away again or if they had just walk into a trap, Pax conceded they had to finish searching the house either way.

****

Juanita and her personal assistant were scurrying down the underground tunnel toward the airstrip.
"What about your brother, ma'am?" he asked nervously.
"He can take care of himself," she answered. "This is where my dear brother and I part ways. Hurry up. You are falling behind."
The stairway at the end of the tunnel led to the utility shed at the far end of the grassy runway. They quickly made the short trip to the staircase descending from the Gulfstream. Elaine, still held at gunpoint, watched in disbelief from the woods nearby as the leader of the Seretus boarded the Pride's plane.

"Hello, dear Robert," Juanita greeted the young Englishman, while Bill observed them through the RC housefly Jeff Harding controlled back in the Den, thousands of miles to the north.

"Ma'am, it's good to finally meet you," Robert lied. "As promised, I've gathered all of the Pride's vis and loose diamonds."

He presented her with an open, black box displaying a series of watches and a generous pile of sparkling, clear stones.

"Although the plane is a little damaged from the landing, I'm ready to take off upon your orders."

She looked at the blinking warning lights and littered aisles.

"Oh, that won't be necessary."

She pulled out a 9mm handgun with a silencer and pointed it at Robert.

"You won't be going anywhere. But thank you for the diamonds and vis."

"But, ma'am—I've risked everything. You promised a life of power and riches."

"Yea, sorry to disappoint you, but we had a change of plans," she said as she offered her assistant the gun. "Manny, shoot the poor traitor so he can't follow us."

"Ma—Ma'am, I've never hurt anyone. I just wanted to be your PA. I—I couldn't sh—"

"I don't know why I keep you around," she barked at him.

She leaned in close to Robert and whispered in his ear, "Sorry about this, dear Robert."

Juanita pulled the trigger and shot his thigh at point-blank range. She stood up, wiped some blood from her neck, straightened her collar, and stepped over the Englishman. After two steps down the airstair, she stopped and turned around to look at Robert sitting in the aisle by the door and pressing on the bloody hole in the middle of his thigh.

"Goodbye, Robert. I let you live so you can pass along a message for me. Give my best to Pax and Bill. And tell them, if they don't chase me, the violence stops today."

She exited the plane with her terrified assistant and hurried down a path towards the open fields where a helicopter and pilet waited in the dark.

****

Without Gary trying to remain invisible or stumbling in the darkness, Maria made it to the top of hill in no time. She could see Bill's back-up plan before she even reached the clearing. Gary, hiding behind a tree, retrieved a device from his backpack and pressed a couple of buttons. The result was immediate. A loud, fiery explosion near the airstrip fence demolished the tree were Gary had placed the putty. Seconds later, an explosion so big it shook the ground went off at the cattle barn behind the house. The third, smaller explosion erupted from the brush only thirty yards away from the crouching Gary. They certainly helped created the diversion Bill had hoped for. Lima's and Carlos' men were all heading to the same area of the compound, shooting furiously at each other without knowing who their enemies were or why it seemed so important to kill them.

****

Elaine received assurances from Bill her rescue would start within seconds, but she felt helpless and vulnerable.

"You don't have a getaway plan. Your boss is most likely dead, and my friends are on their way to save me. Why don't you just let me go and run for cover? I promise we won't come after you," she pleaded.

"Why don't you just shut up before I kill you and go help my boss kill your friends?" he suggested instead.

In Elaine's mind, she heard the wonderful, calm voice of her mother.

"Lainey, honey. On the count of zero, duck as much as you can."

"Well that doesn't sound very fun," Elaine said. "Don't say I didn't warn you."

A few seconds later, she heard her mother's voice again in her head.

"This is it, honey. 3…2…1—duck!"

Elaine elbowed her captor's ribs and bowed at the waist as low as she could. The bullet hit the bodyguard right between the eyes, dropping him on the spot. As soon as Maria verified Elaine's safety, everyone in the compound heard an entirely unexpected sound in the middle of the firefight.

From the enhanced speakers on the Gulfstream and four vis-infused speakers in the sky, Def Leppard's "Rock of Ages" blasted at full volume. Eddie tipped his wings to his scared but relieved sister and turned his modified ultralight around to join the fight. With his Mom spotting for him, he shot strategic bombs that kept the two fighting forces away from his team at the airstrip and house. To anyone not running or fighting for their lives, the synchronization of the fire with the song's lyrics about burning a town to the ground blaring throughout the compound would have been impressive.

****

Even though the noise and gunshots increased outside, the muffled quietness in the house gave Pax an eerie feeling.

The whole downstairs had been checked, except the door nearest the kitchen. The proximity to the center of the house and the soundproof, locked door made Pax assume it protected the security office. Aggie, who couldn't remember ever being so scared and without vis, stood close to Pax and nervously continued to look for trouble to her right and left. Pax reached into his pack and retrieved one of Eddie's keys. Realizing the key might not work if Eddie had used vis to enhance his simple, yet extremely effective tool, Pax felt trying the device would be the easiest way to test it. He had barely placed the key into the lock before he and Aggie heard a latch release. A section of the floor immediately in front of the locked door fell, revealing a trap door.

Aggie fell into the exposed hole and landed badly on the uneven surface below. The sudden pain she felt from at least two broken bones might not have been the worst part. The smell and feeling of sticky, decaying, bodily fluids at the bottom of the pit were unimaginable. Pax's reflexes were a little quicker as he held onto the edge of the opening, kicking his legs in an effort to catch an edge with his foot.

The locked door opened and revealed the large, muscular, Latino fugitive smiling down at Pax.

"Welcome to my South American compound, Pax. How have you been?"

"Carlos, please don't make this any worse. We have almost taken the compound. Your cooperation could be the only thing keeping you from a mind alteration," Pax pleaded.

"Oh, Pax. You should know me better. I don't care about this compound. You can have it. And I have no intention of cooperating with you or any other Attal. I will disappear into the tunnels and live a long and happy life once I know you and Bill aren't around to chase me."

"If it's Dad and me you want, then you can have us. But please leave our Terra friends alone. They have no history with you."

"But you do," Carlos said before stepping on Pax's hands and causing him to fall into the hole.

Pax fell into the dark and landed on his back, knocking him out. Aggie felt him fall next to her, but could not see him in the darkness.

"Pax? Pax, are you all right? Pax, where are you? Pax!"

"He's in the same place you are, my dear Agrata. He is trapped down in my dying cell," Carlos called to her from thirty feet above, before he gracefully jumped across the opening.

Scared, pissed, and totally confused, Aggie did not know what to do. Instinctually, she shouted out to Bill telepathically.

"Bill, help us. We are stuck. We found Carlos. Bill, please help."

"Aggie, we can hear you again. Where are you?"

Realizing she had fallen far enough from the anti-hub that her vis abilities worked again, she searched for Pax's vitals, glad to confirm that, although he was unconscious and his breathing labored, he was not dead.

"Bill, we are in a hole beneath the house. It is in the hallway outside the security room. It's 30 feet deep which must be out of range of the anti-hub. There aren't any guards. Please send help.

"Actually, with all of the dead bodies from my delivery men," Carlos said, "it's likely only 20 or 25 feet. That makes it a little easier to escape, but it does add a rather pungent odor."

****

Bill immediately contacted Gary.

"Pax and Aggie are trapped in the house. No guards, just Carlos. They need help."

"On my way," Gary responded as he started off across the lawn.

"They are in a hole outside a locked room. Be careful and remember, no vis in the house."

"Roger that," Gary answered as he half-jogged, half-ran through the compound, bending over and zig-zagging from tree to tree.

There were constant explosions and gunfire on both sides of him. Less than halfway to the building, he got knocked over by a fireball, compliments of Eddie. Def Leppard still blared in the compound while trees fell, men screamed, and debris flew in every direction. While attempting to right himself, with bullets buzzing past his head, Gary realized Eddie's modification to his suit had worked. His cloaking device repelled bullets, just not explosions. Getting back to his feet, he threw caution to the wind and sprinted to the rest of the way, leaving a ghost image behind for anyone who cared to notice.

****

"How can you kill like this, Carlos? What about our laws?" Aggie asked.

"Since I've been alive, I haven't killed even one hundredth of one percent of the Terra that have killed each other in their silly, little wars."

"That's beside the point. We have laws. What about the Attal you've killed?"

"We have flawed laws, Agrata," Carlos stated. "But I don't have time to talk with you about politics. Plus, the smell is making me sick. You won't have to sit in the stench very long. I've rigged this whole compound to explode in ten minutes. The authorities will assume I'm dead, and I'll start over—rich and free. Enjoy your last, few minutes. I just wish Pax's health allowed him to share it with y—"

One of Eddie's firebombs shook the house, interrupting his speech.

"Who *is* that?" Carlos asked in disgust.

"That would be my boyfriend," Aggie answered defiantly.

"And my son," Carlos heard from behind.

Before he could turn to see who spoke, Gary swung his baton with two hands and struck him in the back of the head. There was no doubt this time. Carlos fell dead into the hole and landed on top of Pax.

"Pax, Aggie—are you two all right?" Gary asked, yelling down into the hole.

Chapter XXXVII

Bill's van was not cloaked as it bounced across the pastures and broke through fences. After checking on Aggie, Gary ran outside to communicate with the Pride.

"The whole compound is going to blow in nine minutes. Pax and Aggie are trapped in a hole thirty feet down. She's injured, and he's barely holding on. What's the plan? Someone tell me there is a plan."

Elaine responded first.

"God, no. Not Pax. I'm on my way. Do something Dad!"

"Elaine, stay with the plane. There's too much gunfire. You will never make it," Eddie told her.

"I've got to get to Pax. I've got to tell him that—"

"He knows, honey," Maria interrupted. *"We will save him. Stay with the plane and get it ready for take-off."*

"But, Mom—" she protested.

"*Bill and I will get the kids,*" Gary yelled. "*Elaine, stay with the plane. Eddie, we are going to need a clear path to the plane.*"

After the ending, evil laugh from "Rock of Ages," Eddie's voice came in loud and clear over all of the speakers.

"The compound has been rigged to self-destruct. Save yourselves! Run now and I'll quit fighting. If you don't, you will die where you stand. You have five minutes to leave the compound."

With Maria's vison and Eddie's skills, they perfectly targeted their bullets and explosions to encourage evacuation while not injuring anyone else.

As Eddie made his last turn before heading back to the airstrip, he contacted Aggie, "*How you doing, Link?*"

"*Not so good. I have three broken bones, it's dark, and there is no way to climb out. And I'm doing a lot better than Pax is,*" she reported. "*He doesn't have much longer. Contrary to what your Dad keeps telling me, there is no time to get me out of here before it blows.*"

"*Are we even sure it's rigged? Maybe it's a bluff,*" Eddie suggested.

"*I don't think so,*" Aggie said. "*Besides, it doesn't matter. We can't risk the rest of your lives in the hopes Carlos might have bluffed. You need to get off the compound, Link. Please do that for me. Remember me always. And make sure Juanita gets caught.*"

"*Of course I will remember you always,*" Eddie responded. "*But don't give up hope, yet. I have one more trick up my sleeve. Dad has my latest toy. I didn't have time to test it, and it might technically be illegal—but it's our best plan. I gave it to him to use in case of an emergency. I think this counts. I promised to always come back for you. I just didn't make it in time. I just hope—I just—*"

After an awkward pause during which Eddie could not come up with the proper words to express his feelings, he simply said, *"Dad knows what to do."*

"I knew you'd come for me. You're my juke box hero. You've made me the happiest person on the planet," she responded before going silent.

The commandos in the courtyard accepted Eddie's warning, reinforced by continual explosions and gunfire. The remaining seven soldiers were running as fast as possible, in two different directions, away from the compound. Eddie landed the ultralight and boarded the Gulfstream, clearly upset.

"What's wrong?" Elaine asked when she saw her brother with tears in his eyes for the first time since grade school.

"I may have just killed my girlfriend and your fiancé," he answered.

"What? Why—What did you do?" she yelled as she left Robert's side to attack her brother.

"If we do nothing, they're both dead," he told her the blunt truth while she pounded on his chest. "Pax is almost dead, Elaine. I had to do something. But there's still a chance. Dad has my—Well, there's still a chance,"

He grabbed his sister and pulled her in for a hug instead of the beating she gave him.

"How much of a chance?" she asked through her tears.

"I'd say fifty-fifty," Eddie lied, since very few of his inventions ever worked right on the first test.

He continued to hug his sister and hated himself for what he had to do next. He contacted his Dad.

"We are out of options, Dad. Aggie is ready. It's time for the last resort. You know what to do. Right?"

"Yea, I know. And I'm sorry, Eddie."

Bill came to a skidding stop outside of the house when he saw Gary sitting on the front porch and staring at the burning compound.

"What's wrong? What are you doing?"

"There's no time to save the kids, Bill," Gary said slightly louder than a whisper.

"I know," Bill admitted. "I've come to stay with them. It's time for you to go be with your family. I'll stay with mine. I'm so sorry I got you involved in this mess. You are truly the best friend a guy could ask for."

"You, too, Bill, but I can't let you do that," Gary responded.

"It's over for me, Gary. I'm just glad I will have the opportunity to die in action and be with Pax and Aggie at the end."

"You underestimate me and my family," Gary said with barely a hint of a smile through his tears and pain.

"I wish I would have never included you. I wish I would have found someone I liked less. I'm so sorry. I'm going to miss you, Maria, and the kids."

"You and AJ included us Terra because we are unpredictable and don't follow your rules," Gary continued, ignoring Bill's sentiment.

"What?"

"The White boys aren't done breaking Attal rules," Gary told his friend.

After Gary explained Eddie's plan, Bill asked, "And he thinks it will work?"

"He gave it about a 25-30% chance. He said to only use it as a last resort," Gary admitted.

"I'd say this qualifies," Bill admitted.

Gary entered the house, took two black, metallic, semi-circle devices, each twenty-four centimeters long, out of his backpack and yelled to Aggie from thirty feet above.

"Place these devices above both of your ears and press both buttons simultaneously. Remember, do Pax's first."

"I know," Aggie said. "Thanks, Gary. Thanks for everything. Pax and I love you so much. We are so lucky to—um—We—Well, I really hoped someday I would—"

"Aggie, you know that whether this works or not, it will—"

"I know, but it doesn't really matter. I'm dead either way. It's my only chance. You and Bill go save yourself, Maria, and my best friends. I love you all so much. Thank you for making me Terra."

Running out of time, Gary and Bill honored Aggie's wishes and made their way through the fire and debris toward the airstrip. Meanwhile, Aggie placed one of Eddie's units on Pax, followed the instructions, and then placed the second unit on her head. She unlocked her Link-Ink to Eddie and requested his company.

"Hey, Link. I'm about to test your genius. I love you. Thank you for everything."

"You don't have to thank me for falling in love with the best girl on the planet. I just pray I got it right. I hope the end is peaceful, and, God, I hope I see you soon."

"The end is peaceful because I get to spend it with you. I have no regrets. I've come as close as anyone to being totally Attal and totally Terra. I just wish I would have had the chance to go to Pax and Elaine's wedding. And to make love to you."

"You are totally Terra, yet helped me experience being an Attal. You will always be my one and only true love," Eddie said. *"Good luck, Link."*

"Goodbye, Link," Aggie said and pressed both buttons as she closed her eyes.

She barely felt the prick on the side of her head when the probes entered her brain. In an effort to make the user's last seconds peaceful, Eddie had chosen his own memories to implant for each Pride member's last, conscious thought. In the dark, dank offensive hole filled with death and decay, Aggie laid back with a smile on her face as she relived a moment from the pleasure hub. Her cerebral self sat on the edge of the cliff in the French Alps, kissing Eddie in the brisk, clear outdoors. After thirty seconds of experiencing the blissful, physical passion and the emotional bonding with Eddie, Aggie died.

Eddie felt his link with Aggie break and knew, pass or fail, he had just killed his best friend and his girlfriend.

****

Gary and Bill climbed on board and saw the mess on the Gulfstream. In addition to all the debris in the aisles, an emotionally spent Elaine sat holding her knees, and a weak Robert had a belt around his thigh and blood all over his pants. A crying Maria quickly wrapped her arms around Gary and laid her head on his shoulder.

Over the roar of the Gulfstream's engines, Gary asked, "Is she seaworthy?"

"I think we are about to find out," Bill answered. "We have less than two minutes, if Carlos actually planned to blow up his compound."

"Hold on to something. This is going to be ugly," Eddie warned.

They bounced down the runway as fast as the grass and dirt would allow. The conditions worsened the further they went, until the plane pushed through an open field.

"I don't think they planned for anything this big," Eddie said as he gave the engines one last chance to speed up before the field became an impassable pasture.

The last forty yards were so rough Maria fell out of her seat and Elaine banged her head against the overhead storage, but they did get enough speed to get airborne. Eddie climbed to five thousand feet and started a 180-degree turn to a northern heading. When the Pride flew back over the compound, they confirmed the last words of the fallen Seretus leader had been truthful. The explosion originating in the basement of the house sent a fireball more than 25 feet in the air. The following 4 explosions demolished the entire compound.

Eddie expected the flight back to Ohio, including a scheduled stop to refuel, to take more than sixteen hours. Everyone on the Gulfstream experienced an uncharacteristically quiet flight, filled with pain, worry, and guilt. Unfortunately, information about Eddie's device would not be available for hours. Due to the illegality of the portable transporter Eddie had developed, it had to send its energy signatures using a completely new and substantially more time-consuming method. Adding to the estimated time frame, the station had to receive two signatures.

Eddie's plan was to first get the signatures to the closest transport office disguised as a procedure update and hide them in a sectioned-off location in the station's transporter. He would then create a file using small, systematic, and hopefully untraceable bursts of energy. Waiting for a member to transfer, it would piggy-back the files on a normal transfer to the main surface station's transporter and hide them. Later, if one knew where to look, he could recall the fake files and create what would hopefully look like two normal transfers, even though they came from inside their own transporter. Because of the illegality the final transfer would certainly be exposed without an inside conspirator.

Seven hours into their quiet, solemn flight Eddie checked on the progress for the second time.

"*Any update, Ivan?*"

"*Do you think I would have an update and not tell you?*" the station leader answered. "*There is a Brazilian transfer scheduled in an hour and a half. Assuming it doesn't get rescheduled, I'll come up with an excuse to take over the surface transporter and look for your hidden files. As soon as no one is available as a witness, I'll attempt to create the transport. How is everyone holding up?*"

"*Robert has lost a lot of blood, but I've repaired his wound and he'll be fine, if Elaine's evil eye doesn't kill him,*" Eddie reported. "*Mom, Dad, and Bill are worried but fine. I'll chat with you in a couple hours.*"

Eddie refueled in northern Venezuela, had the Gulfstream set on auto-pilot somewhere over the Atlantic, and used some of his nervous energy to repair and clean the plane from its miserable first date with Brazil. He lay on the floor of the cockpit rewiring the damaged landing gear release when he heard the best lecture he had ever received start in his mind.

"*I swear, if you don't learn to follow our rules, I'm going to lock you out of the Den and find a new best man for my wedding.*"

"Holy shit, it worked! Man, it is really good to hear your voice. Is anyone else there?"

"*I'm right here, Cubby,*" Aggie reported.

"Cubby? What happened to Link?" Eddie asked with a large smile.

"*I left it in South America,*" she said. "*Do you think you could re-link me?*"

358

"Oh, I'm going to do more than that," he said as he sat up and announced to everyone on the plane, "Elaine. Guys, they are both alive. They're alive!"

The Gulfstream's speakers immediately played the Eurythmics' "Sweet Dreams (Are Made of This)."

Chapter XXXVIII

The next two weeks were filled with much-deserved, blissful relaxation. It took two days of meetings for everyone in the Pride to learn all of Ivan's and Bill's plans relating to their last mission. Although Juanita remained free, the Pride had successfully ended the Seretus' reign. Robert walked with a limp, but did not feel any pain during his and Aggie's walk around the property.

"I know I've lost you, but I'm glad I lost you to a great guy. You look really happy. I just want you to understand what Ivan and I were doing and why I had to keep it a secret," he admitted.

"I'm sorry I lost faith in you," Aggie said. "As I always knew, you are truly a great man, and you will always be my first boyfriend. I hope you find happiness, and I hope we remain friends forever."

"We will. And, well, actually, after a Moonlight meeting tomorrow, I have a date with Elizabeth," he said, suddenly studying his shoes and trying to hide the pinkness of his checks.

"That's great," she said as she stopped him, stood on her tiptoes, and gave him a kiss on the cheek. "Whether it works out with her or not, you and Elizabeth both deserve to be happy. Your lives have been anything but, since learning about us."

"You're wrong," Robert corrected her and returned her friendly kiss. "Living with a secret, alien race on earth validated all of my studies, and I got to do it with the most wonderful girl and save the world. You've made me very happy and very content. Thank you for teaching me about Terra love."

Not everything was blissful at the surface station. After many tearful hugs and welcome parties for the arrival of the Attal Homeland Delegate and personal friend of the Pride, there were many unpleasant activities in store for AJ. He had important services and arrangements to preside over due to the Attal massacres. He had dozens of debriefing and planning meetings about the apprehension of the remainder of the Seretus Ligare. And most importantly to the Pride, he had to enforce any disciplinary actions for all the breaking of Attal rules Eddie insisted were more like bending.

Sitting in Eddie's bedroom-office in the Den, AJ continued his argument, "We can't do nothing."

"Why not?" Eddie asked. "How about just punishing me? I don't need to be involved anymore."

"It's not that simple. I'm the Homeland Delegate now. You guys broke at least twelve laws. Someone has to be responsible. The Council is looking at a twenty-year-old, confused, young man with no authority and a two-hundred-year-old leader of an advanced race who helped him break our laws. Who do you think they are going to hold responsible?" AJ explained.

"So, you traveled for years to come here just to punish Ivan?" Eddie asked.

"Oh, hell, no," AJ corrected him with a devious smile he had learned from his time with the Whites. "I traveled years to come here and save my friend Ivan and to preside over your sister's wedding next month. Do you think you have one more illegal move in you before we put your illicit ways to bed?"

Eddie chuckled out loud.

"I love you, man. Whatcha need?"

****

In an effort to accommodate all of the Attal who wanted to witness this historic event and the Whites' Terra friends and family, Elaine decided to hold her wedding at the property, overlooking the pond. There was not a dry eye when Elaine, with her hair dyed Pax's favorite shade of red, stood in front of her family and friends in her strapless, tight fitting, silver dress beautifully studded with small seed pearls, and recited her vows.

"I have already loved you 'til death and after. And, if you never do that to me again, I'll love you even more."

After a brief pause she continued.

"I promise to never be boring and to share everything with you—the believable and the unbelievable. I won't take your love for granted and will always honor the historic merger our marriage represents to both of our cultures. Thank you for allowing me to be me, but more importantly, thank you for being you. It is my honor to join your family and have you join mine."

She took a step backwards, clasped her hands in front of her at her waist, tilted her head slightly to the right, and bowed to her new husband.

Pax and Elaine enjoyed a week-long, proper Terra honeymoon in the San Francisco area and then were granted a four-hour pleasure vis hub as a wedding gift from Ivan. Two weeks after their return, they held a final Pride meeting to announce AJ's departure and some leadership changes within the Attal.

Although Ivan attended the meeting, AJ led it.

"I feel strongly the turmoil facing our society is finally behind us. We still have one more task to complete before my departure, but I thought you all deserved notice of the changes taking place in a couple of weeks. Even though our fellow members believe he is returning with me, Ivan's petition to remain on Earth has been granted. Per his request, he is going to remain on the surface and live as a Terra. He will not have a position within our society and will not have communication with any Attal not currently in this room.

"After one more mission next week, Bill will take over the responsibilities of Surface Station Leader while still serving on the Terra Relations Council, whose necessity will become even more important moving forward. Coming here has been an honor. I cherish every opportunity to spend time with everyone in this room. But, I sincerely hope Bill is too busy in the near future raising grandkids to cause mischief and call me back."

****

Eddie pulled his 1972 Ford Mustang Mach 1 into the Venice Beach, oceanfront condo. He and Aggie were on their way to meet Robert and Bill in Naples, Florida, to complete Bill's last mission. Even though they knew what to expect, they almost fell over with shock at the 35-year-old, smooth-skinned, young, beautiful brunette who opened the door.

"Mema?" Eddie asked.

"You better get used to calling me Lucy," she answered with a hug.

"What's all the commotion out here?" Pax's twin brother asked as he entered the room.

"How are you, Ivan?" Aggie asked.

"Healthy and stress free," Ivan answered.

"I'll be the judge of that," she said as she started her health scan.

"You mean you didn't just come for pie?" he asked with a smile.

"Mema made pie?" Eddie asked.

****

Juanita sat poolside at her Naples condo with her assistant.

"Manny, be a dear and get me a bottle of water."

Her eyes were closed when his shadow blocked the sun from her face.

"Sorry, luv, but they were all out of water. I did bring you a present, though," Robert said as he pulled out a 9mm handgun and pressed it against her exposed thigh.

"Robert, how did you—but—"

"Hello, Barry," Bill said, joining the reunion.

"But there is no way—"

"Oh, there is a way," Aggie said, surprising her from behind. "We knew you couldn't resist taking Bill's money and vis. He knew your arrogance would be your downfall. Robert worked with us the whole time."

"But I took nine different flights under three different names. I traveled on a train and two buses. I only used cash and stole the car that brought us here. How—What—How where you able to follow me here?" Juanita asked, startled and confused.

"It wasn't blood you wiped off your neck on the plane," Bill explained.

"It was Link-Ink, and you were linked to my boyfriend," Aggie added.

"Hello. That would be me," Eddie said, joining the party growing at Juanita's chaise lounge.

"Speaking of Link-Ink," Aggie said, retrieving a small spray bottle of clear liquid and applying it to a little tattoo on Eddie's arm, "it's time to get that bitch out of you."

"I was caught by a Terra?" Juanita asked.

"Technically, you were caught by a whole pride of Terra," Eddie corrected her. "But we decided to let Robert do the honors of either bringing you in—or not. It seemed only fair. After all you did shoot him."

"Dear Robert, I still have all the diamonds you saved for me," Juanita said. "Why don't we take them, run-a-way and live a life of luxury together. We could be very rich and very happy."

"Sorry to disappoint you, but I've had a change of plans," Robert said with a smile.

"Well it looks like Bobbie has everything under control here," Eddie said. "Juanita, even though you are about to leave our planet, let me share a quote with you: 'It's best after a mission that's dangerous and long, to be thankful you survived and to always end with a song.'"

Suddenly the soft relaxing steel drum music playing over the bar speakers was replaced with the loud and immediately recognizable song featured during the last scene of the 1985 movie Breakfast Club. As Simple Minds sang "Don't You (Forget About Me)", Eddie took Aggie's hand and escorted her off the patio. He sang along as the song played and twirled Aggie as they danced out of sight.

Authors' Note

I sincerely hope you enjoyed the Whites' adventure and I'm honored you chose to spend some of your time following their quest with the Attal. If you wish to get a more in depth feeling for the music that inspired Eddie's subconscious, I invite you to listen to the more than 20 songs referenced in this book.

I would like to thank my Delegate Donor from book one The Secret of the Attal, Rosemary Hickin for helping pick the last song. "Don't You (Forget About Me)" was the perfect song to end the book.

I'd also like to give a shout out to Ed Fortney and Kathy Dreher for being the first to complete the scavenger hunt given at The Secret of the Attal release party. Well Done!

Completing a novel is a long, complicated process. Finishing a series is even more so. Thank you to Jennifer and Artie at J. Arthur's Edits for all their skills and guidance.

Most importantly, I'd like to thank my wife Jeanne, who also has the undesirable burden of being the sounding board forced to deal with any of my frustrations during the creative process. The character of Maria should be the benchmark of excellence for wives and mothers. Everything good about her I learned from watching Jeanne.

Also by Michael Chrome

The Secret of the Attal

Authors' Biography

Michael Chrome is a long time proud Ohio native who attended the University of Akron from 1984 through 1989 where he received a B.A. in Business Management with a second major in Marketing. After marrying his high school sweetheart he continued his education at the University of Akron where he earned a M.B.A. in material management before entering the workforce and managing companies in both the non-profit sector and the wholesale distribution industry.

In 2001, in an effort to be closer to his family and fulfill his dream of owning his own business, he and his wife purchased a neighborhood store.

In addition to running the family business, Michael recently became a self-published author. He is enjoying the excitement of starting a new career and exploring his creative side. He just finished the second book in the Attal series and looks forward to continuing to follow the adventure wherever it leads.